Praise for *A Delirious Sum...*

"Quirky characters keep the reader interested . . . Blackston's tongue-in-cheek hum...
Christian singles will grab the attention of readers."

Publishers Weekly

"Amusing adventures among the questing ladies . . . [who] practice serial churchgoing, 'hopscotching' from Pentecostal to Methodist to Southern Baptist in search of the elusive Mr. Right."

Booklist, starred review

"Lean and breezy style. This sequel to *Flabbergasted* is top quality lad lit, straight from the guys' hearts to yours. The first half of the book is witty and funny, followed by a second half full of wise insight."

Romantic Times

"Blackston brings back some of the same quirky cast of characters from *Flabbergasted*, including larger-than-life blonde Darcy Yeager and unorthodox Alexis Demoss. Offer[s] the rarely seen perspective of the young, single Christian male trying to balance his emotional and physical needs in the dating world with his spiritual calling and growth. Recommended.

Library Journal

"Fast, funny, and quirky . . . A deliriously good book."

ChickLitBooks.com

"Combining unforgettably quirky characters with wacky situations and lots of humor, Blackston parades for the public a tale fit to rival his first. This laugh-out-loud read is laced with spiritual insights and misadventure romance. If you've ever scanned the sanctuary for prospects, let *A Delirious Summer* buoy your spirits—but be prepared for the ride of your life."

ChristianBookPreviews.com

"Blackston has brought his inimitable and delightful humor back to this novel. While most of the action revolves around the Presbyterians, no denomination is left unskewered. Blackston doesn't take religious trappings too seriously, and neither do the Ladies of the Quest, Greenville's young single women trolling for potential husbands: they will attend any church so long as the single male pickings are good. Most important: these characters build community. Whether they're in a South American city, the rainforest, on a beach, or in a parish hall, they take each other as they are and find ways to love each other. What could be more Christian—no matter what denominational stripes are donned?"

FaithfulReader.com

"Takes you into the psyche of a single man. A humorous yet thought-provoking novel about dating, church-hopping, friendship, and missions, *A Delirious Summer* is an enjoyable romantic escape that single as well as married individuals won't want to put down."

Charisma magazine

The Buzz on *Flabbergasted*

"Amazing. A novel with no illicit sex, bad words, racial slurs, or crime that is simultaneously serious, hilarious, and impossible to put down."

The Dallas *Morning News*

"Blackston's first novel is refreshingly honest in its portrayal of young, single Christians. Good writing and an ample dose of humor make this as charming as *Bridget Jones's Diary* from the male point of view. Highly recommended."

Library Journal

"Imaginative first novel . . . sometimes brutally honest but always refreshingly funny."

Library Journal, Best Genre Fiction 2003, Christian Fiction

"Blackston's tale is a zany take on twentysomething life in the shadow of the steeple—and proof that when it comes to courtin', less can definitely be more."

Fort Worth *Star-Telegram*

"Ray Blackston [finds] humor in the absurdities of American dating rituals while weaving a healthy dose of religion and romance through both. An ideal reading choice."

Bookpage

"If you only read one novel this summer, let this be it!"

Crossings Book Club main selection

"Lad lit with great buzz and a voice very much like Nick Hornby, *Flabbergasted* is well worth checking out."

Bookreporter

"This is one of the feel-good novels of the year. A fun, lighthearted and thoroughly enjoyable 'relational gumbo' of a novel . . . quirky and very satisfying."

CCM magazine

"Intelligently funny."

Singer/songwriter Andrew Peterson, *Love & Thunder*

"Ray Blackston takes an amusing look at the Christian singles scene; the story proceeds at a leisurely, episodic pace."

Romantic Times

"Full of quirky characters, including our slightly jaded hero, this book made me laugh out loud. Fasten your seat belts and get ready for a wild ride!"

Liz Curtis Higgs, best-selling author of *Bad Girls of the Bible* and *Bookends*

"The bugs were bad, my friends were stupid, and my boyfriend was a mystery."

My name is Darcy, and I drove

"I was not leaving until I saw at least one kangaroo."

My name is Allie, and I was in charge of photography

"I drew the map. I followed the map. I obeyed the map."

My name is Steve, and I like my directions firm

"I was only trying to be romantic . . ."

My name is Jay, and I will be your narrator

Also by Ray Blackston:

Flabbergasted
A Delirious Summer

Lost in Rooville

A Novel

Ray Blackston

Revell

Grand Rapids, Michigan

© 2005 by Ray Blackston

Published by Fleming H. Revell
a division of Baker Publishing Group
P.O. Box 6287, Grand Rapids, MI 49516-6287

Second printing, June 2005

Printed in the United States of America

Library of Congress Cataloging-in-Publication Data
Blackston, Ray.
    Lost in Rooville / Ray Blackston.
        p.   cm.
    ISBN 0-8007-3057-7 (pbk.)
    1. Wilderness survival—Fiction. 2. Australia—Fiction. I. Title.
    PS3602.L3255L67 2005
    813'.6—dc22   2005002936

For my "Grace" friends

A discerning man keeps wisdom in view,
but a fool's eyes wander to the ends of the earth.

—Proverbs 17:24

Act 1

"This fellow is wise enough to play the fool."
—Viola, in Shakespeare's *Twelfth Night*

1

With apologies to the heat, what I remember most is the color of the dust.

After the shuttle bus pulled in that morning, a fine coating of orange dust settled over the town of Alice Springs. But unlike the dull, transient dust I'd seen in America, this dust looked provincial, as if for centuries it had been proud to rise and fall in the exact same spot.

I had climbed aboard that shuttle some twenty minutes earlier, one of four excited faces, all of us twentysomething, all of us peering through tinted windows; two of us about to discover that Australia can be a stealer of bliss. Before we could say "down under," the landscape flattened, momentum slowed, and our driver braked us to a stop. The four excited travelers stood and grabbed for luggage.

The third, my buddy Steve Cole, pressed his leather hat on his head. Ahead of him, a duet of girlish giggles filled the aisle. Steve's longtime flame, Darcy, led the way, blond hair swishing side to side, her height blocking our view. Right behind her was my brunette girlfriend, Allie, who eased between the seats with her year-round tan, toting two bags of luggage and her journal. Allie and I worked together in a remote region of Ecuador, and our dates were nothing if not adventurous. Today, edging forward on an Aussie shuttle, we peered once more through tinted windows, stunned at the absence of rainforest.

Last off, I tipped the driver with a five and stepped from air-conditioning into an early February heat wave. Not just any heat, but desert-quality heat.

For here the seasons were inverted, or perhaps the season never changed. From the baked look of the terrain, every month was summer.

"Did you tip him?" Allie asked over her shoulder. The weight of her luggage pulled her arms straight, and already the sweat beads had formed on her cheeks.

"He's happy," I assured her, turning to give the driver a thumbs-up.

We all stood in the road for a moment, blinking our disbelief, hoping our sneakers wouldn't melt.

Darcy reached into her shoulder bag and drew out her sunglasses, aviator frames with mist-green lenses. She was tall and not easily given to embarrassment, the kind of girl who could paint her car an odd color and not care what you thought, then sell that same car and use the dough for charity. Now adorned with her mist-green lenses, she looked quite Hollywood but spoke pure Southern. "Y'all, this land just goes fo-evuh."

Steve grabbed her heaviest bag and grunted with the effort. "Yep, so big you might lose the rest of your r's."

Darcy frowned, slung her camera strap over her shoulder, and asked Allie to share the sunscreen. Our long-traveled foursome shoved luggage to the sidewalk and stared up at a sign beneath a wooden awning: OUTBACK ADVENTURES—RENTAL FOUR-BY-FOURS, AND GUIDED TOURS.

The last guided tour I could remember was a field trip back in the third grade, when our class toured a Texas fort and after lunch I hid with Michael Stokes beneath a cannon. All afternoon we'd pretended to shell the Union. A search party of teachers found us just before sunset.

Twenty years later, I, Jay Jarvis, stood on the other side of the planet, in the Northern Territory, just outside of a discount rental agency, discussing with Allie, Steve, and his independent girlfriend whether to rent one four-by-four or two. Travel all together or in separate vehicles? This was the only relevant question. After flying fourteen hours across the Pacific and losing an entire day of our lives to boot, no way were we going on a guided tour.

We took all of sixty seconds to decide.

Allie reached out and took both of my hands in hers, swinging them persuasively, in the way she always did when she wanted me to see things her way. "Jay, I'd like to be able to engage in some girl talk every now and then," she said. "And lots of alone time with you too." She let go of my left hand and reached up and pulled away some dark hair sticking to her neck, hair that had grown long and uncooperative, semiwavy and unfit for heat. She tugged at the bottom of her shirt and enticed some air inside. "So I vote for two."

Darcy Yeager, in all her height and blondness, stood with hands on hips, looking around as if she could not believe we had actually arrived here. Finally she sniffed the hot air, gazed over her sunglasses, and nodded her approval. "And I want some alone time also, just Steve and me riding together."

Steve moseyed over beside me—he'd gained a good ten pounds since I'd seen him last, and he'd cut his hair military short. Together with the hiking shorts and the outback hat, he looked like a stocky, twenty-eight-year-old Boy Scout, ready to explore. He put an arm around my shoulder and winked at the girls. "And Jay and I are gonna need to talk sports every once in a while."

I left them in the shade of the awning and stepped into the rental place with our order memorized: Two dependable Land Cruisers, please. Extra gas. Hold the guides.

Cheap vinyl flooring and a pair of chrome chairs masqueraded as a lobby. Motown music piped low and nostalgic from the ceiling. Outback Adventures had a retro feel to it, and atop the counter a chrome bell was the only available employee. I stepped forward and rang the bell.

From a back room came an angular fellow with leathery skin and sun-streaked hair. He reached across the counter and shook my hand, in a manner that told me I was about to get charged too much. "I remember you, mate," he said after I'd told him my name. "You're the Jay who called in from South America, right?"

"Ecuador, right. You spoke to me and Allie."

"And the other two out there," he said, pointing out his front window. "They look American too. That tall girl, the blonde, she'd be his sister, I hope?"

"Nope. His girlfriend."

"Me luck," he muttered and began filling out the rental forms. "So I guess you need to see what you'll be driving. Right, mate?"

"Right . . . mate. And how much per day? 'Cause we're gonna need them for four days."

Rental Guy produced a calculator and began a tally. "One hundred twenty-three dollars and eighty cents per day," he muttered. "So that would be—"

"Four hundred ninety-five dollars and twenty cents," I said, smiling. "Times two."

He looked up from pressing the buttons. "Good at math, are we? Well, let's see how good ya are at navigating 'Stralia." He motioned for me to follow him outside.

Rental Guy led our foursome around the side of his building, where he summoned us together and began espousing the capabilities of his well-used fleet: Four-wheel drive. Spare gas cans. Spare parts. Two-way radio to talk to the other vehicle. A tent and sleeping bags folded in back. "And if you happen to break down or get stuck while camping or out carousing," he said, pointing toward the barren interior of his country, "do not leave the vehicle. Our heat is a killer. Three of every five people who try to walk in, die. But four of five who stay with the vehicle, live."

Allie stepped in front of me. "But what if you're in mixed company and you have to *go*?" She stood on her toes and peered as far as she could into the colossal blank that was central Australia.

Rental Guy's answer was quick and dismissive. "You sheilas just go behind a bush or a rock formation, hurry back to the vehicle, and no worries, aye?"

Aye. No worries.

He then pointed to the last three four-by-fours he had available. The silver one sported a flat tire and a cracked windshield, though the other two looked in decent running order: A burnt-orange Land Cruiser that was obviously not its original color, though it did remind me of the University of Texas, my alma mater. And then a white one, a bit newer and boasting symmetrical mud stains behind the wheel wells. Roof racks and oversized bumpers topped off the rugged look.

"V-8s, mate," our host said to Steve.

Steve dropped to all fours and examined the undercarriage. Then he stood with orange kneecaps, kicked a back tire, and gave his approval.

"Saucy," Darcy said, smiling at the discussion of our rides. Darcy was the worst driver in our group, but also the most insistent upon driving; she'd spoken of little else all the way across the Pacific. After the four of us initialed the rental forms, she climbed behind the wheel of the white Land Cruiser and left Steve to load their luggage.

Not that I didn't help. Allie and I loaded similar gear into our burnt-orange chariot—the one to which we would entrust our lives in hundred-degree heat. While loading, I kept glancing over at a thermometer that hung on the side of the building, wondering if the thing was broken. "That's the temperature in the shade, mate," warned Rental Guy, who lifted the hood and began checking the oil level. "So take plenty of bottled waters. But we cool off quickly in the evening."

I opened the driver's door to inspect the interior, saw a rag on the floorboard, and used it to wipe the collecting dust from the side mirrors and windshield. "What's with the big bumpers?" I asked.

Our host placed one foot on the front bumper and pressed hard. The vehicle barely bounced. "No worries. After sunset you might see roos and wallabies hopping about. They'll cross the roads, snoop around campsites. These bumpers here'll protect you and the sheila."

Next he reached in under the dash and pulled out a walkie-talkie, small and black, not much bigger than a cell phone. "Jay, this here's your best friend," he explained, turning the squawk control on and off. "You and the other vehicle can talk to each other if ya get lost. I checked her out just this morning, and she's got a good range to her." He demonstrated how to work the thing and then stuck it back under the dash.

While he and Steve checked all the fluids in the vehicles, Allie hurried around the passenger side, toting a backpack and a frown. "Jay, I wish he'd stop referring to me and Darcy as 'sheilas.'" She set the pack in the backseat and turned to speak. "Doesn't that mean 'hooker' in Australian?"

After we had all of our gear situated in the vehicle, I called Rental Guy aside and asked him, in a low whisper, if "sheila" did indeed mean "hooker" in Australian.

"No, mate," he whispered back. "Means female. A few Aussies even use the term for female kangaroos."

"Aye," I said, not sure if he was telling the truth but trying my best to adapt to the carefree lingo. "No worries."

They say Australia is about the size of our lower forty-eight. But the similarity stops there. For if maps of the two countries were overlaid, Maine to Maryland would comprise the Great Barrier Reef; Sydney would envelop Savannah; Melbourne would be Miami; and across the country, in the role of windswept San Diego, would sit Perth. Now that we all have our bearings, I'm here to tell you that we were not in any of those places. Not even close. Where we launched from was, in effect, Kansas, which in Australia means the Northern Territory and this town of Alice Springs, gateway to the outback.

The plan was to spend four days driving in and out of arid wilderness, during which we would visit some famous rocks, King's Canyon, and an Aboriginal settlement. Then we would return the vehicles, fly down to Melbourne and depart three days later from Sydney. But how often does the reality-map overlay the plan?

Darcy and Steve pulled away first. After a stop to buy groceries and two cases of bottled water, they led us down a two-lane highway, a dull blacktop coated in familiar orange dirt. It was early afternoon, and the tourist town behind us faded rapidly, in contrast to the view ahead, a rocky horizon that seemed to just keep growing and growing.

Minutes later Allie reached over and put her hand on mine. "Jay, this is the free-est I've felt since we floated off in the Atlantic with our eyes shut."

"Don't remind me. We almost became human sushi."

"It was a test. . . . I would only date a risk taker."

I rubbed her fingers and tried to adapt to driving on the left side of the road. "If you don't mind, let's say yes to vision in Australia."

Pursuing her had meant saying no to a six-figure offer to work on Wall Street, yes to risk, and maybe to Ecuador. It also caused a wedge in my family. In Dallas lived relatives mired in shock over my leaving the investment world to go work in a jungle village with a Carolina girl whom they'd never met.

And because of what I'd given up, I often teased Allie about what our dating life might have been like if she had been the one who'd moved. "Hey, do you realize that had I stayed on as a stockbroker, we could have afforded to come here twice a year? Twice a year down under?"

Through a curved section of road she remained silent. Then she opened her journal, wrote a line, and spoke without looking up. "And you'd have been traveling with someone else . . . twice a year."

She had this mind-set, this theory ingrained in her that if a person was passionate about something—in her case helping to raise a bunch of orphans—that everything else, including who she ended up with, would flow from that service. Perhaps she was right.

I followed the white Land Cruiser along a straightaway—already Darcy was speeding—and pressed the issue with my girlfriend. "So, you're certain that you would never have moved to New York City to be near me?"

Allie closed her journal and gazed out of her window. "No way," she said, not a hint of tease in her voice. "It was either going to be me working alone in the village, or me and you working together in the village, but it was never going to be me living in New York City."

Such brown-eyed convictions not only attracted me but produced in me a challenge—to convince myself that occasionally men have to leave career and relatives in order to cleave to the right woman. And right now, as we drove between sparse fields of grass and stone, my thoughts were growing very cleavolicious.

Darcy and Steve rolled on ahead of us, pulling in their wake a hovering copper dust that settled on and blended with our burnt-orange hood. The road out of Alice Springs had begun smoothly enough, but now the pavement looked tired and scorched, like it was ready to give way at any moment to packed dirt and gravel. For the next hour we drove between plains of golden grasses, weathered rocks, and, I imagined, lots of scaly things that crawl.

Allie began writing on a page of her journal, and a few miles later she caught me peeking. I only saw the first two lines—the beginning of a poem—before she hid them with her hands.

16

Aussie foyer, red welcoming road
What lies beyond, in your arid lands?

"Don't," she said, clutching the journal to her chest. "It's not good yet."

Convicted, I caught up to the others on yet another straight stretch of highway—and saw Darcy reach over and squeeze Steve on the neck, as if to thank him for letting her drive. She sped up, and I accelerated through their dust.

With Darcy feeling the pressure of steering the pace truck, the next fifty miles became the vehicular equivalent of ADD: tall blonde slowing to see everything; tall blonde speeding up so as not to miss anything.

Soon the deficit and the disorder caused me to level off at a reasonable speed, and it was then that Allie leaned into the console and looped her arm around my elbow. "Jay, did the rental guy ever explain what sheila means?"

"He said it means you resemble a female kangaroo."

And here, just when I was feeling all romantic about this journey, Allie reached into the backseat for one of her bags and said, "I think it's time for some girl talk. Catch up to Darcy and I'll switch places with Steve."

After Allie alerted them on the two-way radio, I honked twice and waved Couple Number Two to a stop.

Both vehicles stopped on the shoulder and sat idling. Allie started to open her door, then reconsidered and leaned across the seat to kiss me good-bye. "G'day, Jay."

At the parting of lips I winked and reminded her to wear her seat belt.

There would be lots of switching of drivers on this trip, but if I'm honest I'll admit that I was so distracted by what I was planning to do that I almost missed Australia.

The entire ordeal seems a blink, a breath, and yet it is memoir and forever.

G'day, Allie.

2

I had bonded with Steve Cole over sports, a love of great seafood, and the startling fact that both of us once went to church solely to meet girls. I'd met him in South Carolina, as he drove us to the beach on a Memorial Day weekend that greeted him with a speeding ticket. Today, however, rolling along through the middle of Australian Kansas and tailing our girlfriends, he was steering one-handed and humming to Lynyrd Skynyrd, confident that no cops patrolled such a vast expanse of desert.

"Oldies stations, Jarvis," Steve said, turning down the volume. "That's all they have here. Besides eighties music and country, me 'n Darcy could only find Bing Crosby and the Osmonds on the dial."

"Maybe the Aussies are just way behind America."

Steve shook his head and kept driving. "Nah, way in front. It's like those old crooners are serenading us as we roll across the outback, reminding us to take our time. I could never cross the outback to heavy metal."

"Or to rap."

"Or, or . . . to punk."

He seemed restless, and for no reason at all he drove off the road and onto the shoulder and back again. Our four-wheel drive hardly strained as the oversized tires kicked up and spewed a mixture of sand and rock.

I shut my eyes and tried to retrieve the day we'd lost on the flight across the Pacific. "Just don't kill us, Cole . . . and don't fall too far behind the girls."

Steve steered us back up on the road and pointed at the girls rambling ahead. "Whaddaya think they're talking about up there?"

I only hesitated a second. "Us."

"Just us?"

"Allie says most girls have a preordained pattern of chatter. They start with the heavy stuff—all the relational tangles—then move toward the trivial. You know, food and fashions, then news and movies."

Steve let the data settle on him for a moment. "I had no idea. I stay firmly within the trivial." Then he slowed our pace considerably and began staring into the rearview mirror at his lips. He kept saying, "'Stralia, 'Stralia, 'Stralia."

It took me a moment to figure out what he was doing. He was practicing the native tongue by leaving the "Au" out of "Australia."

"So you got it down pat?" I asked, amused at how precisely he was trying to pronounce the word. "You're now an expert in the lingo?"

He repeated the word three more times. "I just figured it out, Jarvis. If ya say it just right, it's like the first syllable is in there even though it's not. It's a stealth syllable."

"I don't think there's such thing as stealth syllables."

Steve sped up again, drafting just beyond the backwash of Darcy's rear tires. "Well, at a minimum it's a lazy syllable. But I didn't fly halfway around the world to argue language."

His linguistics took root, however. I rolled down my window, sniffed the hot air, and with a hint of Texas pride muttered, "'Merica."

But it lacked the intended effect and, truth be told, my heart wasn't in it. If there was one time when I felt distanced from the trivial, it was now. Part of me didn't even want Steve and Darcy along on this trip. Part of me wished that they had stayed in South Carolina. Because at some point in this baking-hot excuse for a continent, when time and scenery allowed for privacy, I was going to drive Allie far away from Couple Number Two. I would wait for a memorable moment, no, a magnificent moment—perhaps a sunset in the shadow of some scenic hilltops—and produce the little black box hidden in the clutter of my duffel bag.

I, Jay Jarvis, had toted a rock to Australia. And something—whether it was fear or pride or a need for accountability—made me want to share this information with my buddy. In a barely audible voice came my confession. "I brought a rock with me, Steve-O."

He tipped up the brim of his hat, stared intently through our windshield at a distant range, and replied as if barely interested. "Ya brought a pet rock to 'Stralia?"

"No, a real rock."

At this news he pushed his brim even higher, like his mind was now turning faster than our knobby tires. His eyes darted quickly from the road to me and back again. "Jarvis, you're not talking about a . . . a ring?"

"That's what I said—a real rock."

His grip on the steering wheel tightened. "Man, we gotta have a talk."

"Don't worry, bro, this gem ain't intended for you."

Steve slowed further, and in seconds we fell a quarter mile behind the girls. "Hold the steering wheel for me a sec."

"What for?"

"Just hold the wheel. I gotta show you something."

I leaned over and held the wheel steady with my right hand as Steve turned and dug through a bag behind his seat. I figured he was just hungry.

Instead he produced a small box, the shell lined in black velvet. He flashed it open, grinned, and shut the lid. I immediately let go of the wheel, and we swerved toward a ditch. Steve jabbed the brakes. Tires skidded on loose dirt, and we stopped sideways in the road.

"You cannot be serious," I said, raising my voice, glaring at him in a way that said *how could you?* "This was my plan, and now you're copying me? I've been planning this since the day we booked the trip. I'm gonna find the right spot when Allie and I are off alone and far away from you two, and then I'm gonna, you know . . . pop the question."

"Well . . ." Steve's mutter trailed off as if he had no real rebuttal.

"Well, what?"

"I've been planning a similar thing since last Thursday, when I bought my hat and packed my luggage."

I pointed a finger at him. "You are not going to steal my idea. I thought of it first, so you'll have to wait till after I'm done."

After some contemplation he pointed back. "But if I wait on you to go first then I'll look like the copycat."

I stared out the window and did not bother to hide my frown. "Oh, man," I mumbled to the dirt, "two gems in one truck."

Steve set his black box in his lap and gripped the steering wheel with both hands. "Yep, Jarvis, little Stevie brought a rock to 'Stralia."

I went numb for a minute before urging him to get going, that we surely didn't want to lose track of lead-footed Darcy and my poetic flame. Steve turned us straight again and drove quickly toward an orange horizon. Neither of us said a word for miles.

I sought relief in geography. I opened the glove box and unfolded our map and began to look for unique places, private places, memorable places where Allie and I could split off from Steve and Darcy.

WEEBO, WAGGA WAGGA, and STREAKY BAY caught my attention, though all were hundreds of miles away. Termination Island, off the southwest coast, eliminated itself by name alone. Draw your own conclusions, but apparently lots of Aussies descended from criminals, misfits, and crazies. The whole place was once a prison.

Rolling along through the uncluttered center, I envisioned the early settlers not seeing another soul for months on end. Nearly everyone lived at the coast. Out here, marsupials were said to be the more populous species, though we had yet to see any.

Even stranger was the plant life. Patches of spinifex, a prickly strain of Australian grass, grew defiantly through seared earth, and beyond it the land rolled out as a lonesome carpet, only an occasional ripple interrupting the flow, as if never pressed flat by feet or tire. The region boasted an emptiness that begged wonder, oozed privacy, and prodded the curious to explore. We, of course, were the curious.

Steve sped up, caught the girls, and in a straightaway that went forever, eventually passed Darcy, who honked twice and let us by. I blew a kiss through the dust at Allie, and she sent back three. During the entire fifteen months we'd been together she'd never sent back more than two, so maybe three meant something.

Another few miles and I could stand it no longer, could not distance myself from Steve's confession. "I still can't believe you brought a ring with you. What cut?"

"Teardrop," said Steve, nearly smirking through his reply. "You?"

"Big and oval."

He pursed his lips and accelerated again. "What gave you the idea to propose in Australia?"

"An elderly friend said it was exotic," I said, wondering why he even had to ask. "You?"

"Same."

All I could figure was that we were two nervous males who'd been enticed by simple math: Australia + Woman + Ring = Good Plan.

Visibly unsettled, Steve gripped the steering wheel with both hands and squeezed. "How much did you spend?"

I tried to imagine him in his khaki Boy Scout shorts, dropping to one knee. "More than you."

He checked our speed. "No way. You're a poor mission worker."

He was right, though he didn't know everything, certainly not my finances. "I still had 272 shares of Microsoft left in my old brokerage's savings plan, so I sold 68 shares to pay for my plane ticket and 200 shares to pay for the ring."

"That only adds up to 268 shares."

"I know that."

We rolled along for miles before Steve spoke again. "Jarvis, why would anyone keep just four shares of stock?"

My answer sprouted from Wall Street and its excesses. "Someday those four shares will split two for one, and then I'll have eight shares . . . and then it'll go up and split again and so I'll have sixteen, and then thirty-two, sixty-four, one hundred twenty-eight, two hundred fifty-six, and finally, five hundred and twelve, at which point I'll be about seventy-five years old and can bring Allie back to 'Stralia and go on a guided tour."

22

Steve rubbed his temple, as if my head math had confused him. "You're a genuine nutcase. You need a wife even worse than I do."

I let the map slide onto the floorboard. "So, does this mean I get to go first?"

After much consideration, he nodded his head. "Fine, go first." He looked longingly at his little black box, then reached behind the seat and stuffed it back in his travel bag. "We'll work out a schedule and you'll have an entire afternoon to do your thing."

I smiled inwardly, outwardly, and into my side mirror. "Cool."

Having only one couple from whom to distance myself was really not so difficult a task. This plan of mine could have been much more complicated to pull off, with a third couple planning to join us for the journey. My former Spanish teacher, Neil Rucker, and his off-the-wall girlfriend, Alexis Demoss, had originally bought plane tickets with us way back in November. But a week later Neil and Alexis turned into the Couple Who Could Not Wait. They simply had no patience to wait much longer to enjoy the union that God had sanctioned. They were engaged on December 5 and were married in Greenville, South Carolina, by the Reverend Asbury Smoak, on January 22.

How romantic.

And how nonrefundable their tickets.

So they convinced Qantas to move up the departure date of their trip from February 3 to January 23 and left for Australia without telling any of us when they would return stateside. For all I knew, Neil and Alexis were somewhere within three hundred miles of Alice Springs—camping, exploring, and using various and scenic locales to enjoy what God had sanctioned.

Steve had been a groomsman. I was the envious best man.

Few bachelors will ever admit this, but as we stand around at wedding receptions with our second and third glasses of punch, we are all envious.

Three hours had passed since we'd left Alice Springs, and in the monotony of the landscape, Darcy grew bored. She began weaving ahead of us. As if privy to the protocol of desert flirtation, Steve swerved right and accelerated past the women, making one half of a figure eight. Then he cut left and she right, the women passing us back and completing an elongated ocho.

Imagine a long line of giant, dusty figure eights, laid end to end across central Australia, and that was our pattern for the next half hour. Steve was enjoying himself so much that I hesitated to engage him in conversation. Like a madman set free for one afternoon, he grinned wildly and let Darcy pass us once more.

"It's just stored-up energy from flying for all those hours," he said, as if this was some kind of excuse for running ragged across the outback. "We gotta live this trip to the max."

Our windshield slowly caked with dirt and dust, and we wobbled to the swerves and passes. "We're not even to our first stop, and already we're to the max?"

"Yeah. We gotta make up for the lost time, because I heard your girlfriend say that we lost a whole day of our lives when we landed."

"That would be true."

"So there's no February 4? Today is the fifth?"

"Yeah, but the Aussies give you the day back when you return to the States. It's like they just borrow it, then decide they don't want it."

Steve began nodding to himself, as if all facts had registered clearly. "So, so, that means I'll land back in the U.S. even before I leave Australia. . . ."

"That's as near as I can figure it."

He honked through the dust and passed Darcy again "'Stralia is gonna be great, Jarvis."

"Yeah," I said, sucking on the word but still miffed that he'd copied me. "'Stralia."

Without warning, Darcy passed us back, and tiny pebbles pinged off the hood. My guess was that she and he had planned this swerve-a-thon in advance, just to scare us.

But I was too preoccupied to be scared. I was planning a magnificent moment and trying to stay calm, which is an elusive state of mind for any bachelor contemplating happy-ever-after with his favorite sheila.

3

I suppose that many happy-loving-couples start out as secret-liking-couples. Some even go so far as to not admit they are dating. So it had been with Steve and Darcy. They had done such a fine job of hiding their relationship that it took a chance discovery by me before Steve would own up to the romance. I'd caught them at the beach in South Carolina, two houses apart, standing on separate rooftops and signaling each other with flashlights.

Presbyterian beach trips . . . not quite what you'd expect.

No matter the relational history, I considered it a privilege to hang out with a couple who were laid-back enough to switch riding partners in order to visit with their best friend's flame.

"For an hour or so?" Steve asked.

"An hour's good."

The women slowed ahead of us, and Darcy signaled with her left blinker. Here in the Northern Territory, switching hour was preceded by Steve pointing out, for the third time, that the highway never widened beyond two lanes. Except for the occasional trucker—in Australia they pulled up to three trailers and were known as road trains—the asphalt was barren in both directions. The view grew similar to driving west through Arizona, only there were no golf courses in midroute, no casinos in the next state, and no L.A. waiting botoxed at the far end.

At Darcy's wave, Steve pulled to the left shoulder, and below a billboard we stopped in the shade of an insult: AYERS ROCK (ULURU): 110 KILOMETERS (THAT'S ABOUT 68 MILES FOR YOU AMERICANS).

Beyond the wording lay nothing but dirt and grasses. They say that if you stare across such a barren expanse for any time at all, you'll start seeing things, leisurely images that shimmer and dance. Ever hopeful, I stared. And stared. But there rose no waterfalls or palm trees or blue pools of comfort, just a vision of married life that was, like this outback, uncharted acreage.

The thought of it—another life beneath my roof—had me bouncing in my seat as I pondered not only union but monogrammed towels and filing jointly. I glanced over at Steve, and he too looked as if his thoughts ran wild.

He stared up at the billboard for a moment before killing the ignition. "Just remember, Jarvis, you cannot give Darcy any clues about what I brought, or what I'm planning."

My hand paused on the door handle. "Only if you leave all mention of rings out of your discussions with Allie."

He made a fist, I made a fist, and we tapped knuckles like athletes.

"Then we're agreed?"

"No worries."

I climbed out from the passenger seat of our orange Land Cruiser, only to be scolded by the Aussie sun as I stretched my back. Out here, in a matter of minutes a person could feel crispy like a French fry or dry roasted like a peanut, although in my ring-obsessed state of mind I could not be sure, just that you'd be some sort of snack food and very hot.

Steve waved a plastic bottle out his window, and I went over and took it from him and slung some water on the windshield. He switched on the wipers, and in tandem they produced a streaked, orange mess. Paper towels proved effective, and after a check of the tires our pit stop was complete.

The girls remained chatting inside their vehicle, its engine idling. Steve leaned out his door as I gave one last wipe to the windshield. "Jarvis," he said, tugging his hat down low, "you not only make a good window washer, but someday I might even use you as a groomsman."

"Vice versa." I turned to wave the girls out and commence with the switch. Ahead the white passenger door opened slowly, and I watched

26

a lithe and familiar hand ease out of the interior. She signaled with one finger that I should come hither.

I arrived thumbing, like a hitchhiker, and pulled her door wide. "You ladies headed my way?"

Allie turned in her seat and placed her feet on the running board. I loved the way she looked here, windblown and adventurous, the angled sun catching her face aglow, the squint of her eyes communicating that she didn't want to be with anyone but me. Then, "Jay, first of all, I can't believe you changed into that purple Hawaiian shirt."

"It's the nearest thing I had to island wear." She looked confused, so I pointed end to end across the continent. "We're driving across a big island, ya know."

With the back of her hand she brushed off a fly, then, just as quickly, the subject. "Darcy and I think the four of us should camp out in the desert tonight, preferably near some photogenic cluster of rock." She turned and met the affirming gaze of her driver. "Isn't that right, Darcy?"

Darcy was busy tying a scarf around her neck. The scarf was lime green, and she tugged it up over her nose to where she looked like a bandit from JCPenney. Her voice turned nasal. "Yep, if you men can find us some scenic, sandstone rocks, we might even make dinner for you."

I peered inside the truck and gave Darcy a thumbs-up. "No arguments with that."

Allie stood and put a finger to my chest. "But one more thing," she said, tapping out each word. "We all need to respect the traditions of this country."

"What, you two want to grill a goanna lizard?"

"Not the food; the place. According to my travel book, the Aboriginal name for Ayers Rock is Uluru, and so from now on we've all gotta use the correct name."

Darcy leaned across the console and pointed at the billboard. "Yeah, Jay, the dumb Americans will count down the miles to Uluru."

"Oo-la-roo," I repeated, wondering how any guy could be expected to memorize the traditions of a foreign country while his brain was in the

27

relational blender, being mixed, whipped, and pureed by thoughts of dropping to one knee.

"Uluru, Jay," Allie said, insistence in her tone. She pulled me onto the dirt shoulder and turned me to where we were face-to-face. "Don't forget."

She didn't wink, and she didn't exactly smile, but she looked at me as if she were searching for something in my countenance. My legs shook. My brain fogged. But I made myself think about nachos with cheese and somehow managed to blink my innocence to her.

I could never tell what she was thinking. Once in our Ecuadorian village, we were walking to pick bananas after giving English lessons to the kids, and just before we began climbing I sensed that something was bothering her—and that the problem was, as usual, me. So I asked her what I had done wrong that day, or the previous day, or even the previous week. She shrugged and said, "Oh, little Isabel misspelled Amazon on her test today, and she's never misspelled Amazon before." Then Allie told me to interlock my hands and stoop over so I could hoist her up the tree.

But here in the outback there were no trees worth scaling, only mile after endless mile of baked red dirt, clumps of golden spinifex, and a sky stretched so wide that it had exhausted its supply of blue and inserted violet as a substitute.

Brunette Allie, in desert camouflage, and blond Darcy, in white shorts, navy T, and her lime-green scarf, allowed for one hour, and one hour only, of boyfriend swap. Allie strode back to her original vehicle, coerced Steve from behind the wheel, and asked him to navigate. I climbed into the white Land Cruiser with Darcy, who would not let me drive.

As soon as I hitched my seat belt, Darcy pulled her scarf down from around her nose. "We're gonna leave those two in the dust, Jay-bird."

"Um, yeah . . . the dust."

She mashed the gas, and we sped into the flatlands, our two-lane highway tapering in the distance to a fine black point of pilgrimage.

Ranking high on the list of awkward situations for a guy is how to converse with the girlfriend of a best buddy when he knows that within the next few days she might well be the object of a proposal.

I began with something safe—the flight over the Pacific.

Darcy adjusted her rearview mirror and told me the flight over the Pacific should have been lower, nearer the ocean, and that it was boring.

So I moved to the weather and the ovenlike temperatures.

Darcy fiddled with the radio. "Australia is less sticky than I'd thought, though very scenic, and now that we're here the flight over the Pacific seems even more boring."

Almost out of safe subjects, I brought up her car—she'd owned an old Cadillac convertible for several years, and it was always a hit on beach trips—and how I could not believe that she'd parted with it.

Darcy acknowledged this fact with a nod of her head. She lowered the sun visor and began steering left-handed. "Jay, the only way I could afford to come to Australia was by selling that car. Half went to restoring a coffeehouse, the other half to this vacation. But one day I'll have enough to buy another convertible, and I'll probably paint it lime green too. The odd thing about selling it was—"

She cut off her sentence as Allie weaved around us and spewed grains and gravel onto our hood. Under the dash, our radio squawked to life. My girlfriend spoke only two words: "Dare ya. . . ."

"You were saying?" I asked Darcy.

"Just a sec, Jay. I've been challenged."

Right there in the middle of the wilderness, the two women commenced with another bout of figure eights, white swerving behind orange, orange gunning its engine and honking its horn. These eights were longer, smoother, and far less jolting than Steve's version, even a bit feminine in their shaping.

But that didn't last long.

"Hold on, Jay," Darcy said, and she not only passed the others but also went right off the road, behind a dune and out of sight, through soft sand, onto hard dirt, bounced us through a dry ditch, and reemerged behind them. Darcy leaned on the horn and spoke into the radio. "Try that, mates."

She seemed in a great mood—which was nice to see. This was a girl who could just as quickly retreat into her own private Idaho, or perhaps I should say private Carolina, although private Carolina has too many syllables and would get blackballed from the American lexicon for its lack of efficiency.

"Darcy?"

"Yeah?"

"You're in a great mood."

She nodded and passed Allie again. "I'm definitely in a great mood. That huge rock, even though we can't see it yet, just keeps luring me onward, urging me to drive faster, like it has something it wants to tell me."

I swallowed my first sentence and retreated to safer ground. "That ol' Caddy you had would be fun out here with the top down. You miss it?"

Like a fainting starlet, Darcy put the back of her right hand to her forehead and in her best Southern accent said, "Oh Rhett, Rey-utt dahling, it still hurts me to know my cah is gawn, long gawn . . . gawn with the wind."

For the record, the word *wind* contained two syllables. We-und.

Before lead-footed Scarlett could utter another word, a mammoth shape began ascending against the horizon. Uluru looked out of place, as if a rust-colored boulder, five miles in circumference and shaped like a collapsing loaf of bread, had just decided to fall from the sky and plop down in the middle of nowhere. In fact, there was nothing preparatory on the landscape. No mini-Ulurus or granite siblings lying about. No cluster to admire, as with, say, Stonehenge. This thing before us was gigantic, historic, and very much a loner.

Darcy sped up, then she reconsidered and slowed way down, as if the extra time would magnify the experience. "Jay, that has got to be the biggest, most gargantuan rock I'll ever see."

Again I gulped the sentence that wanted to come out, took a drink from my water bottle, and began again. "Yeah, probably so. But I'd imagine there'll be lots of rocks on this trip."

She glanced left, out my window, then right out of her own. "Maybe, but this one will be the most memorable."

As tempting as it was to respond, I kept my mouth shut.

To my slight disappointment, we were not the first people to arrive at Uluru. More like the five hundred and first. Dust-covered four-wheel drives of many makes and colors, as well as tour buses, had done their best to surround the rock. Like an oversized tailgate party at a college football game, vehicles were strewn singularly and in clusters. Tourists climbed from air-conditioned comfort onto parched ground and stood transfixed, staring with squinted reverence at the southern and western walls. Flanking us to each side were tripods erected on sand mounds, people snapping photos of friends and family, others pointing, posing silly, the rock blushing now, embarrassed at the attention. Deep grooves, smooth edged and vertical, marred the surface of Uluru, as if God had taken an ice cream scoop and proceeded to carve away, just because he could.

If I were God, I'd do lots of stuff just because I could. Though I'd still be nervous about proposing to Allie.

Here in late afternoon, the sun seemed to exist solely to highlight this one inert spectacle of stone. Allie and Darcy parked the Land Cruisers a quarter mile back, amongst orange-red dirt and hardy clumps of spinifex. The four of us got out, coupled off again, and leaned against our substantial front bumpers, Steve and Darcy to Allie's and my left. Sunglasses on, gazes fixed in awe, we could only mutter the obvious. "Man, it's so big and old and reddish-looking."

Minutes later a middle-aged couple began walking toward the rock, as if intent on hiking up it. They wore matching light-blue caps and marched for hundreds of yards across crusted earth. But when they reached the base they stopped, glanced up at the sun, and turned back for their air-conditioned bus. Rental Guy was right—this heat was sneaky, and water was more valuable than opals.

Steve was the first to begin comparing—and Americanizing—Uluru. "Jarvis," he said, one hand gripping a bottle of Gatorade, the other fingering Darcy's left thumb, "that rock is a thousand times bigger than the Louisiana Superdome. In fact, if it were a stadium, it would be the Super-duper Dome."

"Sports," Darcy muttered, pulling her hand from his and folding her arms. "One of the great landmarks of Australia sits before us, and you have to compare it to American footbawl. Such a pity."

"Yes," Allie chimed in, "a genuine pity." She scooted closer to me on the bumper and removed her sunglasses, her right hand shielding her eyes while she concentrated on our find. "If anything, Steve, that rock deserves its own poetry."

Steve shook his head. "No way. Sports is the true comparison, right Jay?"

I scanned across blue sky and reddish rock and took a deep breath of the Northern Territory. "Don't pull me into this, bro. I'm just admiring the view." My long whiff reeked of hot soil and dry grasses, the smell of Kansas in July.

Steve and my girlfriend could not be stopped. "It's like this, Allie," he said, leaning forward from his bumper to make eye contact. Persuasion filled his voice. "Even if you took the lengths of all of Babe Ruth's home runs and laid them end to end, they wouldn't reach around that thing."

Allie stared upward and blinked astonishment. "Silly me. I was thinking of all the pages of Robert Frost laid end to end."

Steve gulped his Gatorade and continued. "Even if Tiger Woods stood atop that rock and hit his most mammoth tee shot, he wouldn't be able to clear the other side."

"Oh wow, Emily Dickinson, where are you?"

Perhaps he was full of nervous energy, or perhaps he just needed to distract himself from the fact he'd packed a little black box and lugged it halfway around the world in hopes of a yes. No matter the motivation, Steve stepped in front of us and, like a preacher reaching a crescendo, pointed with both hands at Uluru. "And one more thing, y'all. If the Civil War had been fought across this rock, none of the bullets or cannonballs from either side would've reached the enemy."

"My goodness," Allie muttered, feigning amazement. "General Lee in iambic pentameter."

I left them at the bumpers for a moment and returned with a fact-filled paperback. From Allie's travel book I read to them the Aboriginal beliefs about the rock, that it was a product of Tjukurpa, their version of the creation period, and that what we saw before us amounted to a mere glimpse; there were miles of this thing wedged underground.

Certain spiritual beliefs were attached to Uluru, although the travel book, like all politically correct travel books, did not expound on the beliefs beyond mentioning a sacred route to the top that dated back somewhere between twenty thousand years and prebrontosaurus. This route would wind through the crevices and rise steeply over eleven hundred feet, a trek so strenuous that more than twenty tourists had expired in midclimb. Two of five who climb the rock, die?

Steve glanced over at me, waited until neither of the girls was looking, and pointed at the ring finger of his left hand. Then he pointed to the top of that wind-scarred monolith and raised his eyebrows.

I shook my head no. Three times I shook it. No this was not the day, no I was not going to be hurried, and no I was not going to climb the sacred route to Uluru and risk expiring in the same hour that I pledged lifetime devotion to my girlfriend.

After a long silence and much gawking at the rock, we took group photos and sat down in the shade of the orange Land Cruiser on a light-green blanket that Darcy had spread out on the dirt. Daylight seemed suspended, and our long-traveled foursome began pining for naps.

And nap we did.

At sunset Uluru glowed deep red, nearly maroon in the grooves and crevices. Steve woke second. In the shade of the white Land Cruiser, he signaled to me to meet him at the rear of his vehicle, where he opened the hatch and slid a cooler out onto the ground. I was already tiring of his impatience but nevertheless excused myself from the waking women and strode back there and opened the cooler. Through melting ice I dug out sandwich meats and another bottled water.

He and his khaki Boy Scout shorts moved close and whispered from behind me. "Well, Jarvis . . . what about tomorrow? Could that be the day when you pop the question to your poet babe?"

"Don't rush me," I said, flinging water in my face to cool off.

Steve dipped his hand to the bottom of the cooler, sprinkled some drops in his outback hat, redipped, and dripped some inside his shirt collar. "But you can't wait too many days, 'cause that'll leave me no options. I don't wanna have to do it in the airport just before we fly back to Carolina."

I made the most casual face possible, even poked out my bottom lip. "Maybe tomorrow, maybe the next day."

He sucked on an ice cube for a moment and tossed it into the dirt. "I have an idea."

Mercy.

"Not another one of your engineering ideas," I said. "Those always misfire." I tried to ignore him while searching through plastic bags for bread and paper plates.

"No, really. This is a good one." He gripped my shirt sleeve above the elbow and gave it a tug, as if his idea really had merit. "Let's split off tomorrow morning. Take different routes to the next point of interest."

I removed my arm from his overanxious grasp. "What is the next point of interest?"

"I saw a sign that said there's a wildlife sanctuary a hundred and fifty kilometers down the highway. But for us Americans I guess that would be, um—"

"Ninety-three miles." I dug a plastic package from the ice before turning to address the women, who were seated together on the blanket and comparing their digital cameras. "What would you ladies like on your sandwiches?"

"What do we have?"

With curiosity I read the contents. "Looks like Oscar Mayer low-fat emu."

Darcy pulled her blond hair over one shoulder and spoke through the strands. "I'll have that," she said, traces of doubt in her voice.

"Double that emu," said Allie.

My girlfriend was the most contented person I'd ever known. After working in the wilds of Ecuador and living in a wooden hut for two years (I'd been there in my own hut for fifteen months), she was used to eating whatever was available, used to getting by with less, and fond of poking fun at the average American consumer.

What Allie was not used to, however, were bush flies.

Whether they were attracted to the meat, my jars of peanut butter and jelly, or Darcy's yellow tube of sunblock, swarms of small, brown flies descended upon our picnic. I figured the flies were making the rounds, using Uluru like peddlers use New York City—it was where the people

34

gathered. The flies didn't bite, just pestered our lips and eyelids with teasing flits and mocking flybys.

"Bugs," said Darcy, fanning them in exasperation. "Everywhere I go on this planet there's a bug. Bugs in Carolina, bugs in the Bahamas, bugs at Litchfield Beach, and now bugs in the outback."

Soon after Darcy overemphasized her point but well before we had finished our sandwiches, the majority of the pests moved on to harass another party. It was then that Allie decided it was time for something poetic.

Just off the right flank of our bumper, she found a stick and, a few feet farther away, an oval patch of dirt devoid of grasses. She pointed her stick at the soil and spoke to no one in particular. "The outback's word processor."

We watched amused as she carved a title in red earth, at one point bending so low that her lengthy hair tickled the dirt. She looked back between her knees. "This one's for you, Stevie." And she didn't say anything else until she was done.

Ode to Uluru

A rock of imminence, a rock of girth
Cannot be cloaked in the sports world's worth
Stevie Cole can't understand
That roots go deep in this Aussie land

We the privileged, invited here
To the Aboriginal hemisphere
Stare and gawk and feel your thunder
Dumb Americans . . . adrift down under.

Steve walked over, read the poem, and without comment went and sat back down on the blanket beside Darcy. "Hmmph," he mumbled. "No poet could even hit a baseball."

"But the poet could hit you," was Allie's smiling retort. She came over and pinched a piece of bread from her plate, balled it up into a doughy

35

marble, and hurled it with great accuracy into the side of Steve's head. He almost retaliated, but Darcy spread her arms wide and called for peace.

Allie's two stanzas were not earth shattering—nowhere near her best stuff—but then she hadn't spent any time at all on them. The meter came out of her just like it appeared. No rubouts. No rewriting. She'd been carving with her stick for three minutes, tops.

After finishing the first half of her emu-on-wheat, Darcy had the last word on Uluru. Seated Indian style to the left of me, she chewed a bite of her sandwich, tugged down her mist-green sunglasses, and stared out at the majestic landmark. "Alexis would say it's a spaceship . . . a spaceship disguised as a rock."

All nodded and continued eating.

With a plastic knife I cut my second pb&j sandwich in two halves, then summoned Allie back to the blanket. "Good writing, dear," I said to her. "Much better than the first one."

She came over and picked up her plate. "Ya know, Jay, a rock that size really does deserve its own poetry."

When she sat down beside me I set my plate on my knees and pushed the two sandwich halves back together, to where jelly and peanut butter bonded. It was the most subtle sign I could render, the two halves becoming one.

But Allie didn't notice. There in the fading light she just put her head on my shoulder and asked me why we hadn't seen any kangaroos yet.

4

Nightfall brought closure to our first day down under, and the mass fronting our campsite was now little more than bulk interrupting the sky. Never had I felt temperatures fall so quickly—from the hundred-degree heat of afternoon to perhaps sixty by the time we had snuffed out the bonfire and gone and stood in line in the dark to use the only bathrooms within fifty miles.

After brushes and flushes we walked back over hardened earth to our campsite. With his toothbrush in one hand and Colgate in the other, Steve turned an ear to the night air and stopped to listen. "Jarvis," he said, pointing over a sand hill, "a pack of dingoes could invade our camp if we don't take preventive measures."

I rolled my eyes and grudgingly agreed. And while our measure was not totally preventive, it did seem to soothe Steve's nerves—he and I moved the two vehicles to where they were parked in a V, the front bumpers nearly touching.

"Safer now?" asked Darcy. She stood in the middle of the V, turned her own ear to the bush, and gave a mocking howl to whatever was out there.

"Don't entice them," Steve said into the back of her head. "This isn't Carolina."

Allie and Darcy unloaded the gear from the back of the white Land Cruiser and decided that the long, empty space—with the hatchback raised and the backseat folded down—would make them the perfect bed. The girls insisted on sleeping in there, saying that it was a tight fit but a good fit for two best friends with lots of catching up to do.

But before crawling in, Allie put on a navy warm-up jacket and summoned me out away from the vehicles.

In darkness we stood together, silent and staring up at the heavens. Through experience I'd learned not to rush her. Finally she lowered her chin and said, "The stars in Australia are incredible, aren't they?"

I gazed across the night sky and saw a bazillion diamonds sparkling, twinkling, urging me on. "Yeah . . . incredible."

She took both my hands in hers and once again swung them gently, persuasively. "Jay, sometime tomorrow I want us to have a talk about our working together, and our lack of financial support. We said we were going to—"

"I know . . . communicate."

Allie stopped swinging our hands but retained her grip. "Do you know what I value most in our dating?"

"Being good communicators?"

"Right. And you have been . . . sorta."

I almost challenged sorta, but then I pictured the talk detouring into far tangents, off into areas where females exhibit uncanny memory for behavioral lapses. So I just nodded to her and glanced over at Steve and Darcy, who were practicing the South Carolina state dance, known affectionately as the shag. In the dark and without music, they made for a comical sight, especially with Engineer Steve lending mechanical rhythm to the steps.

Allie jerked my hands—and attention—back to her. "One other thing, Jay."

"You wanna dance too?"

"No, I misplaced something. I had written a note to Darcy and must have dropped it in one of the vehicles. You didn't find an envelope, did you?"

"Nope. Is it important?"

"Not really. Just girl stuff."

The air continued to chill, yet what felt like centuries of stored heat seeped upward through the sand. I corkscrewed my sneakers into its warmth and stumbled through the question I'd wanted to ask all evening. "What did Steve talk about with you while y'all were riding together earlier?"

Moonlight paled her frown, and she took a moment to answer. "He kept asking me to look at distant boulders and tell him what shape they were. He said one looked like an oval to him. But I just thought it looked odd shaped, like a bald man's head."

What a friend we have in Stevie. He'd be dealt with later.

I squeezed Allie's hands. "And that was all Steve said?"

"No, a mile later he pointed at another big boulder and said it looked tear shaped. He seemed obsessed with Australia's rocks. I think the heat really got to him."

"Yeah, sure . . . the heat." After a few minutes of absorbing the emptiness that is inner Australia, I led Allie back around to the open hatch of the white Land Cruiser. There she kissed me good night and crawled inside atop a thin foam mattress.

I should have turned to go unwrap my sleeping bag.

But I did not. Instead I lingered and thought of what it would be like to crawl in there with her, to have her as my wife. As a single man my greatest struggle was how to contain sensual thoughts about my girlfriend. Imagistic advice had come from Ransom Delaney, who told me once that sensual thoughts about girlfriends should be bound and gagged, held captive. Tonight I tried to apply his careful phrasing while admitting to myself that having a ring in waiting and Australian stars twinkling as Allie crawled onto a mattress was a situation far beyond captivating, and instead of careful phrasings what I really needed was a leash.

That's when Steve coughed from behind me.

I turned just in time to see him give Darcy a smooch g'night. Over her T-shirt Darcy pulled a gray USC sweatshirt, then she patted me on the head as if to say "It's been a good first day." The long-legged blonde crawled inside with the brown-haired poet, and the women laughed and pulled a blanket over themselves.

Laughter subsided into schoolgirl giggles, and they waved us away. *Shoo, boys. Make your own bed.*

No way was I staying in the back of the other vehicle with Steve Cole. At the passenger door I dug through my duffel for a long-sleeved T-shirt. Steve opened the opposing door and glanced across the interior. "I know what you're thinking, Jarvis, so don't worry. We ain't sleeping together in the back of this orange Land Cruiser . . . or any other color truck."

"So glad to hear you say that."

He assured me that he had a plan—Steve always had some kind of plan—and that last summer's beach trip with our buddy Neil had renewed in Steve a real passion for camping out in tents.

Rental Guy had included a four-person tent with the vehicles, a gesture I'd considered generous, if not presumptuous. The tent was a desert camouflage of brown and tan. Steve reached in, hoisted the folded canvas from the rear of the Land Cruiser, and turned with an offer. His voice stayed low as the girls settled further into their makeshift bedding. "You can sleep on either side of this tent, as long as it's not the left side."

I stared hesitantly at his offering and reached out to finger the thickness. "I dunno, bro. I tend to roll around a lot if I'm on the right."

He pointed firmly at the right edge of the canvas. "You'll do no rolling around. I need my rest if I'm gonna plan the perfect time to—" He motioned to the other vehicle. "You know."

My sense was to try and ease his anxiety. "Just enjoy Australia, bro. No worries. When the time is right, you'll know it."

The words were spoken as much for myself as for Steve. "When the time is right" were words I had heard ever since high school, words I did not trust. I used to think that even if the time *was* right, I'd somehow be distracted and miss the moment, and that life would thus be relegated to a series of Plan Bs and mediocrity. But not anymore. Tonight, I felt I had all the time in the world.

Steve and I unfolded the camouflage canvas and made ourselves an abode. We erected the tent on a patch of grass next to Allie's poem, just off the front bumper and out of earshot of the girls, who I was sure were not sleeping. A plastic smell welcomed me to the innards of the canvas, like the thing had never been used. Two poles in the middle functioned as support and separator, and I settled into the right side, still in shorts and sweat socks, still thinking of Allie, still capturing my thoughts, holding them hostage, and periodically whipping them just for spite.

Minutes later Steve crawled into the left side and sat up and rubbed his hands together, as if the friction in his palms would stir me into conversation. "Jarvis, I thought you might hike up Uluru this afternoon and propose up there."

I lay back and shut my eyes. "Never crossed my mind."

"No?"

"Nope. Besides, I wanna be a long ways from you and Darcy so I don't have to see you making goo-goo faces at me when we return."

I heard him do the palm thing again, though I figured wrongly that he had a case of the chills. "Are you nervous about it, Jay? 'Cause I'm kinda nervous about it. I didn't think I'd be this nervous, but I am. Both for you and for me."

"Will you just get over it? Please? There's not as much hurry or anxiety when you know you've found your soul mate." He stirred, and I opened my eyes.

Steve was adjusting the support poles; in many directions he adjusted them. He tilted one his way, one my way, and did not lie down until completely satisfied with his tent tweakage.

"Okay," he said. "I gotta know."

"Know what?"

"The soul-mate thing. Is there only one person? I mean, I'm sure Darcy is the right person for me, but what if I was born in California—would there be a different right person?"

"Our little friend Lydia covered that topic thoroughly on the beach trip, remember?"

"That was just the female view. I have to look at it more logically."

I could feel what was coming, knew I should just roll over and turn my back to him and go to sleep. But Steve and logic had always been inseparable, and since this was our first night, I mumbled a halfhearted, "Okay, let's hear the logic."

Steve cleared his throat like he was stepping up to a mic. "It's like this: what if a guy—let's call him Tom—is supposed to marry Susan, and this union is ordained from the heavens. But Tom's wandering eye causes him to get the hots for Doreen, and they end up marrying. So . . . you see where I'm going?"

"All I see are camouflage splotches on our plastic-scented tent."

"I need you to follow along."

"Okay. So Tom is ordained for Susan, but he marries Doreen."

"Correct. So now you have three potential undoings and—"

"What's an undoing?"

"An undoing is what God would have to do to set things straight again—if there really was just one person for everybody. Now we have three of 'em: Tom, who married the wrong woman; Doreen, who got swept off her feet and married Tom; and then of course Susan, who by now is really mad because she can't find someone to replace Tom, and so she's going online every night to scan the dating services. She's closing one match after another because she knows what should have happened."

"Poor Susan."

"Yeah, but do ya see my point?"

"I think so, but I'm all for clarity."

Steve took a deep breath, reached out, and readjusted a pole. "My point is that if one person messes up and gets hitched to the wrong person, then the whole diagram of 'who should be with who' gets knocked out of whack. Because what we haven't covered yet is Doreen's right man. He is now online as well, trying to communicate with Susan, who is not interested because she knows her guy, Tom, is hitched to Doreen. So this new guy is trying to find his Doreen online and has no idea that she's messed up and married Tom, the wrong guy. So now in desperation Susan finds some wrong guy to replace Tom, and now this guy misses his best, and so on and so on until the bridal stores are chock-full of wrong women picking out dresses to impress wrong men. I'm tellin' ya, Jarvis, I have my doubts about the only-one-soul-mate thing. Like ping-pong, it's far too likely that the dating ball will careen at some strange angle, get stepped on, and *crunch* . . . game over."

I lay there blinking rapidly, trying to follow engineering logic applied to male-female relationships and the intangibles of ping-pong. "So, um, how does all this relate to you and Darcy, and to me and Allie?"

Steve rubbed his palms together again. "Ah! That's just it, Jarvis. It doesn't relate to us at all, because we're patient men who found the right women and brought diamond rings to 'Stralia!'"

At this he reached across the tent and high-fived me.

In a buddy-buddy sort of way, I loved this guy.

I let the night air calm him for a time, and when he indeed seemed calmer I lay flat on my back and changed the subject. "Now tell me, bro, why'd you point at boulders earlier today and ask Allie to guess their shape?"

He hesitated like the guilty Carolinian he'd become. "I was curious."

"You were trying to give her hints, weren't you?"

Another pause. "Nah, I really thought the boulders were oval and tear shaped. I couldn't get my mind off of rocks, so in my weakness I gave in and started asking her what she thought of the scenery."

"You were giving her hints."

"I bet you tried to slip in a hint with Darcy."

"Did not."

"I know you, Jarvis."

My turn to hesitate. "Okay. One teeny, very vague hint, but she was driving and swerving so crazily that it slipped right past her."

Steve pulled out a tiny penlight and shone it into the top of the canvas. "This is not a well-made tent. It's only double stitched. My old pup tent back home has triple stitching."

"You must really be trying to distract yourself."

He cut the penlight off and mumbled, "Perhaps."

I was almost asleep when I heard him fidgeting with the poles again. I turned over and saw him sitting up, one hand on each pole. "Jarvis," he said, "it's not that women are wired differently than men, it's that they're not wired at all. They're . . . wireless."

"Yeah," I said, just hoping he'd get quiet. "Wireless."

43

"And what about Neil's new bride, Alexis? She's gotta be the most wireless woman in history."

I agreed wholeheartedly—I had gone on a date once with Alexis, to a French restaurant where she had slurped her merlot and rearranged the silver. Somehow she and harmonica-playing Neil had fallen for each other. And now, late at night inside a tent pitched in central Australia, I pondered out loud the adventures of the Couple Who Could Not Wait. "I honestly cannot picture what it would be like to live with her. Neil wrote me an email before their wedding and said Alexis had used her real-estate license to buy them this little house, and when he went over to see it she had painted their initials in giant script on the bedroom ceiling."

"He showed me that room—bright blue paint on a white ceiling. But that wasn't the half of it. Alexis got ol' Beatrice to help her clear out a flower bed by the front door and plant seeds in a pattern of letters. So next spring when the flowers bloom they're gonna spell out LOVE SHACK."

Affection expressed botanically. Hmmm. Gardening was not my thing, although I could picture Allie planting seeds that would blossom into a poem.

Thoughts of Neil on his honeymoon, serenading his bride, had me wondering about my lack of musical talent. Perhaps Steve was thinking likewise. "Ever serenaded Darcy?"

Steve turned on his side. "It's all I can do to learn the steps to beach music; I'm a long ways from any serenading. You?"

"Maybe once or twice."

"Like what? You sang to her?"

"I'm not tellin'."

"Oh man, I can't believe you sang to her. Mission workers make horrible singers. They warble like Tarzan."

"I'm an exception."

Steve clicked his penlight on again and rustled some papers in his bag. "I found something you need to see, Jarvis. Under the passenger seat I found a note that I thought was from Darcy to me, but when I opened it, the note was really from Allie to Darcy. It's most interesting."

I rolled back over and faced the camouflage. "If it's not for me I have no interest in reading it."

Steve grew insistent. "Jarvis, you'll want to read this. It was an honest mistake that I opened it. I really thought it was for me."

"Did the envelope have your name on it?"

"No."

"Did the envelope have my name on it?"

"Nope."

"Then I don't want to read it."

"But the envelope didn't have anyone's name on it. It was just a blank, lime-green envelope like Darcy always uses whenever she writes me something."

I rolled over into the middle of the tent. "Well, if that's the case, maybe we can share one little peek."

Leaned forward between the two poles, Steve shone his light onto cream-white stationery:

"The two of us shall become one." That, Darcy, is the way we women want to hear it from our men. But nooooooo. Instead we hear secondhand, from Neil and Alexis, that "a tangelo soared over the jungle as an act of commitment." We, the objects of Jay's and Steve's affections, are not even present for the event, and they would pretend to commit to us with a piece of fruit? Darcy, do you realize how sad this will be to have to share with our grandchildren? That is, if we ever have grandchildren. I agree with what you said on the flight over, that it will likely be at least three to four months before either Jay or Steve get around to seriously discussing marriage.

This trip down under is just for fun . . . so let's just
have all the fun we can.
G'day, sister,
A. K.

Steve looked at me with a blended expression of excitement and disbelief. With similar sentiments I tucked the note back into its envelope. Then
I crawled outside into chilled air, ambled over to the orange Land Cruiser,
and wedged the note in the backseat, beneath Allie's camera case.

Back in the tent, I could only glance at Steve and shake my head.
Further talk was unnecessary. From all the available evidence, we were
indeed going to surprise our women.

Steve lay flat on his back, and I let him have the final words on this,
our first night in Australia.

Again he rubbed his palms together, rapidly and with great enthusiasm.
"Just think, Jarvis, this could be the last road trip of our singleness."

5

If anyone thought I came up with the idea of proposing in Australia, they'd be wrong. I had help—and not from a fellow twentysomething.

She was at least eighty.

Her age and globe-trotting optimism made up for a deficiency shared by all members of our foursome: none of us—not Darcy, not Steve, not Allie or myself—had a living grandparent. Yet we rarely lacked for home-made cookies or relational advice. The source of the chocolate chips and the wisdom was the same woman who had donated the flower seeds that would blossom and spell out LOVE SHACK.

Beatrice Dean had returned from Australia in late September, after three weeks touring with the members of her gardening club. I'd known her for years, having been her stockbroker before I met Allie and said adios to Wall Street. Beatrice had even come to Ecuador once.

She had the habit of phoning me as soon as she got back from a trip, usually gushing about the scenery, the food, and the strangers who talked funny. This call had come while I was living in Quito.

"Jay . . . Jay, is that you?"

"It's me, Beatrice, about to eat my cereal. Where are you?"

"Jay, can you hear me, dear?"

"Yes. It's me. Where are you?"

"Back in Carolina. We've been to the down under."

Figures. "I've always wanted to go there. Did you see any roos?"

"Yes, dear, I did ruin my shoes. And the hiking is bad on the ankles."

"I said, did you see any kangaroos?"

"At sunset from the tour bus. We had just left the big red rock. I believe the locals call it Waterloo."

"You're thinking of Napoleon, Beatrice."

"Well, just imagine—sunset in the outback, and not a man on the bus with us. A pity and a shame. Just women."

Simple math began that very second: Sunset + Australia + Woman = Romance. "You say the sunsets are nice in Australia?"

"More reds and oranges than in my roses." And here she snickered. "Why do you ask, Jay? Are you getting serious with that jungle girl?"

"Yes. Quite."

"Planning something I should know about?"

"Probably."

Again she snickered into the phone. "Then I have some wisdom to share."

"Tell me."

"Qantas Airlines has nine-hundred-dollar, round-trip tickets on sale, although their pilots take forever to get you across the Pacific. They must play video games. But they do turn down the lights and let you sleep, and their breakfast fruits are fresh. And . . . and, oh dear."

"What is it, Beatrice?"

"My bladder is urgent. Can I call you back another day?"

"Certainly."

She never did call back. But her beauty lay in her unpredictability. After we'd hung up, it took no time at all to get Allie enthused about the possibility of an Australian trip and the affordability of tickets. The next day she contacted Darcy, and before I could think of an excuse for just the two of us to go by ourselves, both women were contacting Qantas. All Steve and I had to do was show up at our respective airports, and the four of us connected in L.A.

By then I had owned the ring for over a month. And by then, of course, Beatrice had called Steve and given him the same advice.

Thanks, Grandma.

What wakes you in Australia is not the morning cackle of birds but the heat resuming its authority. The chilled air of nightfall had long since departed, and the muggy air inside the tent grew muggier by the minute.

I poked my head through the flaps and saw Steve Cole a hundred yards from camp, seated by himself on a dirt hill, his back to me, his leather hat low on his head. To his right the Aussie sun rose monstrous and yellow, as if, like a snowball rolling down a slope, its girth had enlarged as it arced across the Pacific. I crawled out onto baked earth, stood slowly, stretched slower still—my first yawn in Oz.

The girls were still asleep, and from a nearby camp the smell of coffee eased past the tent. In the distance Steve rolled onto his stomach and pulled to his eyes a pair of binoculars. Something had grabbed his attention.

He peered intently through the lenses, refocused, and lay still again. From in front of the tent I watched him—the nervous Boy Scout of the previous night—now calm, all by himself and concentrating. And then, just as my curiosity peaked, he brought his left hand up behind his hat and signaled with two twitches of his finger that I should join him. I put on my sneakers and stumbled as I tied them in haste. With flopping laces I jogged toward daybreak, my posture crouched, my eyes unable to see over the red hill to whatever had caught Steve's fancy.

I'd covered most of the distance when he waved for me to stay low. "Get down," he whispered. "Stay down."

I dropped to all fours and snuck through clumps of grass and loose rocks. Beside him at 7:00 a.m., I lay on my stomach and borrowed the binoculars.

I had never even seen a wallaby in a zoo. But across the plain, between two bushes, a plump gray wallaby nibbled on grasses, offering only its profile, hiding its belly.

With much impatience Steve and I exchanged the binoculars, nudging each other and muttering "gimme 'em" after each five-second viewing. I had them back again, the strap dangling over my head, when the wallaby offered a full frontal view.

For a moment I thought I'd watched a mother give birth in the wild—

the momma looked relieved, the joey looked happy to have landed on the warm end of the planet. Then I realized that the momma had simply let the joey tumble out of the pouch.

"Wanna see a baby wallaby?" I whispered beneath the eyepiece.

Steve's jerk of the strap nearly pulled my ears off. Perched on his elbows, he focused, awestruck. He watched for a long while before whispering, "This is a sign, Jarvis."

I dismissed his comment and tried to see the happenings with the naked eye, but distance reduced the animals to featureless balls of fur.

"We should have woken the women," I said, knowing that Allie would savor such a sighting.

"Nah," Steve whispered back, lowering the lenses and squinting as the sun crept higher. "This is just for us. Don't you see—it's a sign from God."

I sat up on my knees and shielded my eyes from the glare. "Watching a momma wallaby feed its baby is a sign from God? For two soon-to-be ex-bachelors?"

Steve nodded. "This is preparation for daddyhood."

Finally I convinced him to share again. With borrowed binoculars I peered west and east, at long, barren expanses of dry plains and random chunks of granite. "But I don't see a daddy wallaby around anywhere."

This time Steve asked politely, and he took the binoculars back and wiped the lenses. He gazed at the momma and chose his words carefully. "We're not going to see the daddy, Jarvis, because he's out doing his thing, becoming a hunter-gatherer."

"Is that what we're in for? In addition to taking out the garbage, we gotta become hunter-gatherers?"

"Shhh. You'll scare the momma."

At this early hour I was not prepared for lessons on raising young 'uns, be the lessons from God, Steve Cole, or plump gray wallabies. But when are single men ever prepared for such a leap? Here in the Aussie sunrise, I did not have the ring in hand to hold up to the rays, but even without it I imagined new meaning in its core, extra depth to its luster. My goodness . . . daddyhood.

Steve must have been thinking the same thing. With a blank, squinted expression he caught my glance. "Think we'll ever—"

"What, be parents?"

He scratched a day's worth of stubble. "Probably, but not together."

I asked him if he wanted to hike back to camp, but he shook his head no and began adjusting the band on his leather hat. The quickness of his shake was all it took to let me know that nerves were again creeping up on him.

He sat up and wiped the morning sweat from his brow. "I think we need to go ahead, right now before the girls wake up, and make a plan for how we'll split off."

We were facing opposite directions, my back to the sun, arms wrapped around my knees, Steve still on his belly and watching the wildlife. Beyond our campsite Uluru sat patient and orange, too big to yawn, too old to care, just a loaf-shaped spectacle awaiting more gawking tourists. "I'm up for suggestions. Wanna just meet in a small town at dusk?"

"We have to set a specific hour," Steve said, "not just dusk. What about 8:00 p.m.? I already looked at the map, and there's this tiny town called Kulgera. It's on the far side of the Musgrave Ranges, which is a hilly bunch of—"

"If they're called ranges, Steve, then that implies hills."

"Just let me finish."

"Go ahead, finish."

"I figure if we both have all day to wait for the . . . what did you call it?"

"The pristine moment to propose?"

"Yeah, that. If we both have all day, then that means we can look for that moment and do it right, and then when we meet up in the evening, no one will feel like they've copycatted, 'cause everyone will have a surprise for each other. That's what you're thinking, right?"

I retied my left shoe and nodded. "You're a fine logician, but you're also a binocular hogger."

He never acknowledged my comment, just kept gazing across the plains and expounding on his plan. "On my map there's a scenic section where the road splits, so Darcy and I can go one way, and you two the other. The roads meet up again after a hundred miles or so. This way you can take Allie wherever you want, and we'll be separated all afternoon."

I sat up and turned to watch the wildlife again. "Sounds like you have it planned. But what if I don't sense the pristine moment to propose?"

"C'mon, Jarvis! This is the outback, and the sun is out. Today is perrrrfect."

I laughed. Then I coerced him into amending the plan. "Here's how I see it. We tell the girls we're splitting off to have a contest."

He looked worried. "What kinda contest?"

"A photo contest. Both Darcy and Allie love their digital cameras. Plus we'll say we're using our disposable cameras for—"

"I brought two."

"Fine. Three for me. So we tell the women we're having a contest to see which vehicle can get the most pictures of wildlife in one afternoon. You and I start driving west into the barren regions, me following you, and when we get to that split in the road, you go left and I'll go right. We'll trace the entire route on your map. Cool?"

Steve raised his eyebrows, twitched his upper lip. "Yeah, okay. Cool."

I reached for and took the binoculars from him. "And if you don't see us in Kulgera by 8:00 p.m., call me on the little radio, just in case something goes wrong."

Steve nodded slowly and with confidence. "And you do the same for me."

He made a fist, I made a fist, and again we tapped knuckles.

My last glance through the binoculars revealed momma wallaby nudging the joey back into its pouch. When I stood for a better view she hopped off into the bush, as if remembering she was nocturnal and had stayed out too late.

Animal hour had ended, so Steve took back his binoculars and stuffed them into their case. "Jarvis," he said, pulling the strap over his shoulder, "this day is gonna be magnificent. Can't ya just smell it in the air?"

For a brief second I put my hand on Steve's shoulder and gave him a squeeze of encouragement. Anxiety buzzed through his shirt like electrical current, but he just shrugged and pointed me toward camp.

Together we strode back to the tent, and in midstride I raised my nose to the blue sky and sniffed.

"Yep," I said to the morning. "Magnificent."

6

Our exodus from Uluru began when Steve poured the last ounce of orange juice into Darcy's plastic cup, clinked his own cup against hers in a toast to the morning, and told her that he'd be doing the driving. At the back bumper she shrugged and gulped the juice and tossed the cup into a grocery sack that I held in offering. Steve added the empty container to the trash, and the two of us went around to the front of the Land Cruisers to wipe a night's worth of dust from the windshields. We males were neither hunting nor gathering—at 10:00 a.m. on the day of magnificence, the most we could manage was hospitality.

Steve leaned across his white hood and cleaned beneath the wiper blades. "You nervous?" he asked in a low voice.

With a bottle I flung water across my windshield. "A bit. You?"

"Very."

That was all we said. Like a pair of car-wash employees shining up new clients, we wiped in tandem and made our way to the side windows. In the reflection I saw my girlfriend—Allie was walking back from the camp's restrooms, a yellow towel draped around her neck, dark hair hanging limp over terrycloth. From some fifty yards behind me she waved and blew a kiss. I sent back three.

Breakfast with the girls had consisted of very little talk, mainly yawns and cinnamon rolls. Though I craved an opportunity to be split off from Steve and Darcy, I had concerns about the two of them driving around in the outback unescorted. Both were city folk—she in advertising, he an engineer—and these city folk were going very rural.

In contrast, Allie and I were accustomed to harsher environments, to hosting the jungle version of Romper Room and going without the amenities of yuppiedom. But I kept these thoughts to myself and feigned confidence in the decision Steve and I had made over the map: we had planned our work, and we would work our plan.

In the V of the two Land Cruisers I helped Darcy fold her green blanket, which had been the setting for breakfast, the only meal our foursome would share on this our second day down under. We had just centered the first fold when she suddenly let go with one hand, tossed her blond hair over one shoulder, and pointed behind me at Uluru. "Jay, we're about to say good-bye to the most fabulous rock we'll ever see."

I could only nod and double the fold. Her timing could not have been more perfect, her innocence any more becoming, the irony any sweeter. Darcy Yeager was the product of an atheist father who had tried many times to manipulate her with money, even buying her the Caddy convertible that she had eventually sold.

That Steve—the steady, logical engineer—could commit to her, love her, and fix her lawnmower gave me no shortage of confidence that the two of them were a match.

Next Steve and I took down our tent, divided the groceries and the two cases of bottled water, and loaded it all in the rear of the vehicles.

My back was turned when a towel popped me in the leg.

"Mornin', Jay," Allie said into my ear. Fresh washed and rested, she ran a hand through waves of damp hair. Then she spun her towel into a rope, looped it around my neck, and pulled me close. "I think we should ride together all day today, agreed?"

Nose to nose with her, lost in her brown eyes, I used my foot to shove an Igloo cooler farther into the hatchback. "You read my mind, jungle woman."

In minutes the campsite was empty, our footprints and Allie's poem the only evidence that dumb Americans had spent the night. Steve opened the passenger door to the white Land Cruiser, motioned Darcy inside, and smiled as he closed her door. With the orange door I did likewise for the lithe woman who I hoped did not suspect a thing.

Allie climbed in, and I pulled her seat belt to her hand. "Such gentlemen this morning," she said.

"No worries," I whispered before closing her door.

At the rear of the vehicle, Steve locked the hatch, flashed me a nervous grin, and held up eight fingers.

I nodded through my windshield. Eight p.m., Kulgera.

Steve and Darcy pulled away first, onto a curving frontage road that allowed one last look at the mighty rock. I handed Allie one of my disposable cameras and asked her to get a picture. She lowered her window. Whiffs of hot sand rolled swiftly through the interior. "Gonna be another scorcher today," she said. She snapped the pic and motioned me onward.

"Yeah . . . a scorcher."

As we left the park I honked once for Uluru, once from sheer adrenaline, and once for the momma wallaby who was out feeding her joey with no help at all from the male.

We tailgated Steve and Darcy toward the exit, where we all stopped for gas. The concrete and neon of the Yulara Quick Stop looked out of place amongst its earth-toned surroundings, but it was the only store in sight. With a handful of two-dollar Australian coins, Steve and I purchased ice for the coolers and colas for the women. Too excited to wait for our change, we bolted out of the store.

"Calm down," I said, striding behind him and between the gas pumps.

"I can hardly breathe," Steve mumbled just before pulling open his door and handing Darcy her drink. She was wearing those mist-green aviator shades again, and neither her smile nor her posture led me to believe she suspected anything.

I opened my own door and handed Allie her Sprite.

"Since when do you unscrew the top for me?" she asked, pausing with the drink at her lips.

"Oh . . . the Australian bottling companies . . . put on the caps tighter," I fumbled.

She gulped once, paused again. "Oh."

Ahead on the frontage road, campers, buses, and four-by-fours merged slowly into a convoy, all of them turning east for the long drive back to Alice Springs.

Except for us—Steve and I turned west. From the Yulara Quick Stop and onto desert highway the long-traveled foursome went west, out to where pavement lost the center line and replaced it with trust, out to where the Northern Territory kissed the border of Western Australia. Out to where humanity was scarce, wildflowers were plentiful, and wilderness could pose as backdrop for a magnificent day.

Allie turned in her seat, glanced briefly out the rear window, and said, "Wow, looks like we have the pavement to ourselves." After we passed the domed rocks known as the Olgas—the plan was to hike them on our fourth day—she opened her journal in her lap, began writing, and caught me looking at her first sentence. "I'm recording details from my first day down under. Keep your eyes on the road."

"The road . . . sure."

She tapped her pen on the journal. "You'll nudge me if something wild bounds across, won't you?"

"Of course . . . anything wild."

I continued to ease up on the accelerator, allowing Steve and Darcy to get farther and farther ahead. Their tires spit dirt and dust, and at times I lost sight of them completely. I tried to catch Allie glancing at me again, to see if suspicion had crept into her countenance. But she just kept writing, didn't suspect a thing.

I savored the anticipation, guessing at the place, the scenery, time standing still, and most importantly, the look on her face. I also loved feeling anticipatory while at the wheel of an old Land Cruiser, the rugged look of its roof rack and oversized bumpers forging details for a future memory. An old SUV fit the portrait in my head, its burnt-orange color a near match for our sun-drenched surroundings.

Several times I glanced over at Allie's left hand, at the soft skin of her ring finger, all ringless and feminine and lovely. The very thought of adorning that finger with three-quarters of a carat—it was with great joy that I sold those shares of stock—had my head fogging again. Words, even simple chitchat, became a burden.

"Allie?"

She tucked her journal between the seats and gazed out her window at the desert flowers, a carpet of tiny yellow blossoms. "Yes?"

"I, um, I wish we had some nachos and cheese."

She turned from the blossoms and frowned. "But we just ate breakfast."

"Yeah . . . right. We just ate."

I shifted into four-wheel drive as the road grew bumpier, the roof rack rattled, and Steve drove ahead of us like he knew where they were going. From a distance I followed them into noontime, where the redness of the sands seemed to melt into the blues and purples of a western sky. To our right a range of boulders, nearly teetering on their perches, paralleled the highway. Perhaps Uluru, like the gray wallaby, had reproduced after all. Ulurettes? Wind carved and peculiar, they served as a reference point, until red dirt widened into opportunity, and the highway split into two forks.

When Steve kept going on the wider left fork he tapped his brakes three times—three flashes of brake lights were our preordained signal—and I flashed my headlights and veered right, onto a red dirt road. I smiled a confident smile at Allie, then glanced in the rearview to see only a swirling cloud of dust.

The split had gone smoothly, and all systems were go. Houston, we have liftoff.

I knew from the rapid clicking of Allie's pen that she was going to need some explanation, and need it fast. Not that I volunteered anything; I just waited for her to ask. Seconds later she leaned up near the dash and turned to watch the white Land Cruiser rambling south, the gap between the trucks widening by the second.

Finally she sat back in her seat and crossed her arms. "Okay, Jay, why are we going this way while Steve and Darcy went left? Aren't we supposed to stay together?"

My answer was deadpan and succinct, if not well rehearsed. "Steve and I planned a surprise for you girls today—a contest, taking photos of wildlife. Then both couples will compare their pictures and count the number of animals and . . . then, um, then late this evening the losers have to buy dinner for the winners."

She nodded approvingly. I knew that a wildlife-loving girl like Allie would embrace such a contest.

She looked left and right out the windows. "Sounds interesting. But y'all should have told us earlier." Then, a minute later, "Do we get extra points if we get in the shot with the animals?"

Hook, line, and sinker. "Oh . . . sure. Double points for that."

She unhitched her seat belt, turned to the backseat, and began digging through her stuff. I heard a rustling of paper. She sat straight again. "How strange. I just found that note I'd misplaced yesterday. It was under my camera case."

Without cracking a smile I said, "Glad you found it," and drove farther into the right fork, a baked two-laner that marked the beginnings of a two-hundred-kilometer, U-shaped route. Steve and I would pass through the curve of the U hours apart, after the forks merged again. Despite his nervous energy, Steve was good at reading maps.

An hour passed, but no wildlife showed itself. Not even any humans showed themselves; we hadn't passed another vehicle since the split. My exotic plan would only be exotic if we found some animals, and preferably some that hopped.

Allie kept scanning the plains, her hands on her digital Nikon. I could already sense her disappointment.

But the more I thought about it, the more I didn't want to stay on Steve's logical, planned-out course. This course seemed too structured. This course lacked spontaneity. This course was like driving west from Kansas, turning south toward Amarillo, and taking the interstate back east to Dallas. *Nah,* I thought, *I don't want to go to Dallas; that's where my family lives, and they never did approve of my leaving Wall Street to go work in South America with a woman they'd never met.*

I fought discipline and struggled to keep to the route.

Still we saw no wildlife. The road continued as a mix of smooth dirt and baked corrugations. Soon the road roughened further, and the steering wheel began to shimmy in my hands. Perhaps those vibrations were my first warning, but I kept driving west, determined to find the remotest spot possible, determined to visit what was, in effect, Aussie Arizona. "Got plenty of memory in that camera, Allie? 'Cause I predict today is gonna be memorable."

"Plenty," she said, tweaking the settings on her Nikon as we bumped along. "And I'll hang out the window and snap pics while you drive right up beside whatever we find out here." She was doing her best to stay positive. Just like me.

Our first detour was nothing spectacular, just a veer onto a smooth expanse of orange earth—ground that barely rattled our four-wheel drive. We passed rocks but no wallabies, bush but no kangaroos.

Had the entire continent gone into hiding?

Soon I had driven far to the west of the Petermann Ranges, a bit off course from where Steve would think us to be traveling. In the side mirror I watched the main range shrinking in size, though it was not much as far as ranges are concerned, especially if you've seen the Rockies, which according to Steve are the Yankee Stadium of all things mountainous.

Lost in my thoughts, I aimed the vehicle at the smoother sections of dirt and tried again to make conversation. "You're really gonna hang out the window?"

"Absolutely." And she stuck her head out and let the wind whip her hair across her eyes.

The landscape continued to flatten, shaking out its wrinkles, leaving only remnants of granite. Allie stared wide eyed through the windshield. "This is like discovering a lost continent."

"A very dry and empty continent," I said, looking ahead at the scale of uninhabited earth. "Looks like no one has been out here in decades."

She raised her camera and snapped the first photo—of me driving. "I think we'll win the contest. Free dinner from Steve and Darcy is all the motivation I need." She saved the picture and peered out her window. "But we may have to take some chances."

We were racing the sun westward—and losing badly. The ground became crusted, our windshield specked with seed pods, dirt, and dead flies. No sign of humanity. No tire tracks anywhere.

Take some chances, she'd said.

Immediately into my head strutted the male nemesis—the tendency to try and impress the woman, to be the so-called hero. The feeling was irresistible; even more so after I pulled back onto that barren road and the second detour presented itself.

A square, dented road sign identified the route as the Gunbarrel Highway. It must have been named for a sawed-off shotgun, because its asphalt ended after only two miles, as if the road crew just ran out of tar and decided to go on walkabout. Not that the highway ended, just the paved surface. Semismooth red dirt took command, bisecting the flora and pointing us to a panting landscape.

There was scant evidence that anyone traversed this route, only an occasional drink can on the side of the road, gleaming in the sunlight. I cut off the air and lowered my window, looking far and wide for anything furry, bouncy, and indigenous.

"Haven't seen a thing."

"Me either," she said, looking humored and impressed at my detour. "Just grass and rocks and dirt."

Patches of green spinifex dotted the acreage, and a familiar orange dust boiled up behind us. Allie took a long swig from her water bottle and pointed north—she'd spotted two house-sized boulders off our right flank.

I turned right and drove, clumpity-clump, across desert grasses and lonely earth. The geography was matching up with my magnificent plan, although the animals had yet to cooperate. We parked beside the boulders, and she beat me out of the vehicle, Nikon in tow.

"We'll start small . . . with lizards," she said, striding quickly toward the first boulder. "My travel book said big rocks with a mix of sun and shade are where we could find them."

"Lizards?" I parroted, walking fast to catch up. "We get points for lizards?"

She stopped, frowned, put her hands on her hips. "It's your game,

61

silly. Didn't you and Steve discuss what kinds of wildlife counted for a photo?"

Beside her I took stock of the sunlit surroundings. "Sure. Yes, lizards are definitely in this game."

Already sweaty, we wandered slowly around the first rocky mass, peering into crevices weathered by wind and time. On our second pass, a stocky orange lizard with bony spikes protruding from its body came swaggering out at waist level, stopping in the sunlight as if it were expecting us. Allie quickly identified it as a thorny devil, and she got a close-up shot of my finger pointing at its back.

"Perfecto," she said, snapping a facial shot. "First points go to the Jarvis team."

There in the ninety-five-degree heat, her words stopped me cold. The Jarvis Team. Team Jarvis. The Jarvis family. The Jarvises. She had said the words only in reference to the photo contest, but I heard them as future union.

My camera shook in my hand. My head fogged again. Only the *clickwhirr* of her Nikon brought me back to reality. This was not yet the perfect setting. Besides, the ring was in the vehicle, tucked in a new pair of socks inside my duffel. The moment had yet to arrive; I was waiting for sunset.

To relax, I feigned great interest in the lizard and snapped two shots with my disposable. Even when I was two feet away the lizard never moved, just continued to bask, unblinking, posing in the rays like a reptilian supermodel.

Who knew what would prey upon such creatures. Imagine biting into a hot dog pierced with tacks, and that would be the equivalent of trying to eat a thorny devil.

Ten more minutes of snooping around sandstone produced no more photos, just a frustrated Allie who warned that we were now probably losing the contest, simply because long-legged Darcy could cover ground faster than either of us.

I leaned against the rock and wiped the sweat from my face. "You really care about winning this thing?"

She winked. "Wanna go exploring the real Australia?" Bright brown twinkles danced in her eyes, and an air of mischief tinted her voice.

I climbed atop the second boulder and gazed across the outback at distant hills and a copper horizon. "You mean go—"

Below me she tucked her camera back into its case. "That's right. Even farther off the beaten path, out to where the average tourist never thinks to explore."

This sense of adventure was one of many reasons why I loved this girl. She had none of the practicality of Steve Cole, none of the bug fear that had kept Darcy always close to a vehicle and, to my delight, none of the suspicion of the average American female.

I climbed down from the boulder. Without speaking I took Allie by the hand, and we walked over baked Australia toward our trusty four-by-four. Geography was secondary now; my thoughts were centered on the ring.

In seconds we had our map spread across the hood; in minutes we had plotted a new course; and in an hour we'd driven so far from the original route that I was beginning to doubt the possibility of finding our way back.

She made sandwiches on the go, and we ate while I drove. No sign of humanity. No chance of my being interrupted. We had entered the Gibson Desert, where in the distance both rock and topsoil appeared to shimmer in the heat, that floating-on-fumes phenomenon that I should have recognized as our second warning.

But my thoughts were centered on the ring, so I just ate my sandwich and kept driving.

Lizards. Lizards. Lizards. By midafternoon we had seen only lizards. And for my competitive girlfriend, this was not acceptable. After pulling a bottled water from the backseat and setting it in her lap, Allie freed waves of brown hair from sticking to her neck and gathered her mane in one hand.

"Jay," she said, tying back her hair with a band, "we've been in Australia for a day and a half and haven't seen a single kangaroo. The travel book says there are over a hundred million of them on the continent, and so wouldn't you think we'd have seen some by now?"

"You'd think." I was driving slowly now, trying to pace things just right.

Eager to make things happen, she reached under the dash, grabbed the car-to-car radio, and turned it over in her hands.

"What are you doing?" I asked, hoping she wouldn't try to use it.

"I'm calling Darcy to see how many photos they have."

"No. Don't do that. Please don't do that."

Too late. She'd already pushed the talk button. "Darcy. Miss Darcy. Come in Miss Darcy." She playfully stuck her tongue out at me and repeated her call.

Only a static squawk 'came back. Allie studied the radio, turned it upside down. "The sticker on the back says the range of this device is from three to five kilometers, depending on terrain."

This new fact produced in me the dual effect of fear and delight. Fear that no one could contact us, and delight that no one could interrupt us. "Forget it, babe. You have no chance of reaching Darcy."

Allie frowned hard. "How far do you think they are from us?"

I could only offer a guesstimate. "At least a hundred miles. They were circling back to the southeast when the road forked, and that was three hours ago."

She wedged the radio back into its holder and looked at me blankly. Suspicion had finally crept its way in. "Are you okay? You seem distracted."

"I'm, um, worried that Steve and Darcy might have found a herd of wallabies and have ten times as many pictures as us."

"Just stop."

"Stop talking?"

She leaned across the console and took hold of my arm. "No, stop the truck."

I braked quickly, and the orange dust overtook us and whisked ahead before losing its momentum and spreading like powder over parched ground. "Okay, why stop here?"

"We need to rethink this."

"You wanna turn back?"

She gazed out of her open window, then turned and peered past me through the driver's side. From all indications, her creative mind was trying to think logically, and this forced on her a pause. "We just need to take our best guess at which direction is most likely to contain a herd, or a brood, or a pack, or whatever they call assembled masses of kangaroos. And then . . . how much gas do we have?"

"Over half a tank."

"That'll be enough, won't it?" She didn't wait for me to answer. "So which way? To the left and toward those hills, or to the right and the grassy plains?"

"Don't roos eat grass?"

She tilted her water bottle to her mouth, swallowed the last drops, and set it under her seat. "I think so."

"Well then, I'd pick right. You?"

She licked her lips and nodded. "I'd pick right as well."

I unfolded the map over the console and checked our bearings. "One warning, poetess—if we go right that will take us even farther into the barren regions."

"You're scared?"

I shook my head. "No, not at all. You?"

"No. We'll just have to watch the gas level . . . and pray that there are kangaroos somewhere in those plains."

She folded the map and slid it into the glove box. Winning the photo contest was now an important priority for me—simply because it was an important priority for her. I pulled the gearshift into drive and gave Allie a wink of confirmation.

But regardless if there was any wildlife out here, I figured a grassy plain in central Australia was a fine place to wait for sunset and a pristine moment. So the last thing I did before driving farther into the outback was to silently rehearse my well-chosen words of proposal.

7

We found them napping in desert grasses. We found them after hours of searching. We found them in the middle of nowhere, as I drove in wide circles, like a wayward farmer in a hay field, leaving in our wake a pressed lane of passage. In a country that hosts one hundred million kangaroos, we should not have been surprised.

But I was very surprised. Amazed, actually. Not just at finding them but at the strength of their hind legs, the height of their jumps. Having only been around domesticated dogs and cats in Dallas and Carolina, I was in near shock at seeing wild kangaroos hopping ahead, startled from their naps and scattering in twelve directions. Nothing in North America, including our zoos, prepares you for such sights.

Still circling—Allie had already filled her first memory chip and reloaded—I slowed so as not to endanger any of our subjects. Confused marsupials, some of them more than six feet tall, bounded left, right, and beyond us, all of them cast in a golden light.

Allie could hardly contain herself. She shouted directions while shooting through her window. "Look, Jay, a whole family of 'em! Turn right . . . now straight."

She snapped photo after photo.

Click-whirr; click-whirr. "Circle behind the herd. Don't slow down; they're getting away."

Click-whirr; click-whirr. She lowered her camera and glanced at me in frustration. "Will you hurry up? You're the worst roo chaser in history."

Allie leaned halfway out the window as we rolled through the grass-lands, waking and scattering the last of what must have been eighty kangaroos. I felt like an African nature guide, steering an overzealous client through the bush.

Directing frequently and aiming constantly, she laughed like a kid at what was unfolding. At the peak of her excitement I reached across the seat and took hold of her belt loop, just so she wouldn't fall out.

In just ten minutes she had used up her second memory chip. She then set her Nikon in the backseat and employed my disposable.

"To the right," she directed. *Click-*pause*-whirr.*

With impatience she thumped my cheap camera. "This thing is too slow. But we'll still trounce Steve and Darcy. They'll never find any sights like this." *Click-*pause*-whirr.* "Unwrap another disposable, Jay. Take a whole roll."

With husbandlike obedience, I unwrapped the second disposable, drove one-handed, and snapped photos through the windshield. Soon I was so into the shoot that my agenda lay with my luggage in the back-seat.

Roos bounded in haste—adolescents following adults—and across the plain more had joined the herd. It was as if the animal kingdom was in on my plans, bouncing with untethered glee to the news that Jay Jarvis was going to propose.

We had stirred up plenty now—a dispersed family reunion was my guess—and I pulled out of our circular path, set the camera in my lap, and drove parallel to a dry creek bed. We rolled along at twenty miles per hour, doing our best to balance caution and pursuit.

Allie squinted and steadied herself for some up-close-and-personal shots. "Closer," she said. "Just a little closer."

Dumbstruck mommas bounded beside us before veering west, parent and joey all doing the pogo toward a sinking sun. Between the bumps Allie lowered her camera, reached across the console and, without looking at me, placed her hand on my arm. "Jay, it's like we really have discovered a lost continent."

Hers was the gesture of couples, and the warmth of her hand on my arm and the speed of the roos through the grass rendered me nearly speechless. "Incredible, isn't it?"

She was too distracted to reply. I steered with both hands on the wheel as more red granite formations appeared over a rise, directly in our path. It was like driving in a video game.

Three kangaroos veered right of the rocks. In an effort at surprise I veered left—and directly into a yellow glare. We were close now, *National Geographic* close.

Again I squinted. Again the dust rose and the steering wheel shimmied in my hands. Sunlight fractured on the windshield, red boulders blocked our view. Lost in a maze of glare and high grass, I never saw the adult roo angling in from our right.

Only Allie saw the collision path.

"Brake, Jay! There's a—"

I swerved left to avoid him—and did, by inches—but the detour plunged us into the dry creek bed, jolted us to the point of bumped heads and spilled drinks, and sent us careening up the opposite bank. The vibrations continued as the tires strained for grip, a jackhammer on wheels.

We emerged on the opposite side of the creek bed from the objects of our pursuit. And now something in the engine didn't sound right. But this was a Land Cruiser, tough and sturdy, so I ignored the issue.

A rattled Allie rubbed the top of her head. "That . . . that was too close." Then she grabbed a towel from the backseat and wiped spilled water from the dash, her legs, the gearshift.

Embarrassed, I turned us around and eased back through the waterless creek, allowing one wheel at a time to angle down and find its footing. "We gotta slow down," I said, negotiating the climb back to flat ground. "That roo would've ruined the afternoon."

Allie stuffed the damp towel under her seat and rubbed the top of her head again. "I would've cried, Jay. Cried all night."

Don't make her cry, Jay. Don't do anything—or hit anything—that could make her cry.

Amid inner Australia's diminishing light, I wondered if Steve had already found his moment, or if he and Darcy had found a way to bungle the afternoon photo shoot. When the day began—as the wallaby fed her joey and we watched through the binoculars—I thought I'd be engaged by now. Who knew, maybe Steve really had gone first.

Across rocky earth I drove us farther into the plains, only to find that the kangaroos had vanished. Golden grasses swayed in the distance, waving the opposite way, as if snubbing us for our recklessness. "Wanna keep looking for 'em?"

She grabbed her digital camera and began reviewing her photos. "I have a ton of pics already," she said. "You?"

"One whole roll." The moment drew nearer, and I watched the sun redden and highlight the rocks. "I was thinking we could have a picnic."

Allie stared out through her window at the landscape. "Sure," she said, talking absentmindedly to the glass. "A picnic . . ."

After another few minutes of bumps, rattles, and corrugations, I spotted a sandstone mass that faced the sunset. Shades of russet and orange and reddish-brown glowed at its edges, and at over ten feet in height and concave in shape, this rock formed the ideal amphitheater.

With the truck facing west, I parked so that the rock was on Allie's side. A preview for her; a stage for me. I cut the engine and ignored the heaving sound from its innards. My mind was on the ring, and if there were anything that needed attention under the hood it could wait until yes.

Allie climbed out and pulled a yellow blanket from the backseat, and together we spread it in the shade of the sandstone. In minutes the bread and snacks and lunch meat surrounded us on the blanket. She sat Indian style to my left and pulled the crust from her bread.

To keep her in a good mood was rarely a difficult task. Even so, I felt that my best move was to add a margin of safety. Besides the ring and the photos, I also wanted her to have a story that would capture this day in its totality. So while she made herself a sandwich, I tried to think of a story. But my mind went blank. The only idea came when I looked south across the plains and spotted the gathering marsupials. The roos we had chased stood grazing again, several looking back curiously, ears twitching as if trying to snoop on our conversation.

This sighting alone—it still felt so strange to be here among them—inspired me to involve Allie. What I had in mind was a kind of legend-with-a-twist; and the character names were a no-brainer. "While you dissect your sandwich, I think we should coauthor a story."

Allie peeled two slices of sandwich meat from their brethren and plopped them on her bread. "Is it a sad one or a good one?"·

"Can't sad ones be good ones?"

"I suppose, but not today."

I reached for my Pepsi and popped its top. "No worries. This one will probably be wacko. Ready?"

She nodded and took a bite of her sandwich. "Go ahead, gimme the first sentence."

I took a quick swig of my soda. "Steve and Darcy are driving through the outback, searching for kangaroos to photograph."

She swallowed her bite and never hesitated. "They need lots of photos, 'cause they need to win a contest over their married friends, who just happen to be Neil and Alexis—the Couple Who Could Not Wait."

My turn again. "So Steve and Darcy veer off the Gunbarrel Highway in search of a herd, and they drive and drive across miles of flat orange ground until they are a hundred miles from anywhere."

She tossed the crust over her shoulder and blurted the next line. "Soon they spot twenty kangaroos grazing in the grasslands and unaware that two Americans want to get some close-up shots."

"So Darcy takes over the driving, and quickly she's in hot pursuit. Steve leans out the window and starts taking pictures, telling Darcy to get closer."

Allie nodded and continued. "Then Darcy says she wants to feed the animals, so while the roos bound beside the truck, she tosses grapes out the window, and the roos catch them in their mouths."

An unexpected plot twist. "Do roos eat grapes?"

"In this story they do."

Keep going, Jarvis. Get her in the best mood possible. "Steve starts throwing ten grapes at a time, and soon they have run out of grapes."

"But now ten more kangaroos show up, and they haven't eaten all day."

"Not even any grass?"

Allie finished her sandwich and leaned back on her elbows. "A fire had burned the grass."

"Oh." More plot twists. "So . . . so these new roos are really hungry?"

"Famished."

My swig of soda coaxed the next line. "Now Darcy grabs Steve's box of cinnamon granola bars."

"Wow," she said, "these are some health-conscious kangaroos."

"Yes, and now Darcy has one of the bars unwrapped, and the hungry roos are bounding next to Steve's window."

She grinned and exhaled the next line. "But Steve takes the bar from Darcy and refuses to give it to the roos because cinnamon-flavored granola bars are his all-time favorite."

I leaned back beside her and mimicked her posture. "True. But the roos will not stop begging, and they hop along at ten miles per hour while Darcy begs Steve to not be so selfish."

Allie quickly kept the momentum going. "But Steve will not give up his granola bars, and so the roos get mad."

"Yes, very mad. For they work for the Australian Tourist Bureau, and their contract calls for them to hop beside American tourists in exchange for food."

Tickled, she beat her feet on the ground. "The ten hungry roos are panting now, having hopped for miles to please the tourists but without the benefit of food."

"Darcy begs Steve to give up his granola bars. But he has his arms wrapped around the box."

"So Darcy stops the Land Cruiser in the middle of nowhere."

"And ten hungry roos circle the truck."

"And Steve refuses to feed them even a smidgen of a bar."

"So two roos at a time hop on the hood and bounce up and down until the hood is smashed and steam is pouring from the engine. And out of sympathy and fright Darcy throws the whole box to the roos, who gobble the granola in seconds. But now the truck won't start and so Darcy and Steve are stuck out there, all because Steve was stingy. . . . The end."

Just then my magnificent moment peeked out from behind its stage curtain and saw a full house—the curiosity of the roos, the vast smudge of sunset, and the hilarity beaming from my girlfriend's face.

Just as I rose from the blanket to proceed with my plan, Allie gazed into twilight and waved at the herd. "Jay," she said, talking over her shoulder, "you've been so gentlemanly today that I'm gonna let you have more practice. This thirsty tourist could use a cold drink."

Nerves laid claim to my innards, so I left her at the bumper and went around to the driver's side and opened the back door to get her a drink. But before I dug into the melting ice I reached into my duffel bag, found the new pair of socks, and checked to make sure the little black box was still stuffed inside.

Satisfied, I left it there and delivered to Allie a bottle of semicold Sprite. I sat beside her on the blanket again and unscrewed the top for her. Just a few more minutes. *Quench her thirst, then quench her singleness.*

She drank heavily, swallowed hard. "Ahhh. What an afternoon, yeah?"

"Yeah. And your rating on my story?"

She gulped again before offering me a sip. "Your coauthor is fabulous," she said. "And who knows, that might really happen to Steve and Darcy."

The sky dimmed to a dark pink, streaked with purple brushstrokes and teeming with urgency. The moment pulsed. My legs shook.

My instinct was to turn sideways so she wouldn't detect the nerves. Again she lifted her drink to my lips. She tilted the bottle and I drank.

That's when I excused myself and went back to the driver's side and opened the door and reached into my duffel for the socks. I pulled out the little black box, opened the lid, and admired the brilliant gem. Then I tucked the box into my back pocket and stood there, hidden by the truck's girth.

At the back of a burnt-orange Land Cruiser I fought emotion. My jaw quivered. My eyes watered. These were the last minutes of singlehood, the fleeting seconds before commitment. I peered through the rear window and across the interior and out the windshield to see Allie gazing off at the curious herd that stood in silhouettes on the hillside.

Doesn't suspect a thing.

I took a deep breath, counted to ten, closed my eyes. I asked God to help me remember all the words. I walked around the driver's side, past the side mirror, and around the orange hood.

Before we even made eye contact she reacted. Seated Indian style, Allie brought her hands to her face and covered her eyes. She gasped once, twice. Her hands dropped from her face, and she looked up at me with fear in her pupils. Her jungle tan had vanished, replaced with a pale stupor.

How would she know? I hadn't even kneeled yet or pulled the black box from my pocket. I stood before her, dumbfounded. "Allie, what is it? Aren't you happy that we didn't hit the kangaroo?"

She pointed past my ankles and under the truck.

I kept staring at her. "What is it?"

She pointed more firmly.

I turned and peered under the front bumper. My first thought was that it was just water formed from the air conditioner. But this liquid was dark, and it dripped into the dirt.

To glance beneath a truck and spot a small problem was one thing. But to glance beneath a truck and spot two major problems—in this case the hole in the oil pan plus the broken serpentine belt hanging down in the dirt in front of the oil—had me wishing we'd turned around after the first few photos.

I dropped to my knees and inspected the underside of the truck. Hot oil pooled in the dirt, glistened black, and seeped below ground.

It felt like a cruel joke, but I knew we had brought it upon ourselves during the chase, and that my swerve through that creek bed had caused the damage. Dumb Americans, adrift down under.

I stood again and exchanged nervous glances with Allie. Go ahead, Jarvis. Don't let circumstances delay the moment.

The outback lay still, massive, vacant. The roos had disappeared.

Darkness was descending, and the rocks and plains lost their definition. Everything was a haunting reddish-gray, and beyond us the limber desert grasses swayed in all directions, mocking us, laughing in hysterics.

I stared into a fading Aussie skyline, blank faced and unbelieving, numbed by the reality that we might have lost our means of locomotion.

At the rear of the Land Cruiser I used a bottled water to wash my hands, the back window to tidy my hair. Truck problems could be cured later; these were the last minutes of sunset, and my girlfriend was seated on a blanket in the outback.

To simply whip the ring from my pocket did not feel right. So for a second time I eased around the Land Cruiser; only this time I approached Allie with the black velvet box held reverently in both palms, an offering.

She immediately tossed her drink bottle into the dirt. "That's not what I think it is . . . is it?"

"Yes, a set of wooden earrings carved by the Mugu Mugu tribe."

She was not smiling; her lips had parted until they formed a small oval of unbelief.

As soon as our eyes locked I forgot my lines. All I could remember was to kneel before her. "Allie Kyle . . ."

Her eyes widened not into saucers but frisbees. "Yes?!"

"You're not supposed to say yes until I ask."

Briefly she shook her head. "I meant 'go ahead, continue.'"

"Oh. Okay." I scooted closer and took her hand in mine. But my memorized lines had gone on walkabout. "Allie Kyle, um, jungle love is driving me mad, it's making me crazy."

She smiled politely and squeezed my hand. "Jay?"

"Yes?"

"Those are the lyrics to a song by the Steve Miller Band."

Panic. Nerves. I was choking. Not even my esophagus would cooperate. "Sorry. I'm nervous here."

"Just take a breath and ask me what you need to ask me."

My inhale was long, my exhale nonexistent. "You are my mostest match, the, um, caramel to my latte. Plus, you're kind and pretty and good at poetry, so I guess you're also the meter to my rhyme, although I'm too nervous to think up rhymes, not even a romantic stanza of Dr. Seuss, so will you just forget how bad I've bungled this and accept that I want to spend the rest of my life with you, and will you please please oh please marry me?"

Her hand trembled so much that I missed her finger. Twice. She arched that finger upward as I slid the ring over her nail. Then her eyes followed the diamond's short journey over her knuckle as if viewing life's entire timeline. "Yes, yes, and of course yes."

She kissed me hard, then fell forward and hugged me around the neck. Never before had she squeezed that firmly. I expected some whispered words of affection. My back was to the truck, however, so all I got was, "Jay, that oil is really draining out under the truck."

Act 2

*"Clowns to the left of me, jokers to the right,
here I am . . . stuck in the middle with you."*

—Stealers Wheel

8

She said yes.

This is what I could not get over—along with nine kisses, six hugs, one cry, and "you really know how to pick your spots," Allie Kyle had said yes.

Two hours had passed since I'd snagged the magnificent moment, and now at 9:30 p.m. she sat with me on the roof of the Land Cruiser, our legs dangling over the back end, both of us in gray sweatshirts, the moon our lone spectator. I felt elated to be engaged, ecstatic to be engaged to her, and frustrated by our inability to drive across Australia and share the news with every person we passed. Instead we turned our attention to our plight.

But even before we dealt with plight we had to deal with Allie's relapse of guilt. Like all her emotional extremes, this one gathered in haste, her thoughts a cresting wave, spilling its length and breadth at once. While for me these moments always lent an air of comedy to her frustrations, for her it was pure and utter release.

She clasped her face in her hands, the ring hidden in her hair. "Jay, my excitement probably killed us. And not only that, but we'll be dead. In three days when the water runs out we'll dry up like prunes and then wild vultures will eat our flesh and we'll never get to experience the joys of marriage."

I rubbed the back of her head. "We'll figure out something."

She reached up and pulled my hand away, as if she needed to suffer alone. "No, it was me who urged you to take chances, and it was me who got so enthused about chasing the kangaroos, and now the engine is messed up and the truck won't start. What I did was stupid, not normal everyday stupid but a whole new realm . . . dehydrated, rock-hard stupid. Why couldn't I have had even one of those rational thoughts that taps a girl on the skull and reminds her that she's urging her boyfriend to drive farther and farther into wilderness?" Her eyes widened, and she clutched my wrist. "Jay, what'll become of all those children? I'm failing them as a guardian even while you and I . . . this is probably not a good time to talk about wedding plans, is it?"

In the ebb of her word spillage I sifted through the many possible responses. I settled on comfort and put my arm around her. "We share the blame."

But before I could say anything else, Allie's posture slumped. Then, just as quickly, she sat upright. "Isn't there a box of spare parts? I'm sure I remember the rental guy mentioning a box of parts."

Embarrassed, I gripped the roof between my knees and rocked myself into confession. "That's another reason we share the blame. The box of parts is in the other vehicle."

"Please don't say that."

I rocked for a few extra seconds before speaking again. "When we rented the vehicles it was assumed we were staying together, so Steve and I put the box of parts in their truck. Same for the tent. This morning I was so nervous and excited about proposing to you that I never thought about it. And besides, I'm no mechanic. We broke something major."

"We could've tried."

"I'm really sorry. I think it's the transfer case."

My fiancée winced, stared at the moon, and shut her eyes. For a long while she remained still, as if the extra time would help settle her. Then, in a voice just above a whisper, "Remind me never to pray to St. Jarvis, patron saint of spare parts."

She squeezed my arm as her next wave swelled. In contrast to fear, this one flowed from hope—and it too erupted without warning. "Jay, the radio! Maybe the two-way radio will still work with the truck not running and we can call Steve and Darcy."

It was probably the ring that made us both forgetful. I jumped to the ground and opened the front door and pulled the radio from its holder. One press of a button and it squawked to life. Just for spite I also pressed the on button of the cassette stereo. It too lit up. I shouted to her on the roof. "Yep, the little red lights are on."

A rejuvenated Allie scooted across the roof near the windshield, legs dangling inside the open door, her feet clapping their approval. "See, we have our way out."

And here I had to squash our hopes. "But honey, the range of the radio is still just three to five kilometers."

She leaned over the driver's side of the roof—she was on her stomach now—and peered upside down into the front seat. Her face flushed. "Well, is it three or is it five? That might be the difference."

I gripped the steering wheel and looked east at endless dark plains, north to the craggy rock casting moonshadows to the base of our front tire. Tonight the moon was three-fourths full and bursting with light. "I would guess five kilometers in most directions."

Brunette hair dangled toward earth. Still peering in, she raised her eyebrows, which in this case meant lowered eyebrows. "Well?"

"Well, what?"

"Push the talk button and ask for 9-1-1."

I started to speak into the radio but stopped and reconsidered. "What if they use different emergency numbers in Australia? What if down here it's '9-4-4,' or '8-6-5,' or simply '1-2-3 our butts are stranded'?"

Allie said nothing; I don't think she even heard me. A new wave—this one drowsy and thick—had washed over her, and now she slid backward across the roof and down over the windshield, her back against the glass, her head on the hood. Just as hope had washed away fear, so now enchantment flooded her entire world. She gazed longingly at her ring and lost herself in its luster, floating off to that mindless void in which all newly engaged women reside.

I left her to her diamond distraction and pressed the talk button.

"Emergency 9-1-1. We're Americans and we're stuck. Emergency 1-2-3. Anybody?"

Only static replied. Just monotonous, inhospitable static.

I tried again. "Steve . . . Darcy . . . hey, Steve . . . we need help. We took a detour into the Gibson Desert and now we're stuck. I'm not kidding. We've broken down in the outback and need you to come get us."

Just static-filled, inhospitable monotony.

My third attempt was not even sincere, for I knew no one could hear me. My third attempt was just a lame attempt to hide, if even for a brief moment, from reality. "Steve, help. We won't be meeting you at eight in Kulgera because it's already quarter till ten here and her answer was yes. Did you hear me, bro? She said yes. . . . Allie said yes."

We couldn't even share the news.

Dejected, I dug a cassette tape from the glove box and without even looking at the title, nudged it into the stereo. It began to play. And to my surprise, it played an oldie, a goodie. It even played irony. From a dormant Land Cruiser, among our pitiful circumstances and our fleeting minutes of bliss, Barry Manilow crooned "Can't Smile Without You."

Allie stirred from her enchanted place, grinned through the windshield, and flashed me her ring. "I love this song, Jay. We should dance."

I peered around the door frame. "We should first find a rescuer."

"No, first we should dance." And she climbed down over the hood and came around and pulled me by the arm, mouthing the words to "I feel glad when you're glad."

In red Australian dirt we slow danced, celebrating engagement as Barry sang to the night, to the roos, to the seventies and the eighties, to leisure suits, to love itself, and now, beneath three-quarters of a moon and three-quarters of a carat, to us.

It wasn't even our tape. Rental Guy had left it in the glove box.

I dipped my fiancée in dramatic fashion, she dipped me right back, and we continued the dance, cheek to cheek.

9

Slow dancing barefooted for three more songs was the most I had danced in my life. But Allie insisted, and it was the least I could do after nine kisses, six hugs, and a yes.

After the last song we put our shoes back on, and I kissed her and told her again that I loved her, never mind the immobilized truck. Then I sat in the front seat and turned off the cassette player so as not to run down the battery.

In seconds she was tugging on my arm a second time, leading me around to the front of our dusty Toyota. On the oversized front bumper we sat together. The night air turned crisp and cool, and she pulled her sweatshirt sleeves over her hands and snuggled up next to me. I could tell she wanted to talk.

She looped her arm through mine. "Jay, remember yesterday when you recited that 'four of five people who stay with the vehicle, live'?"

"I remember."

"Well, can we make sure that both of us are included in the four?"

I paused and rubbed her hand. "Are you wanting the math or my personal hopes?"

"I want to be comforted."

My fingers stroked her sleeve. "If four of five who stay with the vehicle, live, that means an eighty percent chance for each person." Unsure if she would be able to follow the logic, I squeezed her hand but failed to get a reply. "So, if two people stay with the vehicle, then it's eighty percent times eighty percent, which would mean a sixty-four percent chance that both will survive."

Allie stared across shadowed plains, and soon her steadied expression retreated to a frown. "So, we have only a sixty-four percent chance that both of us will make it through this?"

I raised her hand near my chin, kissed it, and tried to be encouraging. "Honey, sixty-four is much better than fifty-fifty."

She pulled her arm from mine, and her shoulders slumped and she stared at the ground. "That's barely a difference, Jay. Sixty-four minus fifty is only fourteen, so that means we only have a measly fourteen percent chance of being better than fifty-fifty at survival."

"Our kids are gonna be brilliant."

She glanced at her ring again. "Are you still going to marry me?"

"Of course."

She looked like she was about to doze off. But then a third wave hit, submerging her back in her enchanted place. She giggled to herself and gazed at the ring again. She shut her eyes, giggled softer, leaned into me. While she fought the whimsical pull of slumber, I replayed the specifics of the proposal—me on one knee, in the middle of Australia at sunset, her left hand trembling in my own. Magnificent.

Allie's head nudged against my shoulder, and in seconds she was fast asleep.

Still seated on a front bumper that lacked the power to bump, I couldn't help but wonder what kind of proposal Steve Cole had dreamed up. Regardless, at least he and Darcy could allow their moment to linger, as opposed to Allie and I, who would have to forgo enjoyment and figure out how to avoid our inevitable wilting.

I did my best to dismiss doubt in favor of faith, although my experience with faith was quite limited. Back in the days when I was wandering into church just to meet girls, I thought that a successful test of faith eliminated a person from further testing. But of course I was wrong. All that does is up the ante. All a successful testing does is qualify you for a more extreme test.

Silently I asked God not to submit us to any testings during the first week of engagement. I made the request that there be no tests of thirst, no tests of hunger or, for that matter, of survival. And when nothing but a gentle wind blew across my face, a doubtful voice in my head whispered that no one had heard me, which led me to do what I always did when I was unsure—I tried to *think* my way to the least sufferable scenario.

Perhaps God needed me stationary for just a day or so.

Perhaps he had a purpose.

Perhaps he had something to say that I could only hear while stranded.

And perhaps I was merely comforting myself with comfortable thoughts, sucking on them like a pacifier, as if I, the patron saint of spare parts, could ascertain the ways of the Omnipotent Purposer.

I took a mental inventory while Allie slept against my shoulder: Thirteen waters. Two Sprites floating in the cooler. Loaf bread and a package of meat. Peanut butter and jelly. Some fruit. A bag of chips. But it was the water that had my attention. In this heat, we'd each consume three bottles minimum per day. Six per day between us—two days' worth of liquids, plus one extra and a couple of soft drinks to get us through the first half of day three.

Without rainfall, I figured we had sixty hours, a strange and alarming conclusion, since over my adulthood I'd averaged two trips to a grocery store per week and never thought twice about how the food and drink arrived chilled and packaged, when all I had to do was choose debit or credit.

I figured on a dry and dusty night. I figured Steve and Darcy would just think us to be loitering. But I never figured on engagement overlapping with demise.

In the moonlight I gazed at Allie's left hand resting in her lap, at her ring finger all ringed and feminine and lovely. My buddies would be proud.

Hey, Steve. Hey, Neil. I'm engaged . . .

Within minutes I too began to doze off, plunging into a dreamscape of swirling colors, all of them shaped like marsupials, some hopping, some flying, all backdropped by laughing plains of grass. A camera clicked and whirred. Rolls of film rained from white clouds. Then the sky cleared, and my UT cap floated to earth. But just before the cap touched down, the wooden bucket of a waterwheel turned up beneath it and swooped it away. I looked down from the aerial view of dreams and counted thirteen wooden buckets spaced symmetrically on the waterwheel, all of them in slow, steady rotation, all of them empty except for the one hoisting my cap. The other twelve buckets held nothing but dirt grains and air as each reached the apex and circled down, trying to help, trying to offer sustenance, trying to be a waterwheel in a place ill suited for waterwheels, trying in vain to scoop water from crusted earth.

"Mmmm," Allie mumbled in my ear.

"Mmmm, just dozin'," I mumbled back.

At that she woke me fully, and I stood in the dark and yawned and pulled her to her feet. She let her head bob like a sleepy child while I led her to the back door. Her yellow blanket lay across the backseat, and I made a bed for her and gently nudged her inside. Then I rolled her window down an inch, stepped back, and shut the door. Allie was so sleepy she didn't even say g'night.

I went around to the rear of the Land Cruiser and pulled out my sleeping bag and unrolled it across the roof and climbed up top. Aerial sleep for aerial dreams.

I dozed off to twinkling stars and groggy numbers.

Sixty hours.

Thirteen bottled waters.

A half inch of steel and three feet of air between me and my favorite sheila.

10

The dawn did not crack; it exploded over the horizon. From my sleeping bag on the rooftop the view was fantastic—an ascension of pink and yellow light commingling on the desert floor, sand art at sunrise. Morning's sheer girth distracted me from the parched reality—dry mouth, dry voice, dry acreage for as far as one could see. I watched the haze burn off to the east, then turned and saw Allie fifty yards to the west. She had changed into beige shorts and yellow T-shirt, and in the distance the morning light crept behind her as she gathered dead grasses. She moved deliberately, as if to conserve energy, each step producing an ankle cloud of orange dust. Ours was an arid form of stranded.

I watched her for a long while—my best friend, my co-conspirator in desert shipwreck, my loyal Mary Ann.

This comparison was inescapable, or perhaps just another diversion. Regardless, I lay on the roof and retreated to childhood. At least Mary Ann and Gilligan had coconuts. At least they had shady palms and a fresh water supply. At least they had the professor to help them figure out what to do. They even had lagoons and fertile soil, as opposed to stubby plants that offered no fruit, craggy rock that was stingy with shade, and a baked terra firma that forced us to ration bottled waters.

I had woken mad at Mother Earth. Mad at her stinginess. Mad at her size. Mad at myself for not respecting her.

But then I looked out at Allie walking back with an armful of grass and twigs, and I knew we would build a signal fire and knew we would build it well. She had always been an early riser, and she was quite aware that our time was limited. Once again I smiled at thoughts of this virtuous woman, a second time at the replay of our engagement. I may have even giggled.

I fought the yawns, jumped down off the roof, and hurried to help her. I felt grody and was therefore hesitant of physical contact. "Mornin', wife-to-be."

Sweat beads rolled down her forehead, and I wiped them away before they could reach her eyes. She handed me half of her bounty, spilling some in the process. "Mornin', husband-to-be."

"I'm supposed to be doing this."

"Doing what?"

"Being the hunter-gatherer. Steve said it was my duty as a man."

Allie rolled her eyes and looked around for a place to build the fire. "Then you and Steve should learn to wake up earlier. I'd bet he and Darcy think we're dead."

We selected a patch of flat ground some fifty feet from the driver's side of the vehicle, and there we dumped her humble collection of grass and twigs. Allie kneeled to arrange them in a pyramid but stopped suddenly and pointed at the Land Cruiser. "You or me?"

I stooped beside her to help. "Need matches?"

"Have matches. One of us needs to siphon gas for some fire starter. Surely you're not gonna ask your little woman to suck unleaded through a hose?"

"We don't have a hose."

"Yes, we do. The rental company left one rolled up under the seat." She motioned for me to go, and as I rose and loped away she offered something that sounded vaguely like encouragement. "It'll fit easily into your mouth, Jay, and it's clear so that you can see the gas coming before it gets to your throat. These Aussies think of everything."

"Yeah," I said, speaking to the sky, "everything but a quality two-way radio."

I pulled open the driver's door of the Land Cruiser and tried our cheap communication device a second time. I fiddled with the channels but found only static. A change of channel brought no change of signal.

Three to five kilometers . . . in Dallas the dogs could howl farther than that.

Disgusted with two-way radio, I leaned across the console and reached under the passenger seat to pull out the clear hose that would fit easily into my mouth and was ideal for siphoning because I could see the gas coming before it got to my throat.

Allie already had the gas cap off of the Land Cruiser, and in her hands she held two water bottles—one empty, to catch the gas; the other full, to give me a rinse.

I threaded one end of the hose down into the gas tank, knelt, and pulled the other end to my chin.

She stood over me, holding the water bottles and trying not to break into a grin. "You can do it," she said, noticing my hesitation. "Do it, Jay. Do it like a good hunter-gatherer."

On my knees near the back door, I brought the hose to my lips. "You have no idea how tough life can be as a male."

She shook the full bottle playfully, like a nurse with bad medicine. "We women endure childbirth; you men siphon gas. It's not even a fair trade." She waved the bottle in front of my face, then she pointed at the hose. "Now do it. Do it before the gas evaporates."

I did it. I sucked hard. I got the gas coming and nearly, nearly, pulled the hose out before the unleaded bit my tongue. I filled the empty bottle, hacked once, spat twice, hacked again.

"You look pale," Allie said, handing me the bottle of water.

I filled my mouth quickly, sloshed the water, and spat in the dirt beside the rear tire. "Sickening way to start our first week of engagement, eh?"

"You did good, honey. You're an excellent gas sucker."

I wiped my lips on my T-shirt sleeve. "That killed every germ in my mouth," I said, on my feet now, edging close to her. "Doesn't wife-to-be wanna kiss?"

"No way. You have gas breath." Then Allie gasped and put her hand over her mouth. But her gesture was not to mute my flirtation. Her eyes grew wide and, just as she'd done when she assumed all the blame was her own, she got that oh-no look about her.

I spat the last trace of gas into the dirt. "What now?"

"Please don't hate me."

I searched her eyes for an answer. "What is it?"

"Oh, Jay, I'm so sorry." She grabbed my arm in earnest. "We forgot about the extra fuel can in the rear of the truck. I guess you really didn't need to siphon any gas."

Backed against the driver's door, I stared blankly into red dirt and accepted my lesson—getting stranded and engaged in the same instance does awful things to short-term memory. And, to my astonishment, the phenomenon seemed to strike man and woman with equal ferocity.

Allie's hand found mine, and she squeezed her regret. "You mad?"

I shook my head. "Marriage is gonna be interesting."

Reeking of fumes, I went over to our grassy pyramid and doused it with the collected gas. Beside me, still apologizing, Allie ripped a page from her travel book—a page about Perth, which was useless to us—and stuffed it under the twigs. We stepped away in unison, and she reached into her pocket and produced a pack of matches. One flick of her finger and our fire erupted.

In my ongoing efforts at hope, I dropped to my knees and blew on the embers. The smoke smelled like medium-rare rescue, and I watched it curl upwards and prayed it would blacken.

But as a summoner of help, the smoke was puny—and limited to sight and smell. Allie, however, thought to add a third sense. She hurried back to the Land Cruiser and climbed into the driver's seat and blew the horn in long blasts, three at a time.

She then tried tapping out an SOS, even though neither of us knew the code.

Dit dit dit, dot dot, she honked. She tried four different variations before leaning into the horn in frustration and giving the outback an all-encompassing, ten-second blast. This honk traveled quickly through the heat and across dry acreage before exhausting itself down under, up above, all over.

Our fire crackled weakly and collapsed into low flames and pulsing embers. From my kneeling posture at the fire I dodged the rising ashes while watching Allie for signs of despair. For a long time she sat with her hands in her lap, her forehead resting against the steering wheel. Slowly she made a fist and whopped the dash. Then, from fifty feet apart, our eyes met in a locked gaze of perplexity.

What now? I thought. What would an able hunter-gatherer do here?

I figured that a hunter roams the land and searches for tracks like Daniel Boone, although Daniel was raised in the woods whereas I had been raised in a Dallas suburb, where the kids wore Walkmans instead of coonskin caps. Nevertheless, I made up my mind to search for tracks. But I was distracted by engagement and not yet ready to roam.

Behind the Land Cruiser I opened our cooler to find lukewarm water supporting lukewarm Sprite. The water smelled like plastic. I dipped a towel in the water and washed my face, followed by my neck and under-arms. Then I applied deodorant, just to make myself tolerable. Fresh shirt too. Then, with the half-empty bottle of drinking water warming on the roof, I grabbed my toothbrush and toothpaste. Side to side, lower, upper, molars twice. Rinse and spit, rinse and spit. Stranded or not, I was deter-mined to qualify for some smooch before I set off in search of help.

And at our dining table of a front bumper, over a breakfast of loaf bread and single slices of low-fat emu, I qualified.

"Mmmm," Allie said, pulling her lips away, "Gas Boy sweeps Fire Girl off her feet."

I brushed a crumb from my chin and tried to laugh. But it was forced laughter. Neither of us was fooling the other. We were both using every tangent possible—flirtation, breakfast, even scenery—to avoid discussing the possibilities.

"Did you use some of our water to bathe with?" she asked.

"A little. You?"

"Just one bottle. It was before you woke up this morning."

Thirteen minus two. "So . . . so we're already down to eleven bottled waters, and it isn't even 10:00 a.m.?"

Allie winced. "I didn't want to stink on the day after you proposed."

Our fire had burned poorly, the smoke dissipating before it reached even ten feet in height. I estimated its visibility at less than the range of the two-way radio.

Allie frowned at her diminutive fire. She rubbed her left foot on my right and kept her gaze there. "We'll figure something out, Jay. We always do."

I returned her foot pat. "Sure we will, babe . . . sure we will."

I ate a second piece of bread and tried to summon the courage to tell her that I was going to break the number-one rule of Outback Adventures. I was going to leave the vehicle.

No other option appeared valid. To backtrack was impossible, so varied was our detour. But there was just no way that I could remain passive when ahead of me lay a lifetime of jungle love and possible fatherhood, not to mention that I figured Steve and Darcy were by now in full-fledged panic. By now I assumed they had alerted some authorities—whatever that meant in these remote parts—and the authorities had mounted a search.

My fingers tapped nervously on the bumper. Still seated beside Allie, I perused the sky but saw only stray clouds.

So I listened hard for sirens.

What I heard was a bird.

In seconds its shadow passed over our smoldering fire, wings flapping in a whoosh. The bright red on its belly looked to be of the male gender, and in his haste his line of flight never wavered. In the distance he chirped again, this time cheerfully, as if announcing his daily commute.

"Colorful bird," Allie said.

We both turned to watch him go.

"Yeah . . . and fast."

11

By 10:00 a.m. I still had not left the vehicle. By 10:15 I had tried the two-way radio a dozen times, all to no avail. By 10:30 the diminishing, angled shade near the rear tire had become a kind of dirt-floored chapel, where Allie and I leaned back against hot orange metal and uttered "amen" seconds apart, finishing off our pleas to the Almighty after ten minutes of intensely focused prayers.

And now, with our eyes reopened, the vast emptiness of Australia lay before us as a buried puzzle, the pieces strewn, each one measured in square miles and hidden beneath dirt—but with no box top to show us the pattern.

Allie slapped at a fly and drew her knees toward her chest. "Where exactly do you think we are?"

My hesitation to answer was itself an answer. I tipped the brim of my cap down low, for the day grew brighter by the minute. I could only make a rough guess as to our location. We'd driven so many miles off the Gunbarrel Highway—so far from anything that resembled a road—that to pinpoint ourselves was as difficult a task as my repairing the truck without the parts. Truth was, we were but a single pixel on the flat screen of Australia. "Want me to get out the map again?"

Allie set her chin on her knees and offered a half frown. "It'd make me feel better."

I got up and opened the driver's door and found the map wedged between the console and the passenger seat. When I spread the map over the hood, the shadow of my head sent an eclipse from Melbourne to Brisbane. My neck began to warm under the risen sun, but I ignored the rays and leaned forward to read the topography.

"Okay, babe, you want the bad news or the mediocre news?"

From the front bumper I could sense her anxiety. This was evident in her longish pause and the pebbles she kept throwing at a clump of grass. She'd remained seated in the dirt and shade. Finally she threw a dirt clod at misfortune and said, "Just give me your best guess."

I scanned the map and tried to calculate. At this point my faith was bouncing between God and my math skills. "We're two or three hundred miles west of Uluru, so we're probably in Western Australia, which is actually a state . . . a very large state."

Her voice came weakly. "And is Western Australia heavily populated?"

"Maybe near Perth, which is on the southwestern coast and over a thousand miles away."

More throws of frustration. She wasn't throwing at anything in particular, but her velocity had increased. "Then what's nearby?"

"Dirt, rock, clumps of grass. Pretty much what we're surrounded with right here."

Another pause. "And that was the bad news?"

"No, that was the mediocre."

"Oh." Minutes passed before she spoke again—she had stopped her tossing in favor of deduction—and her questions reflected her fears. "How far to civilization?" she asked.

A gust of wind fluttered the map and flustered my bearings. I pressed the paper smooth again. "Over two hundred miles back to Uluru, at least two-fifty to Kulgera. That's to the east."

"And to the south?"

"For five hundred miles to the south lies the Great Victoria Desert. And to the north lies the Great Sandy Desert."

"And how big is that?"

"Bigger'n Texas."

Allie threw one last dirt clod. "What about to the west?"

"Across the Gibson Desert, after eight hundred miles of hiking, we would walk right into Lake Disappointment."

"You're lying."

"I'm not lying. Come see for yourself."

She came around to the front, brushed off her fanny, and leaned over the hood beside me. "Where?"

I motioned to the northwest corner of the map. "See," and here I pointed, "directly to our west, some eight hundred miles."

Allie backed away from the map, pulled some sweaty strands of hair from her face, and stood with hands on hips. "Why would anyone in their right mind name a lake that?"

I fumbled with the map and made light of the name. "It's obvious, isn't it? A couple gets stranded and starts hiking across the outback and runs out of bottled water. So they pant and grow thirsty as they stumble onward, mile after mile. Then they drop to all fours and crawl while the sun scorches and the desert chokes, and soon even the skin on their ears is blistered. They exhaust themselves on hands and knees, and their tongues drag in hot sand. And then, finally, they make it down to the shore of Lake Disappointment and find that all the water has evaporated."

Allie sat down on the bumper. I could tell from her posture that she was not thrilled with my ad lib. "What a depressing ending. If we live through this and return to the village, I'll be approving the content of your stories."

I finished folding the map and spoke over my shoulder. "My stories are not that bad."

She crossed her legs and peered across the red plains. "Jay, if a child were to hear that tale at bedtime, they'd cry all night."

Creativity was not my strength, and I struggled to revise my tale. "Well . . . what if at the end of the story I have a tanker truck drive up and fill Lake Disappointment with grape Kool-Aid?"

She almost smiled. "That'd be a start."

"And what if an eight-foot straw was handed to the thirsty couple and—"

The clench of her lips and the drop of her chin halted my feeble attempt to distract her from the present. Whether intentional or from the subconscious, this was how I dealt with crises, and if such tangents relieved Allie's anxiety for even a minute, if even she shook her head in mild amusement, then I had succeeded. I truly wanted to comfort her, desperately wanted to be the hero.

That's when I decided to leave the vehicle.

Allie stood in front of the Land Cruiser, her back to me, and stared across the flatlands. She was rubbing sunblock on her arms. "Jay, while you were reading the map I was rethinking things."

I remained seated on the bumper and crossed my legs. "Now you don't want to marry me?"

"Just the opposite. I think Darcy should be my maid of honor, and I'm wondering, with all their past turmoils, if you think Steve and her will still be together in June? If so, Steve can escort her down the aisle."

"Oh, sure. They seem, um, quite happy. In their dating, I mean."

Allie nodded and went around to the back door. She pulled her beige floppy hat out of her luggage and put it on her head.

Off the passenger side, shadows from the sandstone retreated by the minute. The rock was nearly two stories high, and by afternoon we would have shade again, but for now the sun appeared hung like a picture, stuck on a nail.

Time mimicked the sun like the two had joined in on a hazing. These were not the normal revolutions of time. This was time at ease, time looking over its shoulder and whispering, "Ah, I'm slowing down today, just to roast you two a bit extra."

Allie walked to the rear of the Land Cruiser, and there she made the drinking motion and looked at me as if asking permission.

I answered her pantomime and followed her back to the open hatch. I opened the cooler and unscrewed the top from another bottled water. "We don't need to ask each other," I said, offering her the first drink. "Let's just sip some when we feel thirsty, and keep praying and keep thinking of ways to signal whoever might be out there . . . surely someone is out there."

She swallowed hard and handed me the bottle. "Surely. And I'm gonna restart the fire and burn some empty bottles, make blacker smoke."

I took one more gulp, set the bottle on the back bumper, and took Allie by the hands. "Ya know, you look good in hats."

She tugged the brim at an angle over her left eye. "Uh-oh, a compliment. What's up?"

"I've decided to walk a few miles and look for help. . . . One of us needs to go search."

The squeeze of her hands told me her objection would be stronger than anticipated. "No, Jay. Absolutely no."

"But babe, I can—"

"Don't 'babe' me, Jay Jarvis. You told me, you looked me in the eye and told me that four of five who stay with the vehicle, live. Did you not say that?"

My right foot scuffed lines in the dirt. "Yes, I said that."

"And three of five who leave the vehicle, die?"

"I said that too." More scuffs and a pursing of lips. "But I'm different, and I'll know when to turn back before I get into trouble."

She tipped my chin up to hers, locked her brown-eyed gaze into my blue-eyed sincerity, and shook her head. "No, no, and no again. You're just desperate to be the hero."

"But someone needs to go search for a road or a train track. Our map isn't very detailed."

"No, Jay. We both stay with the vehicle, remember?"

I pulled away from her and stared off toward Rooville. Words failed me.

"Remember?" she repeated. She had hold of my shirt now.

No longer able to look into her eyes, I knelt to retie my sneakers. "We might be only a few miles from an unmarked road, and I have to go look while I still have my strength."

She leaned over and spoke to the top of my head. "No."

I pulled the knot tight. "Have to, babe."

"You'll reduce our percentage."

"Will not."

She tugged at my shoulders, and I stood to face her. Her grip above my collarbones firmed as she once again fixed her gaze into my own. "Yes, you will. We'll then have only a seven percent chance of being better than fifty-fifty at survival."

I pulled her close, hugged her, and spoke into her ear. "I'll only be gone for a few hours. You stay here and try the radio every fifteen minutes . . . and maybe work on your math."

After I kissed her forehead she pushed away and stooped to retie her own shoes. "I'm going with you."

"No. We'll consume too much water if we both go."

She finished tying her right shoe and started on her left. "I'm going."

"No way. Besides, it's still morning, and I can explore to the east before it gets too hot."

"It's already over ninety."

Whether her next comment was spontaneous or an attempt to get me to reconsider, it did manage to stun me into delay. Her chin dropped slightly, her eyes unblinking—this was a new look, the blank-faced, still-mouthed look of a woman who wants to introduce an even more serious subject. "Jay?"

"Yes?"

She flashed her ring in the sunlight. "I want us to set a wedding date."

I'd already moved back a few steps, almost sneaking into my departure. "Now? Right now when I'm about to go on walkabout?"

"It would give me something happy to think on while you're gone."

"So it's okay if I go . . . now you're approving?"

"No, but you're so hardheaded I know you're going to leave the vehicle no matter what I say."

I felt my defenses drain off. "So, when?"

She played with her ring and spoke as if distracted. "When should you leave? I thought you were leaving right now."

"I meant, when do you want to get married?"

She gazed deeply into cut, carat, color, and clarity, as if the four Cs held her answer. "In June, of course."

"I can do June."

"How about June eleventh?"

"Is that a Saturday?"

Allie rolled her eyes. "Of course it's a Saturday. Any engaged woman is going to have all the Saturdays in June memorized."

I had no idea. I didn't even have next Saturday memorized. My mind was locked on heroism, being the hunter-gatherer, and if I could not be that, then at least I could approach my walkabout in a daring manner and call myself an alpha-male, a phrase without clear meaning but welcomed into the American lexicon for its wonderful brevity and aggressive connotations.

Jay Jarvis, Outback Alpha-male.

Allie could not stop at just a wedding date. We stood ten feet apart, both of us with hands on hips, waiting for the other to say something. Finally she cocked her head at an angle, like she'd just conjured a new thought. "Have you picked all of your groomsmen?"

"I've been too busy fantasizing about the honeymoon."

"I'd like you to pick your groomsmen."

"Right now? While we're roasting with only a two-day supply of water?"

"I need to work out the height thing, who should escort whom."

The height thing? We haven't even talked about the birth control thing. "Why does it matter who escorts whom?"

"So the pictures will look symmetrical."

"And you have to arrange all this today?"

She sat on the back bumper and sighed, her shoulders and lips combining in a kind of persuasive shrug. "A bride-to-be must use her time wisely."

I looked off to the east, where the grass plains lay still and the red dirt dared me to search its breadth. "Okay. Steve Cole will be one groomsman, and then—"

"You need to pick four."

"Count on Ransom and Neil . . . and I might ask Neil to play some music on his harmonica. I was thinking something like—"

"Violins, Jay. Only rednecks use harmonicas in their weddings."

"Oh."

Allie had what she wanted—a set date and three-quarters of my grooms-men—so I left her at the bumper and went around to the side and fetched my UT cap from the backseat. A rub of sunblock and a lukewarm bottled water completed my luggage.

Thus supplied, I pulled her to her feet again and held her close. "I won't be gone more than four hours. I love you, and I promise I'll be back soon. Try the radio every fifteen minutes."

She squeezed me hard before backing away and easing into the front seat. A small wave, really just a flex of her fingers, was her parting gesture.

Already the sweat stung my eyes. I walked southeast, past the low hill where the adult roo had vanished shortly after forcing us into the creek bed. But like Lot's wife, I couldn't walk far without looking back. "Any sounds on the two-way?" I shouted.

From the open door she shook her head. "Just static."

For a moment I watched her stand near the hood and rub the sunblock on her neck. She looked up in midrub and waved me to go on. *Just get it over with,* her look conveyed. *Just go and do your thing, my hardheaded future husband.*

I had walked for only a few more feet when Allie allowed her matri-monial obsession to blossom fully. She raised her voice and asked me if I preferred the name Sean or Micah for a son, followed by her assurance that either would work fine although I shouldn't be getting any wild ideas from my Greenville friends, especially that surfer couple who named their firstborn Wally Kahuna.

Without looking back I gave her a thumbs-up and kept walking.

After hiking over the rocky hillside, I was suddenly out of sight from the vehicle. In that dry and boundless wasteland I searched for a road. After another twenty minutes of walking I unscrewed the top from the plastic bottle and sipped something that tasted warm, like bathwater.

There weren't any roads out here.

Not even a tire track.

An hour into my walkabout I was not feeling like a hero. More like the flat plains drifter. I plucked the cap from my head and tightened the band, for my sweat alone had loosened its fit. The damp ring expanding above the elastic reminded me that water was leaving my body much faster than I was replacing it. This was a drier heat, and it was nearly impossible to tell when you were dehydrating.

Then I convinced myself that I was young and strong, and so I kept walking east, wandering aimlessly over parched ground. The heat melted my thoughts, boiling them into strange conclusions, the most prominent being that I was about to experience the opposite of claustrophobia.

Outbackobia—the fear of never-ending orange dirt.

I walked on, often turning to look back at the way I'd come. Silent prayers went up for Allie's safety, that she would have success with the two-way radio, that she would stay in the shade, and that she would refrain from chasing any more of Australia's national icons.

Each time I came to a wind-carved rock or boulder, I scrambled atop it, using the increased height to scan for distant roads.

But there still weren't any roads. Not even any litter.

After climbing down from the fourth boulder of the day, I discovered, to my dismay, that I had lost my bearings. Perched straight overhead, the sun had reached the one o'clock hour, where it functioned poorly as compass for the wandering but expertly as roaster of mankind. I turned in three directions before focusing on yonder sandstone—the diminishing, craggy landmark that stood beside the Land Cruiser.

I walked on. My bottled water grew hot to the touch, and my sneakers turned orange from the sand and dirt. I looked back every minute or so at my landmark, only to watch it shrink, like a sailboat on far seas, completely out of sight.

With the heel of my sneaker I drew a long arrow in the dirt, pointing back across the plains in the direction of Allie.

A few hundred yards later I drew another, some time later another, and in this manner I plodded—looking for roads, sipping warm water, and carving my arrows.

12

The roos had spent the night here; their footprints were everywhere. Two hours east of Allie and the burnt-orange Land Cruiser, I had found no trace of humans but clear evidence of roaming marsupials. The footprints were clustered in a crude circle, as if the more gregarious ones had hosted a square dance in this very spot, a late-night party to toast their supremacy over dumb Americans.

I searched the ground for tire tracks but found only a dark purple rock. The rock seemed a good souvenir, and when I stuffed it in my left pocket its heat penetrated the fabric and warmed the side of my leg. To make sense of the footprints was an exercise in frustration. Whether the footprints were fresh or three days old was a mystery to me, a guy raised in a Dallas suburb and unsure of his survival skills, unaccustomed to being on foot, and unfamiliar with the tracking secrets of Daniel Boone.

I sipped another ounce of warm water and scanned the geography. Red earth and clumps of spinifex lay in every direction. Each glance brought duality—increasing my fear at being separated from Allie but bolstering my hope of spotting a rescuer. I considered turning south, but to press on to the east seemed the better idea. Just one more mile.

One mile eventually became two. And two, three.

Inner Australia baffled me with its red illusions. I simply wanted out—no miracles, no magic, maybe the hocus without the pocus.

The sun slid into its three o'clock angle, and my shadow grew stunted and deformed. I stood among golden grasses and empathized with Jonah—for Tarshish bobbed on the horizon, the agenda was my own, and I was squirming in the belly of the outback. I had the feeling that no matter which way I turned, my situation would worsen. And surely Allie was worried.

Soon the wind kicked up and stirred the topsoil, tiny grains popping me on the cheeks, legs, and arms. Suddenly I wanted long sleeves and pants. Exposed skin recoiled at each sting, and I hid my face in my arms; it was like being sandpapered to death.

And just like that, the winds stopped. All went quiet again. Not only was this region unpredictable, it was unsteady, unsociable, and, I must admit, unparalleled.

I kept walking. Ahead of me stood yet another granite formation, this one also of sandstone but odd shaped, like the side of a candle melted unevenly. Its surface first appeared rust colored, then bronze, then brown as I found the shady side. In this shade I sat against the rock and rested.

Briefly I tried to get my mind off our dilemma by focusing on Couple Number Two. By now I figured Steve and Darcy were fighting emotional extremes—the rapturous glee of engagement and the horrible fear that their best friends would appear next in the obituaries.

I leaned my head back against the rock and closed my eyes in my best why-me posture. I replayed the photo shoot, the elation of driving in circles through high grass, kangaroos bounding in twelve directions, Allie leaning out the window with her Nikon. And now I felt guilty for letting exuberance squash reason, for bringing grief to loyal friends, and for tainting not one but two engagements.

In a measured voice I said, "Congrats, Steve. Congrats, Darce," and imagined a hot breeze carrying my words three hundred miles to wherever those two might be celebrating. Or agonizing.

My only company was lizards. I sensed them watching me. I craned my neck and looked above and saw a young thorny devil peering down, curious and sullen, not used to having visitors. I asked him if he had seen anyone in the vicinity. He apparently viewed me as dangerous, for he scurried inside the rock and out of sight.

One more mile. I rose to my feet and with my right sneaker drew my twenty-third arrow of the day.

I walked on. Only rocks littered the landscape. Not even a candy wrapper or a faded drink can.

Across the next plain I arrived, sweating, at a eucalyptus tree, a thing so ugly that it looked to have been coughed up from Middle-earth. I knew it was a eucalyptus because Allie had pointed out a gnarled specimen in her travel book, and the sheer uniqueness of its shape had pressed itself into memory. I was hesitant to even run my finger against the eucalyptus, thick and deformed as it was, the bark pale and wrinkled, like old skin. This was surely the Elephant Man of the tree world, and even its shadow looked grotesque.

Grotesque shade, however, was better than no shade at all, and so I sat at the base and drank some bathwater and gazed across central Australia. The afternoon light pooled and shimmered across the red center. So wavering and substantial was the mirage that one could envision taking a swim in it.

I didn't picture myself swimming alone. I saw my future children standing on the shore. Three of them. The youngest, a girl of four, dipped a toe in the water and glanced at me nervously, finding a lack of assurance in my words, "Daddy will hold you up." Across this liquid mirage I saw a diving board. She walked tentatively to its end, goose bumps on her arms, shaking with the first-time nerves of children. I was right below her, looking up through wet blond hair and saying, "I'll catch you."

The nameless little girl wouldn't jump. She couldn't move. She looked left, then right, then back down at the pool, and stood fear struck—because I was no longer below her. I was right here, stranded against an ugly eucalyptus tree, a daddy wannabe unfit to be a daddy, unable to figure out how to get Mother and Father out of a searing perplexity.

In minutes a cloud appeared from the south, big and lumpy and drifting. I prayed that it would blacken, float over Allie and the Land Cruiser, spill rain, then come my way and spill more rain. But immediately the cloud disobeyed and drifted randomly to the north, leaving me with the rare vacation experience of detesting a blue sky.

For a few minutes I tried to nap. Then I jumped to my feet when I thought a train had blown its whistle.

But it was just a dry and distant breeze, teasing me with rumors of rescue.

I gave up on finding a road and decided the smart and romantic thing to do would be to journey back to my waiting fiancée. I'd already journeyed farther than good judgment allowed, and my water bottle, hot and clear, sat empty at my feet.

Before I left the eucalyptus tree to begin the long walk back—my estimate was a good four to five miles—I perused the trunk and branches again and strengthened my opinion of its homeliness. In fact, I thought this particular specimen so ugly, so incomparable to what I'd seen in the travel brochure, that I broke off a limb and stuck my empty water bottle over the remaining nub, doing all I could to discourage the tree from reproducing.

I couldn't bring myself to litter, even in the vacant outback, so I stuffed the bottle in my pocket. Then I turned and saw spots, yellow and black flickers. Dizzy, I leaned over to prime the blood flow, touching my toes as the sweat dried around my eyes. These flickers were telling me yes, I'd walked too far, and yes, I'd best get back to my beloved, and yes, I'd best be careful on the way.

For a moment I stood there teetering, convinced I would never understand this God who pulls me into jungle missions one year, then has me fainting under a eucalyptus the next. But then my stance firmed, the blood circulated, and I recalled that God hadn't been consulted before I drove off the Gunbarrel Highway and across miles of empty plains just to get more photos than my best friend who had also toted a ring to 'Stralia.

I'd only taken a few steps homeward when the yellow flickers reappeared, and I stopped and asked Australia to go ahead and give me my lesson and clear my head and send a dark cloud that would burst on me fully.

But I felt so unqualified to extract lessons from circumstance. My preferred method was to have a self-help book inform me how to improve my life, and for the book to do so in condensed, fifteen-minute time frames. Brief, three-page chapters, please.

I had no book, just fleeting shade, dripping sweat, and the present tense. The only lesson I could conjure on this, the first full day of my engagement, was that God was showing me my inability to add a single cubit to my life. The lesson felt costly—I had already arranged all of my cubits; they were stacked on my own timeline, each waiting its turn in my head. However, as a math guy I preferred to call them cubes, small cubes presently condensed but capable of rapid expansion into the bliss I surely deserved. Each of my cubes was stored away as a future magnificent moment. Currently in my stack were marriage and family, health and happiness, reasonable income, and island vacations. But today in this oppressive heat my cubes began melting one by one, liquefying right alongside my optimism. They were no longer stacked high in my head and waiting for their appointed hour but instead were draining down my throat, just another slippery form of rumor.

My legs wavered. Sweat stung my eyes. Stripped of creature comforts, I saw myself for exactly what I was—a guy who would detest blue sky in want of rain, then detest rain in want of blue sky, all the while powerless to initiate either.

I licked parched lips and pressed on. Each step seemed to drain water from my body, as if walking was counterproductive. *Pace yourself. You're not living just for Jay anymore. You're living for a wife and future children.*

Wobbly in the orange dirt, I acknowledged to God that I could add neither cube nor cubit to my life, followed by a request that he hurry June 11—when there would be plenty of refreshment during a Caribbean honeymoon. And right now fruity drinks with tiny umbrellas looked nearly as appealing as consummated love.

But not quite.

The yellow flickers came again but soon faded. I tried a few leg squats to check my strength. I remembered my arrows and squinted across a dry riverbed to see my most recent one. Nothing moved in any direction. The grass lay limp, the winds died down, and not even a lizard made an appearance. Every creature seemed to have dug underground, burrowed into cooler earth, as if they too had taken a peek at blue skies and shaken their furry and scaly heads. *No rain today, maybe tomorrow. Time for a group nap.*

Alone and thirsty and stumbling, I found my twenty-third arrow and began the dry trek home.

13

When I reached the eleventh arrow I could no longer spit. My mouth was so dry and my stomach so empty that I considered, for the first time in twenty-odd years, turning over a rock and eating a bug.

But I did not eat a bug. I kept walking, looking for arrows, and fighting thoughts that this was it, my appointed time to expire.

Back past the rock formation, past the footprints where the roos had held a party in my honor, I gained new appreciation for the scale of central Australia. Here the possibility of finding help seemed about as likely as finding fresh-squeezed lemonade.

My pace slowed, my stomach growled, and optimism dragged behind me like an anchor in dirt. I hoped for a Jeep to come skidding over a hill, and when I saw no Jeep I prayed for a train, and when I heard no train I prayed for a horse, and when not even a dingo showed up there was nothing for a wayfarer to do but scan the sky for planes.

All I saw was that red-streaked bird, flying high overhead in his return commute. He seemed unaware that two humans, who had been given dominion, had misused that dominion and now needed him to be a carrier pigeon. But he could only be what he was. He never chirped as he flew, unwavering, into a languid afternoon.

Assurance came in the knowledge that I was more valuable than many sparrows. Yes, I tried to convince myself, I'm much more valuable than a lone, red-streaked bird. But as that bird flew strong and far, it seemed to command the higher bid.

I looked for the tenth arrow and found it not quite as deep as I remembered; intermittent winds had begun filling it, a few grains at a time. This arrow also held a present for me. Some curious creature had stopped by to see if I had left any food in the furrows and, finding none, had left me a small pile of white droppings. The excrement seeped into orange dirt, right in the shaft of my arrow.

Again the horizon floated on fumes. I turned in a circle and saw the same desert grasses and patches of orange.

A new cloud appeared to the west, thick and white and alone. In my thirsty and famished state I envisioned this cloud forming itself into puffy letters and spelling out "Walk north, young man, and there you'll find help." But of course the cloud did nothing of the sort. It just continued to drift westward until it dissipated into the atmosphere. It could only be a cloud.

The distance to the ninth arrow fooled me. I kept searching near a termite mound, knee-high and familiar. But there were many termite mounds, and many were knee-high. The earth looked the same in every direction.

I walked a zigzag into the sun and searched the ground. Still no arrow. The way back was not visible. The way to water was an unsolvable maze.

Panic set in. Dehydration had snuck up on me. And I feared for Allie.

Halfway into a circular walk, I stumbled upon arrow number nine. It was spaced unevenly from the others, though it was indeed beside a termite mound. The one with the white rock at the base. Of course.

Past the ninth arrow I removed my UT cap, found it damp with sweat, and balled it up in my hands. One hard squeeze, and a single drop fell at my feet. In my exposed posture the sun embroidered my neck with rays of hot thread. And now my legs had weakened further. *This walkabout was such a stupid idea.*

At the eighth arrow I began regretting that I'd picked Australia for the site of my engagement. A simpler setting, perhaps a national park affixed with phone booths and surrounded by convenience stores, seemed so much more appealing.

I tried to spit again but could not summon any moisture.

At the sixth arrow I stood atop a boulder and saw in the distance the sandstone formation that marked the site of my proposal. At the time of Allie's yes the rock seemed so stately and encompassing, our amphitheater. Now it looked so miniscule, a lone pebble languishing on a blank and unforgiving continent.

Half an hour later, walkabout was over. My strength had faded, my search had failed, and even worse, my fiancée was not waiting at the Land Cruiser.

I hurried around all sides of the vehicle, thinking Allie might be napping in shade. An empty Sprite bottle, green and topless, teetered on the rooftop, a hot breeze trying to tip it from its perch.

I searched the seats and dash for a note. No messages. As usual, I was shortsighted. I had approached from the east and never looked past the vehicle. If only I had kept walking I would have seen her. Allie stood some two hundred yards to the west, out past our morning fire and in the middle of a particularly flat and orange patch of ground. She had a stick in her hands, and every few seconds she'd lean over and carve something in the dirt.

I opened the hatchback, then the cooler, and found eight bottled waters. Took me only seconds to gulp half a bottle. Hunger kept me from making a proper sandwich. I just spooned gobs of jelly and peanut butter on bread, devoured it, and washed it down with lukewarm Sprite. I even took off my sweat-soaked T-shirt, washed myself for a moment, and changed into a fresh gray T. Then I moved to the driver's door, reached in through the open window, and honked the horn. Allie looked up from across the field, waved heartily, and went back to her writing. My guess was a list of bridesmaids, paired off with groomsmen according to height.

I couldn't wait to hold her. My steps found a new spring as I strode across the dirt.

She waited until I was within forty feet of her to speak. "You said four hours."

I couldn't walk fast enough. "Yes."

She checked her watch. "You were gone over six."

"Yes."

"You had me worried."

Just thirty more feet. "I needed time with God."

"So how was it?"

"Time with God?"

"No, your search for roads and rescuers."

Twenty feet. "Empty. I found kangaroo prints and a eucalyptus tree."

"Get thirsty?"

Ten. "Saw spots."

I extended my arms.

"And what about—"

I reached for her shoulders and stole a much-needed kiss.

"Gosh . . . you really missed me."

"Yes."

"I knew you'd be back."

I hugged her tight. "All my life I've wondered about the exact location of the middle of nowhere. I found it three hours ago."

"Did you leave your initials?"

"No. Just arrows." We let go of each other, and I turned to look at her carvings. "What are you writing out here, a love note?"

Without answering she reached down and picked up her stick and finished off her last line. I read the three stanzas and recognized the first of the three. She had it posted on the wall of a hut back in our Ecuadorian village. The previous summer a fire had torched the rest of the poem shortly after she'd composed it. I had never seen the whole thing—and she had never bothered to rewrite the balance. Until now.

Each letter was a good five feet in length, and Allie had even titled her composition. She called it simply "The Sand Dune Poem."

Sand dunes blown with heavenly breath
Make for fleeting, aloof congregations
The hot winds are vocal, the sermon is swift
And the grains do not wait for amen.

But what of that grain who is stuck down below
Who has never seen the sun rise?
Having heard all the rumors, it aches to take wing
For a taller, more glorious mound.

Yet each anxious grain is helpless to move
Unless heavenly breath sets it free
Though it squirm, though it shout, though it
    complain to the dune
All must wait for the heavenly breath.

To decipher her verse had always been a challenge for a math-oriented male. And in this moment, this peaceful and scorching and stranded afternoon moment, I was determined to be an accurate decipherer. I took Allie by the hand, walked her to the first stanza, and pointed to the third line. "That phrase, 'the sermon is swift,' refers to you and me getting stuck, right?"

She smiled as if amused.

I stepped back with her and pointed to the next line. "And the next, 'the grains do not wait for amen,' that's you and me turning off the Gunbarrel Highway and driving out here into the wilderness without thinking of the consequences?"

This time she cocked her head to the side and raised her eyebrows.

I was on a roll now. I led her beside the second stanza and nodded at the wording.

"You and I are 'the grains stuck down below.' The 'sun rise' is help on the way, 'aching to take wing' means our anxiety to get out of here, and a 'more glorious mound' is us finally making it to Sydney."

She restrained a grin and said, "Keep reading, professor."

Emboldened by my skill and insight, I walked Allie back to the third stanza. "We are the ones who are 'helpless to move,' and even though we can squirm and shout and complain to the dune, which is really God, we have to wait for his timing and his mercy to send our rescuer—the 'heavenly breath.'"

Allie let go of my hand and clapped sarcastically. "Bravo, professor. You have totally misrepresented every line of my poem . . . except for the part about mercy, which was obvious because any ol' slob could get 'mercy' from 'heavenly breath.'"

She walked past the last line and picked up her stick and carved her initials in the dirt. Then, assuming the role of teacher, she pointed at me with the stick. "Wanna know the real reason behind this poem?"

"Only if it doesn't embarrass me."

She pointed the stick at my belly. "Do you promise to never leave the vehicle again without me?"

"I promise."

"Then sit at my feet like an obedient first grader."

I paused in midkneel. "You're kidding."

"Sit."

With her stick she pointed some sixty feet away to the first stanza. She cleared her throat. "What you must understand, husband-to-be, is that I was not thinking of you at all, but of others."

I looked up at her like a hungry puppy. "Oh."

"And therefore, given the fact that you and I may not make it out of this outback alive, I wanted to leave one last piece of encouragement for a neglected part of the world."

"Wayward Australians on walkabout?"

Allie rolled her eyes and nearly snorted. "Single people, Jay. The poem is for singles."

"Oh."

"It has nothing at all to do with you and me being stranded. The sand dunes represent the millions of singles who try to barter with God over finding their mate. The fleeting, aloof congregations are the church hoppers, and the hot wind is the pressure to make things happen."

I nodded rapidly at her explanations, rose to my feet, and started for stanza number two. Allie tapped my shoulder with her stick. "Sit."

"But I was about to decipher—"

"Sit." She tapped me back to a sitting position. "The 'grains do not wait for amen' are those desperate Ladies of the Quest that Darcy and Alexis were part of last summer." Allie paused and frowned. "Did you know they would never forward me that list of churches with single men?"

"Never ever?"

"Alexis said it wouldn't do me any good in the jungles of Ecuador."

"Well, you still managed to snag me. And all I had to do was hop from one plane to another."

"I'm so glad you did."

"Me too."

"Are we about to get mushy?"

I stood again and pulled her to me. "Probably."

"Wanna know some more about my poem?"

"Kiss me first."

"Like that?"

"Again."

Next she pointed at the first line of the second stanza. Her ring sparkled in the sunlight. "That grain who is 'stuck down below' represents the single girl who never gets asked out on dates, who feels at the bottom of the pile. The 'sun rise' here alludes to a relationship, and the 'more glorious mound' is, of course, marriage. As for the third stanza, well, that should be obvious by now."

I stood shoulder to shoulder with her and tried to follow along. "And this sand dune poem was the one that got rejected by those publishers?"

"They thought it was about the Mojave Desert."

"Dumb poetry publisher."

She pointed up to the first stanza. "Yeah . . . dumb. Of course, the only reason I used the sand dune as metaphor was because you and I met on that beach trip at North Litchfield when we walked back down the deserted beach next to the dunes after we'd floated off to sea with our eyes shut."

"That was great."

"I thought you were cocky."

"But you invited me."

"I just didn't want to drift alone."

"But now you can't wait to marry me."

"It took a while."

I watched her toe the dirt again, knew her mind was turning. "That's not all, is it?"

She shook her head. "Someday we might be parents, Jay, so we won't be able to go off on these kinds of . . . risky ventures."

"But you said you would only date a risk taker."

"Yes. But that was dating. For marriage and parenthood I'll need you to switch over to stability."

"Stability?" I asked before recovering. "Oh, I mean, yes, I'm as stable as they come."

Allie dropped her stick and wiped her hands on her shorts. "Sorry. I didn't mean to bring up parenthood so soon after our engagement."

Still side by side with her, I stared out at sunlit desert grasses. "No worries. I even saw future children in a mirage today. The youngest, some nameless little girl, was standing on a diving board, shaking."

"Did you catch her?"

"I blinked and I was back here, sitting under the homely eucalyptus."

Allie was about to say something else when she turned and looked south over my shoulder. She pointed, gasped, and pointed again. Over a distant hillside and moving against blue sky, the speck appeared first as a dot, then a rising dot, angling across the plains to the north.

To describe the view properly requires Steve's baseball perspective. It was as if Allie and I were behind home plate, and the plane was angling across from right field toward center. The main difference being that we were at least twenty baseball fields away.

Neither of us yelled, "That's a plane!"

Time was too fleeting.

We sprinted toward the Land Cruiser, toward the radio and gas and matches. I passed Allie in my haste and looked back to my left at the slow-moving speck. I figured it was five miles away, and we had maybe three minutes to get its attention.

I leapt into the front seat, grabbed the radio. "Emergency. Can anybody hear this?"

Static filled the truck.

I tried again. Same result.

So I flashed the headlights. And flashed and flashed and flashed.

The plane kept going toward center field, its wings never tilting.

Allie ran with the spare gas can to the spot of our morning fire. She doused some pages she had ripped from her journal, covered them with handfuls of dry grass, and lit a match. The flames leapt waist high, but it was a skinny fire that quickly consumed its kindling. She tossed two empty water bottles on the flames and drew black smoke.

In desperation I flashed the lights faster, honked the horn longer.

Still the plane kept going, never veering, locked into a course that appeared neglectful and bullheaded and inhumanly selfish.

I was out of the truck and to the hatchback in seconds. There I yanked the tire tool from its mount and ran to the front seat. Turned awkwardly, I hacked at the plastic mount behind the rearview mirror, missed once, and cracked the windshield. Two more hacks and the mirror fell onto the dash. With this mirror I climbed atop the Land Cruiser, held the mirror up to the sun, and flashed reflections at the plane.

But the aircraft was over the outfield stands now, heading not for the middle of nowhere but perhaps just left of center. There was no way to tell if it was a patrol plane or a private craft out for a leisurely flight.

My fiancée stood amid gray smoke and yelled, "Come baaaack."

I flashed reflections as fast as I could.

As the speck became smaller and the fire became ashes, Allie collapsed back on her butt. There in the dirt she drew her knees near her chest and wrapped her arms around her knees and tucked her head inside—the identical posture she'd assumed when the truck broke down.

I continued to flash sunlight until the plane, like that white, fluffy cloud on my walkabout, dissipated into the atmosphere. Arms at my side, exhausted, I remained on the rooftop and considered Beatrice's advice of taking a guided tour.

The outback lay silent again. But this was no ordinary silence; this one had an undercurrent, like the silence of ants marching.

On the dirt patch near her poem, Allie sat motionless. Seconds later she lifted her head, glanced up at an empty sky, and tossed another dirt clod at misfortune.

14

We ate little that afternoon. The last two slices of low-fat emu had spoiled, forcing us to dine content with peanut butter and warm jelly on loaf bread. So visceral was our plight, and so verbal were we in complaint after the plane disappeared, that neither of us spoke for the entirety of a very late lunch.

Seated again on the oversized front bumper, we chewed slowly, swallowed occasionally, and stared out at a world that seemed to turn without us. I was certain that we pondered the same consequence—that we would never be discovered. We'd just end up a couple of piles of bones crumbled beside each other, bleached white skeletons that missed out on the joys of marriage. Allie's diamond ring would rest in the dirt, glowing in the Aussie version of an endless summer.

From dust you are, and to dust you shall return.

Sensing pessimism, Allie nudged me to look at the ground. She had eaten most of her sandwich and had just tossed the remaining morsel into the dirt. A horde of brown ants boiled over the exposed jelly, and as we stared at them I knew we needed to think of something or risk a similar fate.

Allie was the first to think of something. She gently elbowed me and said, "Ever hot-wire a car?"

"No. You?"

"No. But a good husband would try."

I donated a piece of crust to the ants and considered her request. "First you ask me to siphon gas when we already have a spare can, and now you ask me about hot-wiring when the problem isn't even electrical?"

She set her plate on the hood, strode around to the driver's side, and propped herself against the door panel. "I'm sorry. It's my poet brain trying to think mechanically."

I joined her back there and leaned against the back door with her. Mired in frustration, I watched the sun go down over the outback. For a second evening in a row, orange rays settled across orange earth and a burnt-orange truck, a monotony of color to highlight our lack of locomotion.

That's when Allie's survival instincts kicked in. She opened the back door, rummaged through her stuff for a minute, and emerged with her travel book. She stood beside me again, both of us propped against the truck and facing the sunset.

"Jay," she said, flipping through the pages, "I read something interesting in my book after you left this morning."

"About the wild camels? Haven't seen any of them, either."

"Not the camels. The book says that in the arid regions of Australia there is a species of small, slick frog that endures droughts by storing water in its skin till it gets all bloated, and then it just burrows under the earth and waits for the next rain."

"That's a hoax if I ever heard one."

She found the page and pointed to the second paragraph. "It's true," she said, tapping on the page. "They call it the water-holding frog, and it can hold over an ounce of water. And if the next rain is long in coming, then the Aborigines have been known to dig the frogs from the sand and squeeze the water out into their mouths, which must be terrible for the frogs but I guess if you're thirsty enough you'd squeeze too."

I pondered these Ziploc frogs for a long time. "Only in desperation would I squeeze one."

She closed her book. "It'd be gross. But yeah, if I absolutely had to . . ."

For a minute I still thought she might be joking, trying to ease our burden for a while. But when I borrowed the travel book from her hands and began flipping to the index, she folded her arms and said, "Page forty-seven."

She had told the truth—the frog went by two names, the burrowing frog or the water-holding frog, and it lived in a wide region of the outback. "Hmmm."

"Hmmm?" she parroted.

"Just wondering, now that we're engaged, if you'd squeeze a frog for me."

"Tonight? We still have seven bottled waters and a Sprite left."

"I meant if I was dying of thirst and couldn't lift my arms to drink, would you hold the frog over my mouth and squeeze?"

She tilted her head onto my shoulder and sighed. "For you, Jay Jarvis, I dunno . . . maybe."

For a newly engaged couple down to seven bottled waters, and considering what we might well miss out on if circumstances did not change, there was an issue that continued to creep, hour by hour, to the fore.

Our 10:00 p.m. issue was this: if a twenty-eight-year-old man loves a twenty-seven-year-old gal deeply, and vice versa, and the two of them have yet to know each other physically, and when his bones and her bones are about to become dust of the outback, mixed with roo dust and wallaby dust, Uluru's dust, and even the dust of scorpions, and when the Couple Who Could Not Wait are likely holed up in a Sydney hotel enjoying their union, does true love still wait?

Put yourself in our position. Think on it for five minutes. Think hard.

We had been discussing the issue for a half hour, she sprawled across the backseat with the door open, me in the driver's seat and trying the radio at ten-minute intervals.

"I must admit," Allie said, reaching up over the seat to stroke my hair, "the thought of dying out here without ever enjoying intimacy with my intended is . . . well . . . depressing."

I was only trying to nod my agreement when I accidentally leaned into the horn. I jumped at the blast, startled like a teenager caught parking.

But not so startled that I could not sit there in that hot driver's seat and feel Allie's fingers in my hair and know that we could take a few of the bottled waters and wash ourselves clean, climb into the backseat atop her yellow blanket, and do what the world urges everyone to do. Even out here in the barren interior, with no billboards to titillate, no commercials to fan the flames, the cumulative effect of sexual bombardment shouted for us to do it.

Do it. Do it, Jay. Do it like a man. Or, at least like the celluloid definition of a man. Do it like Sheen, do it like Cruise, do it like Baldwin, Travolta, and Smith. Do it do it do it do it do it do it do it. Just do it. The bombardment was relentless. *Give up your convictions. You may not live. Die happy. Die spent. Just do it.*

Some time later Allie took her hand away from my hair and lay back in the seat behind me. Her next exhale spoke of frustration, and the next one of resolve. She wouldn't have let me even if I'd insisted; and I wouldn't have done it even if she'd asked.

It wasn't fair to have engagement overlapping with demise.

As the moon rose more than three-quarters full, and I measured my sunburned arms against Allie's, we sat together against the back tire, shoulder to shoulder in our dirt-floored chapel, and prayed again for a way out. Then we drank another bottled water, passing it back and forth until the tears on Allie's cheeks were flowing faster than she could swallow. It was her first sign of true panic, the first evidence of withering hopes, as if she were conceding marriage, motherhood, maybe even life itself, to a land that refused to love her.

Her head rested in the crook of my neck, and I tilted the plastic bottle up for her to have the last ounce.

At this hour I had given up for today the idea of being her hero. For now, I could only be her best friend, her waterwheel in a place ill suited for waterwheels.

15

I woke to the sound of roaming marsupials. From my sleeping bag on the roof of the Land Cruiser, and in the wee-est of wee hours, I heard them shifting about, even snorting. They tend to snoop around campsites, Rental Guy had told us.

My peek over the side revealed shadowy shapes lingering some fifty yards away, the whole herd of them hanging back on the edge of visibility, sniffing the air, jostling for a better view. In the moonlight I could not tell if one was the male who had forced us into the creek bed. In the night air I could not tell if they smelled as bad as rumors would have me believe. But in seconds I could tell it was time for me to put on my sneakers and jump down off the opposite side of the roof, hide behind the Land Cruiser, and try to provide for my fiancée.

Actually I was growing a bit tired of trying to be the hero. I wanted to wait for morning, try the radio again, and have someone answer to "1-2-3 our butts are stranded." There was no way of knowing if we would need food—and we certainly had no way to store meat—yet I had to try. Could at least cook some burgers.

From behind the hood I peeked out, squinting for clarity and searching for a victim. I was all for respecting animals, but what if we found water but ran out of food? What if we needed the meat? I searched the herd for a young male. If it was him or me, it was going to be him. And if it was him or Allie, then it was definitely going to be him.

Waking Allie was not an option; she needed her sleep, and it was 3:20 a.m. Her head was at the far end, behind the driver's seat and against the door panel, her yellow blanket pulled up to her chin.

I snuck around the back end of the truck and peered out. The roos were still sniffing around the ashes of our fire.

Then I stooped, retied my sneakers extra tight, and took a deep breath. I even stretched my quad muscles. Then behind the back tire I found a good rock, a bit larger than a golf ball. Its heft felt good in my palm. One shot, Jarvis. Sprint hard, fire the rock at his skull to knock him out, then kill him as quickly and painlessly as possible.

Pocket knife? Stranglehold? I had no idea; I just had to provide.

In the waning seconds before my sprint, four young roos hopped a step closer to the Land Cruiser, maybe forty yards away from me. Behind them, tentative and lurking, several larger roos stood watch. It was too dark to select the weakest animal, and my only chance was surprise.

Again I bounced the rock in my palm. I took another deep breath, gripped the rock like a baseball, and sprinted for the herd.

For the first two seconds they all stared in amazement, ears twitching.

In the next second the four closest roos bolted to my right. I ran hard and straight for the lurkers, who had just caught on to the happenings.

They panicked. I charged.

Hind feet thumped on hard earth, surrounding me with percussion. Most bounded left toward the plains, but three went right, toward the hill. Swathed in moonlight, one adolescent slowed to look back at his pursuer. I ran straight for him. He saw me and bolted. When he angled left I had my chance. In full pursuit I cocked my arm, slowed to leverage my weight, and hurled the rock at a point two feet in front of his head.

Instantly I knew I had not led him enough. The rock whistled through the air, tailed like a fastball, zipped behind his ears, and thudded into dry ground.

By the time I had found another rock, the roos had all but vanished. Over the hillside I saw the last jumps of the adolescent before he descended over the top, chasing quickly after the herd, his silhouette a whirl of black.

It was like watching Dracula on a pogo stick, bounding from the scene after a particularly eerie encounter.

In a last-ditch effort I ran to the top of that hill. But down the other side it was like running into a vacant dream. Rooville offered nothing. No animals. No sounds. No evidence at all of confrontation. Except for their footprints—and of course my heavy breathing, my gasps for air, and a Texan's obligatory spit of frustration.

At sunrise on the second morning I woke to find Allie facing the vehicle from the front bumper, her hair a mess, her hands full of orange sand, her elbows where you'd expect a hood ornament. Except that Land Cruisers don't have hood ornaments, unlike Darcy's old Cadillac, whose lime-green hood had a huge one fashioned up there to help first-time drivers aim the tonnage.

Allie let the sand and dirt sift through her fingers and out of her palms. She dumped the grains on the edge of the hood and watched them slide off and tumble to the ground. She heard me stir but did not look up, just continued to sift scoop after scoop on the front of the hood.

Finally she spoke. "Why would any self-respecting rental company rent us a vehicle that was the same color as the dirt?"

From my bedding on the rooftop, I could only shake my head.

"Don't they even think about it?" she asked, reaching down for another scoop. "Don't they want to be able to spot the people who rent from them?"

This time I shrugged and climbed down from the roof, stood beside her, and scooped my own handful. "You do have a point."

Allie did not greet me with touch. Instead she turned and raised her empty but stained palms to the Northern Territory. "We just had to rent the burnt-orange truck, so now we're nearly invisible and no one will ever find us, or if they do they'll just find our bones all dried up like the fossils that were in my textbook in eighth-grade geology at Riverside Junior High, which I made a C in because I was always scribbling stanzas in my notebook."

That's how she always talked when upset, and it only got worse when a crisis was upon her.

122

It was a quality I'd grown to appreciate, though it made journaling our relationship somewhat difficult. She most definitely had a point. I mean, who would paint their Land Cruiser burnt orange, knowing that the dirt and sands of inner Australia are also burnt orange, and that people like us frequently get lost out here?

My quick search through the glove compartment revealed the answer. There was a registration certificate, made out to one Edward Batalee. Typed onto the back was a line that said "for personal use only."

Perhaps Rental Guy had rented us his personal vehicle.

Anything for the tourist dollar, I figured. Or maybe he just needed the income.

Breakfast consisted of warm jelly on loaf bread, plus the sharing of our lone apple. Allie continued to fret throughout the meal, so when we finished I took her by the hand and led her back to the front bumper and tried to calm her.

By this time the sun shone so vivid it throbbed. The earth seemed to have swallowed everything but granite and those stubborn clumps of spinifex, whose roots were probably sucking their sustenance from two miles underground.

Sweaty and without answers, Allie stood and resorted to her comfort zone, which was, in nearly every instance, her creativity. With her index finger she wrote words on the hood, in the dust and grains that covered warm metal. She wrote slowly, and she wrote but one line:

Here lies a boundless pothole on the road less traveled.

"Nice," I offered, trying to be complimentary.

"Don't talk to me right now, Jay. I'm in a mood."

For the next few minutes we passed her bottle of sunblock back and forth, repeating for a second day an act that I had always associated with white sands, seawater, and watching an old friend, Ransom, surf the waves at Litchfield Beach.

As I slathered the goop on my neck and arms I tried to picture a crazed and worried Darcy leading rescuers back the way we had come, an outback convoy retracing the split-off via Steve's map. But I had driven so far west of where they would think us to be that I just could not picture them getting any farther than that fork in the road.

That's when my mind just shut down, unable to process an optimistic thought.

All I could think of was going for another walk and maybe stumbling across someone. Allie seemed to sense my deliberations. Again she glanced blankly in my direction. "What now?"

"Wanna go on walkabout with me?" I asked.

Her answer was delayed, her mood waffling between downcast and melancholy. "Are you serious?"

"We could try south," I explained, pointing yonder way. "In the direction the plane came from."

She wiped her dirty palms on her shorts, checked them briefly, wiped again. "But how far could we—"

"Depends on how thirsty we get."

She frowned at the twin orange smudges on her shorts. "But what about 'four of five who stay with the vehicle, live'?"

I had tired of that mantra. And besides, every cell in my body was urging me to be a man, to find a solution. I wiped the excess goop from the bottle top of SPF30 and spread it on my earlobes. "We won't walk more than a couple miles. Three or four at most."

Allie turned and looked hesitantly at each empty quadrant, struggling to concur. When finally she spoke, she neither agreed nor disagreed. "I tried the radio three more times before you woke."

"I won't even ask."

She leaned back against the hood. "Only static, and it's getting weaker."

My next move was to edge up beside her, shoulder to shoulder, and tell her the truth. "I have a small confession."

She rolled her eyes and tried to smile. "You bathed with three of the last five bottled waters?"

"No, of course not. The roos came back last night. They were snooping around the fire, and one even sniffed the last line of your sand dune poem."

Doubtful, she shook her head. "You were dreaming."

"Was not. I woke up around 3:00 a.m. and saw a dozen of them snooping out there around the ashes."

Her eyes widened, and her mouth opened, though no words came out. Finally she blinked herself into speech. "So . . . you didn't think to wake me?"

"No time. I grabbed a rock and gave chase and tried to knock one out. But I missed."

"I can't believe you threw a rock at them." She ran a hand through her hair and looked out past the ashes. "Those poor roos. You almost hit one once before, ya know."

I pushed away from the warm, orange metal and turned to face her. "Allie, if I would have knocked a roo out with that rock, slayed him, and made roo burgers, you would have hugged me and kissed me till the cows came home."

She stood motionless for a long moment before an agreeable nod overcame her. Then she gazed past me at the sun, elevating by the minute. "You ready?" she asked.

At 10:30 a.m., after two more attempts with the weakening two-way radio, we left the vehicle and headed south, hand in hand. Bouncing on my shoulder blades was Allie's backpack, stripped of everything but two waters, one pb&j sandwich, and our diminishing tube of sunblock.

When entering the valley of the shadow of death, best to travel light.

16

We had only walked a mile from the dormant Land Cruiser when Allie saw the bones. Between clumps of spinifex and atop the orange soil lay the ribs of a perished animal. So bleached and old were the bones that they looked like props left behind from a fifties western. All the scene needed was a wagon wheel half buried in the dirt.

Allie nudged the ribs with the tip of her sneaker. "What do you think it was?"

I leaned down and ran my finger along the edge of the smallest rib. "Don't know. Wallaby, perhaps. Or a young roo." I glanced upward, saw the concern on her face, and quickly added, "Maybe it died a peaceful death."

She did not believe me. She didn't even nod her head. She just turned her back and looked away. "No, Jay, it did not die a peaceful death. Whatever it was expired slowly and with great suffering, probably with its tongue dragging, just like in your depressing account of Lake Disappointment."

I stood and pointed at a distant rock formation. "Let's just keep walking."

The sky offered no clouds to shadow a wayfarer; it was just blue and bright and empty. In fact, the days here seemed so similar in comportment that the Weather Channel might need to broadcast only once a week.

Allie strode briskly across the parched earth, two steps ahead, as if she needed to be alone for a minute. She frequently did this when she was thinking on a new topic. Seconds later she slowed and allowed me to catch up. "Do you have a will?" she asked.

I reached for her hand. "You mean a legal will?"

"Yes. Do you have one?"

"No."

"Me either . . . but we should."

I squeezed her fingers, but her return squeeze was halfhearted. "No big worry," I said, "you're a missionary with few possessions."

"Still, I should have a will. I have that old red Beetle back in Greenville."

We stepped across the spinifex and kept walking, kept looking in all directions. Small talk became our welcome distraction. "I thought Darcy was driving your Beetle ever since she sold her Cadillac."

"She does drive it, and she's added another dent. So I should probably go ahead and will it to her, just in case."

Beneath that relentless sun I counted my own possessions, found them few and of little value, and so began counting my footsteps, summing in my head how far we could walk in one minute. Eighty-three paces was how far. "I could've willed Neil my old Blazer, except for the fact he bought it."

She admired her ring at many angles, then she held it up to the sunlight. "I still can't believe he moved to South Carolina, and that he and Alexis are now married. I may have to have a cry."

"Because Neil and Lex got married?" I asked, oblivious to the emotions boiling within her.

"No," she said, pulling her hand from mine and using it to accentuate her point. "Because they're on their honeymoon, we're stranded, and who knows where Steve and Darcy are." Allie tried to blink the sweat from her eyes but gave up and used her T-shirt sleeve. Somehow she also wiped away the topic. "Don't you still own some stock?"

In midstride I reached for her hand again, knowing that as we talked of willing possessions to friends, we were already falling into negative thinking. "Four shares of Microsoft," I muttered almost to myself. "Maybe I'll will that to one of the kids in the village. Start a college fund."

We walked on, scanning the outback and kicking at rocks. Through the glare and across the hot soil, vague shapes that at first looked human soon revealed themselves as six feet of sandstone or sapling eucalyptus. This heat was a fooler.

"Thirsty yet?" Allie asked. Her pace had slowed, as had mine.

"Yeah. You?"

"Yeah. Let's drink some and then head for those tallest rocks."

One dab to the south of Smack Dab, which all Southerners—and most Northerners—know is in the middle of nowhere, we stopped. Here I pulled Allie's backpack from my shoulders. We removed our waters and unscrewed the tops and gulped with closed eyes.

"What do you think Steve and Darcy are doing right now?" she asked.

"Panicking," I replied, stuffing my bottle into the backpack. "I'm sorry about causing them panic almost as much as I'm sorry about veering off the Gunbarrel Highway."

"That highway wasn't even paved."

"It was built by explorers, and lots of people died before it was completed."

She pushed her half-full bottle into the pack. "And just how do you know that?"

"Page eighty-three of your travel book."

At this point I turned and looked for the Land Cruiser—which was now just a tiny bump on the landscape—and used my heel to draw our first arrow.

We walked toward a distant rock formation, this one bulky and imposing. We were hoping against hope that when we got there, the other side would reveal a road, or some campers, or some backpackers, perhaps even a ranch. Neither of us spoke, because by this time nearly everything had been said that needed saying. Let's face it, when you're a pair of stranded, engaged twentysomethings, and you've already had the sex talk and the will talk, there ain't a whole lot left.

My guess was that she too was thinking of family. Allie had four brothers, all of them older; thus she was not only a daughter and a sister but also an aunt six times over.

I had spoken to her father three days before we left for Australia, telling him what I had planned. Mr. Kyle was an elder in the Presbyterian church, and after he had gently reminded me of the responsibility that lay ahead—a man must love his wife as Christ loved the church—he had given his approval. He wished me well and advised me to propose early in the trip, so as to be free to enjoy the balance.

And now I had thanked him by endangering his daughter, never mind the fact that she'd been overzealous for close-ups of startled marsupials.

As for my own parents, they had sounded noncommittal as I shared thoughts about Allie while on the phone with them two weeks before the trip. Yet I still loved them. Still craved the chance to share my news. But neither my family nor Allie's would have a clue as to our whereabouts. They might just as well think us to be sightseeing in Sydney by now, me in khakis and a dress shirt while listening to world-class musicians at the Opera House, Allie next to me in a little black dress. No worries.

I was in khakis all right. Dirty khaki shorts that had remained on me ever since I'd ignored the warnings and driven four hours west of the highway in search of a herd, or a brood, or a pack, or whatever Australians call assembled masses of kangaroos.

"We've already walked too far," she said, barely gripping my fingers.

"Hang tough; we're almost there."

And soon, just ahead, that rarest of commodities—shade.

Allie hurried on toward the rocks, literally reaching her hands out to the shade, as if to hug it, to finger it, to thank it for existing. There we both leaned our backs against a wall of dimpled granite. There we hid from that relentless sun. There I even tried to inhale the shade, thinking my innards could use some after getting nearly cooked on our transdesert hike.

Allie cupped her hands as if pleading for rain. She leaned her head back and shut her eyes. "I'm wilting, Jay."

"Here, I'll water you." And I poured a lukewarm ounce over a sweaty brunette.

She almost smiled as the water ran down her forehead and toward her scalp and soaked into wavy strands of hair already damp with perspiration.

"You do know," she said, motioning for me to pour again, "that a certain deacon in the Presbyterian church would now consider us to have bathed together."

"Ah . . . Stanley." Verbose, theologically obsessed Stanley. It was much too hot for legalism, so I poured the next ounce and let the subject evaporate.

Allie and I had arrived at a cluster of wind-carved boulders, all of them massive, all of impressive height. After a few minutes of resting in the shade, we climbed atop the only boulder that was scalable, and from twenty feet up saw nothing but the vast province of a land that refused to love us. Ahead lay no roads or campers or ranches, just another hundred thousand square miles of red earth, sandstone, and swaying clumps of grass. Atop that very warm boulder, it was like sitting in a mirrored room, where every view is a duplicate, and confusion reigns as mean, median, and mode.

To proceed any farther would have been meaningless. And stupid. We'd be but wandering dingoes, lost in the desert and chasing our tails.

Allie stood for a minute and looked in every direction, squinting into the brightness of our plight. Finally she sat back down. "Wanna eat our sandwich now?" she asked.

I nodded and set the backpack between us. She pulled out the muggy sandwich, divided the halves, and volunteered to pray us a prayer. She prayed for our stamina and prayed for Steve and prayed for Darcy and thanked God for the meal. She even prayed for Neil and Alexis, who may or may not have still been in Australia on their honeymoon. Allie continued to impress me—mired in heat that threatened to melt us into broth, she could still be thankful. I tried to emulate her, but my mind was too busy scrambling for solutions, too busy trying to think my way to the least sufferable scenario.

So scrambled were my thoughts, and so desperate was I for answers, that fate and providence and folly became indistinguishable, like three strands of a cord I could not unravel. None of the three made sense, either woven together or singular: God's providence should not include such calamity. Our folly did not deserve such extremes. And fate—fate was simply too rigid a word, as if our desert shipwreck had been unavoidable.

But indeed it had been avoidable. All we had needed was a do-over by the author of providence, a second chance to realize our folly in the millisecond before folly muted the still, small voice whispering that we really shouldn't test the hand of fate by insisting on more close-up shots of wayward kangaroos.

Convoluted thoughts from a convoluted mind. Every one of our strategies had failed. And now I had serious doubts about the truth of four of five who stay with the vehicle, live.

Allie nudged me and pointed at my half of the sandwich. "Aren't you gonna eat?"

I removed my UT cap, wiped the sweat from my brow, and pushed the cap back low on my head. "What do we have?"

She rolled her eyes. "Where were you? Daydreaming again? We only had peanut butter and jelly left in the cooler, you made one sandwich to take on our walkabout, and now you sit next to me on this boulder and ask 'What do we have?'"

I took my first bite. "Sorry."

"You were doing it again, weren't you?"

"No."

"Yes, you were. You were trying to figure out if God did this to us, or if we did this to ourselves, or if it's some of both."

"It's some of both."

"Eat your sandwich."

I chewed slowly and scanned the earth, overwhelmed by the amount of iron oxide dotting the acreage. Surely this was the land where old rocks came to weather and die.

After a time of meditating on our circumstance, we drank the rest of our waters and climbed down from the boulder.

Reunited with hot ground, I pointed back in the direction of the Land Cruiser. Allie nodded and offered to tote the backpack. I shook my head no and started walking.

But then she reached out and grabbed the side pocket of the pack, halting me in midstep. "I'll carry it, babe," I said.

"Sunblock."

We squirted the goop in each other's palms and spread it once again on our arms and faces and necks.

Halfway back we passed my third arrow. Just another mile of trekking, I figured.

We were within sight of the truck when something—instinct? providence? boredom? fate?—made me turn around and look back toward the boulders.

Above and beyond those rocks, way off in the area of right field, a familiar speck-with-wings angled silently across the sky.

In one motion I dropped the backpack in the dirt and spun Allie around. "It's back."

Her glance began blankly, then morphed into shock. Her eyes widened. Immediately she stood on her toes and shouted, "Over here!"

We yelled. We jumped. We waved our arms and yelled some more.

The plane kept going.

I quickly filled my empty water bottle with dirt and hurled it skyward. Allie filled her own. We threw them without the tops on, so that the trail of dirt spilling out might somehow catch someone's attention.

I was stunned at how high Allie could throw. Of course, from the plane's vantage point, the orange dirt spewing from our bottles fell against a matching orange earth. *And why didn't I think of that,* I thought just as I reloaded and threw my bottle a second time. It landed, *thud,* behind me, another failed strategy.

"They still don't see us," Allie shouted. "Why don't they see us?"

"Run, honey," I said, snatching up the backpack. "Fast."

We sprinted across the plain, back past Allie's poem and toward the Land Cruiser.

There I grabbed the rearview mirror from the seat and scrambled atop the roof. Allie tried the two-way radio. When again the radio did not work I flashed reflections as fast as I could. I flashed with confidence and determination, then with urgency, then with desperation at this plane that flew selfishly to the southeast. But it kept going, that negligent plane, and its wings never wavered, retracing the same right-field-to-center-field route it had taken the day before.

Between flashes I glanced at my watch to see if the pilot might be flying at the same time every afternoon. But the time was 3:35, and the day before, it was 6:10. Like everything else about inner Australia, aeronautics and flight schedules were at best unpredictable. I watched that speck progress against blue sky, the kind of slow-motion flight that can be a delight to watch on normal days; now it appeared as betrayal.

"Turn arrrrrrounnnddd," Allie shouted. She was not a great shouter.

After the plane disappeared, she sat dejected on the back bumper. The shade grew slowly back there, right next to melancholy. Soon her tears came again, and as they fell she leaned down and picked up a dirt clod. But instead of throwing it she just crumbled it in her hand, allowing the grains to spill randomly on dry ground and dirty sneakers.

I came around beside her and put my hand on her shoulder. "Are you okay?"

She licked her lips as if her mouth was dry. "No. I'm scared and I'm thirsty and I'm hungry and I'm worried about the kids." She didn't need to tell me that she was weakening. I saw it in her eyes, heard it in the lightness of her voice.

She was emptying the dirt from her shoes when I reached into the hatchback to get her another water. Our consolation prize.

We shared this one, along with a handful of tortilla chips left in a cellophane bag. Allie ate for a time, then she drank quickly, gulping in the manner of marathoners. She looked like she wanted to say something, yet all she did was stare out toward "The Sand Dune Poem" and shake her head. Some minutes later she changed her mind. "Maybe that poem really is about us."

I finished off the chips, took another swig of warm water, and nodded my agreement. "Maybe so, wife-to-be . . . maybe so."

If I had been back in the leafy confines of our Ecuadorian mission, or perhaps even the balmy shores of South Carolina, and someone had told me I'd be stranded in the outback with my fiancée, I would not have been scared. No, in my vision the second afternoon would have produced a good-natured Aborigine strolling across the red earth, perhaps a cane in his hand, dust covering his hat, a knowing smirk rising between unshaven cheeks. He would walk slowly, squinting into the sun, as if he'd seen similar idiots in similar predicaments all his life. This man would be our rescuer, our John Wayne, our dark-skinned Indiana Jones. He would lead us to his camp, give us drink, tell us stories, point the way.

Such was the effect of movies, and my brain retrieved the caricature like a favorite song.

17

Though we'd done our best to keep to the shade, we were by now sun-burned and famished. The condition proved contagious, as both the radio and the horn had all but died. The last rays of the day ignored our silent pleas for mercy, and so Allie and I split off—she in the backseat, me seated on the front bumper. Both of us rested our heads in our hands, the posture of shared frustration. Alone, maybe one of us would conjure a solution.

I was still juggling providence, folly, and fate. I was doubting my faith. I even entertained the brief thought of throwing a dirt clod at God himself. If this barren wilderness was where I was to seek first the kingdom, then the things that had been given unto me—a roasting engagement and a wilting joy—were not the least bit impressive. I didn't deserve this lot. I'd never pictured a God who would slay me in the prime of my life, who would cut me off from bliss, whose will brandished a serrated edge.

And so the sun went down on a second day of desert shipwreck, sinking not in a blaze of glory but definitely in a blaze. My thoughts boiled with comparison. At least the sun still has its locomotion. At least the sun didn't lose its engine and get stranded at the noon hour, sautéing everyone this side of the equator.

I began to regret my life. I regretted that I hardly knew God at all. I even regretted my math skills. For with my math skills I kept dividing time by ounces of water, trying to pinpoint the zero hour.

Math distracted. Math had me cornered in a human house of deduction. Math could so easily replace faith—which was exactly what consumed Allie as I sat on that front bumper and sulked.

I knew what she was doing in the backseat. She may have been scared, may have been thirsty and hungry and worried about our future, but the woman could pray. Allie Kyle could always pray.

And then into my convoluted mind flew Elder Kyle's advice. Allie's father was a pleasant fellow but a staunch Presbyterian, so his counsel was rather startling, especially for me, a guy who eighteen months earlier was going to church just to meet girls. What he told me was that in order for a man to love his wife fully, he might one day have to die for her. And yes, Elder Kyle, I heard you, and yes, I believe what you said, and I even wrote it all down, and I know you're right, but how do I love your daughter when shelter and sustenance are more fleeting than the wildest of roos?

Just before dark, Allie and I rose from our lonesome and frustrated poses. We'd been sitting apart for over an hour, and now she made her way to the front and stood facing me. Her yellow T-shirt was smudged with dirt stains, and her eyes were still red from her afternoon cry. She held some papers in her hands. Her stomach growled.

"Jay, I wasn't going to show you these, but . . ."

I started to reach for them but could tell she was hesitant. "What are they?"

"Rejection letters."

"For your poetry?"

"I have three. I packed them to show to Darcy." Allie looked down at the papers and pursed her lips. "Want me to read one?"

After a smile of sympathy, I nodded and pulled her beside me. I knew why she was doing this. She would show me the papers just to lighten the mood, to distract us from our dilemma.

I squeezed her shoulder. "Who could ever reject a volume titled *Allie Kyle's Deeply Philosophical Jungle Poetry for Kids*?" I asked, hoping to ease her uncertainty. "That title is so, um . . . resonant."

"Yes," she said, agreeing much too quickly. "So resonant."

"Would you rather I read the letters?"

136

She plucked one from the bottom, handed it to me, and turned her head as if unable to watch.

I was about to read it when she turned back around and snatched it away. "No, I have to learn to accept this stuff. I'll read them myself."

"Sure?"

She flicked an illiterate fly from the page and cleared her throat.

Dear Miss Kyle,

Our editorial department has reviewed your submission, but unfortunately we do not see the marketability of your work. Specifically, a book titled *Allie Kyle's Deeply Philosophical Jungle Poetry for Kids* should not contain poems that slice and dice corporations for their greed, insult the average American worker, and hint that everyone over the age of twenty should leave the United States, learn Spanish, and do mission work in remotest Ecuador.

Allie stopped halfway down the page, her frown twitching from left to right. Then she glanced at my mouth, as if hoping my lips would produce encouraging words.

I pointed at the paper and did the best I could. "Well, honey, maybe that's all the negative stuff up front. . . . Keep reading. It probably gets better."

"No. That one gets worse." A drop of sweat fell from her forehead and soaked into the salutation. She ignored the smudge and shifted that paper to the bottom of the stack.

With two hands she shook the next letter, removing the center crease.

To Allie Kyle:

Although we are not in a position to publish your vast volume of jungle poetry, we would like to make you an offer for one of your poems. Each year we publish a collection of poems which we cull from submissions from across the nation. We only ask that those whose poems are selected purchase a special leather-bound gift volume. Your friends and relatives will be so proud to see your work displayed in all its splendor. Three easy payments of $29.99 will secure your volume. Pay in full by January 7 and receive as a bonus a certificate announcing you as a published poet. The poem we have selected from you is "The Sand Dune Poem," which our editors thought to be excellent in its meter. There was mild debate over your subject matter, but regardless, you should be so proud to be included in this special leather-bound gift volume. Remember, Allie Kyle, just three easy payments of $29.99, and you are on your way!

She thrust the papers into my chest, and I held them up by the corners, like they were tainted or were about to tinkle. "They want you to pay to get published?"

Allie reached over, pulled the one she had just read, and wadded it into a ball. "Never."

I watched her fling the paper in the direction of the setting sun. The beige wad tumbled to earth just ten feet away. "Never will you pay to get published?"

"Never ever."

She reclaimed the rest of the papers and prepared to read to me the last rejection. "At least this next woman cites individual lines to make her points."

"I'm all for individual lines."

She glanced skeptically at the paper, stalling. "What's needed from editors is more clarity."

"Of course."

She looked nearly too weak to read. "This one has good clarity, but it's very negative."

"How negative?"

"Very. You're ready?"

"Bated breath."

She started to read but coughed dryly. Her eyes watered. "My mouth is dry."

I began to get up and make for the hatchback, but she shook her head no. "Only read it if you want to," I said, shouldering up to her again. "And then we'll drink another of the waters."

To see her suffering was almost too much. I nearly stopped her from talking further. But she held up a finger to my concern and made her point. "You know I only brought out these rejections to distract us."

"I know. But I still want to hear what the editor cited."

Allie again cleared her throat, this time in the haughty manner of academia. She read:

Dear Miss Kyle,

I have not quite recovered from the shock of reading stanzas like "How shallow their roots, they chase only careers. These neighbors seem date-stamped, like cartons of milk." I thought I had heard it all. But here you have expanded the boundaries of poor taste. Who has the audacity to compare the American worker to a dairy product?

Although we occasionally publish poetry, it's never anything as antimaterialistic as your work.

I congratulate you on your command of meter, and I'll admit to being impressed by your footnote—that you created this poem on a sandbar, with only a piece of driftwood for a writing implement. But I think you should reconsider your intended audience.

Rethink your title; reconsider your motives; and resubmit when you've figured it out.

All the best to you.
Sincerely, Sarah Wiley

Allie folded this one in half, and then the first letter as well. Then she walked dejectedly around the side of the Land Cruiser and dropped them in the backseat.

She stood there by the driver's door and looked at me across the hood. The distraction had been nice, but like most distractions, it was easily dismissed. Allie shrugged weakly, I shrugged back, and for five seconds we tried to simply outshrug each other.

She looked out beyond the plains, into the empty regions of our walkabout. "Oh well," she muttered.

I sat on the hood this time and leaned back on my elbows. "But babe, if two of the three say basically the same thing, doesn't that mean that—"

"Yes," she replied with an affirming nod. "It means that none of these publishers recognize marketable poetry, even when it is right before their eyes. It's because they watch too many TV sitcoms and get jaded by materialistic story lines and the overall lack of morals."

Now that rejection hour was over, she reached into the front seat and drew out her travel book. Then she reconsidered and set it back, unopened. There was not enough light to read anything else, only the orange residue of a day lacking promise.

After we had gulped the water and eaten yet another pb&j, a weakened Allie went to bed in the backseat. I plopped down on the front bumper again and, in a drained and parched state myself, began to question God's plans. I even questioned his motives. Thus emboldened, I got so cocky that I even suggested to him that he did not know what he was doing.

As a kid I had often wondered what it was like to be that astronaut who got separated from his craft in space and spent the rest of his hours (or minutes) floating around in the dark, totally alone, adrift in a galaxy so wide that he would never see the same moon twice—or a familiar face even once. At that moment the astronaut's greatest hope was to hear from mission control, to be assured that a solution was in the works, that someone was on the way.

All that was on the way for us were the wee hours. And, as usual, I needed to wee.

When I returned from the desert grasses it was after midnight—after 1:00 a.m., actually—and in the backseat Allie had been asleep for hours. We were down to two sixteen-ounce bottles, a few ounces of plastic-smelling water in the bottom of the cooler, four slices of stale bread, some jelly.

What I did next could be classified as odd, a maturing in the faith, some of both, neither, or simply the result of too much sun. What I did was, I grabbed my sleeping bag and climbed back up on the roof of the Land Cruiser and thought about hell.

I had heard once that hell is not so much hot as it is lonely. That people who boast here on earth, "See ya in hell, buddy!" are in for a big surprise. What a shocker to arrive there and discover that there are no decadent parties or firelit orgies, but that each person is in total darkness, all alone, no interaction, unable to see even a distant wave from a fellow hellite. Everything is still and black and haunting. And that is your lot, your eternity.

I had read all this in a book titled *The Ambiance of Hell*. Out of sheer curiosity Steve Cole had bought the book for twenty-five cents at a Goodwill, and we had read the first chapter together on the flight across the Pacific. Then, somewhere over Fiji, Steve got scared and stuffed his book behind the Qantas magazine, whose back cover offered tourists fake koala bears in three shades of beige. Those little bears were much more pleasing to discuss than Steve's book, so he wrote down the 800 number and promised to order a tan one for Darcy. Having made the shift from Hades to koalas, we decided to leave the book on the plane in Alice Springs, just before our foursome boarded the shuttle bus. And I was glad we left it—because having been maturing in the faith for only a year, I'd have felt presumptuous walking around Australia and stating with certainty hell's lack of social functions and the particulars of its ambiance.

In some ways, being stranded in the middle of baked Australia was like being in hell. And in many ways it was not. For I had my beloved, our darkness was not total, and the clear skies and sandstone appeared pure and picturesque.

Further into the night I dismissed thoughts of the underworld, although not for thoughts of heaven; I felt so grimy. Even if we did make it to marriage, I was convinced that Allie would never get near me. I'd never wash away all the filth and sweat that coated my body.

I wanted to hold her close again. I wanted to wake her, tell her we were going to make it, maybe slow dance to Barry Manilow again. But I dared not bathe. Baths were not an option, and body odor was now as inconsequential as dirty fingernails. All we needed was a do-over by the author of providence. Or at least a dependable four-by-four driven toward us by some other wandering shutterbug of a tourist.

Immediately I wished I had not thought of the phrase *four-by-four*. Because once again math flooded my head. In this heat we could not go more than six hours without drink; the water we had left would be gone in less than eighteen hours.

I hated my math, the inflexible nature of sums. So I lay there on the roof—only my feet inside the sleeping bag—and thought of the children we worked with in Ecuador. I knew them all so well, knew that at least one would already be scribbling a crayoned WELCOME HOME to tape to the door of my hut. I thought of Steve and Darcy, where they might be, of the anguish I'd caused. I thought again of Allie's father, how he trusted me with his daughter.

I was determined not to drink any more water. Once in South Carolina, in the backyard of my house on the cul-de-sac, I'd watched a male cardinal gather sunflower seeds in its beak, one at a time, then hop over and feed them to the female. I determined that today I would be like that male cardinal—when the time came, I would give the last drops to Allie. In that hour I would try my best to be, in my flawed, human form, her provider.

Didn't I have to be *something*? I had already failed as leader of an unguided tour, had already developed huge reservations about my status as an alpha-male, and was probably not even qualified to be a husband. Perhaps I could dig up a pair of those Ziploc frogs, squeeze us a few extra hours.

Faith, hope, and love. The greatest of these may have been love, but on this night—as the Aussie air cooled, as I licked dry lips, and as Allie slept three feet below—I identified with that astronaut and clung most tightly to hope.

18

By 10:00 a.m. I doubted enough moisture existed in me to produce per-spiration. Yet I continued to sweat into the dirt at the bank of that dry creek bed.

I was on my knees—and perhaps I should have been praying—but I was too busy digging. At the edge of that creekbed, beside a rotten stump, I had located and dug up two of those bloated frogs and was doing every-thing I could to excavate a third. They were cocooned in their own skin, bulging with stored liquid.

Our bottled waters were gone, the risen sun lacked mercy, and Allie had already fainted once from lack of nourishment and the overabundance of heat. I had twice fought off the dizzies myself.

A quarter mile behind me she lay across the backseat of the Land Cruiser, trying to stay as still as possible.

I placed the two captured frogs in the Igloo cooler and added some dirt. The third frog proved more resourceful; he found his secret underground passage and escaped. Despite my frantic attempts to dig deeper with my stick, he vanished in the soil.

Two frogs. Two ounces. Too much for a first week of engagement.

Scared and anxious and deliberating, I stood and scanned again the empty fields, the stubborn clumps of spinifex, and the endless graveyard of rocks that had come to central Australia to weather and die.

The desert grasses had only recently stopped laughing; I reckon they had swayed and chortled themselves to the point of exhaustion. And still there came no squinting Aborigine strolling amongst them and across the parched earth. No John Wayne. No swashbuckling Indiana. Not even a curious wallaby.

At noon we burned the spare tire. I rolled it out past Allie's poem and up atop the hill where the roos had vanished. Then I poured a liter of gas inside and lit a match. The burning tire oozed forth an offensive black smoke, but at least it was black. The odor was only slightly more offensive than my own. Allie and I had voted on what to burn next for a signal, and from her prone position in the backseat, she'd suggested the tire.

But as tread turned to lava and my sweat began to boil, no one saw our smoke, no one showed up. No Jeep or train or horse. No Australian police or forest ranger. Not even a high-pitched wind, teasing us with rumors of rescue.

And here it happened—I gave in.

Caved.

Turned it over.

Let go.

Stopped trying to be the hero.

I told God that I would do whatever he wanted me to do, if only he would allow Allie and me to live. If he wanted, I would go back to Wall Street. If he insisted, I would take ballet; I would even write a nonfiction book for twentysomething singles called *Adventures in Bible-Belt Dating*, and then follow the current trend and pen every derivative product possible, including *Adventures in Presbyterian Bible-Belt Dating*, *Adventures in Baptist Bible-Belt Dating*, *Adventures in Lutheran Bible-Belt Dating*, *Adventures in Pentecostal Bible-Belt Dating*, *Adventures in Methodist Bible-Belt Dating*, and *Why Episcopalians Might Get Kicked Out of the Bible Belt*.

I would do anything. I would manufacture surfboards with Ransom Delaney; I'd paint all the huts in Ecuador sea green; but mostly I'd pledge to never again stray a hundred miles off the Gunbarrel Highway so that we could snap more photos than Steve and Darcy.

That's when I heard Allie cough dryly. When I nearly panicked. Because my own throat was parched, and she was asking me to employ the first frog.

"Come over here, Jay," she whispered. "And bring Kermit with you."

Allie still lay on her back across the backseat of the Land Cruiser, both doors open, her head on the south end, on the side of her carved poetry. She faced the roof and pursed her lips again. "You're going to wet my whistle, aren't you?" she asked. Her voice was barely a rasp. It was like she had sawdust in her throat. "I hope you'll save the other one for yourself."

"No worries," I whispered, leaning in from behind her head and fighting the urge to drink. "You can dig up the next batch."

I backed away and knelt to open the cooler.

When I stood again at the open door, she winced. "Darcy would never allow this."

"But you're not a Darcy."

Allie coughed again. "I . . . I know."

I had the frog around his belly, my fingers pressed up underneath to squeeze him fully.

He was a mixture of pale brown on top and green beneath, pregnant with water and kicking his legs. But he still had dirt and mud under his mouth, so I backed away from the truck to wipe the last grains from his skin. He smelled like warm mulch. I used my hands and shirt, and in seconds I had him clean and ready to sacrifice his storehouse of water.

At the backseat I leaned in over Allie again. Should I squeeze the water into a cup first, or straight from the frog's mouth into hers? I could not decide.

From behind me, the angle of the rays made the shadows of my hand and the frog look monstrous. A ten-gallon toad.

Allie kept her eyes open—she was trying to be a good patient. I ran my left pinkie finger over her lips, and she opened wide. I was about to squeeze when her eyes became saucerlike. She pointed back over my shoulder and through the open door. I thought she was only stalling, so I shook my head and shushed her.

"Relax," I said, "we both need a squirt."

She shut her mouth tightly and pointed harder, this time higher in the sky.

For whatever reason, the speck-with-wings had chosen 1:45 for its afternoon pass. Still some twenty baseball fields away, it once again angled across from right field to center, this time at an even more leisurely pace.

I dropped the unsqueezed frog into the cooler an instant before I grabbed the rearview mirror from the front seat and scrambled back up on the roof. But I was weak, and my head spun. The yellow flickers came again. Still, I flashed well. I was so sure I flashed well. Allie suggested I ad-lib Morse code.

But still the plane kept going.

Out of the corner of my eye I saw Allie emerge from the backseat, look up and out at the plane for all of three seconds, and promptly collapse to the ground.

I knew I should jump down and tend to her, but that would mean giving up the chance to be seen, for someone to notice a burnt-orange Land Cruiser that matched Australia's burnt-orange earth.

Atop the roof my legs shook from lack of energy. Below me Allie rolled over and coughed. I spread my feet wide for balance and kept flashing the mirror.

And the plane kept going.

And what to do now, God? What does a young man do when planes pass unaware and Mother Nature is selfish and his fiancée is collapsed on the earth?

Faith or math? Me or God?

Some of both?

Wisdom was in the numbers, first reminding me that four of five who stay with the vehicle, live. Then convincing me that for a man to love his bride properly, a four-of-five ratio isn't good enough. Not for my beloved lying on the ground with parched lips and the dry heaves.

No, I had a new ratio for the outback: two of two who blow up the Land Cruiser gain the attention of bush pilots.

I jumped down from the roof at the same moment that Allie pushed up from the ground and tried to stand. I took her by the armpits and helped her to her feet. For a second we held each other up.

"I need a T-shirt," I said.

"The one I have on?" she asked, half-dazed and incredulous.

"No, from your bag."

I was an idiot to ask her to do anything at all. Allie was now leaning against the hood, looking like she was about to faint again. In my desperation and near delirium I opened her luggage and jerked out two T-shirts. I ripped them along the seams until I had two long pieces, then quickly tied the ends together. I glanced over my shoulder. The plane continued on its leisurely and selfish flight path.

From the hatchback I grabbed the spare gas can, barely able to lift it.

Allie held herself against the hood and stared at me like I was bonkers. "What are you doing?" she asked in a voice absent of moisture.

"Hang in there, babe."

I grabbed my duffel from the back and quickly stuffed cameras and loose items inside and tossed the bundle over near the two-story sandstone. Kneeled on the ground, I doused half of my T-shirt fuse with the gas, then stood and splashed some gas on the roof and all over an empty black suitcase, which I set on the roof just above the gas intake.

"Jay, what are you—"

"Shhh. Don't strain." I practically leaped in one bound to Allie and half-walked, half-dragged her over behind the sandstone. Our buffer.

"I don't understand," she said.

"Back in a sec."

I stumbled back to the Land Cruiser and used a stick to stuff the gas-soaked end of the fuse into the tank. The remainder dangled to the ground. Then I dug some matches from the console, glanced up at the plane headed for deep center field, hurried back to my T-shirt fuse, and lit a match. Nothing around but dirt, so I never feared collateral damage.

Flame ate cloth, as if it too were famished.

With my last fumes of energy I sprinted, head down, behind that ten-foot rock. We huddled tightly as I covered our heads with the duffel bag and wrapped my arms around her face.

The whoosh of combustion preceded the bang of explosion. The rock shook, and glass rained down, clinking off sandstone and onto my back. From our hideaway I could not see the quadrant of sky in which the plane flew.

And then fire whooshed again. Fresh explosions. I squeezed my eyes tight and covered Allie a second time. Heat blasted around the rock, and I hoped the fireball was huge.

When no more explosions followed and I felt no burns, I propped Allie's head on the duffel and eased around the sandstone to see black smoke billowing from the rear, from the backseat, out the windows, and from the suitcase now ablaze on the roof.

And still the plane kept going.

And going, and going, until the wings tipped against blue skies, that marvelous tipping of wings, mercy aloft and morphing into a Cessna. What a beautiful tipping of wings.

Here he came, banking, descending, homing in, the engine howl growing louder in its approach, the clattering *ratta-tatta* of a Cessna gaining speed as it sheds altitude. He was still a good ways away when I ran out into open ground, grabbed Allie's poetry stick, and carved one word in huge letters: HELP!

I had just finished the exclamation when the plane roared overhead, its shadow trailing the fuselage at an odd angle. His backdraft blew dust in my eyes, and after I had wiped them I looked up and saw the wings tip both ways, which I took as his signal that he'd read my note.

Then I looked back at the flaming truck—which was articulate on its own—and wondered why I even bothered to carve a note.

The plane rose into a wide arc and homed in on me again. I kept waving. The thrill of knowing at least one other human knew our whereabouts was surpassed only by the ecstasy of knowing that Allie would survive, that I'd get to pick out my tux, and at some point just before fruity umbrella drinks on a Caribbean island, a honeymoon would commence, and consummated love would at long last have its turn.

And another turn.

And another.

And, well, here came the plane.

19

When the Cessna roared past a second time and brandished no landing gear, I figured the pilot had either changed his mind or else he was a drug runner.

Fortunately, outback aviators know what they are doing.

He rose, banked, and dropped altitude again, this time leveling off several hundred feet above ground. He homed in a second time. Me, the target. In seconds I knew this guy was not a former Air Force bomber captain, because whatever he dropped out the side window missed me by two hundred yards and went angling off to the west and landed out in the plains, near where the roos had hopped off the previous night.

I jogged, panting and weak, over to the bundle. And between two clumps of spinifex lay the unexploded bomb—an old purse, magenta and very seventies, with little red beads along the stitching, zippered at the top. It looked like something Cindy Brady might have pulled from her mom's closet.

Now I just figured the pilot or copilot was female and had poor taste in fashion accessories. In the role of ridiculous hunter-gatherer, I picked up the purse and unzipped it and found a twenty-ounce plastic bottle of Ocean Spray grape juice, plus a broken Hershey's bar and a note. On ripped white paper was a hastily scribbled message:

We're a sightseeing service. Cannot land. Ground too rough. Low on gas too. Radioed nearest vehicle, 30-40

kilometers away. Wave with both hands
if no one critically injured.
P.S. Please save my purse.

She—or he? No, maybe not—pulled up into the afternoon sun, turned again, and came back for a fourth pass. I stood on my toes and waved fervently with both hands. Again the wind blew dust in my eyes. Again I shut them tight and kept waving. The plane roared overhead, banked toward right field, and faded slowly into blue skies, which now were looking not nearly so detestable.

Now in the role of courier, I was sapped of strength but not the least bit embarrassed at running across the outback while toting a magenta purse with cheap red beading from the seventies. With that purse tucked under my arm like a football, I ran back across the plain and through the third stanza of Allie's sand dune poem and past the smoking remains of the burnt-orange Land Cruiser, which now was the very definition of burnt orange. Behind the sandstone rock I delivered the juice to a shaded and confused Allie. She gulped hard.

"What just happened?" she asked. The sandstone had blocked her view, and in our famished state I doubted either of us could clearly perceive events.

"Magenta manna, honey," I said, kneeling beside her. "Magenta-colored manna just fell from the sky." I tilted the bottle for her, and she drank. She grasped the bottle with both hands and took another voracious gulp.

Next she thrust the bottle at my chest, and I took it and drank. At the instant of my swallow I gushed, "Someone is coming."

Allie slowly sat up and began unwrapping the Hershey's, revealing broken pieces already melting. "Steve and Darcy?" she asked.

"We'll know shortly."

She took a third drink of the juice and shut her eyes to savor the taste. "Ah," and here she sighed and licked her lips. "Much better than frog water."

I smiled and moved some hair out of her face, away from sweaty cheeks that were a shade darker than when we'd arrived three days earlier. She bit into a melty triangle of chocolate, chewed it quickly, and glanced at the package under my arm. "Nice purse, Jay."

"Thanks." I ate a soft triangle myself and washed it down.

Her voice was less raspy now. "But you messed up."

"How's that?"

"This is milk chocolate. You know I prefer dark."

Only a few ounces remained in the bottle now, and so urgent was my own need for liquids that the next sip I took went down like the last remnant from a garden hose. I wanted more. Liters more.

I handed the bottle back to her.

"You sure?"

"I'm sure."

Allie gulped the last of the juice and wiped her mouth. "Please tell me you saved my journal before you blew up the truck . . ."

"Yep."

"Camera?"

"Got yours, got my disposables."

"My shampoo?"

"I think so. Got as much loose stuff as I could in fifteen seconds." I studied the empty bottle of juice for a moment, tilted it above my mouth, and let the last, lingering drop ease down the inside of the plastic and into my throat. "Oh, but your rejection letters are goners . . . total ashes."

She nodded agreeably, like she could care less.

While we sat dirty and sweaty against the sandstone, waiting in the shade for whoever might be rolling across Western Australia, I tried to recall what I'd just done. Yet all my mind could manage was to detach and spin itself into celebratory relief. In fact, the immediacy of relief squashed the memory of suffering, the urgency for food, even the expectation of wedded bliss. Relief draped me like a veil of ice, which I just wanted to lick and savor as it melted over my chin. And when the veil was gone I settled for an air of appreciation, thankful for the new ratio, the one-hundred-percent math that came from "two of two who blow up the Land Cruiser gain the attention of bush pilots."

I loved my math.

Sweat drained into my eyes, and after I'd wiped and dabbed I nudged Allie and spoke into her ear. "Just want you to know I've never before blown up anything of value to impress a woman."

She dismissed my tease, sat up, and wrapped her arms around her knees. "Have you picked your fourth groomsman yet?"

"I've been too consumed with pyrotechnics."

"Groomsman, Jay Jarvis. And he needs to be at least five feet nine."

"Lemme think on it. My brain is fried."

Partially rejuvenated from the sugar in the juice and chocolate, Allie once again allowed enchantment to flood her world. She stared at her ring and held it up out of the shadows and into the sunlight. A prism. "How did you ever afford this gem?"

I stretched out my legs and scuffed the dirt with my left sneaker. "It was nothin'."

"Tell me."

"Okay, okay. I sold nearly all my stock, two hundred shares of Microsoft that I had hidden away in a retirement account on Wall Street—where you claim you would never have lived."

She gazed even more affectionately at her ring. "Wow . . . two hundred shares of Microsoft. That's a lot, huh?"

I nodded in the affirmative. "It used to be a lot. Now we'll have to wait for my four shares to go up and split seven times so that one day when we're seniors we can come back to Alice Springs and go on a guided tour."

Here we both reclined into postures of repose. "A guided tour," she parroted, rolling the words around her mouth as if to sample them. "Sounds nice."

"Yeah. Air-conditioned buses, with running water and potties in the back."

"Yes . . . potties. And soap."

"And coolers full of drinks."

"And a little man with a megaphone, who tells corny jokes and points out all the national treasures."

I paused and thought ahead forty-five years. "Do you think we'll ever play shuffleboard in Florida?"

She put her hands behind her head and looked up at the sky. "Never."

"Never ever?"

"I'll pay to get my poetry published before I ever settle for shuffleboard."

A half hour later I glanced up from admiring Allie's ring and saw a black four-wheel drive bouncing across the southern plain, announcing itself with horn honks and twin boils of dust. This dark and dirty SUV was still hundreds of yards away when Allie and I craned our necks and waved without pretense, preparing to meet strangers by being exactly who we were—the Couple Who Survived Their Stupidity.

20

The windshield was so coated in orange dust that I could not see a face. And for reasons I couldn't figure, the driver stopped some thirty paces away from me, idling on red earth, as if trying to determine if I were trustworthy.

In an effort of greeting, I had walked out into the field next to my HELP! note. Soon I identified the make of vehicle as a Montero and deduced that two heads lingered behind the dust and glass. The truck had a winch bolted to the front. I heard music playing, but still they came no closer. And who could blame them for hesitating? If I came upon a flaming SUV on the outskirts of an Australian desert, my tendency would be to proceed with caution.

The Montero rolled forward and paused again. The music stopped. Then, in a moment that will forever stun me, my newly married ex–Spanish teacher, Neil Rucker, thrust his head and shoulder-length locks out the driver's window. In his right hand he held up a harmonica, and before he said a word he brought it to his mouth and blew the first notes of the *Rocky* theme.

Neil then pulled the instrument from his lips and yelled, "Jarvis!"

I turned my palms up in a gesture of 'who did you expect?' "It's me, bro."

Well tanned and enthusiastic, he leaned farther out the window. "Man, you're so grimy we didn't recognize you. We thought for a second that you were a bandit trying to trick us."

For a moment we just stared at one another through the heat and glare, trying to make sense of it all. I smiled at the thought of committing an unpardonable sin—interrupting a honeymoon.

I turned to my right to look at Allie, who was still propped against the sandstone, on the other side of the burning Toyota. She waved slowly at Neil with one hand, shooed a trace of smoke away from her face with the other. She looked at him and made the drinking motion. With both hands.

"What happened, you two?" Neil continued, shooting twin glances of confusion at the two of us. "But no matter, we'll get you out of here and . . . then I can go back to enjoying my wife."

I grinned first with envy, then with embarrassment.

Neil ducked back inside behind the wheel and turned off the engine to the Montero. And just when I expected to see the raven hair, pale complexion, and pierced eyebrow of his bride, Alexis, appear from the passenger window, out popped the head of Steve Cole.

"Found ya, bro!" he shouted.

I blinked, stared, blinked again. I was too famished to think, too dehydrated to fight hallucinations, but no way would I confuse cute, slender Alexis with Steve's square jaw and crew cut. I stepped forward and placed my hands on their dusty black hood, a prop to support my bewilderment. "But where are . . . where is your wife, Neil? And where is Darcy, Steve?"

Neil jumped from the front seat and came around the hood and hugged me hard. His Birkenstocks smushed my sneakers. "Jarvis, I've been married for seventeen days now. I'm so in the clouds that I don't even care if you ruined my honeymoon for forty-eight hours."

Steve approached from the opposite side and slapped me between the shoulder blades, pounding me twice, in the masculine manner of glad you're alive. "Was worried about you two."

He looked past me and past the burning vehicle and waved at Allie. His voice rose. "We're so glad you survived, Miss Allie."

Again she waved and made the drinking motion.

Neil still had his arm around me, as if marriage had made him overly affectionate and he just could not let go. "Jay-bird, we have a number of things to tell you."

Hot beneath his arm, and hotter still from the proximity to the black hood, I pulled out of his grasp and stood between the two friends. I glanced at one and then the other. "Before any more talking I want to get some liquids into two of my favorite people." I pointed at Allie, then at myself, and kept one hand on the truck as I made my way to the rear. "And what's this about you guys looking for us for forty-eight hours?"

Steve beat me to their hatchback, produced a cold quart of citrus Gatorade, and began walking past the torched Toyota in the direction of my fiancée. He spoke over his shoulder. "It's not just us that have been looking for ya. More like thirty other vehicles . . . all four-wheel drives."

Flattered by this news, I grabbed a second quart from their cooler—they had two cases of Gatorade stacked behind it, plus three cases of water, sacks of food, and a grill. I opened the plastic bottle and gulped half the contents in a haste that surprised even my throat.

The three of us—Crew Cut Steve, Long-Haired Neil, and Dirty Blond Me (call me Grimy Jay)—huddled around Allie at the base of the sandstone. She remained seated, her back against the rock, shadowed and drinking and trying to smile. Neil had made her a turkey on wheat, and she'd already consumed half of it. A minute later I made my own and gobbled it like a caveman going at dinosaur leg.

Behind us the Land Cruiser smoked away, only the front and underside retaining any hint of orange paint. Who knew the costs; right now my friends were here, liquids were plentiful, and I felt oddly free and unshackled.

Allie drank heavily from her bottle and looked up at us. "I think I'm ready to leave now." She pushed off the ground with her hands—and slid right back down on her rump. "But maybe not."

I recalled my approaching pledge—for better or worse—and plopped down beside her.

Steve wiped sweat from his forehead with his Cubs T-shirt. He seemed distant. Finally he took a long gander at the remoteness of our station and sat in the shade to my left. Neil sat on Allie's right. We would give this some time.

Distracted by circumstance, I had forgotten about Steve and his own engagement plans. Yet I remembered that any and all such news was supposed to be a surprise for the girls to share. So with Allie seated there among us all, and neither she nor Neil knowing anything about Steve's agenda, I kept my mouth shut. Did not ask the question.

And just like typical males, Neil and Steve had yet to notice the ring sparkling on Allie's finger.

There in the shade of that tall, rust-colored rock, we all seemed too busy thinking of the questions we had for each other. I had the most and blurted the first one. "What happened to Darcy and Alexis?" I asked of either guy.

"Yes," Allie said, concern creeping into her face. "Where are my girl-friends . . . and your wife, Neil? You're on your honeymoon and you have no wife? No Alexis?" Her left hand turned palm up as she asked, yet they still did not notice the ring.

Neil blew into the front of his madras shirt, trying to cool himself. "The girls are fine. Lex and I ran into Steve and Darcy in Kulgera, a hole-in-the-wall where we'd stopped to eat. That's where Steve told us about you two being missing."

"Yep," Steve chimed in. "And then when it became evident that you and Allie were probably lost or stranded, Neil and I decided to team up and explore the, um, harsher regions."

Allie stared at Neil like he was an absolute kook. "You left your wife in a tiny Australian town while on your honeymoon? On your honeymoon, Neil?"

"Hardly," Neil replied. He brushed the hair from his eyes, and he did so in the nonchalant manner of musicians. "It was her idea. Lex and Darcy volunteered to backtrack to Uluru. Lex claimed that searching for lost friends would be less frustrating with someone of the same gender. So they took off in the other Land Cruiser to look for y'all . . . and so did the other thirty vehicles."

I gulped again and said, "I can't believe we're that popular."

Steve smiled and shook his head, as if amused by our ignorance. "It's not that you two are so popular, Jarvis. After we reported you missing, you were mentioned in a front-page article in the Alice Springs newspaper. Then Darcy found a shop with Internet access and emailed the news back home to North Hills Prez and asked them to pray."

Allie eased her lips from her bottle and searched their faces for sincerity. "Well," she said, "did anyone say they would pray?"

"Oh, sure," Neil said. "Two people said they would. But then something more enticing came back."

"Free admission to a water park?"

"Reward money."

"No way," I said, knowing these guys' ability to play with the truth.

Neil raised a finger of seriousness. "Someone posted an anonymous reward. They contacted the local newspaper and radio station, saying they would pay four thousand bucks to whoever found you two. Plus—"

Steve stopped Neil in midsentence. "There are dozens of four-wheel drives searching for two tourists. But all I want to know is, how'd you get all the way out"—and here Steve gestured to the desert—"here?"

Allie leaned her head back against the rock and sighed. "We wanted to win the photo contest."

Steve shook his head. Then he stood with hands on hips and surveyed the smoldering truck. "And you blew up your Land Cruiser, Jarvis? That's gonna be expensive."

"Yes, I know."

Allie appeared lost in thought. She stared into the dirt and frowned. "So," she said, fingering the soil, "money is the motivation for all those vehicles looking for us?"

"And several motorcycles," Steve said, still looking perplexed that anyone could have strayed this far from the original plan. "The tour companies have been alerted also. Word is out to be looking for an orange Land Cruiser and a pair of American tourists."

Oh, the shame. Guilt. Remorse. This was all so unnecessary.

And so I sat there imagining Aussie trucks rolling across arid plains, caught up in the hunt, hoping to root out the wayward twosome. *We were right here, mates, in an orange truck that matches your orange earth.*

This money issue intrigued me—and I wondered how much it

intrigued my buddies. "So," I said to Steve, "you and Neil get to split the four thousand?"

"Yep." And he promptly reached over and high-fived Neil.

"Any idea who put up the money?"

"Not a clue," Neil said.

I had already finished off my quart of Gatorade and was now stealing sips from Allie's.

At my third sip she took it back and called me a pig. I licked my lips and questioned Steve a second time. "Did you and Darcy try to call us on the two-way radio?"

"That's another thing," Steve replied, standing beside me with his arms crossed, like he had all relevant information stored, indexed, and categorized. "We found out that those two-way radios are barely more than a kid's play toy."

I looked at Neil for confirmation and saw him staring out beyond the plains. He never made eye contact, though I could tell his mind was turning. "Jarvis," he said, still trying to manage his unmanageable hair, "I've been married for seventeen days!"

Allie rolled her eyes and pointed with her left hand at Neil's shirt pocket. "Is that a cell phone in your pocket?"

Neil tapped his left pocket. "Lex and I both have cell phones. We rented them yesterday morning before we split off. So we can talk mushy while we're apart."

This time Steve and I joined Allie in rolling our eyes. And then Allie elbowed me in the ribs. "Why didn't we think to rent cell phones, Jay?"

"'Cause we had the two-way radio."

She reached out and bonked me on the head with her empty Gatorade bottle. "We had a dime-store walkie-talkie and it almost killed us, plus I had to go three whole days without a shower."

Neil flipped open his rented phone and began pressing buttons. He held the phone to his ear and whispered to the group. "Gonna give the girls the news that I found the dumb Americans."

The rest of us sat impatiently, wanting to talk to Darcy and Alexis.

But after a full minute had passed, Neil stared at his phone and frowned. "Probably no coverage out here."

"Yeah, probably," Steve said. He said it as a kind of automated response. But he looked worried.

To get their minds off the possibilities, I revisited the subject of reward, though in an indirect manner. "Steve and Neil, do you love Allie and me?"

Steve blushed slightly. "As much as Chicago Cubs baseball."

I had half the answers we needed. "Neil?"

He shut his phone and tucked it into his pocket. "Almost as much as Alexis's double mochas."

"Do you two love us more than four thousand dollars?"

Neil wiped sweat from his brow and looked at Steve, who rubbed the dry earth with his foot. They both looked embarrassed at the intimacy of the question. "Yes," Steve said finally, "of course we love you two more than money."

I grinned without restraint. "Good, real good. Because Allie and me are poor and we need that reward money to help pay back Rental Guy for blowing up his truck."

Satisfaction fell from their faces faster than that magenta purse from the Cessna. "That's not fair," Steve said. "I'd need to think on it."

Neil kept rubbing his chin, like he could not decide. "Maybe we'll give you half."

I continued to plead. "We might need it all. And Steve is . . . just look at him, Neil. Steve's about to agree with me, because he knows he drew a bad map that tempted us toward this hot and lonely desert."

Allie made her best grim-face and nodded her agreement. "Very hot. Very lonely."

Steve shook his head and tried not to laugh. "Jarvis, this place isn't even on the map." Again he turned and looked in all directions, overwhelmed by this colossal blank. "This is . . . man, this is orange purgatory."

I stood and helped Allie to her feet. "Just get us out of here."

"Yes," Allie said, reaching down for the magenta purse. "Just get us back to showers and refrigerated drinks."

We were about to board the black Montero for the long journey from the outback when Allie peered into the rear windows and spied the cases of bottled water. I knew what she was thinking. She saw Neil fastening his seat belt, folded her arms, and stood outside his door, unwilling to climb into the backseat. "How far of a drive do we have?" she asked.

"At least five hours," Neil replied, fidgeting with the radio.

"Then I need five minutes."

At the hatchback Allie pulled four bottled waters from the case, dug a towel, a T-shirt, soap, and her bottle of shampoo from the duffel, and began walking back toward the sandstone. Suddenly she had a spring in her step, and she never looked back as she toted her loot behind the rock.

In minutes she emerged in a clean white T-shirt, wet hair, and a smile. Thus equipped, she walked a wide path around the smoking truck.

Neil and Steve turned the air-conditioning on full blast while we waited, and when Allie approached I opened the back door like the grimy gentleman I was.

She climbed in and began toweling her hair. Then she stopped suddenly and glanced at me between damp folds of terrycloth. "Well?"

"Well, what?"

She sniffed the air and pointed out the window. "It's your turn . . . go bathe."

Back into the heat. Through closed windows I could hear them laughing. But I dismissed their stink jokes and remembered a forgotten duty. The last thing I did before washing was to release that pair of Ziploc frogs I had left inside the Igloo cooler. I had set that cooler in front of the truck before I stuffed the cloth in the gas intake. The frogs had survived and were buried head-first in the dirt, touching noses.

With both hands I removed them from the cooler and carried them back over to the dry creek bed, where sands did not flow and minnows did not swim and where clay banks were etched with the journeys of snails. There I inserted the frogs into their underground passage, and in seconds they had burrowed out of sight. And without even a *ribbit* of thanks.

"Will you hurry up?" came Steve's shout from his window.

At the rear of a dusty, black Montero I removed my shirt and bathed in angled sunlight, relieved that this was not one of those thousands of times when I needed cleansing with hyssop but instead just a simple shampoo and rinse. I doused myself with cool waters, happy to leave my grime right there with the texture of the memory, with the truck that did not save us, the land that did not love us, and the poem that had two meanings. Not to mention that homely eucalyptus I saw on walkabout.

After I had rinsed my hair and armpits, Allie rolled her window down and flung my balled-up purple Hawaiian shirt across the roof. I slipped it over my head, climbed into the backseat behind Steve, shut the door, and allowed the air-conditioning to tingle damp skin.

I had just stretched my right arm across the top of the seat behind Allie when Neil turned from the steering wheel and glanced at her hands, which were resting in her lap. "Wow," he said, "you two got engaged?"

Allie smiled and wiggled her fingers at him.

From the passenger seat Steve offered hearty congrats, although he would not make eye contact with me. Uh-oh.

Anxious to reunite with Alexis, Neil put on his sunglasses and pulled the gearshift into drive. "Time to locate my wife," he said.

But first Neil offered us one last glimpse of our folly. He turned the steering wheel sharply to his left and drove in a circle around the smoking corpse of the Land Cruiser. "Say g'bye, everybody."

Steve produced a disposable camera from beneath the passenger seat and snapped two pictures. Allie managed but a single wave.

I was tempted to give that Land Cruiser the international symbol of disrespect. But I no longer did such things, for I was now a mature man of the faith, one year into my journey, so poised and content that I could not recall the last time I had doubted God's goodness.

Tendrils of black smoke faded in the rearview, and Neil bounced us across the plains. In the backseat I pressed my nose against the glass and stared across the landscape that had held us captive. It all looked so scenic now, and in the distance three young kangaroos stood grazing on a hillside, half hidden in desert grasses, watching our departure as if sad to see us leave.

Saddest for me, however, was the debt I had brought upon myself for destroying Outback Adventures' prized 1996 Land Cruiser. Rental Guy would surely have a roo, or a cow, or whatever animal Aussies have when something unfortunate occurs. During my youth in Dallas, Mom always had a cow.

I leaned right to whisper. "We'll have to tell the rental company the truth . . . we're responsible for their truck."

Allie sighed and put her head back against the seat. "We were perishing out there, God just sent us a plane, and you're already worried about money? Money, Jay?"

I looked back a second time at the burning carcass. "We gotta at least consider it. What if insurance doesn't cover us? And you should feel sorry for me, what with me down to four shares of stock and being responsible for torching a Toyota."

She shut her eyes. "We'll worry about it tomorrow."

When an hour had passed and we still had not found a road—just rock and spinifex and the endless orange dirt—I realized how far Allie and I had ventured off course during our photo safari. But this knowledge was pure hindsight, nothing like the present-tense thrill of proposal, when a man loses all sense of scale in the midst of his obsession to adorn a ringless finger at sunset, that pastel hour we romantics employ to backdrop our magnificent moments.

By this time Allie had fallen asleep, a towel wedged between her head and the window, her hair drying across her face, her hands losing interest in her Gatorade bottle. I could not wait to marry her.

And I could not wait to ask Steve what had transpired with him and Darcy. Between the shakes and rattles of our drive, Steve kept trying Neil's cell phone in an attempt to reach their women.

And Steve kept frowning, squinting into the sunlight, and redialing the number.

After noting three more failures of the phone, Neil glanced blankly at Steve and raised his eyebrows. Steve answered in kind—with a frown to accompany the brow raise—and muttered that they might have made a mistake when they agreed to let Darcy and Lex take the white Land Cruiser and backtrack toward Uluru.

We were all more valuable than many sparrows. We just shared their IQ.

21

We rolled eastward along the dirt and ruts of the Gunbarrel Highway. Our pace held steady at ten miles per hour—mostly because of the camels. They trotted ahead of us, all fourteen of them.

It was 5:00 p.m., and the cell phone still would not work, the wild camels still would not move, and we were nowhere near civilization. All we could do was remain as we were—the black caboose in a lazy parade. Neil honked the horn, but it did no good. Steve must have thought the photo contest was still on; he snapped two pictures of the camels' golden rear ends.

Allie woke from her doze and informed us that, according to her travel book, such herds were common sights in these regions. Neil honked again, and the camels gained speed, though they never wavered as to direction. It's so much easier to trot in the road.

And that's when Mother Nature—she of searing temps and prolonged drought—laughed the hardest. From the southwest rose storm clouds, nearly black at the core, sneaking up behind us like a favorite sin.

I lowered my window and sniffed disturbed air. Rumbles of thunder preceded the first flashing bolt. And then the soft patter of raindrops, louder by the second, *thump-thumping* the road and pockmarking the dirt.

"Now she sends rain," Allie muttered, gazing out her window. "Three hours after I have a bloated frog at my lips, she sends rain."

Steve held the camera to his eye and said, "I wanna hear all about those frogs."

"Later."

Apparently camels are not afraid of rain, even heavy, fill-the-meteorological-tube-with-one-drop type of rain. Without Alexis on board, Neil didn't say much. He just switched the wipers on high, and we rolled along now at fifteen miles per hour, tailgating wet beasts, failing to shoo them, and swerving around their frequent and steamy droppings.

Happy honeymoon, Neil.

Several muddy miles later the pace camel spotted a ditch filled with rainwater, and his detour dominoed through the herd. A fourteen-hump pit stop. Or maybe it was nineteen-hump; I lost count in the downpour. Figuring this could be our only such sighting, I reached over the front seat, grabbed Steve's camera, and leaned out the window for one last shot.

Oh, the aroma of wet beasts. My shout to the fourteenth camel brought not a toothy grin but an indifferent spit. His amber expulsion splattered against the door panel just as I snapped the picture.

"Gross," Allie said, her nose scrunched in disapproval.

"That's the natural color of camel spit," Neil explained.

"I meant the direction of it."

The way had cleared, and Neil sped up as much as the washouts would allow. I raised my window and felt the air-conditioning mute the damp scent of camel.

How quickly the landscape had changed. Dust got pounded into mud, rocks released steam, and the grit on our windshield gave way to a drenching. But nothing could have been more relieved than the wildlife. I even envisioned the roos extending purple tongues to catch the drops.

"Allie?" I whispered.

"Yes?"

"Do roos have purple tongues?"

"Only after they lick grape popsicles."

Steve continued to try the cell phone at ten-minute intervals, all to no avail. Neil retained the worried look; he had not said a thing for miles.

Ahead, however, lay paved surface, black and wet and spewing its steam, and when I felt the tires gliding beneath us I asked Steve for the phone.

All I did was hit the redial button.

And all that happened was a static-filled voice saying, "Neil? Neil, is that you?"

"It's me, Alexis—Jay Jarvis. Happy honeymoon. Your husband is with two guys and another woman."

Her voice faded, like she had turned from the phone. "Darcy, it's Jay. Neil and Steve must have found them." Then her voice strengthened. "Jay, Darcy and I are going to need some help because we—"

And suddenly Allie had the phone, unable to restrain herself from snatching it right from my hand. Wide-eyed and animated, she spoke into the phone in a stream-of-consciousness banter that was incredible even for her—every other gushed word was proposal or engaged. And girlish screams could be heard from the cell phone, and return screams from my fiancée, and then there followed bursts of speech and more screams.

This pattern repeated itself for three entire minutes before Allie removed the phone from her lips. Her hair had dried unevenly, and after she pulled some dark strands from her face she covered the mouthpiece with her hand and looked across the seat at me. "It's Darcy, Jay. She says they're stuck."

At the utterance of the word *stuck*, Neil mashed the accelerator, and Steve turned to reach for the phone.

But I already had it to my ear, preparing to be the navigational hero. To Steve I held up a halting finger, and in reply he gritted his teeth in mock discontent.

I spoke carefully into the phone, knowing that both my buddies were worried. "Darcy, just give us directions, and we'll find you and get you unstuck."

Her pause was answer enough. "I'll have to ask Alexis where we are."

"You mean you don't know?"

"Hold on a sec." I heard murmurs, fragments of chatter. Then Alexis came back on the line. "Jay, we're off of a rock-strewn road beside a big patch of orange dirt."

Lord help us. "Are you east or west of Uluru?"

"West . . . I think. Darcy was driving into the sun an hour ago."

"Are you okay?"

"I've been married for seventeen days, so of course I'm okay."

"I mean are you and Darcy in any danger?"

"No, except for our front end is down in the mud and Darcy is spinning the tires."

"Tell Darcy not to spin the tires."

Another pause, another muted voice. "Darcy, Jay says not to spin the tires."

Inside our Montero the questions came quick and whispered, peppering me from three of four corners. But I gave everyone a thumbs-up and muttered that I could handle things. Neil made the grim-face. Clearly anxious, he pressed our speed on paved highway, though we could still see only arid plains and sandstone in every direction.

I took a breath and tried to think of how to help. "Alexis?"

"Yes?"

"Listen closely. You're going to have to give us better directions. Where did you veer off the main highway from Uluru?"

"It started when Darcy and I thought we'd spotted a koala."

"But koalas don't live in the arid regions, Lex."

"Well I know that now. It was just a possum thing."

"So you stopped searching for us in order to chase a possum?"

"There was no chasing. Well, just a little. But we had to drive across this soft dirt area to get to the bushes, and then the storm came up and flooded everything and when we tried to turn around the front tires sank a bit."

Both Allie and Steve looked on in a kind of open-mouthed shock, astonished at the half of the story they were hearing.

"How much is a bit?" I asked Alexis.

"At first it was just halfway, but since Darcy's spinning, um, the top of the hood is still a few inches above the mud."

"So the front tires are completely submerged?"

"We're tilting."

"You're what?"

"Just a sec." Her voice became muted again. "Darcy, don't spin the tires."

"Can you get out of the truck?"

"Darcy says we might be in quicksand."

"But can you get out of the truck?"

A short pause. "I think so."

"Well . . . go ahead."

"We're having problems opening our doors."

"Then you'll have to—"

"But we do have a sunroof."

"Can you both climb through?"

"It leaked during the rainstorm."

"But can you open it and climb through?"

"I hate leaky sunroofs. My 280Z has a sunroof and it never leaks."

"Alexis, you and Darcy should crawl through . . . and maybe she should go first since Darcy is taller and can help pull you out."

Another pause, more fragments of chatter. "Darcy thinks we might not fit. We ate a big lunch."

"Can you at least try?"

"Okay," Alexis said in a voice growing in frustration. "I'm going to put the phone in my pocket when it's my turn to crawl out."

"Great. Are you still tilting?"

"Darcy is undoing her seat belt. Hold on, I need to help her climb out." I heard a snap of plastic, like a drink holder had busted. "Darcy has her head out, Jay. Now one arm, two arms and . . . No, Darcy, you're kicking me."

"Is she out?"

"Darcy kicked me in the head. And the rain is coming back."

"Lex, is Darcy out yet?"

"Almost. And we're tilting again. The muck is oozing up near my window."

"How is Darcy doing?"

"She says you owe her a new pair of Adidas because she just ruined hers by jumping off the roof into red mud."

"You might wanna ask Darcy to climb back onto the roof and pull you by the arms."

"I don't want to get my wedding ring muddy."

"The ring will be fine, Lex. Just climb out."

"The Land Cruiser is really tilting now."

"Are you out of the sunroof? Lex?" There was no reply. "Alexis . . . are you out?"

Neil kept glancing back over his shoulder at me, trying to listen and drive, eager for directions and anxious for news. But there were none to give. Allie and Steve acted like they didn't know whether to be amused or concerned. I shrugged at both of them and spoke into the receiver. "Alexis, are you still there?"

"Okay, I'm out. I put the phone in my pocket like I said I would."

"Great, now look around and tell us if you see any landmarks."

"Darcy pulled my arm out of socket."

"What about landmarks? Do you see any?"

"Not yet. And it's thundering, Jay. The beach trips in South Carolina go so much smoother than these outback odysseys."

"Believe me, I know. But we need some kind of landmark."

"Except for that time Darcy got her hubcaps stolen. She was so mad."

"I'm sure she was. Now, about the directions, we're about eighty miles west of—"

"I see one."

"A landmark?"

"Yes. Two tall, pointed rocks that look kinda like arrowheads."

"How tall are they?"

"About six feet."

I fumbled for words. "Alexis, um, we're going to need something bigger. Or maybe a mile marker. Did you and Darcy see any mile markers?"

"No. Since everyone drives on the left side of the road, I think I was looking the wrong way. Hold on and I'll ask Darcy."

Her ten-second pause became twenty, then thirty. "Still there?"

"Yes. Darcy says there aren't any mile markers in Australia because they switched to kilometers during the Cold War."

When I regained my composure I did my best to alter the strategy. "When you turned off the highway to chase the possum that you thought was a koala, were there any road signs or billboards?"

"I remember a Foster's Beer sign somewhere."

"Can you tell us how far west of Uluru it was?"

"Darcy just whispered that Foster's was her favorite back in college. But now she's repented."

"Of beer?"

"No, just Foster's."

"Can I speak to Darcy for a minute?"

"Why? 'Cause you want her to repent totally? I didn't think you were that legalistic."

"I'm not legalistic, Lex. I just want to ask her about—"

"Stanley is the only person I know who is that legalistic. On my first Presbyterian beach trip he found a Michelob in my cooler and made me throw it away."

"I'm not surprised."

"I only wanted one because it was so hot that day and I was bored trying to read Tolstoy. Did you ever get your answer to your question?"

"About the road signs or the Foster's?"

"Your question from that beach trip—when you were curious if Jesus would drink a brew on the beach."

"Opinions run the gamut on that, Lex. Now can I please speak to Darcy for a minute?"

"I think he would. But Stanley said definitely not."

"So can I speak to Darcy now?"

"She's emptying mud from her sneakers."

"Well, as soon as she's done, tell her that I—"

"Those Adidas cost eighty bucks."

"I'm sorry about the sneakers, but Neil says we're now within seventy-five miles of Uluru, and so we need to get some better directions."

"Okay. But tell Neily I love him dearly and that I want us to find another hot spring like we did on day three . . . it was sooo romantic."

In the span of four hours I had gone from gatherer of flying magenta purses to liaison for the lovey-dovey. I covered the mouthpiece and leaned forward between the seats. "Neily, Lex says she loves you dearly."

Neil smiled and said to tell her likewise.

Reclined again in the corner, I put the phone back to my ear and rolled my eyes at Allie, who kept whispering "What?" as events unfolded.

"I'm still here, Lex. And Neily loves you dearly."

"Oh no."

"What now?"

"The sun is coming back out and we left our sunblock in the Land Cruiser."

"Please don't tell us you're gonna climb back in the vehicle. . . ."

"But it's stopped tilting. And now the flies are bad too."

"Lex, if the Land Cruiser is stuck in deep mud, you probably shouldn't climb back in."

"We're girls and we need spray."

"Alexis, please don't climb back in."

"I'm putting the phone back in my pocket now."

"Lex, don't."

"I also need a Dr. Pepper."

"Lex—"

"And Darcy wants a Foster's. . . . Hah! I'm just kidding, Legalistic Jay. Darcy only has Canada Dry. Call us back in five minutes and we'll have better directions."

Click.

Three minutes on the phone with Alexis was nearly as exhausting as three days of being stranded. And I could only hope that Neil was ready to meet the challenge of his next fifty years.

At this point a smattering of other vehicles began to whisk by in the opposite lane, and Australia began to show herself hospitable. Clouds parted in the distance, rain shrank into a mist, and an unusually quiet Steve pointed ahead at a distant service station.

He and I had much to discuss. Most likely in a men's room.

22

The sign above the gas pumps at the Docker River Quick Stop read LAST FUEL FOR 210 KM. The arrow on the sign pointed west, in the direction from which we had come.

As soon as Neil put on his blinker and slowed to turn right, Allie began shaking her knees like she had to go. We had been driving through wilderness for nearly three hours, and this was the first building of any type to appear on the landscape.

Neil parked at the first pump and got out. While he filled the tank he leaned against the Montero and called his wife. Allie and Steve darted off for the restrooms.

I had climbed outside the truck when she stopped at the glass doors and looked back at me. "Four months and two days!" she shouted, one hand feeling blindly behind her for a door.

I shouted back, "And bridesmaids and groomsmen paired off according to height."

She motioned Steve inside the door and grinned at me across oil-stained pavement. She looked drained, sure, and a trace thinner than normal, but I never realized how much one turkey sandwich and three bottles of citrus Gatorade could revive a person.

Make that two persons.

To give Neil a break I finished pumping the gas, and as I replaced the cap he put his hand over the phone. "We need to hurry and get back on the road."

Neil jabbered away to Alexis, trying to determine her location, trying to make sense of what had happened.

"You know where they are now?" I asked when he hung up.

He nodded. "We need to get going."

"I was thinking we might call some local authorities for help."

"Nah. We'll find 'em."

To Neil this day was likely just one continuous quagmire, or perhaps an evolving circus. He glanced at the pump to see how much petrol we'd consumed, and I told him I would pay for the fuel and asked if he wanted anything from the store. He shook his head no.

Inside, Allie counted out change at the register, paying for a bottle of Tylenol and three newspapers.

I came up behind her, reached up through her hair for the back of her neck, and squeezed playfully. Without turning around she said, "Your name had better be Jay."

"Jay of long wanderings."

She accepted her change from the young cashier and thrust the newspapers at me. "Look at these," she said, pointing below the fold. "We're famous."

In a sidebar to an article on tourism was the following notation: TWO AMERICAN TOURISTS MISSING WEST OF ULURU. MORE, PAGE 16.

Page 16. Well. I had never thought of myself in terms of which page of a newspaper the news of my demise might appear. Politicians, celebrities, athletes—I could see their disappearance as front-page news. But what about all the pages in-between page one and page sixteen? Couldn't we make page two? Three or four at worst?

Allie saw me staring at the page numbers. "You're doing it again, aren't you?"

"No."

"Yep, I see the math wheels turning. You're in calculation mode."

I skimmed the two paragraphs of our debacle and noted that they had listed Allie's home state as North Carolina instead of South. "Am not."

174

She tapped the other side of the paper. "You might should take your mind off yourself, and even off of us."

I replied without looking up. "Why's that?"

"Look to the back of the store."

Steve stood motionless—he looked nearly frozen—next to the glass-doored coolers, as if waiting for his dazed demeanor to thaw. His hands were deep in his pockets, and he was staring at the floor.

"Go talk to him," Allie said, tucking her newspapers under her arm. She winked at me and said she was going outside to show Neil the article.

I had left the Question alone while in mixed company. But now I felt the moment of truth needed to surface and become, well, the moment of truth. I approached from the opposite end of the drink aisle and navigated around a waist-high display of Doritos. And though I was sure Steve knew I was there, he did not lift his gaze from the floor. He only turned slightly to his right and faced the glass coolers.

As his friend, I could only do likewise. So for a long moment we just stood there, side by side and staring at the bottom rack of chilled Diet Pepsi. Finally, in a kind of half whisper, half question, I began to probe. "Don't tell me she said no."

Steve hesitated for a second, then he slowly shook his head.

"You didn't even do it, did you?"

Shorter hesitation. Firmer shake.

"And Darcy doesn't even know you have a ring in your luggage?"

He folded his arms and turned his gaze from the Pepsi to the orange sodas. "Nope."

"You had three days in the outback and . . . you didn't even ask?"

"Two of those days were spent looking for you, Bozo. But as for the day of the split-off, well, it's complicated."

"What's so complicated about 'I love you and will you marry me?' Then you either get a yes or a no or a maybe."

Steve turned his back to me and pointed outside. "Go enjoy your fiancée, Jarvis. I don't wanna talk about me right now. Besides, Darcy and Alexis are stuck somewhere and we need to go find them."

I moved beside him again and put my hand on his shoulder. "Look, bro, if there's some kind of commitment issue that you want to talk—"

He pointed again. "Go, Jarvis. Leave me be."

I backed away, palms raised in conciliation. "Fine. Suffer alone."

"Just go. I'll be out in a minute."

I stepped backward between rows of brightly packaged snacks. "We gotta get back on the road. All I want to know is if you really love Darcy."

"Yes." And here he pointed outside a third time. "Now leave."

I left.

Neil had their map spread across the hood of the Montero, and he circled a large spot and told me that he'd figured out the approximate location of Alexis and Darcy. "And according to Lex," he said, sniffing his fingers for gas, "the Foster's Beer billboard was an hour and a half west of Uluru, so all we have to do is determine Darcy's average speed and then we'll know for sure where they are."

Allie peeked around from the open hatchback and said, "Good luck."

"I figure they're thirty kilometers east of here, at most," Neil continued. "And we need to hurry 'cause we don't have much daylight left." Neil turned to scan the humble Quick Stop. "Just what is keeping Steve?"

I reached to open the back door. "He's debating between Pepsi and orange soda."

Into the backseat I settled in beside Allie, who sat with crossed legs, writing notes in her journal. It was all I could do not to look.

And she noticed just how hard I was trying not to look.

She raised her journal with both hands and shoved it to within two inches of my nose. "There ya go, hubbie. Read all you want."

I moved my head back against the seat and noted the words *plane* and *fire* and *Neil with no wife*. Followed by *camels* and *gross amber spit* and *girlfriends stuck in mud*.

Her next line said something about missing all the kids, but she pulled the journal away before I could read it all.

"Steve is kinda down," I said, watching Allie turn her writings upside-down in her lap. "So don't ask him any questions."

Allie pressed the cap over the tip of her pen. "Is he worried about Darcy or is he sick?"

"Think about it—he's feeling like the odd man out. He's with one newly married friend, and with two other friends who just got engaged."

Allie jiggled her pen in front of her nose, chewed her bottom lip. "Well."

"Just well?"

She hesitated, then gazed at her left hand. "Maybe in time Steve will buy a ring for Darcy and take her somewhere exotic and surprise her just like you surprised me."

I had to turn my head. "Yeah . . . maybe."

Steve came out of the store stiff lipped, looking like he would rather remain alone. But by the time he arrived at the Montero he had put on the male mask of indifference, a not-too-difficult task for most of us who claim the Y chromosome. Steve opened the passenger door, climbed in, and glanced at his comrades. We all smiled politely.

"Well?" he asked of no one in particular. "Are we ready to go pull attractive women from red mud?"

"I say we go pull attractive women from red mud," Neil replied. And he stuck the key in the ignition and started the truck.

Into waning daylight he drove swiftly, all of us looking left and right for signs and billboards.

Steve was first to spot the Foster's billboard; it faced the opposite way. When Steve craned his neck and said, "There it is," Neil braked and pulled across the right-hand lane. He drove slowly along the shoulder. Clumps of wet grasses dotted fields of rock and soaked earth. And then far across the acreage I spotted two jagged sprouts of sandstone. One looked vaguely like an arrowhead.

"Left, Neil."

"There?" he said, pointing. "That washed-out excuse for a road?"

"There's the landmark."

He shifted into four-wheel drive, and we bumped southward between low bush and loose rock. After ten minutes of rattling across the terrain we spotted two figures standing at the rear of a very low SUV.

Picture a tall one, blond and drenched, arms outstretched as if to ask *What took you so long?* Then a medium one, slender and raven haired, also drenched, wet hair stuck to her face, pointing to her sneakers and frowning with her lip poked out.

"Pitiful," Neil said. "Both of 'em."

Alexis removed a shoe and waved with it. Darcy gave us her best Queen of England wave. They looked exhausted and relieved and silly in the same instant. Behind them, sitting so low that it appeared to possess no tires or axles, a dirty white Land Cruiser sat stagnant in red mud.

Neil steered carefully around a washout, honked the horn, and parked some twenty feet short of them. Then the waves stopped, and kisses were blown.

I figured that Alexis and Darcy would run up to Neil and Steve and hug their men tight. But such affections were secondary. As soon as we opened our doors to step out, Lex and Darcy rushed over to Allie and began gawking at her ring.

The women gathered at the driver's door, where Neil, Steve, and I stood at the perimeter, looking on with amazement, taking note of turbulent sky and wondering why we weren't pulling the truck from the mud. Allie's left hand had assumed the status of celebrity, and for a moment she and Alexis compared stones while Darcy acted as happy as one gal can be when her two best friends both sport bands of commitment. Her grin began big and exuberant but faded quickly into blank faced and slightly envious.

I looked upon all this with a mixture of amusement and concern, as I knew Steve felt awkward. Yet no one but he and I knew what was in his luggage, so there was nothing to do but enjoy the moment—a moment that contained all five of my best friends, central Australia, the sun setting behind storm clouds, and a white Land Cruiser sunk up to its doors in red mud.

That's when Darcy and Alexis stopped admiring Allie's ring and turned their attention toward causality. And in their minds the cause of all this trouble was, of course, me.

I was leaned against the hood of the Montero, not even considering what they might be thinking.

They approached with their hands behind their backs. I thought they might have some kind of congratulatory gift, something to do with engagement.

What they had were handfuls of mud.

"There," Darcy said, wiping the first handful across the right side of my T-shirt. "That's for getting lost, scaring us half to death, and ruining my new Adidas."

I heard male laughter in the background. Speechless, I looked down and watched the mud drip onto my sneakers.

"And there," Alexis said, pressing her handful into the left side of my chest. "That's for interrupting two days of my honeymoon."

Allie washed off their hands with a bottled water, and soon Neil and Darcy and I had figured out the winch on the front of the Montero and had its cable tied to the rear end of the Land Cruiser. Steve climbed in through the sunroof and shifted the Land Cruiser into neutral. He shouted for someone to begin the tow.

Everyone turned in the muddy road to see Alexis sitting in the driver's seat of the Montero, ready to begin the tug. She started the engine and revved it twice. Neil shook his head at her. Everyone knew that he thought he should do the towing.

Lex shook back mockingly and lowered the driver's window. "I have always, always wanted to do this."

Neil assumed his best hands-on-hips pose. "How much towing experience do you have?"

She revved the engine a third time and spoke over the rumble. "When I was selling real estate last summer I had to free my mom's Saab after she backed over a mailbox. So . . . how much experience do *you* have?"

The rest of us observed them from the left flank, wondering if seventeen days of marriage were about to burst into a full-fledged fight.

Neil looked skyward and scanned the fast-moving clouds. Alexis grinned at Darcy out her window.

But Neil stood his ground. Halfway along the twenty feet of cable that lay at his feet, he looked as if he were trying so hard, so very hard, to find the proper solution.

And with her head out the window again, Alexis had the solution. "I can do this, Neily. Just make sure the cable doesn't hang on anything when I start backing up."

Neil's hands began to fidget at his sides. To his credit, he kept his voice at a calm and measured timbre. "Lex, if you end up getting both vehicles stuck, we'll all be—"

"I know, honey. Up a creek without an outboard."

"Right," Neil said. His stance firmed. "And worse, we're a long ways from the highway and we're still over fifty miles from the next town."

"That's pretty far, huh?"

"Yes, and so—"

"And so I'd better hurry and get Stevie out of the muck." Alexis gunned the engine and waved for Neil to move out of the way. She pulled wet hair out of her eyes, shifted into reverse, and inched backward.

Neil watched the cable tighten beside him. "Lex, please let me do this."

She stuck her head out the window again. "I can handle it, my sweet harmonica serenader."

Darcy and Allie burst into laughter. Neil blushed and stepped aside.

From inside the Land Cruiser Steve yelled, "What is keeping you all?"

Tires spun, and mud flew backward; and mud flew backward, and tires spun. The cable became a tightrope; I could have walked on that thing.

At first the Land Cruiser only rocked on its haunches. But then Darcy and Allie began cheering Alexis, as if gender equality had just this minute reached the hobby of four-wheeling. They clapped for her, even stomped their feet in the dirt. "Lex, Lex, Lex!" they shouted.

The cable tightened further, and tires groped for traction. A gurgly, sucking sound, like pulling a submerged shoe from a swamp, announced the backward inching of the very stuck truck.

Steve shouted, "Keep pulling, don't stop."

Lex must have floored it, because twin sprays of dirt and mud flew from the Montero's tires and did a fine job of tainting Neil's shirt.

Soon the tension became a pull; and the pull, a tow. Sunken back tires emerged from the muck, and Steve begged her not to stop.

"Lex, Lex, Lex!" shouted the girls.

Neil looked on, shaking his head in wonder.

Now with the momentum, Alexis honked her horn, stuck her tongue out at her husband, and pulled uncommitted Steve from the bowels of a bog.

The air was thick with the smell of warm mud as Steve ran up to high-five Alexis. She thrust her arms in the air in victory, and even Neil applauded.

Across the dirt field lay the two-lane highway—just a strip of black tar bisecting the plains—and in the twilight a tour bus rolled past, its headlights on, its route sure.

After checking the engine and the undercarriage, Steve cranked the Land Cruiser, and we all piled in, Darcy in the front passenger seat, Allie and I in the back.

The Montero led the way out, and our foursome followed Neil and Alexis back over the rock-strewn road. Toward the highway we went, a rolling six-pack of weary and heavy-laden. Between frequent jolts Darcy and Allie spoke of hot showers; Steve and I of hot meals.

When we reached the narrow highway we turned east toward Alice Springs, where the next morning I would have a date with responsibility.

Three SUVs go out, two return. A sixty-seven percent return rate.

At first the possible consequences prevented me from napping in the backseat. But as we drove along in the dark, and a sleepy Allie tilted her head to the right, I leaned left, and we rode head to head, exhausted.

A few miles later she managed a whisper. "Thanks again for blowing up the truck, Jay."

"You're welcome, dear."

23

Outside room 121 of the CentreView Motel, the orange dust had vanished, and the moon rose. The afternoon rainstorm had washed Alice Springs of its grit, and here at 11:00 p.m. I stood in a gleaming parking lot and inhaled the damp air.

I needed this air, savored this air. I wanted to share this air with Allie, but she and Darcy had crashed an hour earlier in room 124, immediately after dinner. We had alerted the local newspaper of our rescue, and now I strolled alone around the parking lot, just me and my gym shorts and my shampooed hair. I sent up a silent prayer of thanks, both for the plane and the pilot. I didn't even know her name.

Neil and Alexis had found somewhere else to stay, and since this was still their honeymoon, no one objected. All I knew was that most of us, perhaps all six of us, would fly southeast to Sydney in two days.

Through the open door and the yellowed light of our room, Steve could be seen propped on his back on one of the single beds, watching a rugby match on Aussie television. I doubted he paid attention, suspected he was preoccupied.

I remained hesitant to ask any more questions of him, given his request for privacy and his posture of repose. Yet I had to know. Had to perform the interrogation. After one more perusal of clearing skies, I walked back into the room and stood in front of the TV.

Steve immediately motioned for me to move. "Will you get out of the way, Jarvis?"

I spread my feet wide. "You don't even know the rules of rugby."

"Do too. They all lock arms and wrestle for the ball, and then they sneak it to the fastest guy and he sprints around the chaos while they're not looking."

"Nice try."

"Move, Jarvis."

I turned off the TV, and the room went silent.

"But I was into this rugby," he said. "The blue team was winning."

My feet remained planted. "Answer me this—if you had not spent the second and third days searching for Allie and me, would you have proposed to Darcy?"

Steve plucked the remote control from the bed and stared at the buttons, as if his answer was hiding between the volume controls. "No."

"So our waywardness and zeal for photos didn't ruin your plans?"

"No."

"You just plain chickened out?"

He turned the remote over in his hands and finally set it in his lap. "No again."

A long silence followed, accompanied by male fidgeting and the avoidance of eye contact. Figuring that Steve was no longer interested in rugby, I went and sat on the opposing bed, my feet on the floor. A small, yellow lamp glowed between us on the night table.

"It's not a race, ya know."

Steve folded his arms, extended his thick legs on the bed, and stared at his feet. "I know."

I leaned over and inspected my sneakers, which hosted a handful of orange dirt. "If we had been in a race, rest assured that Neil passed us both three weeks ago."

Steve raised one knee and gripped it with both hands. He was clearly at odds with himself. "Neil and Alexis needed to get married; they couldn't keep their hands off each other. I just got swept up by something more subtle."

I dumped the contents of the shoes into the trash can. "The romance between you and Darcy?"

"No, the romance of Australia. It overwhelmed me."

Maybe I should just throw away these sneakers. "I think you let Beatrice influence you too much."

Steve put his hands behind his head and interlocked his fingers. "Maybe so. Every night in the weeks before the trip I would log on to the Internet and do Google searches for photos and travel journals about the outback. I saw all that wide-open space, the red dirt and the wildlife and the rock formations, and just rushed out to a jeweler one day and bought the ring."

"That's nothing to be ashamed of, bro. Plenty of guys would react the same way."

"What about you?"

I stacked my two pillows and lay back on the bed. "I did the Google thing as well. You and me may have even looked at the same websites. Thing is, before I ordered Allie's ring I had also spent time getting some relational advice."

"From who?"

"Preacher Smoak, of course. He has email now."

"You two did pre-engagement counseling? From South Carolina to Ecuador? . . . With email?"

"Yes, yes, and of course. And sometimes Maurice gave his input."

"I don't believe it. All those old guys do is fish."

"You mean you didn't get any counseling? Did ya even pray about it?"

"I prayed that none of us would get lost in the outback."

"That one sure didn't do us much good."

Steve rolled over in his bed and pulled a pillow over his head. His voice was muffled but his tone sincere. "Jarvis, have I completely blown it?"

My stall was just to make him squirm. And because he was a guy, I doubled the stall and let the room inflate with tension. "Hmmm."

184

He peeked out from beneath the pillow. "You're thinking I really have blown it?"

"Nah, probably not. But maybe you should start thinking up a new magnificent plan."

"And maybe I already have."

I reached over to the yellow lamp and felt for the switch, and the room went dark. "There's still hope for you, Cole. No one but you and me even know you have the ring."

For a long while we both lay on our single beds and said nothing. But Steve could not enjoy the silence. "You still think I'm having commitment issues, don't you?"

I slid under the sheets and turned on my side. "No doubt you have commitment issues. Even seeing the ring around your commode sends you into a panic."

Steve sighed in frustration. "My commode is clean. Besides, I'm trying to think up an even more exotic plan than the outback."

"What can be more exotic for two Carolina boys than Australia? You couldn't get any farther from home if you tried."

"It just felt like the wrong moment, Jarvis. Too hurried."

Sleep tugged at my eyelids, yet I felt the need to nudge Stevie toward his quest from bachelorhood. "Did you see Darcy's face when Allie and Lex were comparing rings?"

"I saw her. She was really happy for them."

"You don't think she felt awkward?"

"Maybe a little. But Darcy's mature enough to handle that stuff."

Darcy had grown in maturity over the past year, even getting involved in community help programs. My concern, however, was that Steve would overestimate her patience.

After a few minutes I concluded that I should get the final word. "I still can't believe you didn't propose."

His bed creaked. "And I can't believe you blew up your truck."

After he had fallen asleep I tried to replay the past three days in my head but stayed stuck on one thought: of how wrong I was when wandering out there by myself, trying to find my arrows. In that hour

I was so certain that this was my appointed week to expire, arranged by God in his Book of Life, which, when you think about all the people who have come and gone since Eve bit into the Red Delicious, must be one huge volume, on a par with all the diet books stacked to the sky.

24

Dawn came and dawn went, and breakfast came and breakfast went, then responsibility came and responsibility slapped me in the face with ethical aftershave.

After the eggs (scrambled), and the waffles (blueberry), and the coffee (black), had been consumed, I looked across the booth at Allie and waited for her encouragement.

She was always so good at this type of thing, one of many reasons I could not wait to marry her. She sipped the dregs from her mug and set it, two handed, in the middle of the table. "Just be honest with them, Jay . . . and pray that insurance will cover the costs."

Darcy and Steve came in from a morning walk—another hot, blue-sky morning in Alice Springs—and sat down in the next booth. They had obviously overheard us. "Yes, Jay," said Darcy, setting a shopping bag on the floor and leaning around to make eye contact. "The insurance issue is huge."

"Huge," Steve said from behind his menu. "Just huge."

"Thanks, guys. I feel much better."

Like a first-time skydiver moments away from his leap, I stood nervously and shook hands with all my comrades. Then I left the restaurant by myself, walked down the street, and stopped outside the front window of Outback Adventures.

I peeked between the travel posters and tried to think of the right words

187

of explanation. Straight to the point, or beat around the bush? Beat around the point, or go hide in the bush?

I peeked again and saw Rental Guy tuning a radio atop his counter; he appeared to be whistling to the music.

At the instant my hand gripped the doorknob I felt newly naked. I was Adam with a mouthful of apple, and Australia offered no fig leaf.

Surely he knew. Surely his wrath was just hiding behind his demeanor. I watched him as I pushed the door open, noting how casually he tucked his sun-streaked hair behind his ears, the nonchalant manner in which he played with the radio. I kept trying to find something in his decor, or his selection of music, anything, to function as icebreaker.

Instead I walked straight in, humming some unidentified song and jingling the keys in my hand. "Howdy."

He turned off his radio, looked up, and waved hello. "Ah, Jay, back already. I'd forgotten if you had signed up for four days or five."

Not the expected greeting. I stopped one pace from the counter and fumbled for words. "Um, it was four. Yes, definitely four. And I guess you've heard the news by now?"

"What news, mate? I've been on my own holiday down in Melbourne. Just got back last night." He was wearing a Men at Work T-shirt.

My lips formed a small O, but no words came out. I stared blankly at his tanned and innocent face. "So, you don't know about the two tourists who got stranded?"

"In the outback?" He pushed the radio to the side and grinned across his empty countertop. "Not unusual, mate."

"The couple drove way out. Way, way out . . . into Western Australia."

"And they've been found?"

"Oh yes. There was a massive search, reward money offered."

This seemed to humor him, and he leaned forward on his elbows. "I haven't seen a paper, Jay. But no worries. You're ready to turn in your keys, yeah? Hope ya had a good time out there. Looks like ya got a bit sunburned."

His chattiness and friendly manner made confession impossible. "Um, yes. Here are your keys." I set them gently on the counter. "But that's all I brought back."

He glanced down at the keys, picked them up, and inspected their worn finish.

"So, you and the lady lost the other set? Quite all right." He pulled out a notepad from beneath the counter and wrote something on it. "Just a small five-dollar charge. I can make another set of keys in minutes."

Toe down, my right foot tapped the tile floor, and I simply could not stop it from doing so. "I meant that I only brought the keys back, period. Nothing else."

He backed away from the counter and stared past me, out the front window to where Steve and Darcy and Allie had just parked in the white Land Cruiser, probably to watch me squirm. "Fill me in here, mate."

"There was a fire."

In seconds Rental Guy lost his casual demeanor, and I watched facts settle over him like a lead cloak. Unable to look him in the eye, I stared at his little brass nametag and read the name Edward. I had forgotten that I'd read this same name on the registration certificate in the glove box.

He had momentarily lost the ability to blink, and he spoke while still staring out the window. "You leave in the burnt-orange Land Cruiser, and you return in the white? Is that what you're telling me?"

"That's what I'm telling you."

"And there was fire you say?"

"Big fire. I'm responsible."

Edward tossed the lone set of keys in the air and, before they clanged against the countertop, snatched them at nose level. Anticipating a conniption, I took one step back. His lips tightened, and his hand shook with the keys. "Lemme guess. You and your friends out there were grilling your cheeseburgers and you had the grill too close to my vehicle?"

I clasped my hands and bowed slightly, like a courteous bellhop. "Actually, Edward, the fire was set on purpose."

This slender gent turned paler than a Nordic albino. His eyes widened to the bursting point. "You burned my Land Cruiser on purpose? On purpose?"

"I blew it up."

"Say again?"

"I blew it up because your math was all wrong, because 'four of five who stay with the vehicle, live' is not a good-enough ratio for a man who just pledged for better or worse to his favorite sheila."

He wiped his brow, ran a hand through his hair. His breaths came faster. "Mate, I've seen lots of better and worse around this town, but nobody's 'worse' ever included blowing up someone else's Land Cruiser."

"I had to signal the plane."

With both hands he reached across the counter, gripped the far edge, and squeezed until his knuckles were white. "What . . . plane?"

"The Cessna that opened its window and dropped the hideous magenta purse with the grape juice and the Hershey's milk chocolate."

Edward backed against the wall behind him, lips moving but not making words. "A bush pilot saw you and air-dropped refreshment?"

"Timely refreshment," I said, fighting nerves. "My fiancée was about to drink frog water."

"You're pulling my leg."

"It was do or die."

Edward shook his head and turned slowly, a full 360-degree turn, as if a full revolution would undo what was done. "You and the lady really got stranded?"

In a play for sympathy I wiped at my own brow. "Three days of torture. Seventy-two hours of the most extreme heat." *Quick, Jarvis, do the math.* "Four thousand, three hundred, and twenty minutes of very intense suffering."

He blinked at me in disbelief. Then he turned in another complete circle, this time with his hands in the air. "And you blew up my truck to signal the airplane?"

"Torched my black suitcase too."

He put both hands over his ears and squeezed, as if to squash all he'd heard. "Now . . . you say you two knew about the water-holding frog?"

"They were mentioned in a travel book. I dug up two and was about to squeeze the first when the plane flew over."

"So you didn't squeeze?"

"I did not. In fact, after the plane dropped the purse I put it under my arm like a football and sprinted across the plains to get liquid into Allie. She had the dry heaves, the very, very dry heaves. And, and . . . so did I."

Now his elbows were on the counter, and with no rhythm at all his fists pounded Formica. "Mate, that was my favorite truck. I only rented it because the silver one wasn't in running order, and I needed the money."

"Very sorry. We're hoping that between our insurance and yours that there might be some kind of coverage. You know, for life-threatening emergencies. I'm really not sure if State Farm has a clause for blowing up a truck to save a fiancée." I had never been good at making a sad, puppy-dog face, but against that countertop I assumed the comportment of a basset hound. "Please tell me your renter insurance covers this."

"It's your insurance I'm worried about." Rattled, Edward pulled a file from a drawer, opened it, and thumbed through a half inch of pink and yellow papers. "I have a one-thousand-dollar deductible on accidents, but that wasn't an accident. Plus I had extra equipment on the truck too—oversized bumpers, my roof racks, and of course my two-way."

I could not stop myself. "That was a cheap, dime-store walkie-talkie."

He did not look up from his papers. "She had a good range to her."

"I've seen paper cups and string do a better job at communication."

"Well, still. Replacement cost is going to be . . . I can't even imagine."

I leaned over the counter to see what kind of fine print he was reading. "Say, when did you buy that Land Cruiser?"

He pulled a pink form from the folder and set it on the counter. "Just last year."

"So you bought it used?"

"Paid 14,500 in U.S. dollars."

There was so much legalese on his forms that I gave up trying to decipher them. "Edward, I'm really sorry about your truck. But if all I end up owing is the deductible, there might be a way for you to come out a couple thousand dollars ahead."

"How is that?"

I noticed he was no longer calling me "mate." Then I pointed outside to my accomplices in the white Land Cruiser. "Reward money, Edward.

There was a four-thousand-dollar reward placed on our being found alive. See that guy outside in the driver's seat?"

Reality had sunk in, and Edward seemed calmer now. He peered outside and nodded. "I see him. He's the one who goes with the blonde. The tall one."

"Right. Steve and another guy, Neil—who just got married and interrupted his honeymoon to go search for us—are claiming the reward cash. But they said since they love me more than money and know that I'm poor, they would give up their reward to help pay you back for my destroying your truck."

Behind the counter Edward backed against the wall again and muttered something that was two parts slang and ten parts idiom, a stream of Aussie vernacular that included a fat man in Sydney, a train ride to Perth, and the gestation period of red kangaroos. "You're not serious?"

"Serious as drought."

He did not seem to believe me. "Your mates would do that?"

"They must really love me. So, what would you do with an extra couple of thousand?"

He stepped back to the counter and pulled a yellow form from the folder. "After I found another '96 Land Cruiser? . . . Maybe take a trip. I've never seen America."

Things were tilting to the positive, and I rode the momentum. "Are you single, Edward?"

"Yeah. Why?"

"Well, back in South Carolina there's this singles group that has great beach trips, so if you ever want to—"

He stopped writing and glared at me. "Jay, it's best that I complete these forms in a timely manner."

For the next five minutes I watched Edward write on the insurance forms and also on a shorter form of his own devising. In midscrawl he said, "You do understand that because there was a vehicle destroyed, I'll have to report it to some authorities."

I watched him pen estimates for my height (5'11"), weight (165), and eye color (sorta blue). "I understand."

"But no worries."

Aye. No worries.

After he had filled out the forms he went into a back room, dialed a number on his phone, and had a short but spirited conversation. Then he returned and began tapping the butt end of his pen on the counter, as if he had forgotten something. After sixteen taps—I counted—he raised the pen and pretended to clang a bell with it. "Say, did you grab the Barry Manilow tape before you set fire to my truck?"

"My fiancée has it. With your permission, she'd like to keep it as a memento."

He handed me the pen to begin signing the forms. "But that's my favorite tape."

I signed the first paper. "Please? We got engaged the night we slow-danced to it."

"Tourists," he said, using the back of his hand to dismiss the subject. "Tourists and backpackers will cause my dementia. Keep the tape."

I was signing my name to the last of four forms when someone coughed from behind me. This man had not announced his entrance. I craned my neck and saw that he was a cop.

But I wasn't sure he was a cop. He just as well could have been a park ranger. Or perhaps a magistrate. I was too scared to ask questions. All I knew was that he was well muscled, dressed in a khaki short-sleeve shirt that matched his pants, had a holstered gun, and spoke with authority. "You would be Jay Jarvis?"

He stopped some five paces behind me, so that now I stood in the middle, between Edward and the Officer of Undetermined Vintage.

"I would be, sir."

He stepped closer. A long, rectangular badge, brassy and reflective, adorned his left pocket.

To my surprise, he was not the next to speak. Edward reached across the counter and tapped me on the shoulder, so that I was forced to turn my back to the OUV. "I'm about to contact our insurance companies," Edward said. "And since I have no idea what they'll cover, you might have a think about what assets you have."

"Yes," came the voice behind me. "We'll need to know about assets."

I turned to face the stranger, who I decided was a magistrate. "I work at a mission for orphans in Ecuador, sir. Very few possessions."

The magistrate let my words settle around the room. He had a full head of nearly black hair, and he kept scratching his scalp with his left pinkie. "What did you do previously, Mr. Jarvis?"

"I'm a former stockbroker, sir, and I own four shares of Microsoft."

"Only four?"

"The rest I spent on a ring and on a plane ticket to your beautiful country."

He nodded past me to Edward, frowned, scratched his scalp again. "We've never had this kind of a situation before, Mr. Jarvis."

I noticed that he had extra bullets in his belt. Large bullets. Just to put him at ease I scratched my own scalp, as if I too was a dandruff sufferer. "And I've never had to blow up a truck before, sir."

He stepped closer and ran his tongue across his front teeth. "Did I hear that you ran out of drinking water?"

"We were down to two of those water-holding frogs."

This time he looked past me at Edward, smiled knowingly, and resumed his interrogation. "Did you squeeze?"

"I did not squeeze."

"Did your lady friend?"

"She did not."

"And why not?"

"Because that was the very minute the plane flew over center field and I blew up the truck."

He stepped forward and took me by the arm. "That's an admittance, Mr. Jarvis."

I turned to Edward for support. He shrugged sympathetically. "Sorry, mate. Not my intention." He held up the pink form and pointed to his list of costs. "All I request is reimbursement."

I was led out the front door, where my comrades and my fiancée all sat in air-conditioned shock inside the white Land Cruiser. They stared in disbelief as the magistrate escorted me, uncuffed, down the hot and busy sidewalk.

Steve, who was closest, lowered his window and mouthed, "What?"

I could only shake my head in frustration. A block away I turned again and saw Edward outside his rental agency, talking to Steve and inspecting the Land Cruiser for damage.

Allie and Darcy stood frozen beside the hood, eyes locked on me, hands over their mouths, not knowing what to do but afraid to get involved.

In the lingo of baseball, I had taken one for the team.

25

The jailhouse smelled like Pine-Sol, the jailer himself like strong coffee. He looked like an Aussie Barney Fife, and he leapt up from his chair as the magistrate handed me over. Like Barney he was short and wiry, only his uniform consisted of navy pants, white shirt, and a better-fitting hat. He looked amused at handling an American tourist. And I knew what he was going to say before he said it.

He took me by the elbow, pointed at a metal door, and said it. "No worries."

Then he led me down an empty hallway, pausing from his whistling to offer me my choice of cells. The first eight were modern and windowless, followed by a pair that looked left over from a century ago, like something you'd show kids on a school tour and tell them that outlaws had clanged tin cups against the bars. "You sure?" I asked.

"Pick one."

Since there was no one else in confinement, and since the song-of-the-day stirring in my head was "Love Potion Number Nine," I pointed down the hall and asked the jailer for the cell to match.

"Very well, mate," he said. He dissected a pound of keys, unlocked the old, musty cell, and gently shoved me inside. "Got a bit sunburned in our outback, yeah?"

"A bit, yeah."

He locked the cell and walked away whistling, and suddenly I felt very alone.

My friends should come quickly; surely they'll come quickly. Allie will come and sit outside my cell and read me her latest. By now she'll have crafted a prison poem.

For a long while I stood and gripped the bars, looking up and down the hallway, scanning the ceiling, and telling myself not to attempt an escape, especially since my sentence had only twenty-three hours and eighteen minutes remaining.

They were holding me for one day to check out my background.

During our four-block stroll down the sunny sidewalks of Alice Springs, the magistrate had repeated three times that he'd never heard of a case like this. That while he sympathized with a couple getting stranded—"We're glad you two didn't perish, mate"—the fact remained that someone had purposely set fire to a rented vehicle, and that the law called for him to detain me.

His guess was just one night in jail. He wanted to feel assured that I would reimburse Outback Adventures for all expenses incurred after insurance proceeds. He called my crime—I couldn't believe he used the word *crime*—a result of a "premeditated zeal for foolishness" and banned me for ten years from renting any four-wheel-drive vehicle in any region of Australia. Outside the entrance to the Alice Springs jail, I had been unable to stop myself from asking him if he had jurisdiction in all regions of Australia. He told me that today he did and that I had asked enough questions.

Maybe I deserved to be here. And maybe I didn't deserve to have that plane fly over, air-drop refreshment, and radio Neil's Montero. But even if the magistrate thought he was right to detain me, he could have at least led my friends here for a visit. Yet nobody showed except for one portly green bug that scampered across the concrete hallway, saw me standing at my door, and hustled back over to cell number ten.

High on the back wall of cell number nine was a small, rectangular window inset with horizontal bars. It was built so high that I would have to stand on the single bed to see out. But first I sat on the bed and tested it for squeaks. Atop a Sealy Posturepedic I considered how the ambiance of

197

prison was much better than the ambiance of hell as described in Steve's little book, what with the free meals, the community shower, and the striped light pouring in through my rectangular window.

Soon the scent of cooked chicken came slithering into my cell. I followed the scent and stood on the bed. Through that window and across the barbed wire and two hundred yards of dirt I saw sunlit pedestrians entering a KFC. Along the sidewalks, tourists loitered beneath blue skies, their cameras dangling beneath shirt collars. People kept emerging from both ends of the street and walking in for lunch. They all looked happy and adventurous, as if preparing to join fifty others on a guided tour.

My stomach growled. But the wiry jailer had not returned to take my order, so I pressed my lips up between the bars of my window and pretended someone could hear me. "Hey, anybody out there wanna buy a mate some fried chicken?"

I heard the metal door open at the end of the hallway. The jailer yelled for me to stop yelling. Said I was too far away for anyone to hear me. Said he would bring me something to eat soon and that I should not make a racket during my one and only day or else he'd make it two days.

Around 2:15 the jailer reopened the metal door at the end of the hall. I heard him say, "Cell number nine. The old one on the left."

The door closed, and I heard the footsteps and knew it was Allie even before I could see her. Before we'd spoken a word she gripped the bars, and then I gripped the bars, and we pulled forward and smooched between cold steel. She wore a burgundy shirt and white shorts, and coupled with her outback tan and wavy hair she looked exotic.

"A female guard searched me before they let me back here," Allie said, still gripping the bars.

I pulled close again, gathered her left hand in both of mine, and fingered her ring. "But didn't you tell her that you were a missionary to remotest Ecuador and cared for twenty orphans?"

"Yes. But she said all had fallen short of the glory of God and so I needed to stand against the wall like every other sinner and raise my arms."

"Embarrassing?"

"Actually, it tickled."

For a while we just looked at one another with little expression. This was engagement? This was the beginning of bliss?

Soon I let go of the bars and leaned my shoulder into them, propped there like this was my daily pose of confinement. "I got a whiff of chicken earlier."

Allie started to sit on the hall floor but reconsidered and stuffed her hands in her pockets. "Hungry?"

"Yep."

"I'll go get you something."

I raised my eyebrows and smiled. "KFC chicken?"

"Is that what you want?"

"Two legs, one breast, with mashed taters and a large lemonade."

She nodded and turned to leave. "I'll be back in ten minutes. Oh, and I'm trying to locate the pilot who air-dropped the purse, but no luck yet."

"I love you, Allison Kyle."

"So much that you went to jail for me," she said over her shoulder. "I'm touched."

Though she was already a cell away and I was aching for food, even worse I wanted her to stay and talk. "Where are the rest of the gang?"

She stopped beside cell number seven. "Steve and Darcy are lunching on grilled crocodile. And Neil and Alexis went off to find a private hot spring because, well, this is their honeymoon."

"Are they going on to Sydney with us?"

Allie smiled and shook her head. "Will you stop looking at me so sadly? You'll make me cry. But as for Sydney and all of us, I think so, yes. The flight is tomorrow at 2:00."

"We should ask for window seats . . . just to reminisce."

She walked backward past cell number five. "What time do they let you out of here?"

"Eleven a.m. at the latest."

"I'll be back in a minute."

I gripped the bars tightly, pulled my head into the space, and raised my voice. "Are you still glad I picked this continent for my proposal?"

"Yes, very," she said, her reply reverberating in the hallway. "And you still need to pick your fourth groomsman." I heard her laugh. Then the door shut behind her, and even the echo was short-lived.

Thirty minutes later I was still alone in my cell, with no chicken and no lemonade, my stomach growling, the cell shrinking, our trip unraveling. I had seen two extremes of this big island—the most boundless wilderness and the most confined concrete room.

I scanned the chipped and yellowed ceiling and yearned to start this trip again. Rewind the clock. Hire a guide. Now here I was in cell number nine—Jay Jarvis, the car bomber who only bombed when totally out of options.

I could hardly blame anyone but myself. My entire life seemed a tangent from the straight and narrow path; every time I aimed somewhere, I ended up somewhere else. Fortunately I had found a woman who shared this same tendency to wander, though Allie at least had some common sense. What I couldn't picture was an all-girls adventure. I mean, if Lex and Darcy and Allie ever road-tripped together, mercy, might as well blindfold Lewis and Clark and spin them around ten times fast.

Right now, I could hardly even think; I just wanted out. I wanted to get to Sydney, put on my good pants and shirt, and take Allie to the Opera House.

I was about to peer out my window again when music began piping into the hallway. My guess was that the jailer had decided to cheer me up by tuning into a radio station. After ten minutes I'd heard Stevie Wonder's "Sir Duke," ABBA's "Dancing Queen," and for a second time, "Sweet Home, Alabama." This was Aussie radio, and it was like being in jail in 1978.

Then the radio cut off, as if nostalgia itself was being rationed.

In minutes I heard footsteps again. The metal door shut at the end of the hallway. And then all five-feet-eleven of Darcy walked toward my cell. She had the food bag in her hand, and as she approached she glanced left and right, examining steel bars and frowning at the emptiness. "I've never been inside a jail before, Jay. So Allie got the jailer to let me play delivery girl. Wow, your cell looks ancient."

"Welcome to the vast down under."

Darcy pressed the box vertically through the bars. Then the drink and straw. "Steve was just bored," she said. "Don't be mad."

"About what?"

"He took a bite of your chicken."

I set the drink on the floor and opened the box. Inside was a note: *Jay, I took a bite of your chicken.*

I shrugged and lifted the meat to my mouth. "I'd have eaten Steve's chicken."

"You look frustrated," she said and leaned into the door.

"I am. But we can't ever tell North Hills Presbyterian about this. They might not want to support a mission worker who's been behind bars."

Darcy nodded. "My lips are—"

"Sealed?"

"Dry. Got any Blistex?"

"The jailer took it when he checked me in."

Darcy ran a finger over her bottom lip. "*Checked* you in? You sound like you just arrived at the Marriott."

"Okay . . . when he shoved me in."

"He shoved you?"

"Just a bit. All jailers are taught the shove. It's part of the job."

"He wasn't nice to you?"

"Yeah, he was nice. Even let me pick my cell."

Darcy dug a wad of napkins from her pocket and handed them between the bars. "Even jailbirds should wipe their mouths."

I sipped the lemonade and pointed to the length and breadth of the Alice Springs jailhouse. "Be glad that they didn't arrest you all for being accomplices. You'd never convince them to redecorate this place. No designer curtains, Italian ceramic tile floors, or premium toiletries in lime green bottles."

Darcy put her hands on her hips and feigned insult. "I am not a froufrou girl." She peeked into cell number ten, turned up her nose at the sight of the portly green bug, and returned to take my trash bag. "That rental guy, Edward, said you shouldn't have been detained."

"Yeah, well, the magistrate didn't see it that way."

"It's not fair."

"Probably not, but this is some great chicken. The Aussies use spicier spices." I chewed, swallowed, and made an attempt to change the subject. "So, has the trip been everything you expected it to be?"

Darcy rolled her eyes and played with her hair. "Didn't expect your engagement."

"I'm full of surprises."

"And I didn't expect to get stuck in red mud with Alexis, especially on her honeymoon."

I slurped the tart and cold lemonade, great ballast for spicy chicken. "According to Neil, you and Lex have a history of mishaps."

"Too many to count." And here her demeanor changed from chatty to serious. "Can I ask you something?"

"Soon as I finish this chicken leg that your boyfriend bit." I ate quickly and told Darcy to go ahead and ask her question.

She stepped closer and lowered her voice. "Ever since you got rescued, Steve has been acting a bit odd. Do you think he feels awkward over his best friend getting engaged, and then his other best friend, Neil, being married?"

I set my drink on the floor and opened the container of mashed potatoes. "Could be. It's not your everyday vacation scenario. Why?"

Darcy raised up on her toes and touched the ceiling. "I just wish . . . no, I can't ask you this."

"Ask."

"I shouldn't."

"Ask. You want some of my lemonade?"

Darcy leaned in close, as if she needed to whisper inside an empty jailhouse. "I want you to tell Steve that I'm not in any great hurry, and that if someday he and I get to the point of seriously discussing marriage, then that time will be the right time."

The spoonful of potatoes shook in front of my lips. I could not eat. "You mean you two haven't discussed it?"

"Not seriously. Maybe joking around a few months ago."

I stuck the spoon back in the container. "Do you think you're ready to commit?"

Darcy pursed her lips and scanned the hallway. "I'm getting close. Steve is probably not as close as I am."

"You don't think?"

She gripped the bars and looked straight at me. "Jay, if Steve Cole had brought a ring on this trip I would have fainted in the orange dirt."

I picked up my KFC box. "Want a bite of chicken?"

"I better get going."

"Why don't you tell everyone to come in and pick a cell? We'll have a party tonight, do the Hokey Pokey in striped shirts."

When I had finished eating, Darcy took my KFC box and napkins and stuffed it all into the bag. Then she shook my hand. Then, in a gesture that caught me off guard, she reached up and patted me on the head. "I'm glad you're marrying Allie, Jay. We'll all be here at 11:00 tomorrow and head straight for the airport. Sleep good."

I turned and looked at my bed. "I'll do my best."

Darcy crunched the paper bag and started to walk away but turned with a last comment. "Just think, one day all of us could be going on a beach trip for married couples, and we'll all have our private rooms. No more singles groups, no more crowded houses."

I met her gaze and returned her smile. "That'd be original."

Darcy began walking backward down the hall. "Just don't stay up all night worrying about what anybody thinks. Lex and I decided that you're a hero for what you did."

She was three cells away when I pressed my head as far as it would go between the bars. "You're a great friend, Darcy Yeager."

"You just love my fried chicken," she replied. And then in her deepest Southern accent, "Scarlett makes such lovely fried chicken."

Her footsteps faded in a dank hallway, followed by the clang of a door, and she was gone.

When I lay on my back and shut my eyes, every thought melted into the baked debacle in the outback. I saw no reason for it, other than stupidity. What was I supposed to do, ask God to boil it all down to a crystal clump of clarity? Somehow I never expected faith in God to entitle me to explanations for every dilemma.

Between the drips of my sink I heard tourist buses rolling through Alice Springs. They sounded so steady, so experienced and dependable. My first hunch was that no one had ever had to blow up a tourist bus in order to summon help. My second was that I had plunged myself into serious debt.

In late afternoon Allie returned with a cheap game of checkers and a newspaper.

She sat on the newspaper in the hallway, and from opposite sides of the bars we played sixteen games before she let me win the last one and break the eight/eight tie.

When the jailer opened the metal door and told Allie she had but one more minute of visitation, she nodded to him, gathered the checkers, and scooted back into the middle of the hallway. There she spelled out I LUV JAY with the red and black discs.

"Ain't I romantic?" she said, finishing off the Y.

I stood and gripped the bars. "I don't deserve you."

After we'd said our good-byes, I tried to doze off by humming "Love Potion Number Nine," which I considered a superb title for the song because "Love Potion Number Seven" just lacks the spunky resonance, not to mention it has that extra syllable.

26

They wanted phone numbers, someone to vouch for me. The wiry jailer came back to my cell—the one that looked left over from the Wild, Wild West—and told me that the magistrate wanted to talk with someone who was not with me on the trip, someone whose name wasn't on the rental forms.

Apparently the testimonies of Neil and Steve weren't good enough. Nor those of Allie and Darcy. Nor that of Alexis, who had reminded the magistrate that her honeymoon had now been interrupted twice, and that Australia owed both her and Darcy a new pair of sneakers.

"One number, Mr. Jarvis," the jailer said. He had a scratch pad and pen in his hand, waiting to scribble.

"Try this one," I offered, showing him a business card for Asbury Smoak.

He eyed the wording on the card. "Who is this?"

"A boat captain in South Carolina," I replied. "And he also preaches."

"I'll be back in a few."

He left me to my thoughts, and my thoughts were many. Most prominent were the differing perspectives on what I'd done. To Allie and myself, the fire was necessary for life and gave hope for our union; to these authorities, it was reckless and juvenile and so very American, a result of our premeditated zeal for foolishness. But I was finished with regrets and tiring of reflection. I would pay Edward back, somehow, and get on with my engagement.

Footsteps in the hallway. The jailer returned shaking his head. "No one home. Got any other numbers?"

I dug out my wallet again. "Try this one. It's for Ransom Delaney."

Again he eyed the card. "And what does this bloke do?"

"Makes surfboards."

He looked doubtful. "Back in a few."

The jailer returned shortly, this time with a frown. "Only got an answering machine, mate."

I gripped the bars and tried to explain. "It's early morning there, so maybe he's not at work yet."

He put his hands on his hips and glared at me. "We'll give you one more chance. I'm getting tired of walking back here."

"Well, you could have taken three numbers the first time."

He rolled his eyes and nodded. "Yeah, I suppose. But we're only going to try this once more."

Again I thumbed through the contents of my wallet. "Okay, then try Maurice Evans . . . he's a cocaptain, along with the preacher." I pointed to the back of the card. "Use this home number."

The jailer took the card, wheeled around to leave, and spoke over his shoulder. "Back in a few."

Next thing I knew, he was unlocking my cell and escorting me to a small room with brain-sucking fluorescent lights, a carbon copy of the room used in police shows and that one episode of *Magnum P.I.* when Magnum wrecked the Ferrari.

The magistrate stood on the opposite side of a small, rectangular table. He held a tape recorder in his hands. Like the jailer who gripped my arm, he looked confused.

"Mr. Jarvis?"

"Yessir?"

"We're confused." He pushed the tape recorder to the middle of the table and motioned for me to sit.

The jailer pulled out a chair for me, and I sat and tried to help. "What's the problem, sir?"

The magistrate placed his finger on the play button and held it there.

"We didn't reach Maurice Evans. We reached his sister-in-law, who was house-sitting for him. Apparently this Maurice bloke is in a fishing tournament off the coast of Florida."

"He does that a lot, sir."

The jailer eased up close beside me. "Mr. Jarvis, we're having a bit of a strain trying to determine what this sister-in-law is saying on the tape. Her name, as far as we can tell, is Quilla."

Anybody but Quilla Jones. No telling what she'll say. Though I had my doubts, I was hoping for a simple affirmation from Quilla that I was a responsible citizen and had few possessions. Then the magistrate told me that he'd already listened to the tape four times and, for all the emotion and accent and strange verbiage, had yet to make sense of Quilla's remarks. He contorted his face and pressed the play button.

All three of us leaned over the recorder, waiting for hiss to end and Quilla to begin: "Y'all done locked the wrong banana. Ain't no way Jay-bird or Fish Stick or any o' them others guilty of nuttin'. I know that boy and he's honest as low tide. Plus I know who put up the 'nonymous reward. And why y'all call me at 5:00 a.m.? Don't y'all sleep? Now y'all let Jay out or else someone comin' to Australia with some attitude. Uh-huh, shaw will."

The jailer and the magistrate, who obviously had known each other for a long time, stared at one another with their heads tilted funny.

"Clear this up for us, mate?" the jailer asked.

"Yeah," the magistrate interjected. "Just what is a 'wrong banana'? We didn't feed you any fruit at all."

I scooted my chair back from the table and attempted a translation. "She says you have a responsible guy behind bars."

"Oh . . . is that right?" said the jailer, not quite satisfied. "Now have a go at why she thinks we have an inmate named Fish Stick."

"Um, that would be Neil Rucker, the newlywed with whom you spoke earlier today. Quilla calls him that 'cause Neil can't fish at all. He's more of a musician."

The magistrate squared his stance to me and folded his arms. He looked at me accusingly. "There's mention of a reward. This the same anonymous reward mentioned on our local radio?"

"I think so."

"Tell the truth, Mr. Jarvis."

I had no idea what he knew, but I suspected he had spoken with Steve by now. "Okay, I've already arranged to collect that four thousand from Steve Cole and Fish Stick, um, I mean Neil."

"And you've committed these monies to Edward?"

"Yes. I told him that."

The jailer mocked the magistrate's firm posture and narrowed his eyes at me. "One more thing. Who is this 'Mr. Shaw'?"

I raised my palms in innocence. "Mr. Shaw? I don't know any such person."

He pointed at the recorder. "At the end of the tape, Quilla states that 'Shaw will.' We need to know what it is that Mr. Shaw will do. Is she threatening us?"

I waved them off. "No, no. No one is threatening. Quilla is just empha-sizing her earlier statement that I should not be held. And 'shaw' is really 'sure,' as in 'sure will.' It's a Southern thing . . . like saying 'footbawll.'"

Both the magistrate and the jailer nodded slowly, in the way people do when they want you to believe they have clearly deciphered everything you've just said.

Then the jailer excused himself and left me and the magistrate on opposite sides of the table. The magistrate pulled a photo from his shirt pocket. "This was taken by your buddy, Mr. Cole."

He set the photo on the table in front of me. Steve had delivered the picture of the burning truck as proof. On the afternoon of our rescue, Steve had managed to snap a photo of the Land Cruiser and license tag as Neil circled the smoking truck.

I examined the photo and shook my head at how I had managed to get into such a predicament. "Does this mean you believe my story now?"

"Your story checks out. But you're hardly off the hook."

"I didn't think so."

He then produced a copy of one of Edward's many forms. This one was a pale shade of pink. "Edward is a longtime friend of mine, Mr. Jarvis, and I felt the need to look after his interests." He tapped on the paper as he spoke. "Edward is just a small business owner trying to make a living, and he can't afford to have a tourist destroy his property, leave the country, and never pay him back."

"I promise I'll pay him back, sir—the reward money plus whatever else I owe."

He shook the wrinkles from the form and handed it to me.

From all I could tell, Edward had gone to bat for me. He had totaled his costs and asked the insurance companies to cover at least half, given that the vehicle's mechanics were partly to blame. Who knew if they would go for it, but at least I had an initial amount for which to be responsible. Half of the vehicle value, plus add-ons, totaled ten thousand, eight hundred, and forty-seven dollars, excluding Edward's personal items. Such as miscellaneous eighties music.

His comments on the matter were written on the bottom of the form:

> The 1996 Toyota Land Cruiser was totaled in a fire that was set only as a last resort, as a signal for help following a horrible mishap by two tourists in Western Australia. After considering the situation and the life-threatening circumstances, I've concluded that I likely would have done the same thing.
> Edward P. Batalee, owner

The magistrate seemed to relax a bit as I finished reading and glanced up at him.

"You'll do the right thing with Edward?" he asked persuasively.

"Yessir. I'll work it out."

No way could I immediately come up with the balance. All I had to my name was the four shares of Microsoft, plus six hundred dollars in checking. I cringed as I realized I would have said most anything in order to convince them.

But convince them I did. The jailer returned from the men's room, and

209

just like that he and the magistrate let me go, even offering a pair of "no worries" as they held open the door.

Released back into society, I walked past the Outback Bar & Grill, then Bo's Saloon, and to the opposite end of town toward our motel, all the while baffled at how many tangents my exotic engagement plan had fostered. Maybe I should have just taken Allie to dinner and hidden the ring in a slice of key lime pie. Yet deep down I knew that our quest to find Rooville was what we'd still be talking about when we were old.

The sun had just set when I reached the motel parking lot, and from the pool area came female laughter, random splashes. The smell of chlorine grew strong, and I peered over a green fence and saw Neil and Steve floating on rafts, Darcy swimming laps by herself. Allie and Alexis teetered on the edge of the diving board, their backs to the water. They were about to attempt a twin back flip when I opened the wrought-iron gate and raised my arms in victory. Both women immediately fell in, limbs flailing, Lex yelling, "Escaped convict!" just before splashdown.

Then Allie surfaced with wet hair in her eyes. "Help," she shouted, "I'm marrying a fugitive."

And without a word I tossed my shoes and wallet to the ground and ran past the pool chairs and dove in in my street clothes. I just needed to be submerged for a moment, a little American fish in a little Australian pond.

At midmorning all of us except Darcy waited in the shade beneath the awning of Outback Adventures, our luggage at our feet, our heads turning left and right as we watched for the shuttle bus to take us to the airport. Edward and I had already met and agreed to simple terms—I was to get him the money as fast as possible.

Inside the building, Darcy leaned against Edward's counter, chatting with him and acting like she was enjoying herself. I had no idea if she was asking about a future tour, or flirting, or both. Beside me under the awning, Steve tipped his leather hat higher on his head and looked up and down the street. He cast the occasional glance inside at Darcy but pretended he wasn't concerned.

I nudged his foot with my own. "Sudden regrets?"

"Stifle it, Jarvis. We'll be leaving in minutes."

Allie was seated on a bench to my left, next to Neil and Alexis. Allie had bought herself a yellow souvenir T-shirt, and while the embroidered koala watched from her sleeve she jotted last-minute details in her journal.

Neil remained lost in the newness of his union and had spoken little all morning. The best he could do was sprawl cozily with his wife and play blues tunes on his harmonica.

"Louder, honey," Lex said to him. "Maybe people will throw tips."

Minutes passed, and Darcy kept talking and laughing with Edward; Steve kept glancing through the glass at Darcy; and Neil kept playin' the blues. Soon the shuttle came thundering around the corner, and we waved Darcy from the rental office and grabbed our luggage.

She turned and waved through the glass at Edward, who waited until Steve wasn't looking and blew Darcy a kiss.

I could not believe he'd done that; but then again, Darcy was bandless.

Allie stepped off the sidewalk first and waited for the shuttle door to swing wide. But before it opened a horn blew from the rear, from the curbside behind the shuttle. Out of a dirty red Audi came a middle-aged woman in aviator sunglasses. She wore a white short-sleeve shirt with bars on the shoulders and approached with a slight smile and a confident manner. "Would one of you be Jay," she gushed, "the fellow who got stranded?"

I removed my own sunglasses and eyed her curiously. "Yes. And you are?"

"I'm Linda. Linda Dooley. And I believe you have my purse."

"Ma'am?"

I saw Allie halt at the bus stairs, shock creeping into her face. She motioned for the rest of the gang to board.

Beside the front tire, bags in hand, I tried to speak. But my mouth would form only a small O.

"My old red purse," Linda said, her hand out as she stood on the sidewalk, as if we should have expected her arrival. "I air-dropped it to you two days ago."

At last, Tweedle Dee and Tweedle Dum had met the Flying Nun.

T Dee remained speechless, but I, T Dum, managed to blurt, "You're . . . Cessna Lady?"

"The one and only."

Before I knew what had happened Allie retreated from the bus and hugged Linda tight about the neck. She held on to her for so long I began to get worried. When finally Allie did let go I went ahead and had my turn. I'd never been much for hugging strangers, but as images of hot sands and bloated frogs and empty waterwheels spun in my head, I hugged that lady like a childhood teddy bear.

Allie unzipped her luggage, began digging for the purse, and promptly shifted the blame. "Jay gave the purse to me," she said, pulling it from under some blue jeans. "But if you need it back, then—"

"Sentimental value," Linda said, reaching to accept her beaded accessory.

What do you say to such a person? Three dozen thank-yous? I owe you my life? Please accept my retirement funds?

The shuttle-bus driver waved at us to hurry, though I felt like we should stay and take this lady to dinner, wash her car, do her laundry, mow her lawn.

In the waning minutes I realized that accepting the grace of another sometimes means not trying to pay them back in any kind of satisfactory manner. The moment felt at once awkward and comic and unutterably fated. Allie then asked for Linda's business card and promised to write and tell her all the details.

Our friends boarded the shuttle, all of them observing the scene from the windows. Forgetting that I had just hugged Linda, I shook her hand like I needed lots of practice.

Several seconds passed. "You can stop shaking my hand now, Jay."

The shuttle driver honked at us. I stepped up on the second stair, set my luggage down, and turned again. "You were great in that plane, Linda, homing in on me like that and waving your wings as you flew off." Like an idiot I held my arms out and waved them up and down.

Linda blushed slightly. "Twenty-two years as a bush pilot. But I must admit, I've never seen any tourists in that particular region. How'd you two get all the way out there?"

"That's what I want to know," Steve said from the third row.

Neil sat with his bride in the first seat and nodded. "It's what we all want to know."

Palms up, I told Linda the truth. "I had planned an engagement."

She peeked in at Steve and winked. "Romance . . . makes all men lose their minds."

Below me on the hot asphalt, Allie signaled to the driver that she needed just a few more seconds. He rolled his eyes, checked his watch.

"I think we owe you our lives, Linda," Allie continued, stealing my next line.

"Yes," I said, still on the second step and breathing diesel fumes. "Our lives."

"Stuff happens," Linda said with a shrug. "Right place at the right time."

Allie picked up her one remaining bag and smiled at Linda. "That's quite a, um, colorful purse you carry."

Linda Dooley nodded. "It's not a purse for wearing. It's strictly for air-drops. You're the fourth pair of Americans I've dropped that purse to in the last three years."

We waved heartily as we boarded the shuttle, although waves felt entirely inadequate. I passed the first seat and tapped Neil on the shoulder. "Great memories?"

He put his arm around Lex and looked up with a wink. "No one can interrupt a honeymoon like you, Jarvis."

I sat with Allie in the second seat as Darcy thumbed through her photos behind us, halfheartedly sharing them with Steve.

Our driver checked his rearview and said, "Everybody ready now, or would you all like to stop off for tea with the prime minister?"

"Proceed," Alexis replied.

The driver closed the door, and I watched Linda and her magenta purse step into Outback Adventures. As she stood at the counter and chatted with Edward, I suddenly realized that she, not Steve and Neil, really deserved that anonymous reward. Or, at least half.

Maybe Linda didn't know about it. Maybe she'd never know. My instincts told me to ask the driver to halt so that I could run in and tell her.

But my excuse was exhaustion, and I didn't do it. Didn't move.

I didn't even tell Allie. Beside her in the second seat, I mentally massaged my debt burden, knowing that Steve and Neil were giving me the money, forgetting that folly is an octopus with many tentacles.

We pulled away from Alice Springs, and I buried my festering guilt in friendships and the memories of engagement. Allie reached for my hand as the shuttle accelerated past a field of dirt and spinifex. I squeezed her fingers and watched the orange dust settle over my integrity, which I'd left on the roadside.

En route to the airport we shared the wildlife photos the girls had had developed while I was in the slammer, handfuls of images passing back and forth between the Couple Who Could Not Wait, the Couple Who Survived Their Stupidity, and the Couple Who May or May Not Remain a Couple.

Act 3

"Bring me your torch . . . the tribe has spoken."
—Jeff Probst, host of *Survivor*

27

In the driver's seat of an old Ford pickup, I fought sleep by rearranging geography in my head, wondering if the outback was in Ireland would the leprechauns and dingoes get along?

We had been traveling for twenty hours and could already smell the jungle. To the north lay farmland, to the east Peru. But I could only afford an occasional glance; we were swiftly declining, curving and swerving through a tire-wearing bout of counterclockwise rotation.

I loved this drive.

"I miss our friends," Allie said. It was early evening, still daylight, and she was staring out the passenger window at Ecuador and talking to the steep, patchwork fields of farmland. "Our friends were a hoot."

Soon we entered the valley and the flattish drive into the rainforest. All of South America looked in bloom. Banana trees grew thick and numerous, and the sky's red tint gave way to purple. Dusk was always colorful in the Andes.

I rolled down my window for a second whiff. "You're not upset that our trip was cut short?"

She leaned her head into her seat. "No, not anymore."

I got voted off the big island. Never made it to the Sydney Opera House. Steve did. Darcy did. Neil and Alexis did. Allie and I, however, got redirected by Sydney airport security. Those uniformed Aussies were cheerful but cautious. They told me to go home and deal with the trouble I'd caused, then I'd be welcomed back to Oz.

And though my pride would never admit it, another one of folly's tentacles had a chokehold on our bliss.

Road weary, I switched on the headlights and re-adapted to driving on the right side. "Sorry you didn't get to see *Twelfth Night.*"

"Don't worry," Allie said, folding a towel for a pillow. "We'll see it next time." Just before she fell asleep she mumbled that if Shakespeare were still alive he could write a play about us and call it a tragicomedy for the directionally impaired.

I laughed. But just briefly.

The road into our village turned blackest just before midnight, and in the headlights of the pickup the entrance was a tunnel of vines and bamboo. I could not stop sniffing the rainforest; the contrasts to orange dirt and sandstone dazzled the mind. Far ahead a pair of torches lit the way. The bugs chirped louder than I remembered.

The native children, the orphans, loved it here. I wanted to jump out of the truck and hug them all. But it was late, and I knew that they—and the whole village—were asleep. At least one of them, however, had expected our early arrival. When I turned in to the left side and shone the headlights at my hut, a WELCOME HOME paper was tacked to the door, its childlike letters alternating in blue and red crayon.

The patron saint of spare parts had been missed.

Allie woke groggy. "Home at last?"

I cut the engine and sighed with the carburetor. "Home at last."

We both sat still for a moment, blinking away the brain fog of travel. She stared out the windshield at my crayoned greeting, turned to look across the dirt road, and saw a similar sign on her own hut. A necklace of wooden beads also hung from her door handle. "My sign is bigger than yours."

I was about to climb out of the truck when the night air turned my thoughts financial. "And my debts are bigger than yours."

Allie yawned, smiled, nodded her head. "We'll pay 'em back. Some-

217

how." She got out and pulled her luggage from the pickup bed. "Next time we take pictures of wildlife, it'll be in a zoo."

From the other side of the truck I pulled my duffel over my shoulder. "I have a small confession about the reward money."

"Let's save confessions for after the jetlag."

"You do know who offered the reward, don't you?"

She came around the back of the truck and faced me. "We both know, Jay."

In the beige dirt foyer that separated the two rows of huts—eight on her side, five on mine—we dropped our bags at our feet and embraced. We'd been engaged for a week, but we'd only been engaged in our village for three minutes.

I held her tight and spoke into her ear. "Which side of the road?"

She pulled away but held onto my hands. "Are you suggesting something improper?"

"I mean which side of the village are we going to live on? There will have to be renovations, ya know." I wanted to slow dance again but lacked the energy.

"Yes . . . and decorations."

After we'd said good night, Allie let go of my hands and picked up her luggage. She moved wearily, and into bug-chirping darkness she shuffled over to hut No. 7.

I stood on the second step of hut No. 3 and looked around at a community in slumber. Allie had stopped on her own steps, though I could barely see her. She was but a vague shape on a moonless night. From across the village our separation felt like miles.

"Let's do it in South Carolina," she said loudly enough to wake neighbors.

"Now you sound improper."

"I meant let's get married in South Carolina . . . at Preacher Smoak's church. We'll combine some premarital counseling with a coastal wedding."

"And then off to the Caribbean?"

She opened her door, and her voice faded. "Just pick an island. Any island."

With a gentle thud her door shut. I loped inside, collapsed in my hammock, and wondered if today was Tuesday or Wednesday. I remembered something about gaining back a day after flying east from Australia, and settled on Tuesday.

There was much I needed to gain back, and right now a day seemed the least of it.

28

At noon the next day I was poked in the ribs after sleeping for eleven hours.

I awoke in my hammock and saw two caramel-skinned kids and one adult standing over me. Plaid-over-Stripes was the adult, and her fashion and nickname were closely related. Today her plaid top was brown and tan, her shorts green and white. Her real name was Orleander Martinez, but she and everyone else (except Allie) preferred the nickname.

"Up," she said. For her, this was a speech; she rarely said anything.

The ten-year-old, Eduardo, reached out and shook the hammock. "Tell about roos."

I yawned in a long and selfish manner. "G'day, senors and senoritas."

Plaid clapped her hands loudly. "Up."

The other child, seven-year-old Isabel, tickled my foot. "Miss Allie say you have story what to tell."

I rolled my legs over the side, rubbed my eyes, smelled soup. "I missed breakfast, huh?" The wood floor felt cool to my feet.

"Tell about roos," Eduardo repeated.

Plaid-over-Stripes shook the hammock again. "Up, Americano."

I raised a finger and told them to gather the other kids and I'd meet them outside.

When finally I stepped into daylight, Allie and Plaid-over-Stripes were getting into the pickup. They waved from across the village. "Back this afternoon," Allie said. "We're going into town for supplies."

I nodded and blew her a kiss. "Check my email . . . please?"

"Of course. Just keep the kids entertained."

The official storytelling spot was an open-air dining area, which contained only three picnic tables and an A-frame roof supported by six poles. It sat outside of the kitchen building, our new kitchen building. The old one Allie had accidentally burned down the previous summer. So on that point—setters of fire—I suppose my fiancée and I were an even match.

I, Truck Torcher, take you, Kitchen Torcher, to be my lawful wedded wife?

In shorts and Alice Springs T-shirt, and without combing my hair, I made it to the center table and sat on a bench. Children saw me and came running from the doors of huts, from behind huts, two from beneath a hut. Due to the abundance of moisture, all of our structures were raised at least three feet off the ground.

What we lacked in convenience we made up for with storytelling. Most everyone had stories, and we told them in English to foster the children's language class. When Eduardo or his younger brother, Pepe, told a tale, the moon would teem with purple oceans, pirate ships, and guns that shot M&M's. When Isabel performed her solo, she acted out a kind of Cinderella in the Jungle, complete with wildlife and a vine-crafted tiara. Today, however, was my turn.

"Wanna hear a new story?" I asked loudly.

Children in mismatched clothing gathered around me, on the benches and atop the table. Hands messed with my hair. Little voices urged me on.

"Tell about kangaroos."

"Tell about snakes."

"No, crocodiles."

"No, giraffe."

I turned to face a table covered with kids. "Who said 'giraffe'?"

Eduardo raised his hand. "No giraffe in Australia?"

I shook my head. "Nope. But I have one new tale about the kangaroos."

Truth is, I did not have one yet. My troubles kept rejecting my attempts

221

at creativity. "Before I start, let's all pretend we're in Australia. Follow me."

I motioned for them to line up, and we marched single file around the village, snaking between huts and looking far and wide for imaginary animals. Isabel held onto my shirttail. "Faster, Mister Jay. I hear the roos, the roos." She shoved me forward, and the kids behind her laughed.

This was my everyday life—the life on which I had not planned when I was pulling a 3.7 in finance at the University of Texas. Now, instead of numbers flashing on screens, there were children bouncing in jungles. Instead of five-figure paychecks came pledges of support from friends and churches. And instead of stucco walls and reserved parking, I taught math beneath green canopies and read to children under the equatorial sun.

The kids never asked about my former life. I think they just figured I was supposed to be here, and cared nothing of the avenue.

Our single-file line continued searching around the village, and I kept getting shoved in the back. "Anybody see anything hopping?"

"I do," Pepe said. "Purple roo hide behind trees."

For Pepe, anything imaginary had to be purple.

The history of the children was rarely discussed and sometimes even off limits, at least according to the native adult villagers. From what I had learned, a few parents had abandoned children at birth because of poverty; other parents had perished in accidents. Two of the kids, Pepe and Eduardo, had been discovered in an overcrowded city orphanage and begged officials to take them elsewhere. Here, two hours east of Coca, Ecuador, was their elsewhere. No one knew if they were really brothers. At ages eight and ten, they looked like brothers. They claimed to have known each other for years.

"Okay, everyone take a seat now." Though I had my doubts that all had time-traveled to the outback, I led them back to the tables and benches. Again they gathered around, scooted close. My thoughts were a mess, juggling debt, the reward money I so desperately needed, and how to make up an entertaining story.

"It's time for the story of Steve, Darcy, and the Rambunctious Roos," I said. Birds cackled in the treetops, and all the kids went silent, expectations high. I returned their excited glances and began. "Steve and his girlfriend, Darcy, were driving into—"

"Senor Steve has girlfriend!" Pepe said.

"Gir-friend!" Eduardo added.

I halted them with adult hands. "Okay, y'all must let Jay tell his story."

I began again. "Steve and Darcy were driving a purple truck across plains of golden grasses in the middle of Australia."

Isabel leapt from the bench and made driving motions with her hands, as if she were steering the truck. She motioned for me to continue.

"It was very hot, and Steve and Darcy were searching for kangaroos because they wanted to get lots of pictures."

Heads nodded at "get lots of pictures," and Isabel closed one eye and pretended to snap photos.

"And then they had to drive way out into the middle of the desert, hundreds of miles from anyone. All they could see were swaying grass and orange dirt. But then Steve honked the horn, and out of the grass ten kangaroos woke from their naps and sprang to their feet."

Pepe joined Isabel, and they began hopping around the table.

"The roos hopped in great bounds across the plains, and the purple truck went *bump bump* as Steve gave chase. Darcy leaned out the window with her camera, but the roos hopped faster and were getting away. Darcy said, 'Closer Steve, get closer.' But Steve was not a good roo chaser, and they fell far behind."

"How far behind?" someone asked.

"Um, really far. So Darcy switched places with Steve and gave him the camera. Darcy was the wildest driver in all of Australia, and she bounced the truck over a hill and went speeding after the kangaroos."

Four kids now bounded in front of me, arms tucked like front legs, Isabel leading the way.

"Soon Darcy had driven right up beside a big male kangaroo. They raced each other through tall grasses as Steve leaned out the window and aimed the camera. But just when Steve was about to take the first picture, the roo snatched the camera with his mouth and hopped away."

A dozen kids gasped. Eduardo looked stunned. "Roo steal camera?"

"Yes, but that wasn't the end."

"Why roo steal camera?"

"Just listen up. The other nine roos joined the one with the camera, and they all began jumping in circles around the truck. They stuck out their tongues at Steve and Darcy, so Darcy stopped the truck and shouted at the roos to bring back her expensive Nikon."

"What's a Nypon?"

"A kind of camera. Now, the roos kept circling the truck until Darcy got so mad she leaped from her seat and said she would have them all thrown in Kangaroo Jail, which is an old jail like in the Wild, Wild West. But they paid her no attention. Darcy was so mad she couldn't speak, so she shook her fist at the roos. She even shook her truck keys at them. But then a smaller roo snuck up behind Darcy and snatched the keys from her hand, so now the roos had their camera and their truck keys."

"And so boyfriend and girlfriend get stuck?" Isabel asked. She had taken a time-out from her acting and appeared concerned.

"Very observant, Isabel."

Pepe raised his hand. "And Steve and Darby die in desert?" He too looked quite concerned.

"Her name is Darcy, and no, neither she nor Steve died. But since they had no keys to start the truck, they had to walk three hundred miles through the desert. And when they got through the desert they came to Lake Disappointment, which, um, was bone dry, not a drop of water."

Isabel dropped to her knees and let her tongue hang out.

"No water at all?" asked Pepe. His young face remained etched with worry.

"None at all. But soon a big Australian man named Phil showed up in a tanker truck and backed his truck to the edge of Lake Disappointment. Then he unraveled a hose and filled the empty lake with grape Kool-Aid."

Pepe nodded his approval, as if grape Kool-Aid dumped into Lake Disappointment was the perfect ending to story time.

"Can't have no grape Kool-Aid in desert," Eduardo said, sure of himself.

"Kool-Aid everywhere," Pepe argued. "Even China got some."

The kids scattered to go start a soccer game, though Isabel stayed behind and sat on the bench beside me. "I'll see the kangaroos someday, Mister Jay."

My thoughts were already back on my debts, and all I could manage was to pat her head and say, "I'm sure you will, Isabel."

She then stood in front of me, eyes down, and pulled something from her pocket. "Money," she said softly, as if ashamed.

In her palm was a one-dollar Australian coin. "Where did you get that?" I asked.

"Floor . . . under your hammock."

"This morning?"

"Eduardo shake you, and money falls out." She handed me the coin and folded my fingers around it. "Miss Allie teach to not keep what not yours."

My hand shook as I gave her the coin, and she grinned and ran off to join the other kids.

When Allie and Plaid-over-Stripes came rolling back into the village, I was still in the shade at the picnic tables, a legal pad and a pen in my hands. They parked beside the kitchen building, and I got up to help unload groceries.

Plaid passed me with three sacks in each of her hands, the plastic pulling on her fingers, her face a grimace. Most of the sacks were stuffed with jumbo boxes of Cap'n Crunch.

I grabbed bags of potatoes and rice and hurried to catch up. "What about my Product 19?"

She paused on the kitchen stairs. "You'll like Crunch."

At the pickup bed Allie and I unloaded the remaining sacks, took them inside the kitchen hut, and tried to explain jet lag to our friend. Plaid was shucking corn and showed little interest in the subject.

Allie shucked an ear of corn with her, yawned, and tried again to clarify why the two of us were dragging. "It's like this, Orleander," Allie said, making a circling motion with her left arm. "You fly back halfway around the world, and the sun meets you before it's supposed to."

Plaid kept shucking, only pausing to hand me an ear.

I stood beside her and ripped the outer leaves off and held the corn by its end, like an airplane. I flew it in a wobbly circle. "You see, Plaid, it's like the earth spins around faster than normal, and so your body feels cheated."

She pulled the remaining gold hair from her corn and tossed it in the trash. "You'll like the Crunch."

After twenty-five ears were fully shucked, Allie and I went outside to talk, and she immediately spotted my legal pad on the picnic table. She walked over and picked it up. "In calculation mode again? Trying to be the financial hero?"

"I don't snoop in your notebooks, Miss Kyle."

"No, but you sneak peeks." She skimmed the page and ran a finger down its margin. "Yep, obsessed with debt and income."

"Wouldn't you be?"

She flipped to the second sheet. "Sure, but I wouldn't take . . ." She flipped more paper. "Six pages to scribble every option."

I motioned for her to sit with me on the bench. "My situation is a bit worse now that I've applied ethics and morals."

Allie crossed her legs and sighed. "Is there ever a time not to apply ethics and morals?"

"Wanna hear my confession now?"

"Sure. Give it."

"When we were leaving on the shuttle yesterday, I realized that Linda Dooley really earned the reward money, not Steve and Neil. At a minimum, she should get half."

Her eyes widened, and she sat perfectly still. "Oh my word . . . why didn't I think of that?"

"You were busy crafting tragic poems in the desert?"

"Do you think she knows?"

"Didn't act like it."

"What about Neil and Steve?"

"I don't think they've even considered it. They've already got it in their heads that they'll claim the money and turn it over to me, and then I'll give it to Edward."

Finally her poet mind grasped what I was telling her. "So, now you might owe another two thousand? Maybe even another four thousand?"

"That's the simple math."

"So the debt is now eight thousand, eight hundred? Maybe even ten thousand, eight hundred?"

"And forty-seven."

"Wow." She handed me the legal pad and stared at the ground. "What are you, I mean we, gonna do?"

I didn't want to say it. Didn't want to tell her that we could be separated for the bulk of our engagement. "The only solution I see is for me to go back to the States, live cheap, and work to pay off the debt."

From the look on her face, I had chosen the wrong time to say it. "Don't you have anything you can sell?" she asked, hope in her voice. "Like some stock?"

"I told you, I sold all but four shares to pay for your ring."

She lifted her left hand to her face and admired her gem. "It really is a beautiful ring."

For the first time since the proposal, I felt unqualified for marriage. Small. Unstable. "Fact is, Allie, I'm no longer the well-to-do broker you first met."

She pulled off her ring and put it in my hand. "Then sell this if you have to. But no way am I going to live in New York City."

I scooted closer to her on the bench, knowing she had misunderstood me. I took her left hand and slid the ring back on her finger. "We're not going to sell your ring, and I'm not asking you to go to New York."

"Then where would you go?"

"I don't know yet. But our little salaries from the mission won't relieve this debt." This felt like our first engaged argument, and I racked my brain for a way to change the subject. "Did you happen to check my emails?"

She nodded. "You only had one."

"From?"

"Steve."

"Anything newsworthy?"

She sighed and shook her head, frustration evident in her body language.

"I printed it but didn't read it. I was too busy emailing friends to share our engagement news. Your email is on the front seat of the pickup."

I went over and opened the truck's passenger door, found Steve's note, and leaned against the hood to read.

Jarvis,

So, how does it feel to get booted out of the friendliest country on Earth? We're spending our last day at sunny Bondi Beach. The girls tell me the play last night was excellent. I fell asleep halfway in.

As for what you and me and Neil discussed on the shuttle, about transferring the reward money to Outback Adventures so Edward can buy himself another SUV, we contacted the radio station. They told us they have not heard back from the anonymous donor, which I'm sure you've by now figured out is Beatrice. Maybe she felt partially responsible for your troubles. I'll keep trying to track her down.

We leave for South Carolina tomorrow. Not looking forward to all the travel, but am looking forward to getting Darcy out of Sydney. She keeps flirting with local men, even one of the actors after the play.

I think she's testing me.

Have you thought about coming to South Carolina and working for a while to pay off the rest of your debt? You could stay with me.

Later, Steve

29

Like gum on the sole of a shoe, financial burdens come with a certain stickiness. But whereas finding a good twig can help rid yourself of the gum, finding good news is often required to rid yourself of the burden. The news was anything but good, and it forced me, finally, to put finances in perspective.

Just four days after Steve's email, a new missive arrived from Neil. I was sitting alone on the steps of my hut, and beyond the banana trees I could hear the children playing on the soccer field.

Jay,

I so hate to do this by email, but as you know, it is impossible to reach you by phone. Yesterday we found out that Beatrice passed away.

She died on a Tuesday, Jay, the same day you flew home. One of her nephews found her in her garden, faceup in last year's flowers. He said it was an unusually warm day, and she'd been installing a bird-bath. We are all sad, especially Steve. I had no idea that she'd been advising him of romantic places to take Darcy.

The funeral is tomorrow morning, and we know there is no way you and Allie can be here. Everyone will understand.

I know this next bit is trivial, but I need to tell you. Beatrice never had the chance to send the reward money to the radio station in Alice Springs, and her relatives have no record of the offer. Her descendants are a feuding bunch, so maybe that's why Beatrice traveled so much. Sorry that there won't be anything to help you with what is owed to Edward.

We know you will be here in spirit tomorrow, and Alexis has already purchased flowers in your and Allie's names.

Grace,
Neil

P.S. Do you remember when Beatrice and Quilla had the debate about pygmies? I know, I know, the news is too raw right now.

I had lost my third grandmother, and worse, there was no one nearby to tell. I stood on the steps, and the tears ran down. I called for Allie, and more tears ran down, clinging to my cheeks for a final farewell before splattering on my bare feet.

Alone with grief and needing human contact, I called for Allie again, forgetting that she was with the kids at the soccer field. The other adults were either with her or had gone into town.

I ran through the center of the village, one hand making a fist, the other clutching the email. I wanted to blame something. Someone, anyone.

Past the ninth and tenth huts, I did just that.

I stopped there in the dirt, the jungle a wet blur. In sunlight that showed no mercy, I raised my voice and gave God an earful. "You've allowed my engagement to get ruined, you've taken my third grandmother, you've taken the reward money that I was going to split with Linda Dooley, and now the debt is even bigger and you're about to separate me from Allie, not to mention kids who need me. Do you enjoy watching this?" I shook the paper at blue skies. "Do you?"

Even with the raised voice and battered emotion, I suspected there would be no explanation forthcoming. But yelling felt better than holding it in.

I ran out of the village and down the dirt road, which seemed longer today. I saw Allie on the sideline of our shabby soccer field, a wide-brimmed hat low on her head. She was laughing at Isabel, who was supposed to be playing goalie but was instead spinning on her heels and jerking her arms, dancing with her back to the game.

Their smiling expressions felt totally at odds with the moment. Allie saw me jogging toward her and tipped her hat high. "I thought I heard yelling. Were you shouting at someone?"

I didn't speak until I was a step away. "Beatrice . . . she's passed."

All the pleasantness drained from her face, and I wrapped my arms around her. She held me as I lost control and sobbed. "Oh, Jay. I'm so, so sorry."

I hugged her tight, not bothering to acknowledge the kids, who had stopped their game to stare at us. "I loved that ol' lady."

"We all did, Jay." Allie rested her head on my shoulder, sniffled, and eased a hand through my hair. "We all did."

After we'd held each other for a long while, I pulled away and showed her the note.

She read the first lines with an increasing expression of sadness. I used my T-shirt sleeve to wipe my eyes and motioned for her to read the rest. "Funeral's tomorrow."

She finished the note, folded it carefully, and handed it back. Her voice was a whisper. "That was nice of Alexis to send flowers."

Aware that I was being watched, I managed to gather myself and wave to the kids, who shrugged and went back to their game. Allie called to Eduardo, telling him to look after the younger children and to have everyone back before dark, that she and I needed some time alone. Together we walked the grassy sideline, our pace slow, the sun high, her hand on my back.

She didn't speak again until we had walked out to where the soccer field met the dirt road. "Your eyes are red, Jay."

The world was spinning way too fast. "Beatrice was my good friend."

The jungle seemed unsympathetic. Then, in a gesture that surprised me, Allie picked up a rock and threw it into the tops of the banana trees. "This engagement is just not going to let us have any bliss at all, is it?"

Forget bliss, I thought. Maybe for today, the best we can manage is community.

My heart wasn't in it, but I needed to be with the kids, those little bronze safety nets who were unaware that they could hold an adult. I grabbed Allie's hand, tugged her once, and we ran out onto the soccer field.

"What are we doing?" she asked, breathlessly trying to keep up.

"Let's be ten again."

From a pack of wildly kicking children the ball came rolling my way. And so with red eyes and forced smile I joined the game—running the field, kicking the ball, and watching amused as Isabel played goalie while practicing pirouettes.

After the game had ended and we were walking the kids back toward the village, I tried to do as Neil suggested—remember the good times with Beatrice.

And, despite her own prediction, it was flowers that got her in the end, not pygmies.

I ground my teeth at the thought of leaving, a second time at the realization that I was poor. While I had once helped support the village with my savings, those savings were gone—spent wisely, I maintained—exhausted on supplies and an exotic engagement.

Today, sitting in sunlight on the steps of Allie's hut with a second bowl of Cap'n Crunch, I felt truth hit me in the face like cold rain: Jay Jarvis, former stockbroker and earner of big bucks, was about to fly off and beg.

Allie returned from giving the kids their reading lessons. She too had chosen a late breakfast; she carried her bowl in one hand and spooned with the other. She sat beside me. "So, Professor Math Brain, how much is your debt now that there's no reward monies?"

"Just over nine thousand. I figured the least I could do was max out the cash advance on my credit card and have that sent to Edward this week."

"How much could you get?"

"Eighteen hundred."

She finished eating and set her cereal bowl behind her on the top step. "How are we ever going to plan a wedding while working on different continents?"

I ate my last spoonful. "Ten thousand Verizon anytime minutes?"

"Be serious."

"We'll manage. Somehow, we'll manage." When she didn't respond, I turned to look at her and noticed what I should have seen earlier. "You had your hair cut in the back."

She reached over her shoulder and flicked her dark mane. "Thanks for noticing. Orleander did it last night. She's quite good with the scissors."

We sat silent for a long while. The moment reeked of awkwardness, as I knew she too was frustrated by our looming separation. "I feel like this is one of those long moments when people say good-bye too many times and just sit and stir their spoons in their bowls instead of getting on with it. I really should go pack."

Allie grabbed her spoon and clanged it around the inside of her bowl. "Good-bye, farewell, adios, let's visit again soon. Who knows, we might like each other and end up dating."

I stood in protest, not knowing what she meant. "Are you being sarcastic? 'Cause that sounded sorta sarcastic."

"I'm sorry. I just want us to have a normal engagement. I want to sit up late with my fiancé and talk about everything and go on dates and feel a sense of momentum about it all."

I stepped down to the bottom stair and watched the kids reading at the tables. "Maybe this is just a test."

She set her bowl in mine and shook her head. "I'm sick of tests. We've been tested with heat, thirst, lust, and even frog water. Then jail, then debt, and now . . . a separated engagement? Don't you think this is enough, Jay?"

"You're my enough." I leaned over, kissed her on the forehead, and walked toward my hut to pack my things.

She caught up to me on my own steps. "Hey," she said, reaching around and touching her diamond to the side of my face, "at least we got engaged."

We watched the kids for a moment, noted the clear skies. "Maybe all the bliss is after the wedding."

Neither of us knew what this would do to our relationship, but getting a job—or begging churches for money from their mission funds—was

233

the only logical option. Our mission board had strict regulations about amassing personal debt while living in foreign countries—puts too much stress on the workers, they insisted.

I saw their point. But the debt was a result of preserving life, otherwise we would be both debt free and dead.

Allie left me to my packing, and with pursed lips I folded khaki slacks, two dress shirts, and the office shoes I'd been planning to throw away for lack of use. I was stuffing pairs of socks into the shoes when I was startled by the sound of scissors snipping the air. I turned into the glare coming from my open doorway.

Plaid-over-Stripes, dressed in her finest clash of green and orange, held the scissors over her head. She snipped them three times in rapid succession. "You need the trim."

I raised a shoe in protest. "No, wait. Orleander, I really—"

"For North America, you need the trim."

I held my duffel bag up for protection. "Orleander, I think I'll just wait till I get to the States."

She entered my hut with confidence and pulled a lone wooden chair to the center of the floor. She pointed to it with the scissors. "Sit."

I sat.

While snips of blond hair fell around me, I wrote out my itinerary, complete with old job acquaintances, my usual dollop of calculations, and a reminder to email friends and ask them to be on the lookout for prosperous contacts.

Even from the Ecuadorian jungle, a man can network. I gave the haircut a B+.

That evening, after a village dinner at the picnic tables, I told everyone what had to happen. More importantly, I told them why. Amid the scent of fish and rice and baked potatoes, a few of the adults nodded, yet none of the kids would look at me. They sat silent, as if they were by now used to the white Americano coming and going. Mostly going.

So in groups of twos and threes I took the kids aside and reassured them I'd be back. The last two were Pepe and Isabel, and I held their hands in mine and walked them over to the kitchen steps.

"Jay has to go earn some money," I told them. "But he'll be back in a short while, and then he and Miss Allie are going to be married, and we'll all sit around here at night and tell new stories."

I squeezed their hands. They did not reciprocate.

Isabel looked at the ground and said nothing. Then, out poked the lip.

Pepe also resorted to lip language. "No," he said between sniffles. "Don't go."

With hesitation Isabel put her other hand on mine and gave it a tug. "I want for you . . . to don't go."

On the morning that Steve and I had watched the wallabies and discussed the various issues of marriage and children, nothing had been mentioned about the crying scenarios. Here I had entered new territory. Here I had to rely on instinct. Here I could only hug Pepe and Isabel and tell them it would be all right.

Here, little ones, it'll be all right.

After my bags were in the pickup and I had given Eduardo permission to sleep in my hammock while I was gone, Allie and I spent a last lingering hour together. It was Monday morning, and we spent it by improving our future home. Behind the supply hut, we fixed the leg of a wooden loveseat and moved it into hut No. 7, next to her bookshelf. Cushionless, the furniture had been built with spare lumber. And just when I was thinking that it looked very hard-on-the-butt, Allie went to her back room and brought out an armful of yellow cushions. "I got these in Coca last Wednesday," she said, stuffing them in place, "while Orleander and I were buying supplies."

I cocked my head to the side and considered for the first time our differing ideas on marital motif. "Yellow, eh?"

She pushed the last cushion into the side and stepped back to admire her renovation. "Better now?"

"Not the most manly of colors, but, yeah, maybe I could watch football on it."

She motioned for me to sit. She snuggled close, flicked a gnat off her camouflage pants, and checked her watch. "You'll let me know as soon as you pick your fourth groomsman?"

The morning air smelled of moist jungle, and I inhaled enough to savor for the journey. "Yes," I whispered in her ear. "Of course."

In the minutes we had before she drove me to the airport, we sat on that old loveseat, sometimes talking, sometimes just holding hands. I could envision her spending her free hours here—writing in her journal, crafting her poetry. She was always writing *something*.

"On sad days I can scribble myself into contentment," she'd told me once.

30

On the evening I arrived in Greenville, South Carolina, to become a hunter-gatherer, Steve Cole met me at the airport in his Jeep. His orange Jeep. We tossed my luggage into the rear, and he eased back into the driver's seat. I, however, remained on the curb, hesitant to climb into anything orange and four-wheel drive. Might be cursed.

Steve lowered the passenger window. "You coming?" he asked and stuck his key in the ignition.

"Maybe." I knelt to inspect the undercarriage, then tentatively pulled open the door and peered inside. "Oh, good, you have a cell phone."

Unusually quiet, he drove us out the exit lane through a thicket of pine trees. He seemed glad to see me but said he was in a hurry. His rearview mirror was adorned with Darcy's mist-green sunglasses, which, given the topsy-turvy romance, was beyond intriguing.

"You have a date tonight?" I asked.

"A surprise."

I lowered my window, and cold air snipped at my nose. So I raised my window, and warm air rose from the dash. It had been sixteen months since I'd last experienced a car heater.

Steve ramped onto I-385 and sped us toward his neighborhood. New construction was everywhere. Roads being widened. Restaurants opening. Greenville looked so unfamiliar. Yet when we reached the North Main area and turned onto his street, recollection morphed into nostalgia, and nostalgia into déjà vu.

Parked in front of Steve's house was a Toyota pickup with surfing stickers plastered on the back window. A roof rack sat empty atop the cabin.

Steve turned into his driveway, and in midturn his headlights cut across the pickup and into the rear of a blue Chevy Blazer. My blue Chevy Blazer, the classic 1981 model I'd left here when I first went to Ecuador—and the one Neil had bought shortly after he took a job teaching Spanish at Greenville High School. I waited for Steve to cut his engine. "You're throwing me a surprise party?"

"Not exactly," he replied. His boyish smirk kept me guessing.

Then I remembered that this was Monday night. When I had lived here, I drove to this house on Monday nights. "Don't tell me you've started hosting that men's group again?"

He unbuckled his seat belt. "I have."

"And now you're gonna tell me that Ransom Delaney still leads it?"

"He does."

"And he and Neil are inside waiting for us?"

"They are."

We got out of the Jeep and walked around the hood from opposite sides. "I can't believe you, Cole. I just get off the plane after flying here to look for a job, and you bring me to the . . . what did we used to call it? The Circle of Nine?"

Steve motioned toward his front door. "Now it's the Circle of Three. But with you here it'll be the Circle of Four."

"You mean I have a lifetime membership?"

Steve nodded. "After you left Carolina, and after Ransom and Jamie had their baby, our group split into two smaller groups. One for the guys on the east side, and one for us downtowners. Last week Ransom even brought little Wally. Said it was good for a one-year-old boy to be around mature men like me and Neil."

I stopped at his front door. Through the curtains I could see Neil and his long hair propped into the corner of Steve's sofa. Ransom sat in a chair to Neil's right, talking away, hands gesturing to spice the conversation. He had wavy, surfer locks and the casual manner of a beach bum.

Weary and in no mood for shared confessionals, I turned to Steve on the steps. "Just what kinda stuff is the Circle discussing?"

Steve reached past me for the doorknob. "Same issues as always. Temptation, lustful thoughts, materialism, and the next beach excursion."

This is the same guy who ate my chicken while I was in the slammer? "I can't wait."

He pushed open the door, and before I could even say hello, he made like an emcee and said, "Contestants, Jay flew in all the way from Ecuador to tell us about his manly struggles."

From the opposing side of a coffee table Neil stood in jeans and gray sweater. He grinned widely. "Jarvis."

"Jay-dude!" Ransom said. He was tan even at this time of year, and the hood of his blue sweatshirt was pulled back behind his neck. "You're now an engaged man?"

"The product of an adventure down under."

He stood and stepped toward me. "So I heard."

What followed were bear hugs and handshakes, offers of caffeine-free Coke, and snack foods spread on Steve's coffee table. And while at first I had felt hesitant about being thrust into this, now I realized that to be in the presence of friends, male friends at that, was just what I needed. The flight had been lonely. Just me and my window seat, no one else in the row.

Ransom Delaney had been married for seven years and owned an extreme-sports outlet. Back when I lived in Greenville, he and his wife, Jamie, were among my closest friends. And only now, with the onset of parenthood, had he succumbed to structured domesticity.

"Get you a drink?" he asked, motioning toward the kitchen.

"Yeah, just anything."

Both Steve and Ransom showed unusual hospitality—they hustled into the kitchen and began pouring Coke into plastic cups. I took a deep breath, sat with Neil on the sofa, and let the hum of jet engines fade from short-term memory. "You got roped into this men's group too, Neil?"

239

He looked relaxed, at ease after nearly five weeks of marriage to Alexis. "It's the best, Jarvis. One night a week to talk with other guys, it's just . . ." He shook his head and smiled at the ceiling. "It's just such a transition to live with a woman."

I thought of Lex pulling the very stuck truck from Australian mud. "Especially an extroverted woman?"

"An unpredictable woman."

I nodded and thought of Allie. "I sure miss my woman."

"Here, have some tortilla chips." This was Neil's effort at sympathy, and he passed me the bag.

Ransom walked back in, handed me my drink, and sat comfortably in Steve's La-Z-Boy. "Did someone mention the transition of living with a woman?"

"I did," Neil said. "It's more than a minor adjustment."

"Dude, wait till you have a one-year-old." Ransom tilted the chair back, like he was ready to hold court. "That's a transition."

"No sleep?" I asked.

"No sleep, no late-night surfing shows, no spontaneous trips to the coast. All I do is work, buy food, and change diapers."

Steve looked very interested in this conversation. He pulled up a wooden chair and rejoined the circle. "And what does Jamie do?"

"Shop, prepare food, and change diapers."

Neil rotated his cup in his hands, smiled the newlywed smile, and said, "All I do is teach Spanish and date my wife."

"You guys just wait a couple years," Ransom said. "Just you wait."

I never told Allie how much I missed these guys. And she rarely mentioned how much she missed her girlfriends. Tonight, on a brown corduroy sofa in Steve's den, I had reunited with my mates.

Ransom leaned forward and pounded on the coffee table. "Jay-dude?"

"Yeah?"

"You look jet-lagged. Perk up."

"Long flight," I replied, still foggy from the travel. "Plus I have to figure out how best to earn some money. There's a kind-of hole in my résumé, you might say."

"Big hole or small hole?"

I had never thought of its size. "Big as South America."

Neil sucked an ice cube from his cup and tucked it inside his jaw. "Want me to climb up on a roof and petition God for you, Jarvis? I'm good at that sorta thing, ya know."

"I thought you only did that as a single man."

He crunched his ice and swallowed. "Nope. Lex and I climb up once a week. Mostly after eating Mexican food."

Ransom set his drink on a napkin, reclined again in the La-Z-Boy, and steered us back to sanity. "I heard about your debt . . . all that mess you got into."

"It's worse than a mess."

"But dude, did you really get put in jail?"

I was halfway into the long-winded explanation when I noticed that no one was paying attention. Six eyes were cutting back and forth. I stopped talking.

Neil looked at Ransom and whispered, "Go ahead; tell 'im what you found."

I held up my hands, palms to old friends. "No way, guys. Don't go telling me you found some restaurant that'll let me wait tables. I was never any good at—"

"Chill, Jarvis," Ransom said. He raised his cup in a kind of toast. "I met your former boss."

Skeptical, I sipped my Coke and eased down into the sofa cushions. "You met Mr. Brophy?"

"He came into my store to buy a skateboard for his son. We talked about you."

"And?"

"And I told him your predicament, that Jay-dude needed a job."

"They'd never hire me back, Ransom. I left the very day my promotion began."

"Slow down your mind, dude. He said he couldn't help you with a job, at least not at his firm. But he gave me a business card for a competitor. Said maybe you should call them about an assistant's position."

"Oh . . . that could work."

Ransom leaned across the coffee table and handed me the business card. Then he reached for his wallet, drew out a twenty, and offered that in kind. Told me it was food money till I found a job, or my old career, or whatever it was I was after.

I shook my head no.

He insisted.

Humbled by the generosity, I wrapped the twenty around the card and tucked it into my shirt pocket. "Okay, guys, since this is the Circle of Four, doesn't somebody need to start confessing impure thoughts?"

Steve tilted back on the rear legs of his chair and nodded at Neil, who ran a hand through his hair and pointed at Ransom, who coughed briefly and said, "Let's get started."

"We've been dealing with the subject of temptation," Neil explained. "The result of not disciplining our eyes."

Steve surprised us and jumped right in. He scooted his chair closer to the coffee table and grabbed the chip bag. "The worst is when it happens at church . . . women in springtime, wearing tight clothing."

"College girls in sundresses," said Ransom.

"Out-of-college girls in red," said Neil.

"You remember that one wore red?" Steve countered. "Shame on you."

It had been more than a year since I'd had any male accountability, not to mention temptation accountability. I began to speak but a yawn forced a restart. "I need to interrupt the debaucherous confessions to ask a question."

From the comfort of the La-Z-Boy, Ransom nodded his approval. "So, ask."

"Whatever happened to Stanley?"

Six eyes rolled clockwise in their sockets before Ransom met my inquisitive glance. "With Stanley-dude, every discussion turned into a theological battle, full of big words I couldn't understand."

"Huge words," said Neil. "So Stanley hosts the eastside group now. We call 'em The Eschatology Eight."

Steve gripped an imaginary bat and made a swinging motion. "When our group gets big enough, we're gonna play softball against 'em."

My eyelids drooped as Steve swung a second time.

Next thing I knew he was shaking my shoulder. But I was sleeping in my hammock in the village, and the kids were knocking on my hut.

Steve shook me again.

The right side of my face was pressed into brown corduroy. I woke and glanced at my watch. I'd been out for over an hour. "Y'all just let me sleep?"

"We let you sleep," Neil said. He was standing at the front door, about to leave. "And now I'll let you say good night."

I yawned again and waved in slow motion. "G'night, Neil-who-just-wants-to-get-home-to-his-wife."

He winked and shut the door behind him.

"You fell asleep during our discussion of temptation in the workplace," Ransom said. He rose from the La-Z-Boy and stretched his back. "But we'll have DVDs of the discussion for sale at the next meeting. Steve got you on camera, dude."

Steve had remained in his wooden chair, rocking on the back legs as if amused at my exhaustion. "Got it all, Jarvis."

I sat up on the edge of the sofa and rubbed my eyes. Then I looked around for a video camera and saw nothing but empty cups and tortilla chips. "You did not film me snoring . . . did you?"

The Circle of Four had been my welcome wagon, my whacked-out but loyal welcome wagon. For a moment I even forgot about why I was in town.

After Ransom left in his surfer truck to go home to his wife and kid, Steve showed me to the spare bedroom. "I've been renovating the place," he said. "Hung those two-inch blinds yesterday."

A set of drums occupied the far side of the room, a room that was painted a familiar sea green. A fishbowl sat atop the dresser, where three baby goldfish hovered beneath fatter adults. The blinds were natural wood, and together with the paint and the near-total absence of decor, the room looked somewhere between spartan and beachy.

Four thousand miles of travel welled up inside me, and I yawned and pointed at the drums. "Playing a lot?"

"Eight lessons," he said. "Neil is trying to get us all to form a band. We practice at the coffeehouse, and he thinks I have potential."

I went outside to the Jeep and got my bags and lugged them through the cold air.

Why is cold air always colder when you're sleepy? Along the sidewalk I thought of how much warmer the weather was in Ecuador. I missed my life.

When I reentered the bedroom, Steve was setting a stack of towels on the dresser, right beside his goldfish bowl. "About Australia and the debt thing," he said, easing back into the doorway. "Too bad you lost out on the reward money. Neil and I really were going to give it to you to give to Edward."

"I know you were." I wondered if Edward's patience would hold out, or if he'd do something drastic in order to collect. I dismissed the thought and hung my shirts in the closet. Exhausted, I sat on the bed. Shoes hit the floor. Feet sighed relief. "Did you go to Beatrice's funeral? I really wanted to be here for it."

"Everyone went. Asbury and Maurice and Quilla drove up for it. Quilla even sang. It was a sad day, Jarvis. But just imagine . . . eighty-one. I probably won't even make seventy-one."

"They say single men don't live as long."

"Funny."

"So, what's the latest?"

Steve gripped the door frame and nodded at his drums. "I can now play four songs."

"Not the drums, bro. You and Darcy."

Steve blinked at the floor. "She plays the tambourine while I drum, so that's been fun. She's currently driving Allie's old red Beetle, and we took it up into the mountains the other day. Very squished, though, for a tall girl to be driving a '73 Beetle."

I lay back on the bed. "That's a fine synopsis of the musical and automotive aspects of your relationship, Steve, but what about the romance?"

More blinks, a rub of the chin. "There's a chance that it might be getting time to possibly consider moving the romance forward." Steve raised an index finger. "But that's enough about me. You're missing your fiancée?"

"Greatly."

Steve turned without speaking and headed down the hall.

After he'd shut his bedroom door and the house had gone silent, I sat up on the side of the bed, staring at baby goldfish and calculating my frequent-flyer miles. I had so little money—a few hundred in checking—but at least I had enough miles to get Allie here before the wedding.

The last thing I did before going to bed was open the door into the hallway and shout, "Hey, you still got the ring?"

His reply came around the corner, and it came in a low, husky voice. "Of course I still have the ring."

31

By the following Friday I had met with six of the eight brokerage firms in Greenville, plus the investment departments of four major banks. The responses were unanimous, spoken in a mixture of male and female voices: "You have a hole in your résumé, so even if we had an opening, we'd be hesitant to hire you."

Undeterred, I sat on Steve's corduroy sofa with the phone in my lap. Three dials and two transfers later, I finally reached the man whose name was on the business card Ransom had given me. Mr. Traynor sounded rushed when we spoke on the phone but told me to drop in after three. "Three is good," I said, speaking way too fast. "And the name is Jay . . . Jay Jarvis."

The business district was only a mile from Steve's house, so I approached this employment maze in the same manner as I had approached being stranded—go on walkabout.

My trek included a walk up Main and over a rise and down into the city's center. The fifty-degree air felt much colder after living for a year at the equator, and now I wished again for the warmth of the outback. My tie would not stay snug. I had not worn a tie during the entire sixteen months I'd been working with Allie in Ecuador, and once again my attempt at tying a full Windsor ended up a three-quarter redneck. My final attempt—in a parking lot, no less—forced me to settle for the lowly half Windsor, which I adjusted constantly until I entered through the glass doors of a twenty-story building. A busy receptionist escorted me to Mr. Traynor's office.

He was sixtyish and well dressed and formal, not even cracking a smile when I shared the reasoning behind my search. "Have a seat," he said, pointing to a chair facing his desk.

"Yessir."

"This will only take a minute."

The walls seemed so close to each other, and the stacks of papers on his desk looked to be the task of twenty. "Yessir."

He accepted my résumé and skimmed it quickly. "You worked with Tate Brophy's firm for six years?"

"Almost seven."

"And now you do . . ." His eyes narrowed as he read my current position. "You teach math and English to orphans in Ecuador?"

"That's right. But I still use some of my financial skills in helping to budget the village's monies and to teach the children sound financial management."

"But they're kids in a village in South America; they can't possibly have any funds to manage yet."

"True, but I'm preparing them. Especially Pepe, who might become a professional soccer player; and Isabel, who we think could end up at Juilliard and act on Broadway. Our village is not exactly prosperous yet, sir. Just happy."

He perused the résumé again, almost flinching when he again got to the current vocation. "It appears, Mr. Jarvis, that you simply cut and ran from the brokerage business in the prime of your career." He glanced above the paper and held my gaze.

I shifted in my chair and accidentally kicked his desk. "Yes, but I'm not looking for a position with benefits, just the opportunity to earn—"

"The reason this will only take a minute—and I only have a minute—is that the assistant's position was filled an hour ago, and there just aren't any more openings." He reached across his ample desk and extended his hand. "Sorry you had to come all this way, Jay."

I sat on a cold, wrought-iron bench beside a sidewalk in the business district, consuming the free donut and coffee the receptionist had offered. Being the object of pity was new to me—and I was certain her offer was partially based on pity. *Oh, look at this poor guy with his half Windsor and his downcast eyes and the hole in his résumé; the least I can do is feed him.* At least the donut was chocolate.

I had assumed my six-plus years as a broker were still worth something; it was the ace I could pull out of my briefcase and use when times were bad. Now the career felt like the three of clubs, with ketchup stains and frayed edges.

From the wrought-iron bench I looked up at the office buildings, at white light in the windows and at busy people in beige cubicles. Their computer screens looked like small blue squares of security. *I can do those jobs.*

The sky turned gray, and the wind pulled nightfall by its ears. The time was only 4:30 p.m., and all I could think to do was go spend a dollar and fifty cents in the café behind me. For my buck-fifty I bought fifteen minutes of Internet time and did my best to avoid pessimism . . .

Poetess,

No employment rhyme has yet matched my meter. And one of the brokerages I spoke with reminded me that if a broker is away for a year or more, their license expires and they have to retest. That would take two to three months. I am still trying to land an assistant's position, which can pay pretty well if the hiring broker has a full book of clients. I have one more firm to try this afternoon.

I wish you were here to talk this through with me, but I will type this out and trust that you'll understand: if I can't land a good-enough job to earn the money to pay back Edward, we may need to talk about pushing out the wedding a bit. The only other option I see is that I could get a nine-thousand-dollar personal loan, send that to Edward, and pay down our debt month by month out of our mission stipend. That would take . . . I know, FOREVER.

What crazy story have the kids told you this week?

I miss sitting on the yellow cushions with you.

Love, Jay

I stepped out of the Internet café and back onto the blustery sidewalk. I almost didn't look to the west. But I had to. Over the roof of a red-bricked advertising firm, the top floor of my former employer beckoned. My ex-brokerage office, home to a dozen hard-selling brokers and a parking lot full of luxury, sat in the very place I'd left it on November 10, 2002.

The sun was setting behind the building, and memories melted into warm fuzzies: Buy. Sell. Hold. Oops. My book of elderly clients. My income. My yellow power tie. What would they say now? Do I dare?

I wondered if Mr. Brophy still had the corner office and the orange golf balls he putted across the fourth floor.

I walked up Washington Street, turned right on Academy, and made my way into the building and onto an elevator. Even after sixteen months away from the investment world, I still had over one hundred stock symbols memorized. I still spoke the lingo. I still knew that my blue button-down shirt would blend in, and that a good move would be to take a bit of water from a hall fountain and slick my hair back above my ears.

The elevator door opened, and I found the water fountain just where I'd left it. But what I didn't know, and what I didn't expect, was that the broker-in-charge was not my former boss, Mr. Brophy. The person in charge was a woman. A mid-thirties woman with TV-anchor hair, black suit, and some wicked perfume that could make the market rise fifty points all by itself.

Her name was Victoria, and I babbled out my name when I first entered her office—her plush, corner office overlooking a water park. It was 4:50 p.m., and she was standing beside her desk, her back to the window. She appeared to be on hold, a phone to her ear. She motioned for me to tell her why I was there.

Again I spoke too fast.

She hung up the phone and told me to have a seat. Then without warning she pulled her phone to her ear again and began dialing a number. "Client call," she whispered. "He's on the road." Her quick nod told me that she was listening for someone to answer.

In seconds she frowned and hung up the phone.

Seated behind an impressive desk, Victoria fingered an earring, tweaked it just so, and fluffed her formidable hair. Her hands returned to a folder in her lap. "And so let me get this straight, Jay. You left this very firm to go work with children in a village in South America, during the same month that you had a job offer to go work on Wall Street?"

The guest chair sat a couple of inches low, so that guests had to look slightly up across the desk. I adjusted my tie and concocted an answer. "That's the major gist of it. But I was also in the early stages of romance."

She appeared stunned by my vocational choices. "And so you chose romance and orphans over a Wall Street trading desk?"

"That's correct."

Victoria shook her head, tweaked her other earring. "I would never do that. Romance is just not worth it . . . and I'm neutral on orphans."

My instinct was to use this moment to begin my request. "Victoria, I came here expecting to find Mr. Brophy and—"

"He's on two-week vacation. Seems he suddenly got interested in surfing, so he flew to Cabo San Lucas. Now, what can I do for you?" She kept glancing up at a wall-mounted TV screen, which was tuned to the financial network.

I knew the markets had just closed and that after-market news was a big deal to brokers. So I tried to hurry. "I came to ask if the firm would consider allowing me to work here for a while on a contract basis, even as an assistant to another broker."

"Not possible. We're fully staffed. Plus, you quit."

I fought nerves and revised my strategy, trying to salvage something from this plunge into my yesterworld. "Okay, you're fully staffed here, and I did quit, but would this firm consider supporting an Ecuadorian village that is underfunded and needs to find new donors? We have twenty kids and seven adults . . . and we're very popular."

Victoria raised a very thin eyebrow. "Popular?"

"Quite. My fiancée and I are so good with those kids that orphans in faraway cities request transfers should we ever have any openings."

"Is that so?"

"Yes ma'am, it's so. And I was hoping that some of the brokers here, or maybe the firm itself, might consider supporting us. You know—trade Dell for profit, help an orphan. Buy low, sell high, donate to Ecuador."

Victoria glanced again at the TV screen and began tapping her pen on her very glossy desk. "Jay, are you a member of the Christian religion?"

"I am."

"And is that the one that says to let your yes be yes and your no, no?"

"It is."

"Then my answer is no. Thank you for stopping by." And she picked up her phone again.

I rose from the guest chair and pressed my lips together in the manner of the flatly rejected. Victoria stood and extended her hand. I shook it lightly and eased away from her desk, still fighting the awkwardness of no.

On the way out I almost turned and begged. I almost told her that I knew Dell's earnings were up in the Pacific Rim, and that laptop sales were booming in Europe, and that I could still make money for their clients. But her no resounded in my ears, and I closed the door behind me.

Walkabout had become rejectabout. I went outside and stood numbly on the sidewalk, where gray skies and a March breeze hinted that I was strangely out of my element, even though I spoke the lingo of that element.

Taking a left on Court Street, then onward to the south end of Main, I arrived in the glitzy section of downtown. Beside me was the Performing Arts Center, and across the street the businesspeople filed into a brick joint called SOBY'S. Its sign advertised fine Southern cuisine.

I hustled across to join them and entered a soft-lit foyer, where hardwoods reflected amber lights hung from rafters.

In the bar area to my right stood loose groupings of patrons in business casual, business formal, and business business. The chatter grew loud. Drinks and talk flowed freely. I figured this was the after-work meeting place for the downtown crowd—which differed greatly from the after-work meeting place for the rainforest crowd, which was an observation tower in the jungle, where Allie and I observed native birds, talked about the future, and smooched above Amazonia. I missed my life.

Just mingle. I wasn't hungry after devouring that chocolate donut. So I stepped into line at the bar, a folder of résumés tucked under my arm.

With the twenty bucks that Ransom had given me at the Circle of Four, I purchased an overpriced glass of sweet tea and proceeded to mingle. A fog of cigarette smoke made my eyes water. Soon someone tapped my arm, and I turned to the pretty faces of two women, both about my age.

They were seated on barstools at a round table. The tapper had dark hair like Allie's, only with highlights. Her short-haired friend raised a glass of Merlot in greeting, a sloshing accessory for her black-and-red pantsuit. "I haven't seen you in here before," she said too loudly.

"Haven't been. Just arrived from South America."

"You came to this bar all the way from South America? That is sooo interesting."

The highlighted one pushed a third barstool from beneath their table and motioned to it. "Wanna join us? You look lost."

"I am. Believe me." I coughed up a whiff of stray smoke from the neighboring table and sat.

"Is that tea?" she asked.

"Yes. But it's extra sweet, with a dash of lime."

Merlot Girl interrupted. "Oh wow. I would have sooo much more money in my checking account if I drank tea." Again she raised her glass. "So, how did you get lost in Soby's . . . what is your name?"

"Jay. Jay Jarvis. And I'm here on a job search . . . from Ecuador."

"A job search all the way from Ecuador? Wow, that's a looong search."

They laughed and clinked their glasses. In the ensuing minutes I discovered they both were bankers. Loan officers, actually. After I told them the beginning of the outback debacle and mentioned clearly and loudly that I was engaged—I had been lightly kicked three times beneath the table—they ordered refills for everyone.

Just as the waitress brought the drinks, the pantsuited one focused in on me again. "You got engaged in the outback? That's really interesting."

I told them the story; breathing smoke and moving my legs to avoid flirtatious kicking, I recited the abbreviated version.

Their reaction was a combination of wide eyes and female romanticism. "Oh wow, a day in jail. And your fiancée played checkers with you in the prison? That is sooo sweet."

Besides my second free glass of tea and a bowl of peanuts, I got an offer for low rates on a home mortgage, an offer to join them for drinks every Friday after work, and a "please oh please tell us the kangaroo story again."

"I'd rather not."

"Oh, pleeeease."

"Okay."

The highlighted one left and returned with three others from their bank, two guys in suits and a much taller woman, all of them sipping mugs of Guinness. They gathered around and urged me to tell it with all the details. "Yes," urged the pantsuited one, "especially the part about the parachuting purse."

"It was an air-dropped purse; the pilot tossed it out her window."

"Whatever. Just tell it all."

To the equity loan department of Wachovia Bank I told the story for a second time, including the rings, the walkabouts, the dwindling water supply, the T-shirt fuse, "The Sand Dune Poem," the Cessna, the purse, the camels, the very stuck truck, and the slammer from the Wild, Wild West.

Bankers toasted the story, and bankers toasted themselves. Then Merlot Girl toasted the roos. "I've always loved kangaroos. They are sooo interesting."

And when I was done I mentioned the village and the kids to them, and how we had a constant need for funding. The bankers looked curiously at one another. Then there was whispering between them, and one by one they reached for wallets.

"Here," the highlighted one said, handing me a ten. "We want to help y'all right away, because we think you need it. Plus we all just got bonuses and so we're in a charitable mood."

"Bonuses," said one of the men over his Guinness, "it's why we're celebrating."

From jovial and charitable Wachovians I received two tens, three fives, and a twenty, all earmarked for the children. I thanked each one personally and stuffed the cash in my pocket. I felt like a beggar, but I also felt like I was sharing the village with people who would likely never get to hike the rainforest on their lunch break.

Their discussion soon turned to company matters. And just when I was feeling out of place again, I was tapped on the shoulder by yet another woman. An older woman. I rose to meet her extended hand with mine. "Remember me?" she asked.

Startled, I shook slowly and let recollection blossom. "Ms. Demoss?"

She was fiftyish and black haired and extroverted—just like her daughter. This professional-looking woman was Alexis's mother, the real-estate lady who had sold me my house on the cul-de-sac back when I first moved to South Carolina.

"I have a table up front," she said, pointing. "Join me?"

"Yes, of course." If there was anyone in this town who was well connected, it was Ms. Demoss.

I said a quick good-bye to the bankers and got hearty waves from all the women. "Every Friday, Jay," said Merlot Girl. "Come back and add more details to your story. You almost had us believing it. It was sooo interesting."

I followed Ms. Demoss toward her table. She was seated at the window, while outside the people continued to stream toward Soby's.

She sipped her drink and said, "I'm sure you want to hear all about my Alexis and Neil. I bet you haven't seen them since the wedding."

"Actually, I have. We all ran into each other in Australia."

She set her glass on the table and thumped the stem in recollection. "That's right . . . you interrupted their honeymoon, didn't you?" She looked amused.

"Yes, ma'am. Allie and I got into a bit of trouble in the outback, and we needed our friends."

She smiled at the mention of Allie. "Alexis told me about your engagement. I can never keep up with you all."

"Me either, ma'am."

She looked around the bar and restaurant, as if waiting to meet someone. Finally she turned her attention back to me. "And what about that Steve Cole . . . are he and Darcy still together?"

"Possibly. They're kinda like two hamsters, running at different speeds on the same wheel."

"Who's running the fastest?"

I took a swig of my drink and tried to sound knowledgeable. "Steve got off to a roaring start, but faded a bit in the back turn. Or perhaps I should say the outback turn."

She was looking around the restaurant again, and I wasn't even sure she had heard me. She dabbed at her mouth with a napkin. "Jay, I haven't asked you why Allie isn't with you."

"She's working in Ecuador, Ms. Demoss. I'm here looking for a job. Just for a few months so I can pay off a debt."

She rotated her glass in her fingers. "You were in financial sales, right?"

"Used to be. Doesn't seem to carry much weight in this town."

She leaned in close, like she had a secret and needed my full attention. "Jay, have you ever considered selling property? Our firm just landed an exclusive contract to handle sales of a new development on the east side. Lex sometimes holds open houses out there. You and me and Lex could all work together. . . ."

"Get a real-estate license, eh?"

"Sure. You have a good financial mind . . . and like Lex and myself you can talk to anybody. That's all you need. Well, except for a few tips on how to prospect for clientele."

I sipped my drink and watched the prosperous bankers continue to celebrate. "You're serious."

"Of course I'm serious. And on Sundays you can network with the Episcopalians and Pentecostals while I hit up the Presbyterians and Baptists."

"Could we switch?"

She paused and checked her watch. "Perhaps. I haven't been Pentecostal in weeks."

I swished my glass and watched the ice cubes swirl. "That whole church-hopping strategy still works for you?"

"Real estate knows no theology, Jay, only profit and loss." Then she stood and waved across the bankers to a middle-aged couple. "That's my appointment. I finally got that Presbyterian pastor and his wife to consider trading up to a bigger house."

What could I do but compliment her. "You're the best, Ms. Demoss."

"Persistence, Jay," she said with a tip of her glass. "Now, one more thing about real-estate sales—if you decide to work with me, it will take you a month to get studied up and ready for the exam, and then after you have your license, expect at least another month before your first sale, and then four to six weeks for the closing. So, just three to four months total before your first check."

And on that happy note she clinked her glass against mine and hurried off to meet her clients.

On the day she sold me my house some two years earlier, Ms. Demoss had told me that her strategy of networking in churches also might work for a single man looking to meet a single woman.

I had taken her advice—and met a young woman named Allison Kyle.

But me in real estate sales? Prospecting in churches? I could just envision myself with clients, walking in the front door of a house, trying to close the sale after intensive training with Ms. Demoss: "You'll notice the very loud colors in the living room, not uncommon since the owners are Pentecostal. Or perhaps you'd prefer the more conservative Tudor style across the street, put on the market by Presbyterians and predestined to bring top dollar."

Nah. Probably not.

32

I did not walk straight home to Steve's; there was still another lady I needed to visit. And before I visited the lady I needed to buy her a flower. The downtown florist was just closing its doors when I rushed in, pointed to a glassed refrigerator, and bought a single yellow rose.

I toted the rose down Stone Avenue, left on Highway 29, past a school and a Red Lobster restaurant. My trek took me down an endless sidewalk, against traffic and away from a brittle sunset.

Cool winds blew, headlights blinded, and in blustery twilight I fingered the rose stem. Separated from the others in its bouquet, it remained just as colorful, at peace even, its bud bobbing in rhythm to my footsteps.

A half mile later I reached the cemetery—a sprawling Nebraska of a cemetery, one that I had seen before but never entered. I had come here to escape. I had come to clear my head. And I had come to pay my respects, which can be difficult to do when acres of headstones lie in no particular order, some weathered, some new, and none of them alphabetized.

The quiet of the cemetery was interrupted by the rush of cars on Highway 29, and soon I passed a headstone engraved with 1977–2004.

Mercy, I thought. *Twenty-seven years. One less than me.* I hurried past, searching for stones etched with longer life spans. How quickly I totaled the ages.

Sixty-eight.

Fifty-seven.

Seventy-four.

Thirteen.

I stumbled on gravel. Thirteen?

The farther I walked along the cemetery roads, the more hushed the traffic became—and the less burdened I felt. I may have been troubled, may have been separated by four thousand miles from the one I loved, but I was moving, with numb precision I was moving, alive and well, among headstones.

Sometime into my wanderings—I had covered the entire southern end and was squinting in the twilight—I spotted a thick cluster of red and pink flowers, far from the highway and set upon a hillside, out among the far reaches of the burial grounds. I was breathing hard after all of the walking, and when I reached the higher ground I stopped and admired the symmetry of polished gray rock. Family plots.

The one surrounded with silk flowers was the newest of all, and this one had the span of years for which I searched. I had walked for miles to get here, and I stood with hands on hips and caught my breath. "Beatrice, you always could find a way to wear me out."

I propped the yellow rose against granite, knelt on brown grass, and read the engraving:

BEATRICE DEAN
JUNE 6, 1922–FEBRUARY 11, 2004
NOW STROLLING ETERNAL GARDENS

Talking to graves had never felt comfortable. But today, as the night fell and the air chilled, I told Beatrice why I had missed her funeral, and that it was okay about her reward money not coming through, since a person never knows when they will leave this earth. I thanked her for being a world traveler, for taking her own trip to Australia with her gardening friends, the trip that had thrilled her to the point that she'd recommended I go there if planning to propose.

The memory of my trip—if my memory could hold out a bit better than Beatrice's—was one I would carry all my life. I shifted onto my left knee and readdressed my eccentric friend. "I know how you always despised fake flowers, so I brought you a real one. And I remember two summers ago, when I told you on the phone that I wanted to go visit a girl in Ecuador, you said, 'Yes, dear, by all means go see the Aqua-door girl.' Well, Beatrice, I want you to know that I'm marrying the Aqua-door girl." My voice began to break. "I did it . . . went down under. And Allie said yes, Beatrice . . . right after we saw the roos . . . she said yes."

No more words would come. I remained there, kneeling, feeling as belated as a person can feel when talking to polished granite.

And then, above the winds and the headstones, I could hear her as if she were kneeling beside me. "Tell me the roo story again, dear."

"Again?"

"Yes, and especially that part about the marinated purse."

"It was a magenta purse, Beatrice."

"No worries, dear."

Then there was the darkness—dark that crept in unannounced. I had only the vaguest notion of how to walk back across town to my sea-green room. For a while I sat on cold grass, lost in my circumstances: a fiancée four thousand miles to the south; a great friend gone home for the eternal makeover; a job market that held little promise. My strength was gone. I had all the resilience of a kicked mushroom.

Far behind me and across the grounds, traffic continued to buzz. Soon one engine whined above all others, the high-pitched engine of an old Volkswagen. It was coming up the cemetery road.

The headlights were on, and so it wasn't until the car got close that I could tell that its color was red, a faded red, and that the driver fit poorly in the seat.

There was no honk; this was a cemetery. Round headlights shone across headstones, and Darcy left the lights shining, illuminating the flowers. The car belonged to Allie, and it was odd fashion for a five-foot-eleven-inch blonde.

Darcy unfurled herself from behind the steering wheel. It was too early in the year for her standard lime-green apparel. She moved around the VW's curved hood in a sage-green dress that was simply striking. "Hi."

"Hi," I replied, rising from the grass and brushing off my derriere. "If you weren't best friends with my fiancée I'd say you looked great, even in a cemetery."

Darcy leaned against the side of the car, her blond hair pushed left in the breeze. "You can still tell me I look great. We had clients in at the ad firm today."

"Okay, you look great even in a cemetery but not quite as great as Allie will on June 11."

"Compliment accepted." She looked up at the sky, back to the highway. "How did you get all the way out here?"

"I walked." Something in the way she looked at me—straightforward and with sympathy—told me that she had not come to bring flowers to a grave. "Darcy, you didn't come here to pay respects, did you?"

"No, I'm afraid not. I paid my respects the day of the funeral."

I could not take any more bad news. Not now. Not tonight. I tried to hold it together by folding my arms and bracing myself with widespread feet. "What is it? You have news about Allie?"

Darcy smiled gently and pulled hair from her eyes. "No. Steve and I both have been trying to find you since five. He said you had mentioned coming here."

Frontlit by the headlights, I tried to imagine who else might be trying to reach me. "By the look on your face, this is not good?"

"An attorney left a message for you. Said to try and call him back today if possible, or at least Monday morning. Steve went downtown to look for you and asked me to look here."

My shoulders slumped, and I sat again on the grass, the left headlight scalping me with its beam. "They're gonna sue me, Darce. I was afraid of this. I can't pay all I owe for destroying Edward's Land Cruiser, and now some Australian attorneys have contacted Carolina attorneys and they're coming after me."

"Edward didn't seem that kind of guy to me."

"Of course not, you were flirting with him."

"Was not. I just liked his accent . . . and he liked mine."

I pulled up some dead blades of grass and tossed them into the wind. "Can you loan me a thousand bucks?"

Darcy shook her head. "If I had it. Australia got nearly all my savings."

Maybe this was rock bottom. Perhaps sitting on your rump in a dark cemetery, thousands in debt while receiving a summons from an attorney who wants your last four shares of Microsoft, represents the underwater gravel pit of adult experience. I wanted to go hide in the rainforest, far away from America and its litigious lawyers. "What, Darcy, do I tell the attorney?"

She extended her arms wide in an expression of give up. "Be honest. Tell 'im you're poor. Tell 'im your money is gone, long gawn . . . gawn with the wind."

"How do you do that?"

"Do what? Keep my sense of humor when a friend is being sued?"

"No. Get two syllables out of *wind*."

"DNA probably." She motioned at the car. "Wanna ride home?"

I opened the passenger door to the Beetle, and Darcy reached across from the driver's side and pulled a tambourine from the seat. It shook loudly as it landed in the back. The courtesy light reflected off its brass shakers and the sun-damaged book on which it landed: *1998's Best Poetry*.

The Beetle's tattered seat belt would barely work. "Ya know, Darce, I've never ridden in this car. Allie left for South America right after I first met her, and the two of us never had a chance to go on a date in this thing."

Darcy reached to start the car but hesitated. "She told me to drive it until I found something else. It certainly gets better mileage than my Caddy did."

Allie's stuff was all in the car, which made being apart that much worse. Wooden beads hung from the mirror, and an old support letter sat crinkled on the floorboard. "I never asked her how long she owned her Beetle."

Darcy turned the key and spoke above the engine's whine. "She got it her junior year of high school. We used to drive it to the Friday-night football games."

For a tall girl wedged into such a small car, Darcy showed amazing dexterity. She shifted and steered in her usual aggressive manner, as if unaware of cemetery speed limits. We pulled out onto Highway 29, and she drove us toward downtown. At the first stoplight her cell phone rang, and not with something common like the theme from *Jeopardy*. Darcy's cell rang with the melody to "Life Is a Cabaret."

She answered at the second "ol' chum."

"I found Jay," she said into the phone. "He was right where you said. . . ."

Yep, I ate something. . . . I can practice in my dress. . . . My tambourine is in the car. . . . I'll ask him. Bye."

Darcy hung up, stuffed her phone in her purse, and shifted into first. "Steve and Neil and Alexis are going to practice at the coffeehouse and want me to join them. Wanna watch some really bad musicians try hard not to be really bad musicians?"

I scooted the seat back a notch. "Beats calling an attorney who wants my last dime."

On Main Street she found a parking place between Steve's orange Jeep and a silver 280Z. We got out and walked a dark block to the Carpenter's Cellar coffeehouse. Even from outside I could hear the beat of drums below street level. Then guitar chords, a blast of harmonica.

In the role of roadie, I pulled open the glass door to the Cellar and toted Darcy's tambourine. She led the way down the stairs as I shook the instrument and beat it against my thigh, hoping music would pull me out of my funk.

The coffeehouse was empty except for the amateur musicians, and we entered the brightly painted room to sloppy rhythms and a song halted in midchorus. On a black stage to my left stood five—including Steve, at a set of drums; Neil, with a pair of harmonicas in his hand; and his four-wheelin' bride, Alexis, front and center, trying to untangle strands of black hair from her silver tambourine. In her enthusiasm she had shaken it too close to her head.

With them were two guys I didn't recognize, a tall man with a cast on his ankle who was giving drum lessons to Steve, and a young guitarist in a Clemson sweatshirt. He and Neil were sharing a music sheet, and they looked up at me and nodded hello.

Darcy quickly cast aside her black heels, reclaimed her instrument, and went up on the stage barefooted. In her sage-green dress she looked out of place among all the jeans and sneakers. She stuck the tambourine under her arm and began helping Alexis untangle her hair.

"Got any scissors, Jay?" Alexis asked. She looked in a bit of pain.

I sat in the front row and crossed my legs. "Sorry."

Soon they had Lex unstuck, and practice resumed.

But I felt alone in this room full of friends. They had their jobs; I had my burnt-orange debt. They had their significant other; I had a folder full of résumés. They had their instruments; I had . . . an egg?

"It's called an egg, Jarvis," Neil said. He pulled the wooden egg from his back pocket and shook it. The thing sounded like it was loaded with BBs. He tossed it underhanded, and I caught it. "That's all we've got for you to play."

Steve raised his drumsticks and beat a three-note *ba-rum-pum* as I joined the girls onstage, a not-so-fantastic shaker.

Facing an audience of empty wooden chairs, I gripped the oblong instrument and waited for the young guitarist to lead us, the tall drummer to get Steve into rhythm.

"Just smile like you know what you're doing," Darcy said. She pulled me to her right side and Alexis to her left, to where we stood shoulder to shoulder, two Pointer Sisters and their car-bombing cousin.

"Yeah, Jay," said Alexis. "Shake the egg next to your ear like it's talking to you."

Chords sounded, drums pounded, and soon I was shaking the egg to a song I had never heard.

I shook it to instrumentals. I shook it to hymns. I shook it to Elvis, to U2, to Third Day, and to James Taylor's "Carolina in My Mind." Didn't matter the song, my shaking rarely varied. Except for the two hymns, when Alexis and Darcy insisted I ease the pace.

"Think slow," said Alexis. "Picture yourself at a Presbyterian communion."

Steve beat another *ba-rum-pum* at her comment, then Neil blew a high-pitched intro into a song I knew quite well.

We were terrible, sure. And we butchered "With or Without You."

But in this manner I spent the next hour—on a stage, missing Allie, worried about lawyers, and shaking my egg.

33

Imagine Steve's shock when he came home for lunch the following Monday and found that the attorney had summoned him too. The message was almost identical to the one left for me—a firm urgency in the voice, wanting to meet soon. His name was Payne Bonner, and he sounded both expert and seasoned. In my head I pictured him a squeezer of human sponges, wringing their last drop of net worth until it soaked into his cardigan sweater. I had no idea what he wore; I just pictured him at home in a cardigan, a Master of the Universe.

I still had not called him back. My morning was spent fidgeting, watching the Weather Channel man exaggerate a warm front in the Gulf, and calling six more investment firms in Spartanburg and Columbia.

But now I watched as Steve made himself a chicken-salad sandwich at his counter, spreading the mixture with a knife while he glanced warily at the phone.

I sat on a bar stool opposite him. He completed his spread but put the top piece of bread on crooked. "You look nervous," I said.

Steve took a hasty bite. "I can't afford to get sued, Jarvis. Just because I signed the rental forms with you in Australia doesn't mean that I blew up the truck."

"I'll explain that to the attorney. And I'll take all the blame."

"They can still take—" A glob of chicken salad dropped from the sandwich and onto his shoe. Steve leaned down and swiped it up and tossed it into the sink. "They can still come after my assets. That's why all that fine print is on rental forms, so lawyers can come after not just one person but everybody who is on vacation with the signee."

"The signee?"

Steve swallowed another bite. "In legalese, you and I are cosignees."

"I thought we'd be codefendants."

"Cosignee defendants then."

My own appetite quickly diminished as I envisioned what was to come. Yet I still managed to make myself half of a sandwich while Steve gobbled his own. "Good chicken salad," I told him.

"Darcy made it." Steve turned and opened his fridge and drew out a pitcher of sweet tea. Since returning to the South, I had been overwhelmed with the proliferation of the beverage. He pulled two glasses from a cabinet and set them on the counter. "Wanna swig o' tea?"

I nodded, and Steve missed the glass. Brown tea flooded the countertop.

"I'll take the blame for spilled tea as well."

He already had a rag in his hands, wiping. "I gotta get back to work, Jarvis. Wanna know what I think about lawyers?"

"That it would take fifty of 'em to get you to sign a marriage license?"

"No. They're as frustrating as horse flies . . . on a beach . . . while you're reading *Baseball Weekly* and trying to get a tan."

"That's pretty frustrating."

"I gotta go. Can you—" He pointed to the crumbs and spills on his counter.

"Finish cleaning up your mess? Okay, but only if you go see the attorney with me. Not separate, together. I might need moral support."

He tossed me the rag, and I caught it. Then the kitchen door closed, and I heard his Jeep start in the driveway.

I felt only a gram better to have Steve sharing the burden. Although to drag a friend into this was not my wish.

Already the mission board was probably voting on whether I should be banned from working with the kids. Debt, lawyers, a day in jail, and a torched Toyota—what a fine résumé I brought to the people of Ecuador.

At least I had enough sense to share my trials with my fiancée. In

265

Steve's den I logged on to his computer, accessed my email account, and discovered that Allie had already replied to the previous note.

Jay,

Please let's not talk about pushing out the wedding. I so want to be a June bride, and if that means I need to come to the States and use my English degree to get a job teaching while you work down here with the kids, then I'll do it. In the meantime, I'll pray your interviews go well.

Oh, for a portion of our wedding vows I think it would be a great idea for us to recite a poem to each other. I'm going to start working on mine this afternoon.

The kids continue to revise your roo story. It now takes place in Brazil, and the roos are paddling down the Amazon with Darcy's camera, and we are all in hot pursuit in pink canoes.

Orleander is here with me, and she asks if you need another trim.

Miss you,
Allie

If she only knew. What was there to do but be honest? I hit reply and typed quickly:

A,

Three thoughts:

1) Last Friday I tried to network in a bar. We should try this when we go fund-raising together. It's much more fun than licking envelopes.

2) The corporate world must be working long hours in the cubicle, 'cause they sure like to hear about our adventures.

3) I'm probably getting sued. Some lawyer has summoned Steve and me to his office. Expect repercussions from whoever represents Outback Adventures. That magistrate with the dandruff is probably involved too. He seemed like the nosy type.

Thanks for the offer to switch with me, but I want to continue the

266

job search. I've had nine interviews so far. Still hasn't happened yet. Today all I could think about was the elasticity of folly, how it stretches into all phases of life and yanks people into doing things they would rather not. Like begging for jobs. But I press on.

Oh, I have learned to play the egg. The wooden, musical kind that you shake. Neil started a band, and we all practiced last Friday. We are beyond terrible, plus Alexis got her hair caught in a tambourine.

Poems in our wedding vows sound great.

Your hunk of burnin' love,
Jay

P.S. Neither Steve nor I would paddle a pink canoe.

Only after the missive was sent did I notice that the screen saver on Steve's monitor was a picture of Darcy beside their rented Land Cruiser in Australia. It was taken the day we split off from Uluru. Also, the task bar at the bottom of Steve's screen was lime green. I took all this as a positive sign. He had said so little in the week I'd been here.

I put off contacting the persistent attorney. I needed to think, and I needed to talk it out with someone wise. I had spoken to my roommate about it, and I had typed it to my fiancée. Yet I craved the perspective of at least one person who had not been in Australia with us. And what better person than the guy who had offered me a part-time job helping in his shop.

Ransom asked me to be there by 2:00, that he needed someone to help him finish, pack, and ship an order of surfboards to Florida.

The back of his shop was filled with long, plywood tables, centered under bright lights and covered in shades of sprayed-on primer. A haze of dust hovered against the lights, and the room reeked of fiberglass and resin. Propped against the walls were surfboards in various stages of completion.

Ransom was leaned over the middle table when I arrived. He did not look up from his work, so concentrated was he on the task. I inhaled the paint fumes and peered around him.

"Dude."

"Dude." He was working on a bright-blue board, and it had a red rock formation embossed in its center. Two Aussie flags were already airbrushed onto the front end. There was paint in Ransom's hair and spray residue on his hands and arms.

"What is this?" I asked. "You get orders all the way from Sydney?"

Without reply he removed his dust mask and pointed to the three kangaroos he had painted earlier atop the rock. Over the flags and the roos he brushed on a clear, acrylic liquid that stunk worse than turpentine. "This one's for you, Jarvis. It's my wedding gift, three months early."

"Yeah, right."

"I'm serious," he said, finessing the finish. "It's for you. And if you never learn to ride, at least you 'n Allie can float on it together."

He didn't allow me to stand there stunned. He showed me to a plywood table on the far end of his shop. On it were new skateboards, without wheels and brackets. "Installation?" I asked.

He picked up a box of wheels, removed a set, and showed me how to measure precisely where to install the screws.

"I thought you said I was going to pack surfboards and ship them off."

"You are. Right after you install the wheels on twenty skateboards. I got a big order from some frat boys."

"A college frat ordered skateboards?"

"Rich kids who live on a hill at Appalachian State."

I picked up a power drill and feigned confidence in myself. "Oh."

"Test track is out back," he said, pointing at an exit door. "Feel free."

Twenty minutes later he came to check on me, and by then he had the surf music cranked loud on a stereo. Even the dust was gyrating. Ransom examined my work and checked the tightness of the screws.

But my initial "Whaddaya think?" came out of my mouth as "I'm being sued."

"Jarvis, what are you talking about?"

"Do you know a good attorney to defend lawsuits?"

"Dude. Aw . . . dude, chill. Why would anyone sue?"

"Because I had to go and get engaged in the outback and torch that truck."

He picked up a skateboard and spun the wheels. "But you told 'em you'd eventually pay 'em back, didn't you?"

"Yes, but it's going to take me forever at the rate I'm going, and that's just not fast enough for the legal profession. They're coming after me, Ransom."

There was a long pause, the sound of Beach Boys music throbbing against the walls. "Wanna hide?" he asked.

"And where exactly would I hide?"

"I know some surfing instructors who run a school in Cabo San Lucas. Lawyers would never look for you there."

I had twelve of the twenty skateboards assembled and began the thirteenth under his watchful eye. "But I'm getting married in June and I want to live down in the village with Allie and the kids."

"Cabo would only be for a while. Till they forget about you."

I installed the second screw and reached for the third. "Gimme another idea."

He paused for the intro to "Wipe Out." "You could hide in my little Wally's nursery. We could throw a mattress on the floor. No lawyers would look for you there either."

"I'm gonna need a third idea that doesn't involve hiding."

A shorter pause. "Then you gotta take it head on."

"Head on?" I stopped work and met his gaze, like I wanted to believe him.

"Dude, picture yourself on a skateboard, on top of a steep, paved hill in a busy city, like San Francisco. And you're flying down the hill and you're in your tuck and the wheels are clattering on the pavement, when eighty feet below, a dumpster truck comes rolling across the street. Can you picture it?"

"I picture it."

"Now, what do you do?"

"Skin my knee really bad?"

"No, you stay in your tuck and go straight for the rolling dumpster."

"Down the Frisco hill and toward the dumpster . . ."

"Exactly. And do you know why?"

"Tell me. My knees already hurt."

"Because by the time you get there the obstacle will have moved. Only if you try to outmaneuver the obstacle will you go *splat*."

I wiped dust from my face and said, "That's really deep."

He pointed over to a row of finished surfboards. "Want me to change my example to surfing and the exposed coral reef?"

"No, I think I got it."

"Cool. So just charge right into the attorney's office and expect the obstacle to move."

My confidence was too low to allow me to do anything but repeat him in monotone. "Charge right in."

"You can do it, dude."

"I can do it."

"March straight in."

"Straight in."

He glanced up at a wall clock and took a step back. "Jay, I gotta go airbrush a psalm on a boogie board. After you're done here I need you to put all the finished surfboards in those long cardboard boxes, then fill the boxes with Styrofoam peanuts."

I spotted the boxes and the boards. "And just where are the peanuts?"

"In plastic bags, under the tables. Then we have to weigh the packed boxes."

For today, this was my lot. Jay Jarvis, former stockbroker and earner of big bucks, was about to stuff Styrofoam peanuts around surfboards—and was glad to have the job.

34

In the parking lot outside of Attorney Payne Bonner's eastside office, Steve and I sat in the Jeep and debated how to proceed. We both wore blue button-down shirts with one button popped off the collar and no tie. The button thing was Steve's idea—let our clothes tell the attorney that we were poor and askew. We had left word with a legal secretary that we would be here at 5:15. The dash clock read 5:17.

"We should have our own lawyer with us," Steve said. He had his hands on the steering wheel, tapping his thumbs on the base in a kind of nervousness that belied his novice drumming skills. "We're gonna get steamrolled."

I opened the passenger door slowly, sniffed ambivalent air. Not warm, not cool, just spring refusing to be hurried. I let my leg dangle but did not climb out. "Ransom said to charge in and confront things head on."

Steve bonged his head back against the headrest. "That's all we need—surfer advice. Ransom relates everything in life to a ten-foot Hawaiian wave. This is . . . man, this is legal stuff, Jarvis. We can't just charge right in."

I stepped out of the Jeep and spoke through the open door. "I'm tired of all of this, bro. I'm charging right in."

Steve climbed out and shut his door and sighed the big sigh. We were walking across the lot when a horn honked. I stopped, turned, stared. Into the lot pulled Alexis in her silver 280Z, screeching the tires and parking crooked. A real-estate magnet-sign was stuck to her door. She exited the car quickly, and a breeze blew her hair across her face. She checked her black slacks for wrinkles and picked a thread from her top.

"You've been summoned too?" she asked, and for a moment she and Steve and I could only stare at one another, dumbfounded.

Then Alexis's cell phone rang—her ring was the theme to *ER*—and she stared at the screen and showed it to us. "Lookie here, guys. A text message from my hubbie. Neil says they've called him too."

"Oh, man," Steve mumbled. "They're gonna bankrupt all of us over one stupid truck."

We stood in the lot talking things over until Neil arrived. He parked the Blazer next to Alexis's 280Z and rolled down his window. "I was grading Spanish tests when some legal secretary told me I should try to be here." Neil did not look pleased.

"Join the crowd, honey," Lex said. "We're gonna have to sell our stuff to pay off a torched truck. Maybe we can all live in a commune together."

Something was amiss, as I knew that Neil and Lex had not rented vehicles with us and therefore had no responsibility.

The four of us had started for the door—the type of imposing, brass-adorned door that attorneys must love—when I heard the familiar whine of a VW engine.

Steve whirled around and looked ready to burst. "Now here comes Darcy too." He waved at her and said, "Aw . . . I've had it. I'm leaving and going to get my own attorney."

Neil reached out and grabbed Steve by the shoulder. "Stay." A short command from a man who plays short instruments.

I had never seen Darcy in pink before. But she opened her door, and there it was—pink dress, pink shoes too. She squeezed out from the Beetle and shouted across the lot. "Yes, I know, it's too early in the season for pink. But if I'm gonna get sued then I'm going to look as offensive as possible."

And now there were five.

For the next minute we huddled in the parking lot and discussed our strategy. Neil suggested that none of us say a word. Alexis suggested we soften Attorney Bonner with Starbucks' finest. Steve remained fuming at what was unfolding. And Darcy, well, her pink outfit shouted clear across the Mason-Dixon Line. She reached for Steve's shirt collar and frowned. "You're missing a button."

I stepped toward the door and heard Steve say, "You do the talking, Jarvis. We just elected you spokesman."

I turned to face them and saw everyone nodding. "Fine," I said, not minding the duty but peeved that this lawyer had dragged my friends into this. "Just get in line behind me, gang. In Australia I took one for the team, and I'll take another one now."

My bravado was not just false; it was the only kind of bravado I knew.

Single file and with a tall, pink caboose, we entered the stately confines of the building that housed Payne Bonner, Attorney at Law. Dark wood and red rugs abounded, flanked by gold-framed portraits of old lawyer types. But no secretary sat behind the front desk.

"We'll be paying for the next gold frame, huh?" Alexis whispered.

"Shhh."

I peeked around a corner and spotted a well-lit conference room. A gray-haired man in a navy suit sat at the far end, writing on papers. He was seated in a chair that stood higher than his head. *Has to be him.*

All I could do was stare. Then he saw me and motioned for me to enter. I turned to my entourage and whispered, "He's in the conference room. Stay behind me and don't say anything."

I stepped to the entrance of the conference room and gripped the door frame with both hands. "Are you Payne Bonner?"

From over a stack of papers he looked up and smiled. "Yes, and you must be one of the five I've been trying to reach?"

"I'm Jay Jarvis, the first party you summoned." Warm breath came over my shoulder from Neil. I glanced back and saw Alexis behind him, Steve behind Lex, and Darcy peering over everyone.

"Please come in, Mr. Jarvis."

I gripped the door frame even tighter. "No."

"No, you're not coming in?"

Neil nudged me from behind, but I stayed put.

Everything—getting stranded, the tainted engagement, jail, debt, and being separated from Allie—welled up at once, and it was like folly's own demon took possession of me. What came out was not just a piece of my mind but a chunk of my frustration and the bulk of my stress. "First thing you need to know is that if I had any money, I would have sent it to Outback Adventures. Yes, I'm responsible for blowing up the Land Cruiser. I did it. Yes, me."

He stared back without expression, and I erupted. "Don't you under-stand? No one else is guilty. But I don't yet have enough money to pay what's owed 'cause I left Wall Street to go work with orphans in Ecuador. And I'm only in this position because I drove a hundred miles off the Gun-barrel Highway in order to find an exotic spot to propose. I'm worn out and I'm poor and I'm separated from my fiancée, plus I've already maxed out the cash advance on my credit card until I have enough to pay off the debt. So, what I need from you people is a little patience."

Even the silence itself seemed to bend backward at the velocity of my words. I felt a temporal relief to have gotten it out, though perhaps ashamed at my tone.

Behind me in the hall, Alexis and Darcy giggled.

Bonner didn't. He nodded slowly, without expression. Then he rose from the far end of the conference table and waved me inside. "Mr. Jarvis, I represent—"

"I know who you represent. You're in with some attorney from Alice Springs and the two of you want to suck the last drops of all of our savings accounts because I blew up the truck to save Allie and myself from dying of thirst. So if you're gonna sue, you'll only get four shares of Microsoft because I've already sold my 1981 Blazer to Neil." I reached behind me and pulled Neil into the doorway. "This guy right here with the long hair is Neil."

Neil waved.

Bonner waved back. "Please have a seat, Mr. Jarvis. You too, Neil. And tell your friends out there in the hall to join us."

Reluctantly, the five of us entered and took seats around the opposite

274

end of the conference table, the long and glossy conference table. We pulled chairs close to each other and sat, boy/girl/boy/girl/boy, as far away from Bonner as possible. He was a good twenty feet across the room from the closest one of us, which was Steve. I stayed far left.

Bonner motioned to a silver pitcher centered on the table. "Water, anyone?"

Everyone shook their heads no. Quick shakes, as much nerves as refusal.

Bonner then lifted with both hands a thick folder and let it drop, *thwack*, back on the table. He called out each of our names as a question, as if to make sure he had the right people. "Jay?"

"Sir?"

"Darcy?"

"Yes?"

"Steve?"

"Huh?"

"Alexis?"

"Present."

"Neil?"

"I'm poor too."

Bonner smiled, raised his elbows to the table, interlocked his fingers. "All of you, please calm down. I represent the estate of one Beatrice Olivia Dean. Perhaps you all remember her?"

Immediately I slid down in my chair. The others were nodding in relief at what he'd just said. But not me; I just kept sliding, sliding, on purpose I was sliding, until I could see old gum wads beneath the glossy table. "I'm so sorry," I muttered, mesmerized by the pink, blue, and yellow fossilized gum.

"It's okay, Mr. Jarvis."

I stayed hidden, felt my face flush. "I'm really, really sorry, Mr. Bonner. I was just, um, convinced you were going to—"

"Mr. Jarvis, please sit up in your chair. It's okay. Really."

I tried to slip up into the chair while leaving my head under the table. This posture hurt my back, however, so I resolved to just face the consequences.

But no one was giving me the evil eye. Only Steve glanced my way. "Thanks for taking one for the team, Jay."

Bonner cleared his throat and proceeded as if this was business as usual, as if it was normal for a client to eyeball the gum under the table. "Each of you is named in these documents in one way or another," he announced. "There are other persons, who reside out of town, that are being notified by mail. But I wanted to get you all together to go over details of Ms. Dean's will and the timing of disbursement of funds."

Whatever he said next simply did not register. I had slumped in my chair, anxiety draining off me like mid-August sweat.

Then came the letter. Bonner said, "Before we get into details, I have a letter from the deceased that I'd like to read to you." He pulled from the folder a page of light-blue, flowery stationery. He looked at each of us as if requesting attention and cleared his throat.

"Today is August 27, 2003, and I have finally concluded that I am slowing down, that there is no fertilizer available to jumpstart these old bones. For the twenty years that I've been widowed, I have seen the world. I've taken friends to Europe, to Hawaii, to the outback, and to see the whales in Alaska. All of it was great fun. But last summer I accompanied seven younger adults to South America, where our hosts had little, and yet never complained. To this day I continue to balance my world with that week. My, how I misspent my working years—always hoarding, always saving for the big trip. But it was a little six-day trip that changed me. There I was in a village in Ecuador, surrounded by huts with glassless windows and no air-conditioning. Children live in those huts. Children! As do the few adults who care for them. But it was all so sparse. I remember arriving and asking, 'No ice?' Nope, said our host. 'No television?' We read a lot, said our host. 'But where do the children catch the bus?' There is no school bus, she said. We teach them over there, at the picnic tables under the A-frame roof.

"I am an old lady now, but every day I think about the fact that children live in those huts. And it occurs to me today that since they are orphaned and living in such remoteness, they and their caretakers might could use a bit of help. I also think of our hosts and their sacrifice, and also the young

276

adults who accompanied me on the plane. It seems strange that my little trip, coming in between all the big trips, is the one that has stayed with me. But I am old now, and few things stay for long. I will cut to the chase, dear. I am revising my will.

"I figure it is much too late in life for me to go into full-time missions, but I think I can do something for those who survive me. I am also indebted to one of our hosts and my longtime friend, Jay Peyton Jarvis, who, while he was my broker, convinced me to sell everything just before the market crashed. The least I can do is return the favor before I, too, take my crash. Of course I wish to help my extended family, but I am dividing my assets differently today, to include a few new friends, and at least one more organization."

He held the letter high, a final salute. The room was quiet but for the sniffling. I wiped at my own eyes, as did Neil. Steve just sat blinking.

Bonner folded the stationery and tucked it back into his folder. Again he looked at each of us, and again he smiled the gentle smile of one entrusted with personal matters. "It's taken this firm over three weeks to compile it all, as Ms. Dean had monies in numerous banks, in shoeboxes, and even several thousand—some of it in gold coins—buried in mayonnaise jars in her garden. We only found them because she left a note inside her passport. She had drawn a map and stapled it to the note." Bonner pulled out the note and flipped it over to reveal a hand-drawn map of a house and yard. I saw dirt under his fingernails. He passed the map around, and when it reached me I read the small handwriting on the bottom.

In case of U.S. banking collapse or invasion by enemies, dig between the dahlias and the rose garden.

"My partner and I found seven jars," Bonner said. He rubbed his back. "There may be more. I'm still sore from all the digging."

I always knew that Beatrice spent lots of money on travel, but I had never figured she could pause long enough to give much thought to a will. And yet I was so thoroughly embarrassed at my earlier outburst, at my sheer propensity for presumption, that I just sat slump-shouldered and numb.

Still sniffling, Alexis leaned across Neil and whispered to Darcy, "Mr. Bonner is about to tell us we're benefactors."

Darcy provided the pink correction. "It's beneficiaries, Lex."

Bonner continued. "Alexis has the gist of it."

Did someone say "beneficiary"?

Alexis had her hand in the air. "Sir. . . ."

Bonner paused from shuffling papers. "Yes, Miss?"

"I need a tissue."

"Me too," Darcy said between sniffles. "Can we be excused for a moment?"

"By all means."

When they returned a minute later and sat again, Payne Bonner rose from his chair and came around behind us and stood in the middle, his left hand on the back of Neil's chair, his right holding a sheet of notebook paper. "Ordinarily I wouldn't show all of this information, but the family said it was okay since you all were close to Ms. Dean. This is her own handwriting, how she wished to divide her assets." He set the paper in front of Neil, and we all leaned in to have a look.

August 27, 2003

37 percent of all liquid assets to family, as designated on page 12.

10 percent of all liquid assets to First Baptist Church, Greenville, SC.

18 percent of all liquid assets to a yet-to-be-named ministry.

5 percent of all liquid assets to the Clemson Botanical
   Gardens and Turf Management scholarship fund.
5 percent of all liquid assets to the University of
   South Carolina Athletic Department. (In case anyone
   asks, dear, I keep my gardening and my football
   allegiances separate.)
5 percent of all liquid assets to my best friend,
   Francine Horner, whom I do not expect to outlive me.
Finally, I wish to split the final 20 percent between the
   friends and fellow team members who accompanied
   me to Ecuador in July of 2003 on my first mission
   trip, and also to my friends who hosted us in their
   village. It is my wish that they enjoy these monies, but
   also that they set a portion aside to afford a future
   trip of service to some needy place on this planet.
   These friends are to each receive two percent. Their
   names are as follows:
Stephen Cole, of Greenville, South Carolina
Alexis Demoss (possibly Rucker by now), of Greenville,
   South Carolina
Neil Rucker, of Greenville, South Carolina
Quilla Jones, of Florence, South Carolina

Maurice Evans, of Georgetown, South Carolina

Jay Jarvis, of a P.O. Box in Coca, Ecuador

Allison Kyle, of a P.O. Box in Coca, Ecuador

Reverend Asbury Smoak, of Pawleys Island, South
   Carolina

José Cepeda, of Mexico City, Mexico

Darcy Yeager, of Greenville, South Carolina

Darcy let out a low whistle and whispered, "Wow."

I glanced across the others at Steve, who had his hands under his chin, his head shaking slowly, as if this afternoon had gotten the better of him.

I'd never been named in a will before. Apparently none of the rest of the gang had either, except for Neil, who appeared emotional himself as he told us about his being a beneficiary after his parents died.

Alexis put an arm around her husband and hugged him. Then she tilted her head way back and looked up at Payne Bonner. "Um, sir, would it be immature and inappropriate and sinful to ask what is the total amount of the liquid assets?"

He smiled, nodded, and went back to his end of the table. He plucked yet another piece of paper from the stack, this one long and legal. "It's perfectly all right. These matters, coming at a time of loss, can help us appreciate the long life and wisdom of the deceased." He ran his finger down the page to a final figure. "Total liquid assets amount to seven hundred and eighty-four thousand, four hundred dollars."

Everyone was calculating. Darcy moved her lips in a kind of numerical silence. Alexis and Neil held hands and scrunched their eyes. Steve had a pen in hand and was writing on his palm. I already had the figure, but out of sheer respect for the proceedings did not speak. One embarrassing moment per day was enough.

"Could you repeat that?" Darcy asked meekly.

"It's right here." Bonner held out the paper and pointed to the bottom: $784,400.00.

Alexis raised her hand again. "Since Beatrice urged us to honeymoon in Australia, and we came back broke, Neil and I would like to state our sincere appreciation for the long life and wisdom of the deceased."

Bonner remained solemn, as if he too were moved by all the benevolence. He was a man respectful of circumstances, graceful in his handling of these after-death issues. After Darcy had blown her nose into a napkin, he moved his calculator to the center of the table and began pressing buttons. "Each of you has been bequeathed—"

"Fifteen thousand, six hundred and eighty dollars," I said while staring blankly at the water pitcher.

Everyone glanced at me. Payne reentered his figures. "Mr. Jarvis?"

"Yes?"

"It's actually fifteen thousand, six-eighty-eight. You left off the two percent of the four hundred."

"Oh."

Alexis patted me on the head. "Nice try, Jay."

Quiet composure was a rarity for this gang. If we had each won fifteen thousand bucks in a lottery, there would surely follow a celebration, perhaps a holler and an impromptu moonwalk. But here among the dark wood and deep, red carpets of Payne Bonner's law office, with a portion of these earthly possessions left for us to use wisely, we only dabbed at our eyes and nodded in appreciation.

Until Alexis raised her hand again. "Mr. Bonner, would it be rude of me to ask how you attorneys are compensated for doing this work?"

He closed his thick folder and rested his hands on top. "No, not at all. Most cases are done for a flat fee, paid by the family. In this case, however, the family asked my partner and me to accept two of the seven mayonnaise jars we dug up." He rubbed his chin as if in remembrance. "Unusual, perhaps, but quite generous."

When he stood we all stood. And the handshakes were firm and the thank-yous excessive. Darcy and her overabundance of pink led the way out. I was last in line to depart, and just before I stepped outside behind Neil, Payne Bonner put his hand on my shoulder.

"Can I have a word with you, Jay?"

"Sure."

Bonner motioned to a couple of overstuffed, gold chairs in his lobby. We sat—he to my right—and he leaned forward, elbows on his knees. "Jay, when you burst out earlier about the truck and the outback, I had no idea what you were talking about. But then you mentioned proposing to an Allie. Would that be the Allison Kyle who is also mentioned in the will?"

He looked very interested in my response, and so I leaned forward and matched his posture. "Yessir. Allie and I are getting married June 11. Why?"

"I'm glad you're sitting down. The will, Jay, if you remember, mentions an eighteen-percent bequeath to a 'yet-to-be-named' ministry. Ms. Dean had written that last August, and apparently could not remember the name of the ministry. But she filled in the blank in October."

Now I was leaning in so close that I was invading Bonner's personal space. "Go on . . ."

"Since Miss Kyle was not here today and I had not gotten a letter out to her, I had no way of knowing that she was your fiancée. But her name, and her mission, is the one Ms. Dean named for that eighteen percent. I don't know why your name is not on that section."

And suddenly this too made sense. "I know why, sir. Allie had been serving in an official capacity for two years, and I had just quit my job and moved there without any preparation, without the knowledge of her mission board. They told me if I stayed a complete year then I could sign on and receive a small stipend. My year was not up until December, and Beatrice knew that. We kept in touch regularly. She may have been eighty-one and hard of hearing, but she had good sense."

Bonner smiled and crossed his legs. "And just where is this Allie at present?"

"Down in the village, teaching the kids and working on our fund-raising letters. She's flying here to Carolina in six weeks."

Bonner rose to his feet and shrugged his sympathy. "Considering what's happened today, perhaps you should move up her flight."

All my life I had been the typical Texas guy who showed little affection to other men. But in that quiet and plush lobby, I stood quickly and hugged that man. I hugged him hard.

When we pulled away he pointed at his head. "I suppose you've already figured out the amount?"

"Nope. Right now I can't even add three plus four."

He retrieved his calculator from the conference room and returned to the lobby. He pressed the buttons and hit the equal sign and turned the calculator so that I could see the result: $141,192.00.

He glanced from the numbers to me and back to the numbers. "Miss Kyle will be pleased?"

"Miss Kyle will write poems about you."

We shook hands on his doorstep, and I joined the gang in the parking lot. They were all huddled at the back bumper of the red Beetle. I approached them as an equal in bequeathment, joining the knowing looks and shared smiles of ones who have received what they didn't deserve. "Everybody shocked?" I asked.

"Astounded," Lex said.

"Stunned," Darcy echoed.

"Delirious," Neil added.

Steve propped one foot on the VW's diminutive bumper. "While you were in there, Jarvis, we decided to do like Beatrice requested. Put a portion aside to afford a future mission trip."

Darcy said, "Too bad Allie isn't here to share in the equal sharing."

I bit my tongue and tried not to laugh. "I imagine she'll be quite happy with her share, Darce." I just couldn't bring myself to tell anyone the identity of what was yet-to-be-named. On this upside-down afternoon, all I could do was suggest a toast to Beatrice.

Neil suggested Italian food. "A quiet celebration?"

Alexis suggested a tangent. "How about we *play* 'Celebration'? Grab our instruments, learn a new song, and eat late?"

"First I'm going home to change out of these pink clothes," Darcy said.

"If I had known what today held, I would have worn my lime-green prom dress."

"Oh, just play in the pink clothes," Steve said. "It's a nice change of pace."

Darcy grinned and told me to hop in and ride with her. I could not wait to shake the egg again. On the ride to the Cellar I borrowed Darcy's "Life Is a Cabaret" cell phone and called information. In seconds I was talking with Delta Airlines, electric with the nerves of reunion, which is much preferable to being electric with the nerves of presumption, which can cause ignorant males to erupt at attorneys without first gathering the facts.

"Yes, one ticket," I told the Delta rep. "And get her a window seat."

Into parking places off Main Street pulled four distinct vehicles: an orange Jeep, a blue Chevy Blazer, a silver 280Z, and a faded red Beetle. I had just walked past the front of Steve's Jeep when he hurried around the hood as if he needed to speak while we were still out of earshot of the others. "Just think, Jarvis, now I can afford another exotic trip."

And he winked at me like I should have known what he meant.

35

The singles class still met at 10:30 a.m., in the little brick building across the parking lot from the North Hills Presbyterian Church.

Long time, no see.

It was Sunday, April 11, and today I did not stroll across the lot alone. On my arm, in a light-blue dress—compliments of a Saturday shopping spree with her girlfriends—was Miss Allison Kyle. She had been in town for a week, after using two thousand of her monies to hire a temporary teacher for the kids, just so she could come home to Carolina and plan her wedding.

In front of us, Steve and Darcy walked side by side, their relationship as undefined as ever.

Allie tugged on my arm as we approached the brick steps. "Are engaged people allowed in the singles class?"

Someone coughed behind us. "I hope so," Neil said. *Strange to see him in a suit.* "Lex and I are transferring in from the young marrieds class."

"Yep," Lex concurred. "They're all having babies, so we're gonna hang out over here."

To open the door felt strange. To see the powdered donuts on the back table felt nostalgic. Inside the room, two semicircles curved wall to wall. Twentysomethings and thirtysomethings stood in clusters, coffee in hand. The atmosphere was way too familiar, though I distinctly remembered three semicircles.

I recognized almost no one. Of some twenty people in the room, I could only name Steve, Darcy, Neil and Lex, and long-lost Lydia. At the snack table redheaded Lydia once again manned the coffee and the hospitality. Allie rushed over, hugged her hard, and blushed as she showed off her ring.

The single guys there just to meet girls were easy to spot, given my experience. They hung out on the perimeter, just past the coffeepot but close enough to reach over and hand a Styrofoam cup to an approaching female. I watched one try to hand a cup to Allie, but she grabbed her own and filled her cup. When she added some Irish Crème flavoring and turned and smiled across the room at me, I wondered if she knew that those five seconds of java theater had made my day.

That's when someone banged on the podium and called us to our seats. At the podium in front of the two semicircles stood the new teacher—Stanley Rhone. Hot coffee ran over my fingers as I rushed my fill.

I left out the flavor and hurried to sit in the back row, next to Allie and the others.

Stanley stepped to the podium and tapped the chrome shaft with his pen, urging stragglers to get settled. He was always the most serious when he wore his black suit. "Please take your seats, coffee lovers, and we'll start on time this week."

I leaned forward to make eye contact with Steve. "How do ya like having Stanley lead the singles?"

"I had no idea Stanley was the teacher," he said, squirming to get comfortable.

"Darcy?"

She sipped her coffee and set it under her seat. "Me either."

"Allie?"

"Hey, I was in Ecuador. How could I know?"

Seated at the end of our sixsome, Neil and Alexis could only shrug.

Stanley held a stack of papers in his hands and shushed us all to silence. "Everyone, this is an abbreviated class today, because the last thirty minutes are needed to plan our beach trip for May. Anyone who wants can stick around. But for now, I would like you all to take my little survey."

He walked over and handed the stack to the front row. "Answer from your own experiences," he said. "Answer with as much brevity or thoroughness as you need."

Across twenty people, take-one-and-pass was a quick success.

We all sat with the sheets in our laps, waiting for Stanley to say go. He went back behind his podium, scanned the room, straightened his tie. "Your former teacher used to distribute a quarterly survey to ask why people attended this class. But I thought Wade's question was always a bit light on substance, that we should dig deeper into the minds of single adults. So, class, in order to determine our relative spiritual maturity, I came up with a new survey question."

Pens clicked to attention. Alexis and Darcy put hands to their throats, as if to strangle themselves.

Stanley sipped from his orange juice and scanned the room. "The question is, 'What has our omnipotent God taught you in the past couple of months?' Do not put your name on the paper."

Singles flinched, and singles pondered. Silence was followed by jottings and sighs and scratch-outs. Ten minutes later, pens lay on papers, and papers, on laps.

Stanley tapped the chrome again and asked everyone to pass their papers, facedown, to the ends of the rows. He gathered the surveys and shuffled them with the thoroughness of a card dealer, except that Stanley would never play cards, because he associated games of chance with hedonism and atheism and possibly even anti-Presbyterianism.

He set the stack on his podium. "I'll read some of these back, and I'll do it in random order. You can judge these responses for yourselves." He lifted the first paper and cleared his throat. "Here, class, is what you claim God has taught you recently."

"That car bombers make the best fiancés."

"That I'm a far worse sinner than I figured."

"That Lydia was right when she said this was a good class in which to meet guys."

"That honeymoons are more fun if you get stuck in mud at least once."

"That the Pentecostals are the only denomination in town with their own cappuccino machine."

"That if I don't plan the beach trips, there won't be any."

"That the Ladies of the Quest must have disbanded."

"To never sit behind a row of college girls in sundresses while the preacher is preaching on Song of Solomon."

"That there are some strange people in this class, and I might need to try the Baptists again."

"Never trust Jay Jarvis to obey a well-drawn map."

"That we are lucky to have Stanley as our new teacher."

"Australia does not reimburse for ruining your Adidas."

"Be nice to elderly gardeners; they might just plant a surprise in your mailbox."

Everyone glanced at everyone else, trying to figure out who wrote what. A stunned Stanley held up one last sheet. "I thought I had heard it all . . . until this."

"Read it, Stanley," Steve carped.

Stanley shook his head and read it: "God taught me that being in jail with a bad case of outbackobia is easier to endure if a good-looking brunette buys you a box of KFC chicken."

For the rest of the class time we tried to guess who had written what. After Stanley dismissed us, I walked up front, and we shook hands. He kept his voice down. "Can't thank you enough for the survey idea, Jarvis. When the pastor grabbed me in the sanctuary this morning and told me I had to substitute, I had no idea what to do."

I picked a piece of lint off his black lapel. "A survey and a beach-trip planning session, Stanley . . . that'll usually satisfy a singles class."

The rest of the gang was headed out the door, but before I turned to go I pulled a wedding invite from my pocket and handed it to him.

"Congrats, Jarvis. It's good to see you."

"You too, Stanley."

Outside under an oak, I caught up to Allie and walked with her out into the sunshine. We stood next to her old Beetle and waited for the others to gather and make lunch plans. Three cars down, Neil and Alexis had everyone huddled and enthralled with tales from their honeymoon adventures.

I rubbed Allie's fingers and remembered how, on the first Sunday I had spotted her, I rushed out to try and meet her—and how this same Beetle had rambled away.

The day had warmed quickly, and a breeze blew her hair back. "Just think, Jay. We're moving into a new phase and out of the singles scene."

"Feels strange?"

"A bit sad. It felt surreal to be sitting there with a ring on my finger." She kept staring at the little brick building, as if her thoughts were far away. "Hey, can you handle one more Memorial weekend beach trip with this class?"

"As long as we don't end up on a walkabout."

She got that mischievous look again. "I was thinking of a floatabout."

"I can do that."

"You buying?"

"The gaudy plastic floats?"

"Yeah."

I pulled her close. "No way. You're the one who got the big bucks."

She laughed over my shoulder. "Those monies are hardly mine, Jay."

She knew I was joking. Allie had discussed the big bequeathment with her mission board, and they had agreed to tuck half of the monies away for a college fund for the children, and earmarked another quarter for updates and equipment for the village. The only surprise was the 5 percent bonus they gave to her—which she had already begun to share.

"Have you finished your giveaways yet?"

She swatted at a fly and leaned against the side of her Beetle. "Nope. Yesterday Darcy and I bought Linda Dooley a new leather purse, and I put a little money inside for her. It feels very odd to go from beggar to philanthropist in one week."

What could I say? I could not relate. "My philanthropy got eaten up by debt."

She paused and inhaled the day. "You think Edward got his payoff yet?"

"I wired the nine thousand, plus something extra for his troubles."

"What kind of something extra?"

"A ticket to South Carolina. He's flying here in late May . . . my fourth groomsman."

Allie smiled and looked over at the singles building, where Lydia was locking the door. I knew what she was thinking. Female math: Lydia + beach trip + Edward = setup.

"Don't even think it, Allie."

"But they might like each other."

We turned to check on our friends, who were still listening to Alexis yap about their trip. Allie took hold of my tie and gave it a small yank. "Jay, you're not going to teach the kids to make wild stock trades with their college monies, are you?"

"No . . . not this year."

Steve started walking toward us, and Allie spoke quickly in my ear. "I still have five hundred dollars to give away, and I know now what I'm going to do with it."

"Hire Quilla as wedding photographer?"

"That's already arranged. I want to do something for Jamie Delaney."

"No kidding?"

She nodded and dropped her voice to a hurried whisper. "I had lunch with her yesterday. She told me they only have that ol' Toyota pickup truck, and it's covered with all of Ransom's surfing stickers. But she's a mom now, and she's just started saving for a down payment on a minivan."

"Ransom would never drive a minivan."

"I'm gonna surprise her."

Steve had stopped ten feet away, giving us space. I caught his glance, and he pointed at his mouth, then to his Jeep.

I kissed Allie on the cheek. "I think Steve wants to go to lunch with me. Do you mind? Maybe he needs more counseling."

Allie laughed and pecked me on the lips. "Be his friend, Jay. You've always been his friend."

"Thanks for the car-bomber compliment."

She took my sunglasses out of my shirt pocket and put them on my head. "No one ever takes those surveys seriously."

She pulled away and walked across the parking lot and hopped in the

Blazer with Darcy and Alexis and Neil. It was good to see her enjoying her friends. She so rarely got to see them. And as she settled into the backseat with Darcy, I just kept staring at her—my partner.

Steve waved his hand in front of my face as if to expel me from a trance. "Ready for a free meal, Jarvis? I'm buying today."

I watched the Blazer drive off, then turned to Steve with my eyebrows raised. "Did you say you were buying?"

He pointed to his Jeep. "Lunch. Let's go."

Five minutes later we were idling in a drive-through. Steve Cole's lunch offer consisted of grilled chicken sandwiches and sweet tea—Biggies—purchased from a teenager at Wendy's.

Even before he took his first bite we were on the interstate, headed south on I-385.

I spoke with my mouth full. "Baseball game?"

"Nope." He took a hasty bite and sped us into the fast lane.

"High-speed relational counseling?"

"No way."

"I don't have my golf clubs, so—"

"No golf either. We're going to Laurens, South Carolina. Just forty miles away."

I sipped my drink and assured myself that all was well. "I see. Just two guys, driving to a small town, forty miles away, in order to eat chicken sandwiches."

"Correct. And you need to finish yours before we get there. So eat."

I ate. And when I was done I washed it down with tea. "Are you gonna make me ask why we're headed for this town?"

"I have to make up for Australia. Find a place more exotic."

I stared out the window at pine trees and kudzu. "Laurens, South Carolina, is more exotic than central Australia?"

"Trust me, Jarvis." Steve slurped through his straw and checked his speed. "I got something to show you."

The sun glared off the Jeep's hood, and except for the smooth pavement this reminded me of our first day in the outback. "I'm not going to guess that you have a rock, because I know you've had that for months now."

He slurped again. "This is true." Settled now on seventy miles per hour, he reached under his seat and drew out a business envelope. "And this is what I have to show you."

The thickness of it was unusual. "What you got in there, a deck of cards?"

"Wrong."

"Cell phone?"

"Hundreds."

"Hundreds, as in dollars?"

Steve veered right onto an exit ramp. "Correct. It's part of what I was bequeathed."

"May I open it?"

Steve didn't exactly answer in the affirmative. I rather think he didn't answer at all. At the top of the ramp he braked, set his drink in the cup holder, and said, "Unless a seed falls to the ground, it remains just a single seed."

This verse had not been the topic of the morning sermon at North Hills Prez, so his quotation took me by surprise. "Are you telling me that the dollars you have in this envelope are seeds and we're going to plant them in Laurens, and that they'll sprout and make the town more exotic than Australia?"

Steve looked left and right for oncoming traffic. "The seed has already fallen, Jarvis. You and I are now the gatherers."

"We're gonna be hunter-gatherers again? Like the wallaby?"

Steve looked at me like I was insane, and cleared his throat. "No, just gatherers."

"And what kind of seed are we gathering?"

"A huge one."

"Bigger than a grape?"

"Much."

"Bigger than a tangelo?"

"Gargantuan." He gripped the steering wheel like a determined man. "Jarvis, we're going to gather a six-thousand-pound, lime-green seed."

I shook my head in bewilderment as I realized what he was doing. "You didn't."

"I did."

I stared across the console in disbelief. "You really didn't."

"I really did. I tracked down the officer who bought Darcy's car. He would only sell it if he could make a profit." Steve handed me the envelope and thumped it with his index finger. "Now please recount the money for me."

While I counted the money, Steve pulled some directions from his pocket and drove us into a neighborhood of small, vinyl-sided homes. In front of a gray one he braked and stopped us in the street. "Have you counted it yet?" he asked.

"You have one hundred and thirty-eight hundred-dollar bills in here."

"Good. The sales price is thirteen thousand, seven hundred. That extra hundred is for gas."

Most of the gang had put the bulk of their funds in savings. But not Steve. Steve had taken the large majority of his and spent it on the most valuable thing he knew, a tall blonde who fit poorly in a '73 Beetle.

Steve pulled into a long and downward-sloping driveway. At the end of the driveway stood a carport, and under the carport—well, actually the rear of the car stuck out from the carport—sat a 1975, lime-green Caddy convertible. The license plate read LWN4CER.

"Lime Law Enforcer?" Steve asked. He made an awful face as he said this, as if the very phrase was toxic.

I opened the door and stepped from the Jeep. "I agree, bro. Doesn't quite roll off the tongue like Lime Sherbet."

Steve honked his horn, and in seconds a barefooted man of middle age and military hair opened his back door and walked gingerly down his steps. His jeans were faded, and his T-shirt referenced the Highway Patrol.

"Never drove it much," he said, pointing at the car. "My bass-fishing buddies said it doesn't fit my image." We met at the back bumper and shook hands. "Y'all don't think it fits my image?"

Steve shrugged at me, and I did my best to appease the man. "I think bass fishing suits you just fine, sir."

That's when Steve noticed the trailer hitch. "You towed a bass boat with Darcy's Cadillac? . . . She'll be sick."

The officer frowned and spat in his grass. "If ya don't like it, have it taken off."

Steve leaned close and whispered, "It's coming off soon as we get to Greenville."

The officer opened the trunk and pulled out a tackle box and a fishing net. "Didn't I ticket you boys a couple summers ago?"

Steve grimaced. "You did."

The officer stood there with the net in one hand and the tackle box in the other, like he didn't know where to put them. "I knew it. I never forget a customer."

While Steve and the officer signed the title and recounted the money, I opened the passenger door to the Caddy and searched for any personal items that needed removing. The car was clean, and the light-beige interior looked as good as it had the first time I'd sat on it.

The exchange of car for money was a remarkably brief affair. After we'd said thank you and good-bye to the officer, Steve stood between his Jeep and the Caddy and jingled both sets of keys.

"Well, Jarvis, which one you want to drive back to Greenville?"

This was much better than picking a jail cell. I ran a finger along the trunk of the Caddy and tried to restrain my enthusiasm. "You're giving me the choice?"

"I'm giving you the choice."

There was no choice.

I got into the driver's seat and moved it back a notch. I cranked the big V-8, lowered Sherbet's top, and smiled as Steve motioned for me to leave first.

A barren interstate summoned me down the on-ramp. Twenty miles from Greenville, I glanced in the rearview and saw Steve grinning in his Jeep. He was tailgating, if only to get a better view of his purchase.

He had told me his plan in the driveway, just before I backed the car into the street. On Monday we would drive Lime Sherbet into the Blue Ridge Mountains and to the top of Caesar's Head, park it at a bluff, and ride back to Greenville in his Jeep. Steve would then pick up Darcy, drive her up the mountain, and present her not just with the Caddy but with a pair of fuzzy dice to hang over the mirror. Inside one of the dice, of course, would be the ring.

According to Steve, all of this was to happen at sunset, that pastel hour we romantics employ to backdrop our magnificent moments.

He was ready this time. I could see it in his face.

In the slow lane I drove one-handed, left arm perched on the door, like I owned the car. Already I could picture Allie persuading Darcy to let us use it to begin our honeymoon. Surely Darcy would agree. With these friends, possessions were less important than the relationships. Beatrice had proven that.

With each windblown mile my thoughts narrowed toward "I do." Ahead was not just Greenville but a great unknown. *Marriage.* I held my breath at the thought of it. Then I exhaled as I realized that what I'd been given was not a label to be feared but a person to be cherished, a poet wife for the math-brained husband.

If some prescient soul had told me back in college that I would graduate from UT with a degree in finance, spend seven years in the brokerage world, move to Carolina, meet a missionary girl, quit my career, move to Ecuador, propose and nearly die in the outback, come back to Carolina to beg for a job, and embarrass myself in an attorney's office while believing I was getting sued, I would have croaked. But now I saw it all in a different light. I saw just enough of the past and just enough of the future to know that Jay Jarvis had control of neither.

It was so useless to predict anything. God has no signature moves. Everything he does is original.

I rolled along in the slow lane with the wind in my hair, Steve still grinning behind me, and the sunlight gleaming on the hood. Orange Jeep followed lime Caddy into Greenville city limits, where I honked to a highway worker seated high on a riding mower. Sweaty in his orange vest, he stopped near the shoulder to gawk at the car. Our two-fingered waves met in a rush of wind. The smell of fresh-cut grass swept past, and I turned on the radio and found it already tuned to beach music.

But of course my life would turn out this way.

Epilogue

Dear singles,

Most of you are aware that over the past year the young marrieds class has grown so large that last month we took over the little brick building across the parking lot, kicked out the remaining singles, and added a nursery. We are painting the new addition this weekend and want to thank you for agreeing to move your class into the preschool wing of the main building.

The nursery comes as a result of a weekend work project organized by Steve and Darcy Cole, Neil and Alexis Rucker, Ransom and Jamie Delaney, and us—Edward and Lydia Batalee.

In appreciation for your generosity in letting us have the building, we would like to invite you to the young marrieds class beach trip over Memorial Day weekend, held, as usual, at North Litchfield Beach. Our discussion topic for this year's retreat is "Keeping Excitement in Your Marriage," which will be led by Jay and Allie Jarvis.

We have four houses reserved, but only one bedroom for single men and one for single women. Some of you may have to sleep on the floor. Also, anyone who wants to babysit little Wally Kahuna Delaney and the other children will be given a 10 percent discount off their house charge, which is $75 per person ($140 for couples). Checks can be dropped off to me next Sunday. Please stop by and say hello, and have a look at our new nursery (formerly the snack area).

Sincerely,
Lydia Batalee, secretary, Young Marrieds Class

P.S. Anyone wishing to convoy to the beach can meet here in the parking lot on Friday, May 27, at noon. Darcy Cole has volunteered to lead the convoy. Traveling mercies to all who attempt to keep pace.

Acknowledgments

Many thanks to the citizens of Alice Springs, and to Heavitree Gap Lodge for their hospitality and cheery manner.

Phil "The Bushman" Taylor drove our group into the far and scenic regions of the Northern Territory. He even let us ride some camels. A hearty "g'day" to Sandy, Matt, Will and Tracey, Sophie, Simon, and Casia. Hilarious hikers all. Singing "Bohemian Rhapsody" in the back of a Land Cruiser while bumping along an outback highway will be a memory to savor in old age. How's the leg, Phil?

The dingoes howl loudest at 3:00 a.m.

Anyone interested in seeing the "real" Australia might consider Way-OutBack Safaris (www.wayoutbacksafaris.com.au).

Two Aussie friends contributed to my research: Linda from Darwin and Taryn from Perth.

Caroline C. of the Bell Shakespeare Company was terrific in *Twelfth Night*.

Once again, Jeanette Thomason and Kristin Kornoelje at Baker Publishing Group gave me wise counsel. Special thanks to Anne McCarthy for test-reading the first half of the manuscript. One day her own books will be published. Of this I am certain.

Breaks from writing are best when I head to the beach with the Bells, Sandy C., Matt K., Tony L., and all the beach bums. And it's even better when none of the gang has a kidney stone.

Every writer needs encouragement, and mine was led by Charles and Phoebe, Dana, Ted, et al. Plus the beach bums, actresses Kristin Jordan and Lauren Suttle (Hi, Cinderella, and congrats to you and Rob!), Joelene Rodriguez, Brandy Jones, Scott Mozingo, Andrea and Reggie Fuller, Allison Pennington, Jim Hamlett, Nancy Parker, Whitney Brown, Christi Larson, Dawn Boggero, Tom Merritt, Joey Fowler, Steve Martin, Wes Cavin, Matt Williams, John and Shari Horner, Bradley and Kathy Wright, Mike and Colleen Haubert, Roger and Amy Throckmorton, Brian and Debi Ponder, and fellow author Brad Whittington.

A shout out to a young fan, Jaime, who urges me to write faster. Also, a big thank you to the Monday night writers group for all the critique and encouragement.

Wes was the tallest drummer in Nicaragua.

Matt G. does a hysterical impression of Donald Trump.

Matt K. won't drink sweet tea.

The "other" Matt K. knows everything about four-wheelin'.

Gee, I have a lot of friends named Matt.

Do not, under any circumstances, attempt to climb Australia's famous rocks if your sneakers have worn soles. Mercy.

And to Him who is able to do immeasurably more than all we can ask or imagine, thanks for letting me write an entire trilogy.

The author confesses that he spends his royalties on golf stuff . . . mostly on eBay, which he learned from Tony, who is addicted.

A cat left a doody on Lime Sherbet. Bad, bad cat.

Maybe I need a pet dingo.

Ray Blackston lives and writes in Greenville, South Carolina. His grandfather, the late Reverend A. F. Smoak, served as pastor of Pawleys Island Baptist Church. Ray invites you to read more of the background for his two intertwining novels, *Flabbergasted* and *A Delirious Summer*, at his website, www.rayblackston.com.

"During my talk at the beach retreat I'm going to insist that all the men write a romantic note to their wife. And since I have to lead by example, I've included mine here."

My name is Jay, and I am a romantic

G'day, Allie

Tell me, dear, of this desert frog
One that burrows 'neath dirt and log.
If we were stranded, famished, dry
Would you dig, for thee, for I?

Would you share and put me first?
You who always quench my thirst.
Would you give or be a hog?
Would you, could you, squeeze the frog?

When your dating life's gone south . . .
what's a guy to do?

"Refreshingly honest . . . as charming as *Bridget Jones's Diary* from the male point of view. Highly recommended."
—*Library Journal*

A NOVEL

flabbergasted

RAY BLACKSTON

from the author of FLABBERGASTED

RAY BLACKSTON

A Delirious SUMMER

A Novel

Don't miss the beginning of Ray Blackston's outrageous series!